LOVE IN PERIL

Dana looked up as Lynette came out, with an exclamation of admiration.

"Oh, you're all ready. That's good, we haven't any too much time to spare. Lynn, this is Miss Smith. You two girls ought to be good friends this summer."

Lynette acknowledged the introduction and turned back to Dana:

"I'm sorry you wasted your time coming after me. I thought I made it quite plain to you that I was not going."

"Nonsense, Lynn. I want you to go. Isn't that enough?"

"Not tonight. It's of no use to discuss it, Dana."

Jessie Belle slid her hand into Dana's and began to pull him.

"Come on Dana. We can't stand here all night. If she won't go, there's no use in our losing our seats. I want to see that picture."

There were tears in Lynette's eyes as she stood in the sunset glow and watched the two walk out the gate . . . .

Bantam Books by Grace Livingston Hill
Ask your bookseller for the books you have missed

BLUE RUIN

Grace Livingston Hill

*This low-priced Bantam Book
has been completely reset in a type face
designed for easy reading, and was printed
from new plates. It contains the complete
text of the original hard-cover edition.*
NOT ONE WORD HAS BEEN OMITTED.

BLUE RUIN

*A Bantam Book / published by arrangement with
J. B. Lippincott Company*

PRINTING HISTORY

*Lippincott edition published in 1928
Grosset & Dunlap edition published October 1954
2nd printing .... November 1956
3rd printing .... November 1961
Bantam edition/July 1975
2nd printing .... September 1975
3rd printing .... June 1976
4th printing .... January 1981*

ISBN 0–553–14533–9

Published simultaneously in the United States and Canada

PRINTED IN THE UNITED STATES OF AMERICA

13 12 11 10 9 8 7 6 5 4

BLUE RUIN

I

LYNETTE went singing about the kitchen like a happy bird let loose, spreading delicate slices of bread, folding them together with mysterious delectable concoctions, cutting them in hearts and stars and diamonds, wrapping them in wax paper, each fold creased down with firm fingers, gladly, as if the task were joy.

In the dining-room her mother crumbed the breakfast table and set the extra dishes away in the rare old ancestral cupboard. She smiled tenderly and sighed in the same breath. How happy Lynnie was! The dear child! Life's morning, and the world before her! Would the realization satisfy her anticipations?

This was Lynette's first day at home after practically four years away at college. Oh, of course there had been vacations, blessed blissful respites from the terror of the long, long loneliness without her. But now she was at home, really at home, come to stay. She asserted it with a glad ring to her voice and a light in her eyes that met an answering light from her mother's eyes whenever she said it. Yet the mother knew in her heart of hearts that she had not really come to stay. This was only another vacation possibly a few days or weeks longer than the others had been, but really after all just a time to get ready to go forever out of the brightness of her girlhood into the goal of every maiden's life, a home of her own. Out of childhood forever, into a woman's life.

The mother's lips trembled at the thought, even

while she smiled. How was she going to stand it when it really came? She had not ever definitely faced the thought even yet, though there had been no lack of reminders in the way of eager admirers among the young men and boys of her daughter's acquaintance, ever since Lynette's primary days.

But Lynette had eyes for only one.

The mother's troubled glance went out of the window, down the sunny road toward a large white house set back from the street, with nasturtiums bordering the path to the gate. A young man came out of the door at that moment and went down the path and out the gate. He was coming with steps that were glad as Lynette's voice.

Was Dana Whipple the right mate for Lynette, her pearl of a girl, heart of gold, spirit of fire and dew?

The trouble grew in the mother's eyes as she watched the young man swing joyously along toward her door, a fine specimen of manhood, noticeable even at a distance for his grace of carriage and his supple symmetrical form. As he entered the gate he took off his hat and lifted his head with a toss as if he enjoyed the play of the breeze in his hair. Yes, he was undeniably a handsome fellow, with his heavy, waving crest of dark hair, his well chiseled features, his great dark eyes, under straight fine brows, the facile lips that could so lightly curve into a smile and show the perfect white teeth that helped to make his expression so vivid. Yes, there was no fault to find with his appearance. "Perfectly stunning!" one of Lynette's college friends had called him last summer when she met him.

Looking at him now, as she had never looked before, with the light of sudden premonition in her heart, Lynette's mother was forced to admit that he was a young man of great charm. Nor was his charm all of personal appearance. He had a mind of unusual vigor. He had taken high rank in college and come off with more honors than she knew how to name, and in seminary was considered the most promising member of his class. It was generally understood that he was in line for a pretty good thing in his chosen profession as a

minister of the gospel. Indeed he was spoken of everywhere as being something most rare and unusual in
these days when so few were choosing to devote their
lives to things religious.

But, of course, Lynette's mother told herself as she
watched the oncoming young man, Dana had a reputation to maintain. There was something in the fact that
he was named for a grandfather who had been famous
as a preacher and orator in his denomination. It was
expected of Dana that he would carry on the tradition
of the family which went with the name. One must remember that in trying to make a fair estimate of his
character. Then as quickly as the thought had come
Lynette's mother rebuked her own soul.

Nevertheless, as she stood there while he came brisk-
ly up the flagging to the door, she felt that something
she had been evading and trying to forget for years,
some sudden possibility of peril or grave mistake was
approaching swiftly. Somehow she felt that this day was
a crisis, a kind of turning point. Today Dana and Lynette would probably settle their future irrevocably. All
through the years they had drifted and played, carefree
and joyous, taking their comradeship as a matter of
course, the future all roseate with possibilities, content
to go through college days with zest and earnestness.
But now at last it was over, and the inevitable time had
come when this friendship between the boy and girl
must have its reckoning, its final consummation, and
the mother's heart contracted with sudden fear and
compunction over the thought. Had she been wrong to
let these two be so close during the years, encouraging
their intimacy because it seemed so safe a thing for her
girl? It seemed that all was as it should be. But *was* it?
Was Dana Whipple the kind of man who could make
her daughter happy? Had she perhaps laid overzealous
hands upon God's sacred plans for the lives of these
two and thought to help them on to please herself?

That the boy and girl had something more than comradeship in their eagerness this morning she could not
doubt. Her fearful heart caught the knowledge of it in
the lilt of Lynette's voice, in the joyous call of the boy

upon the doorstep now. She ought to be glad at this joy that was coming to them today, Lynette's birthday, her first day at home after the college years—yes, she ought to be glad, but there was a sudden sinking of her heart, a fearful realization that what she had done was done, and could not be undone, that made her suddenly feel she could not face the boy, not yet.

She made a stealthy retreat toward the stairs and vanished as Dana opened the door. From the upper hall she opened the back stair door and called down softly:

"He's come, Lynnie. You go to the door. I'll be down in a minute."

"Where are you all?" Dana called in his glad boyish voice that yet had taken on a new manly tone of command. "Lynn! Oh, I say! Aren't you ready yet? I expected to see you waiting for me out on the porch. I'm late. I had to send a telegram for mother after I was ready to start."

There was an instant of utter silence while the mother's heart stood still and seemed to count a million. Then Lynette's gay girl voice, just as always only for that lilt of joy, rang out a saucy welcome, and the mother drew a breath. She closed her eyes for an instant with a hurried prayer: "O Father, take care of my little girl!" and hastened down. The note of naturalness had been such a relief! After all, things were just as they always had been—yet! She wanted to hold the moment and go down and talk to them—just as they always had been—once more, at least.

"There you are, Mother Brooke," called Dana gaily as she appeared, "I almost thought you weren't glad to see me you were so long in coming. Isn't it great for us both to be back again? I declare it doesn't seem real, we've waited for it so long!"

The mother drew a deep breath, and life moved on again as it had been going for years. After all, who could be like Dana? Reassurance surrounded him and permeated the air. Her doubts vanished. How handsome he was standing there with his soft panama hat in his hand and the light of the morning on the crest of his dark hair, his eyes flashing joyous welcome, his whole attitude like a nice big boy out for a lark. She beamed upon him as of old. Who could help it? Everybody loved Dana, and he seemed really to care for her welcome. He was an unusual fellow to be interested in an old woman, even though she was the mother of the girl he loved. Young men nowadays didn't stop to pay much attention to their elders.

Putting aside her misgivings Mrs. Brooke hurried out to the kitchen to help her daughter put the final touch to the glorified lunch basket that was prepared for the day's feast. After all, if one must give up a daughter it was less like giving up to hand her over to a son who loved you. And it would be easy to love Dana. She could just let her natural feelings go and Dana would be like her own boy. She realized that she had never quite done this in the past, for always there had been this dim shadowy possibility ahead of her, that perhaps Dana would not be the right one. Some passing expression, something lax about the handsome lips now and then, a shade of weakness from some thrice-removed ancestor possibly—what was it made her feel so? She could not tell. Only a mother's natural dread perhaps of the man who should finally call her one daughter his own.

There was nothing left to be done to the lunch basket except to tuck in a bottle of olives and the salt and pepper. Lynette had not forgotten anything. She folded the wax paper over the whole and smoothly covered it with an old piece of tablecloth she kept for such occasions, which could be turned into a towel after the picnic when they went down to the brook to wash their hands. Then as if to make up for her sad thoughts of a few minutes before, she slipped out of the back door, and stooping picked a few stalks of cool, waxen lilies of the valley from the lush green leaves that grew by the old doorstep. Coming in quickly with a madonna look upon her face she tucked them down against the snowy cloth, half hidden by a sheathing leaf. Her child must not go forth today without her blessing even though her soul shrank back with premonitions. Lynette would understand. She always had understood.

She watched the two as they went forth gaily carrying the basket between them, Lynette insisting upon taking her share, their hands together on the willow handle, her face looking up laughing, all the dimples playing shyly, a sparkle in her eyes; his eyes smiling down. Did he see how lovely Lynette was? Yes, he seemed to. There was deep admiration, almost reverence—*almost* reverence in his eyes. Why was it she was possessed to put that almost in? Was it just that a mother could never be quite satisfied—satisfied for such a girl as Lynette at least? And what more could she desire? How utterly silly and foolish of her!

"What's become of Dana's fine new car they've talked so much about?" It was the fragile little grandmother's sprightly voice, as the old lady stood just behind her daughter looking out after the two.

Mrs. Brooke turned with a start:

"Why, Mother, are you here? I thought you were still asleep!"

"You wouldn't expect me to stay asleep on Lynnie's birthday, would you?" she asked playfully.

"Oh," said the daughter self-reproachfully, "she wanted to come in and kiss you good-morning, but I wouldn't let her. I told her you had sat up so late last night waiting for her to arrive, that you ought to sleep. I'm sorry I didn't let her come anyway."

"That's all right," said the little old lady with a cheery smile, "I'll see her when she gets back. Why didn't Dana take his grand, new car? I've been trembling all the week thinking Lynnie had to go out in it with him driving. He ought to get used to it before he takes her out. She's too precious. I hate those automobiles anyway. The papers are just full of accidents. I believe they're a device of the devil."

Her daughter smiled.

"Oh, Mother, you and I will have to get used to the modern things. You know our fathers felt just that way about riding on the steam cars."

"That was different," said the old lady with dignity. "But why didn't Dana take it? Seems as if he ought to when he had it."

"Why, I heard him say something about its being at the garage being fixed someway, or washed, or something. They're having company down at Whipples' this afternoon, and oh, yes, that was it, he said his aunt wanted it washed before they came. He did suggest that he and Lynnie wait till it came home about ten o'clock, but Lynnie said she would rather walk this time, it would be more like old times."

The old lady smiled a quivering smile:

"Old times!" she said half jocosely. *"They're gone!"* Then in a change of tone, "But of course, if Aunt Justine wanted the car washed it had to be washed even if it was Lynnie's birthday and she just home from college! It'll always be that way. So many to please! That's what I don't like about it. But I'm glad they didn't go in the car. I won't have to worry about that anyway."

"No, Mother, don't let's worry about anything!" said the daughter with a wistful smile. "Let's just be glad. Lynnie's home! Come, sit down and eat your breakfast now. I'll bring it right in. There are some of those little honey peaches you like so much, and the coffee is on the back of the stove nice and hot."

She bustled about, glad to have something to do just now to keep the feeling of tears out of her throat; unaccountable, glad tears, that choked her while she could not explain them.

There were eager rushing steps outside, and Elim Brooke burst into the kitchen, a fish pole in his hand.

"Muth, where's Lynn? Isn't she up yet?"

"Yes, up and gone. She and Dana went off on a hike, Elim. What became of you, son? We tried to wait breakfast, but Dana telephoned and Lynnie had to hurry."

"Shucks!" said the boy, the light of eagerness suddenly going out of his eyes. "That Dana makes me tired! What does *he* always have to be around for? I was going to take Lynn out fishing. I ben down to the

store to get a new line. The old one broke. I got Lynn's
line all fixed up too. Gee! I didn't think she'd go off
like that! The first day! *Gee!* Now I s'pose it'll always
be like that, won't it? A fella can't have his own sister,
ever fer a day. Not even fer her birthday! Gee, I'd like
to wring his neck!"

"Why son! That's terrible language! I thought you
liked Dana."

"Oh, I useta! Before he went off and got ta highhat-
ting! He makes me tired! Met me down by the garage
last night and when I yelled at him he turned around
with that weary air he puts on sometimes and gave me the
once over before he spoke and then he said, just as if I
was a toad in the mud he hadn't noticed before,
'H'warya, Brooke,' as cool as an icicle. Aw, he's a pain in
the neck! I don't see what Lynn sees in him! Did he
take her in the car?"

"No, they wanted to walk," said the mother feeling a
sudden necessity of defending Dana. "Lynn thought it
would be nice. The car is down at the garage being
washed and they would have had to wait for it."

"Wait! What for? Why'n't Dana get up early and
wash it himself? I ask you, why did he hafta *send* it to
the garage to be *washed?* They gotta hose downta
Whipples'. He oughtta wash his car himself. He hasn't
got too lily-fingered for that, has he? Isn't it respectable
for a preacher to wash his own car? I'll bet Dana *suggested* they walk. I'd be willing to bet my last cent on
that and win!"

"Why, Elim! You distress me!" said his mother anxiously. "You don't sound like yourself. You shouldn't be so
hard on people. You must remember that Dana is growing up. It isn't in the least likely he realized he was speaking that way to you. He has always been very fond of
you. You know how he used to play ball with you when
you were a little fellow."

"Aw, bah, that was nothing! He wanted to keep in
practice during vacation that was all! I don't see why
Lynn wanted to go off with him the first day anyway.
When I gave up the tournament just to take her off fishing and show her the new swimming hole, and a lot of

things. I thought it was her birthday, and I oughtta kinda make her have a good time."

The boy's face was all aquiver with disappointment and anger.

"Well, there, son, that's too bad, and if Lynnie had dreamed you had any such plan she'd have fixed it, I know. She'd have asked you to go with them—or——"

"Go *with* 'em! You suppose I'd go *with* 'em! Not on yer life! I don't care fer kid-glove expeditions. Fat chance I'd have fer a good time with that Dana Whipple along! Last time I went along with those two all he did was *read poetry!* Never again fer mine! Got any cake? I'll go get Pard Wilkins. You tell Lynn I'm off her fer life!" and he dived into the pantry and came out with his hands and his mouth full of gingerbread and disappeared out the back door across the lot toward Pard Wilkins' house.

His mother looked up to see her mother standing in the kitchen door with pitiful eyes.

"It's too bad," she said looking suddenly frail and tired. "It's hard to grow up. If they only didn't have to get separated!"

"Yes," sighed the mother, "it's hard to see it. They were always so close to each other—I wonder——" But she did not say what she wondered.

II

THERE were other eyes watching the two as they started out for their holiday.

Down at the Whipple house with its wide east window looking toward the mountains, sat old Mrs. Whipple, Dana's grandmother, in her padded chair with her crutch by her side, her sharp little black eyes losing nothing that went on up the road. She had been cripple for three or four years, the result of a broken hip and rheumatism, but she was none the less the head of the house which she owned and bossed as much as when she was on her feet and about.

In the background, behind the old lady's chair, watching furtively, the while she dried a handful of silver hot from its rinsing bath after being rubbed in silver suds, stood Amelia Whipple, Dana's mother. There was a belligerent pride in her heavy, handsome face as she watched her boy swing along by the girl's side, grace in every line of his body, every movement he made. They were a handsome couple, nobody could deny that, Amelia told herself. Back in her heart was a latent grudge against Lynette's mother and aristocratic old grandmother, with her cameo face framed in fine old laces, and her soft old-fashioned gray silk gowns. She was almost sure that they looked down just the least bit on Dana. *Dana* who had gone to the most expensive schools, and the finest college in the country, while Lynette had had to be content with a little inconspicuous denominational institution in an out of the way place presumably because they couldn't afford to send her to a larger college. Lynette who lived in a house that had long needed paint! Oh—Amelia *liked* Lynette well enough, knew she was good looking, and sweet and even stylish in her way, though she hadn't bobbed her hair when everybody else did—but perhaps it was just as well for a minister's wife to be conservative, and of course everybody said that bobbing was going to go out pretty soon. But then, land sakes alive, Lynette's folks had no call to look down on her *Dana!* She watched them swing away into the blue of the day with a growing flush of pride, while she wiped and wiped over and over again an old Whipple fork that had been in the family for a century or more.

But it was Justine Whipple in prim high-necked sweeping apron and cap, her hair in old-fashioned crimpers beneath, who stood in the foreground by Grandmother Whipple's armed chair, feather duster in hand, and regarded the revellers with open disapproval. The excursion was to her a personal offense.

Miss Whipple was called "Aunt Justine" by courtesy, but she was really only a cousin distantly removed, being the daughter of a cousin of old Grandfather Whipple. Grandmother Whipple had taken pity on her and given her a home when she was left alone in the world at the age of thirty-five, with only a mere pittance upon which to live. She had accepted the home as her natural right, and referred to the pittance as "my property," but she had been a fixture now so long in the family that no one realized that she had not been born into it. Old Madame Whipple goaded her with sarcasm and scornful smiles, but bore with her from a grim sense of duty. The rest of the family tolerated her and quarreled with her, but she maintained her own calm attitude of superiority and continued to try to set them all right.

Aunt Justine was the first one to speak.

"It seems a pity that those two can't grow up! I should think Lynette would have a little sense by this time, if that was any kind of college at all that she went to. To think that she would take a whole perfectly good day right out of the week to go off like a child on a picnic! Her first day home, too! Of course Dana felt he had to do what she asked him. She leads him around by the nose. I should think Dana would rebel, now he's grown up and finished his education. It's time he was warned that that is no way to manage women, letting them have their own way in everything! I told him this morning that there was no earthly reason why he should not tell her that it wasn't convenient for him to go today. They could have put it off until another time just as well as not, and when I'm having guests come, and there is so much extra to be done. But no! He didn't think he could tell her to change it. He didn't think it would be gallant, he said. Well, I say gallantry begins at home. I declare that girl just flings herself at Dana's head, and I should think it would disgust him. Why don't you speak to him, Amelia, and open his eyes? It's your place as his mother to help him to understand women."

Justine turned her cold gray eyes on her cousin-in-law and looked at her reprovingly from under the long, straight black fringes of her blunt eyelashes that were so straight and blunt they seemed to have been cut off with the scissors and a ruler.

"Well, I should say it wasn't your place, at least, Justine!" replied Amelia witheringly. "Dana has a mind of his own, and I'm sure he has more education than all of us put together. Besides, you're talking in a very strange way about the girl he is engaged to. Why shouldn't he want to do what she wants, I should like to know?"

"Oh! So they're engaged, are they? That's the first time you ever admitted that! You've always said it was only a boy and girl friendship. I thought you'd find out some day to your bitter sorrow! So he's confided in you at last has he? Well, I'm glad we know where we stand, at least."

"Really!" said Amelia, flashing angry by this time. "No, he hasn't confided in me! But I've got eyes in my head if you haven't. But what business is it of yours I should like to know? What difference does it make where you stand? You're standing right here in Mother Whipple's kitchen, where you've been standing for the last fifteen years if I haven't missed count, and it doesn't behoove you to stick your nose into the business of any other members of the family that I see. I didn't know you had any doubts about where you've stood, all these years, or I'd have tried to enlighten you. Besides, I don't quite understand what you mean by bitter sorrow. You didn't suppose I had any objection to Lynette Brooke did you? I'd have made it manifest long ago if I had. There isn't a finer family in this country than the Brookes, and as for the Rutherfords they belong to the cream of the land! Old Mrs. Rutherford was one of the first members of the D. A. R. in this state and I've heard say that her husband owned——"

But Justine had turned away from the window with a disinterested finality and a sigh of amazing proportions:

"Oh, well," she dismissed the subject, "if you're satisfied of course there's nothing more to say. But she isn't the girl *I'd* choose for a daughter-in-law!"

"It isn't in the least likely you'll ever have a chance to choose one," fired forth Amelia with a flame in her cheek, and battle in her eye. "I scarcely think *she'd* choose *your* son—if you had one," she ended with withering scorn.

Grandmother Whipple sat back and took up her knitting, laughing out a dry cackle from her grim old lips. She dearly loved a fight between these two. It was the only amusement she had since she was a prisoner in her chair.

Justine sniffed in token that she felt Amelia had been cruel in her insinuations and started back to her work of arranging the guest room for the expected arrivals that afternoon.

"Well, you can say what you please," she said putting her head back in the door from the back stairway for a parting shot, "I think Dana would have shown a far better spirit if he had remained at home, this morning at least, and helped me put up the clean curtains, and tack up the pictures, instead of philandering off with a girl when there was work to be done. If he is going to be a minister of the gospel he ought to begin to remember that charity begins at home."

"I don't see that he has any call to put up curtains and pictures for your guests," answered his mother furiously. "They're *your* guests, aren't they, not mine? Not his? Not even Mother Whipple's? There wasn't any call to take down those curtains and launder them anyway. They've only been up three weeks. They were plenty good enough, and if you had to be silly about them you don't need to make Dana pay for your foolishness. As for pictures, what's the matter with the pictures that belong in that room? We never had to put up pictures when the Whipples came to visit. We don't change the decorations for the delegates to the Missionary Conference do we? We didn't even have to houseclean when the minister delegates came to Presbytery. You can't get anybody much better than they were. Our house is always in order We don't have to upset everybody's plans when other people come here, why are your visitors so much better? If the house isn't good enough for them I wonder you had them come!"

"They're used to having things nice," said Justine severely.

"Well, so are we. So are all our guests! You don't seem to realize what you imply. If these friends of yours are so grand they'd better pick out some other summer resort to spend their summer in and not come bothering around here. I wonder you didn't entertain them at the grand new hotel. You've got property you know, and could afford it."

"I was told my friends would be quite welcome," said Justine with a premonitory sniff. "I was led to suppose that they would be made comfortable and welcome. If they're going to be such a burden I'd better go and telegraph to them not to come!"

Justine's eyes were like cold chisels behind her straight lashes. Her mouth was hard and straight with fury.

"There's welcomes and welcomes," said Amelia Whipple with a snap. "I have to do the most of the work around here and I say that beggars shouldn't be choosers. I understand your friend were hard up for a home this summer like some of the rest of us around here, but if they have to be so everlasting particular about their decorations even why don't they hunt for other accommodations? Nobody'll be hurt if they do."

"Very well!" said Justine in cold fury, "I'll go right down and telegraph the train for them not to get off." She flung off her sweeping cap and began to take down her crimping pins, tears of displeasure and disappointment beginning to roll down her cheeks.

The old lady had been knitting fast, her lips in their grim smile, now she put in sharply:

"Don't be a fool, Justine! Your hair'll get all out of prink and you'll be as cross as two sticks over it. Go on upstairs and finish your decorating. It can't hurt anybody. You two wouldn't be happy if you couldn't scratch out each other's eyes every few minutes. It strikes me you're all in the same box. The pot shouldn't call the kettle black."

Justine surveyed the old lady thoughtfully, then answered with dignity:

"You may be right, Cousin Hephsibah, but I wonder just what you meant by that last remark? Am I to suppose——?"

"You're to suppose nothing, Justine. I just called you a fool, that's all. Now go upstairs and finish your work. You haven't all the time in the world you know. Prink up your room any way you please and for pity's sake let Amelia alone. She's got all the cooking to do, remember!"

Justine slowly refastened the loosened crimping pin, replaced her sweeping cap after wiping her eyes on its border, and turning reproachfully with a martyrlike sigh, went upstairs.

When her footsteps had died away in the guest chamber above, Amelia lifted an offended chin and swept the old lady a reproachful glance:

"I should suppose," she began with hurt dignity, "That I had a little closer claim on you, Mother, than just a distant cousin. Of course I know we're all beholden to you in a way, for house and board, but I try to do my part. But your own son's wife, and your own grandson——If you feel that way about it I'd better try to get a position."

"Amelia!" said the old lady severely, "the difference is this, *you* weren't born a fool! For pity's sake live up to your birthright! Of couse you got a claim, but remember this, Justine never has much pleasure. Can't you let her enjoy what's she got? She's worked hard enough to bring this about, now if she can get any happiness out of it I guess we can stand it for a couple of months anyhow. Say, don't I smell those apple pies burning? It beats all how you can make so much out of a few fool words!"

"But Mother, she'll go and tell around now that Dana's engaged, and he'll be angry at me."

"Well, isn't he?" snapped the old lady anxiously. "He's a fool if he isn't, that's all I've got to say."

"Well, I suppose he is, I *hope* he is, but he hasn't said anything to me about it," said the mother with a troubled sigh. "You know Dana isn't much for telling what's going on in his life."

"There's some things you don't need to tell, " said Grandma significantly. "However, I'll speak to Justine. She's no call to talk about Dana's business even if he is a fool. Amelia, that pot is boiling over! My soul, I wish I had my good legs again!"

III

Out on the road the two who had been the cause of all this disturbance were walking joyously along. The first day home, the first day together after long separation, all their childhood waiting to greet them out of doors, and a summer day that was perfect. One of those "what-is-so-rare" days described by the poet.

The sky was that warm, clear blue that makes you wonder if you have ever really noticed a sky before. The sunlight fairly seemed a part of the sky, blue all through with fine lacings of gold. One or two lazy fluffs of cloud were drifting almost imperceptibly across the highest blue like tufts of down urged by an unseen draft.

The road they took skirted a hill and wound gently up with pleasant homes on the right at intervals growing fewer and farther between as they went on.

Off to the left the mountains were clear and sharp with touches of gold shimmering over the new green of the young trees that mingled with the darker pines. And one spot they knew where the blue grew deeper with a purple depth marked the beginning of the Mohawk trail. They could pick out the landmarks without any trouble in the clear, bright atmosphere.

And now they came to fields on the left drifting down to a valley where like a thread of hurrying silver strung with jewels all aquiver a river went. And all the fields were broidered with flowers, copper and silver and gold like a princess' garment spread to dry, heavy with gorgeous needlework of buttercups, daisies and, devil's paint brush. Amazing sight to come upon! Broidery of heaven loaned for display.

Beyond the river a dull hill rose, rocky and barren, almost a mountain, dreary except for a drift of blue flowers that rose in waves and seemed to spread and quiver like blue flame, or lovely curling smoke-like insense rising against the gray mass of the barren rock behind.

"Oh look!" cried Lynette her eyes sparkling, her cheeks aglow. "I never remember it to have been so beautiful! How large the daisies are this year! How yellow the buttercups! And see how deep a red the tassels of the devil's paint brush are! This must be a wonderful year for flowers!"

Dana lifted indifferent eyes.

"Oh, you've just forgotten, Lynn. I don't see but it looks about as usual."

"No, Dana! It's bigger, brighter, much more wonderful. I never got that effect of copper and silver threads before, with the gold of the buttercups making a background. It's perfectly gorgeous needle work, Dana, woven with pearls."

"Oh, you're fanciful as usual, Lynn!"

"And look at that blue ruin off on the mountain! Why you can fairly see the smoke rise, and the flames pulsate."

"It's not half as good to look at as you are, Lynn," said the young man turning his glance upon her glowing cheeks, the light in her lovely eyes, and the tendrils of hair blowing about her face. "I say, where are we going today? Have you thought of a plan? It's a shame that car had to go to the garage. You'll be tired before the day is half over."

"No indeed, I'll not be tired," said Lynette. "I haven't been cooped up in the house all these four years, laddie. I've played hockey and skated and hiked over the hills, and worked in the gym. I'm fit as ever I was, and I can walk as far as ever I did and farther."

"Well, I can't." said Dana lazily, stifling a yawn. "Theological Seminaries are not places for physical training. Oh, of course they had some athletics, but I couldn't see going out for anything with all I had to do. Besides, it was time to stop that child's play if I ever meant to amount to anything. One can't play football all one's life."

"Still one must have health," said Lynette. "I hope you haven't allowed yourself to get inactive. It's awfully hard on you to study hard if you don't keep up some sort of exercise. They made us do it out at college."

"Oh, *girls*, yes, I suppose it's a good thing for them. But a man has got to begin to think of more serious things. Besides, it's an awful chore to get cleaned up and get to work again when you're all messed up after sports. I've really done awfully well, Lynn. Even better than I told you in my last letter. Let's see, when did I write? I got so busy in those last weeks. But you got the papers I sent, and the commencement stuff? You really ought to have been there Lynn to hear me preach my first sermon. I can't see why it mattered whether you stayed for your own commencement exercises or not, that little stuffy college! It's ridiculous to dignify it by the name of college! But there, don't get excited!" he laughed indulgently. "It's all right of course, and you were a star student naturally. I only wish it had been Vassar or Wellesley or some big college. You could have made your mark there and it would have been worth while——"

A shade came over the girl's face, and a flash into her eyes.

"Dana! Stop!" she cried. "You shan't say such things about my college! It isn't like you, and you *don't know*, and I *won't* have my beautiful day spoiled! Tell me about your commencement. Some day I'll tell you all about my college, and you will see that it was *great!* Some day I'll take you there and introduce you to my wonderful professors, every one of them masters, and scholars, and every one of them men who are putting their whole soul into their work. But never mind now. You just don't know! You will understand when you know, and you will be glad there is such a place. But now forget it and go on. I want to hear everything you have done from the time you left here last year. No little thing is too small to be told. Don't leave anything out. Did they tell you they thought it would be hard to get a church? Or have you decided to go as a missionary? You used to talk that way you know."

"Oh, I gave up that idea long ago," he laughed. "I think this country needs preachers more than the foreign field. Times are changed you know. A lot has been done for heathen lands in the last ten years. The world isn't nearly as large as it used to be. Travel has become so easy, and civilization has made great strides. Culture and education are everywhere. Why, look what a difference moving pictures and radios have made! The Hottentot in the jungles of the forest can get the latest Paris fashion over night now. There really isn't the need of missionaries there used to be when I began to study for the ministry."

Lynette giggled appreciatively:

"You talk as if the main object of missionaries was to dress up the Hottentots in fashionable garments."

"Well, that had a great deal to do with civilizing them didn't it?"

"I don't know," said Lynette with serious eyes far off on the mountain where the blue incense seemed to rise and fall with the light breeze. "Did it? I don't know. What's that verse about 'where no law is there is no transgression'?"

"Oh, now, Lynn, don't, I pray you, get homiletic. I'm sick to death of arguments and criticisms, and obscure passages. Besides, my dear, you are not fitted to cope with a subject like that. The standpoint from which we used to take our conclusions when we were children is very different when you come to get the student's point of view. Let's drop discussions from now on. We've got a long way to go to catch up in our knowledge of each other. Let's talk about each other. Lynn, are you glad to be at home, or does the old town look dull to you?"

"Look dull? Well, I should rather guess not. Why, Dana, I turned down a whole perfectly good free trip to Europe with side trips and a possible winter stay over there with a trip to the Holy Land and a return by way of the Mediterranean thrown in. Now, will you believe that I'm glad to be here?"

"Lynn Brooke! D'you mean it? Turn down a trip like that? What for?"

"Just because there was no place in the whole world that looked so good to me as my home town—and you in it all summer long!" Lynette added the last words half shyly, half jocosely, and glanced up through her lashes at her companion, with a heightened color in her lovely cheeks. But Dana frowned.

"Lynn, I can't believe you were quite so foolish as that. Tell me about it. Who invited you?"

"Uncle Roth Reamer. He and Aunt Hilda and my three cousins are going, and they wanted me."

"Expenses paid?"

"Every cent. And spending money thrown in! Uncle Roth is always generous and treats me just like the rest of his children when I'm visiting there."

"Well, you certainly are one little fool!" said Dana almost roughly. "Why, Lynn, think of the advantages of culture and study abroad! Think of the prestige of having traveled like that! Why it would do a whole lot toward making up for having been graduated at a little insignificant college if it were known that you had traveled widely. You need sophistication, Lynn. You haven't grown up! You're just as innocent as when you were a child! You really need to grow up. You don't realize that you will have a very prominent position to occupy and need to get ready for it."

Lynette looked up at him startled, a cloud coming over the brightness of her face, her lips compressed with a sudden indrawing of her breath, the color on her face springing up brighter.

She was silent for a moment still keeping that wondering searching gaze on his face, and when she spoke her voice was very quiet, and almost cool:

"Do you mean, Dana, that you are ashamed of me as I am?"

"Nonsense!" said Dana impatiently. "There you go, off the handle at once, jumping to conclusions. That's just what I mean. Like an everlasting thermometer, out to feel of the temperature and be sure it's just at seventy. You need poise, Lynn! And travel will give it to you. If your school had been any good you wouldn't be so utterly childish. If I'm to be called to a big city church, you will need to get poise. There's nothing like that to help you up in the world, and make you able to hold your own."

"I'm afraid I don't understand, Dana," said Lynette in a small distant voice, almost like a stranger. "I supposed you were looking forward to preaching the gospel. What has that got to do with social prestige?"

"A very great deal!" said Dana with the air of a teacher who was condescending to explain to the humblest of pupils. "In the first place a preacher's wife can do a lot toward helping or hindering her husband's progress in his work. She is either an asset or a liability. I have always figured that you, Lynette, with your beauty and your goodness—your most *obvious* goodness—and your charm of manner, would be the greatest kind of an asset. But there is something else. It is something that women of the world have, and that is why they succeed so well." He floundered a little here, for her eyes were upon him, wondering eyes, as if she had never quite known this Dana before.

"There is a verse in the Bible," he suddenly said with irritation, "which you should remember. We are bidden to be wise as serpents! That's what it means, use wordly wisdom. Acquire the poise that the world has and then we shall be better able to cope with——"

He paused, searching for a word.

"Sin?" supplied Lynette questioningly. "I hadn't really ever thought of it in that way."

There was something in her voice that irritated him still farther, for he felt that somehow, while he was attempting to show her wherein she was wrong, she had instead revealed a weakness in himself. Or—could she possibly be laughing at him? He had not made his case as strong as it seemed to him to be. He must try again. You never could force Lynette into a situation, you must always lead her. He ought to have remembered that. She would do anything in the world for him, but of course she did not like his criticism of that little superficial college of hers. That was what was the matter.

"Lynn," he said, softening his voice to its old lover-like strain, "I see I haven't made my meaning plain. It's all because I don't like to blow my own trumpet and tell you all the great prospects that have come to me. You see they've been saying a lot of fine things about my work, and my ability, up there at the seminary, and I've the same as got the choice of two or three prominent pulpits if I just say the word. Let's quit this foolish quarreling and let me tell the whole thing. Don't you want to hear what my senior professor said to me the last day, the man who has the reputation of forecasting the future of his students and never making a mistake?"

"Why, surely," said Lynn graciously, her eyes misty with pride in him, despite her disturbed spirit. "You know I enjoy hearing every thing about your seminary life. But it never surprises me, Dana. I knew you could do anything you set out to do. I knew you would excel. Now, tell me every word."

There was just the least bit of hurt tone in her voice that he had not felt the same about her, but he did not notice it in his eagerness to tell her, and she was too humble in spirit to assert it again.

So Dana told.

Long incidents of class lore. Struggles for scholarly supremacy, days and night of grinding. Self-denial of a kind, Dana's kind, the kind that really got what he wanted. Grudging recognition at first on the part of his associates, instant recognition on the part of the professors. Brilliant accounts of arguments and discussions in class in which he came forward with some original thought, was challenged, and was able to bring notable critics as testimony to substantiate his theory. In short as she listened, Lynette perceived that this was no longer her mate and equal, her boy companion of the years, to whom she was giving audience, but a distinguished scholar who had already made his mark before his career had fairly opened.

Lynette's heart was full of joy.

She forgot for the time being his criticism of herself.

They had passed by the broidered pastures and valleys, leaving the blue flowered smoke behind on the mountain, and as they went up higher into a thick grove of trees bordered by fringes of maiden hair fern unbelievably luxuriant, fragilely lovely Lynette was conscious of a tightening of the muscles round her heart. To think that he was hers, and they were here in sanctuary as it were, alone with the great out of doors to talk together again, and get to know the things about one another that had been withheld through the months of separation!

Her eyes rested pridefully upon him as he tossed off his hat and threw himself down upon the moss at her side, and she was conscious again of the quickening heart-beats, the sudden shyness that made her fight for time——just a little space to get used to his nearness again, to the thought that they were really grown up.

"Tell me something, Dana, I've often wondered," she said, suddenly feeling the necessity to cover her shyness with words.

"Yes, dearest!" He smiled down upon her and reached out to take possession of her hand which lay beside him on the moss. It was his first open acknowledgment of the relation between them, which had been tacitly set aside for the years of their education, the first time he had ventured on that "dearest" since his very young boy love-making which she had gravely restrained with wiser foresight than his own. "We are not old enough for such things yet, Dana, please don't spoil the beautiful time we are having now," she had told him. How well she remembered saying it to him, and having to argue it out for days when he would not be convinced. Yet in the end she had conquered, and their friendship had gone on, with only the tacit understanding that there was to be no more sentimentality until they were done with school days. Nevertheless they had both looked forward to living their lives side by side to the end, and had often referred to the time when that would be as if it were a forgone conclusion.

Dana had wanted to give her a ring, two years be-

fore, the day he was going back to seminary and she to
her college. But she had said no, he must not spend the
money now, and it would be time enough to settle those
things when they both got home for good.

Lynette had known when she came home this time
that she was coming home to face what she had put behind a lovely veil out of sight for a long time, but had
always deep in her heart known was waiting there for
her when the right time came. Today, she had started
out with the knowledge that the time had come. The
lessons were learned for both of them, and they had a
right to let their hearts speak out to one another and to
take their right relations before the world. Yet now that
it had come she felt a sudden strange shyness, as if
Dana were not the same, as if he had changed into a
new man, one that she admired greatly, and respected
and loved beyond all the world, yet somehow she stood
in a strange new awe before him. And so she spoke
breathlessly, marking time for her heart to get steady,
and used to the thrill of his touch in this new way.

"I've always wanted to know just why you decided to
study for the ministry, why you were so sure even when
you were a little boy and I first knew you, that there
was nothing else in life for you. Was it that your grandfather had been such a great preacher, and that you
had his name, and felt you must keep a sort of tryst
with the work he had commenced, or was it— something else?" She finished shyly with her eyes gravely
down, her face almost quivering in her eagerness. "I
think I know the answer, Dana," she lifted her eyes for
a single fleeting look, "but I want to hear you say it, if
you don't mind."

It was very still there in the edge of the pine forest,
with the fringe of maiden hair below them, and the
shimmer of the broidery of copper and silver and gold
out in the June valleys far away. Almost for an instant
it seemed to Lynette that it was sanctuary indeed, with
the whispering winds above in the pines, a bird note
dropping slowly down now and then from the throat of
a thrush, and Dana's eyes upon her in that grave sweet
utterly loving look. Then he spoke:

"Lovely, of course I'll tell you, though there's not so much to tell. As you say you know it already, you've known it all along. Why of course it was Grandfather. I felt the obligation, sort of. I was named for him, he left me his property or at least he left it with grandmother in trust for me, you know. That's the same thing. It was Grandfather's dearest wish. And the family all expect it. A man would be a cad not to carry on after that. I thought about it a good deal when I was in college. There were several other lines I might have taken up where I would have been able to make more money and fame right at the start than seemed likely at that time I could ever make in the ministry. But nowhere would I have had more prestige of course. Really Grandfather was quite a great man. I never really understood how great until I entered the seminary. There were men there who remembered him, enthused over his preaching and all that. More than once he was held up in class as an example of a man who had reached the top of his profession. His sermons too were cited as illustrations of a pure, direct style that was recommended for imitation. You would have been surprised how reverently even some of the more eminent scholars among the faculty spoke of his queer old-fashioned books of sermons. I read them long ago of course when I was a mere boy. They filled me with awe then with their tremendous earnestness. Of course they are quite out of date now, but classics in their way. I almost got my head turned, Lynn, they made so much of it in seminary, I having the same name and all, and following in his footsteps. It did a lot for me in the way of prestige. Lynn, the light on your hair just there where you're sitting is lovely. I don't know but I'm glad you never bobbed your hair, though I confess I'm surprised that you've lived through the fashion so long without doing it. You will have to come to it of course if the fashion doesn't change soon, though, for if I get a city church you'll have to be quite up to date you know."

She looked at him startled, then smiled. He was joking of course. She laughed. "A city church!" she echoed. "You couldn't begin on a city church of course!"

"Brownleigh thinks I can," he said gravely, with conviction. "He says my talents would be wasted anywhere else. So you better be thinking about cutting your hair. You don't want to look like a country parson's wife."

Lynette did not smile. Her eyes were puzzled as she studied his face.

"You speak almost as if you meant that," she said lightly.

"I do," he said gaily, "I think you would be charming with it cut. Haven't you often longed to get it off and be like the other girls?"

"But you used to say you liked my hair," said Lynette.

"Well, I do, but one must be reasonable. You can't go against the whole world of course, and one gets used to those things. But Lynn, I'm hungry as a bear. Why don't we eat? I haven't told you yet, but I've got to go back pretty soon."

"Got to go back!" said Lynette in dismay. "Why, you said we were to stay till sunset! It's our day. It's just four years since we sat up here till sunset and talked so long you know. It's——"

She had almost said, "It's my birthday you know," but he saved her further words:

"You don't say! It *was* about this time wasn't it? Well, it's too bad. But we'll come another time, tomorrow if I can manage it. You see we're going to have company at our house for several weeks I'm afraid, but it won't affect me after today. I gave Aunt Justine warning I wouldn't have anybody wished on me this summer. But I have to go down to meet them on the four-thirty train, the woman is sick and she has her child with her, and they can't walk to the bus line. I offered to pay for a taxi, but Aunt Justine seemed to think that was ungracious when they are first arriving, and she carried on so that I had to give in and say I'd come home in time to cart them up from the train. Aunt Justine is a great nuisance. She knows how to put

the whole household in an uproar with just a few
words. If I had my way she would be sent away. But
Grandmother seems to think she has an obligation so
there's nothing doing. Now, let's see what's in that basket. I declare I've been starving all the way up. I'm
sure I smell chocolate cake and tarts. Are there tarts? I
knew it! Open it quick, Lynn. We mustn't waste any
more time!"

Lynette gravely lifted the white cloth and spread it
on the moss. There lay the neat little wax paper packages as she had placed them, but the glory had gone
out of them somehow. She heard Dana saying funny
things and praising and exclaiming but it did not seem
to mean anything to her. She couldn't quite understand
why. Was she such a silly selfish girl that she had to
hang on to a piece of a day when somebody else needed it? Of course Dana must go after his aunt's company, and of course she must not let him see that she was
disappointed. What was an hour or two more or less
out of a day when it was all to be theirs by and by?
What would it matter if they did go down a little earlier
than they had planned? Dana hated it of course as
much as she did. And he was coming to dinner. It
wouldn't be but a few minutes they would be separated.

She looked up with a smile.

"Well, never mind," she said with a sigh that she
tried to turn into cheerfulness. "It won't take you but a
few minutes, and you'll come right back to the house
after you have got them, won't you? You know you are
to take dinner at our house tonight. You remember I
invited you four years ago, don't you?"

"Am I? Why, sure, you did, didn't you Lynn? How
you keep little details in your mind don't you? That's
going to be a great asset in a minister's wife. Lynn, I
can see you're going to be a great help to me."

"It's what I want to be," she breathed almost inaudi-
bly, as if she were registering a long-contemplated vow.
"I haven't forgotten that my own father was a minister
you know, too."

"Why, so he was!" said Dana taking a great bite out
of a chicken sandwich. "We'll be quite following in the

way of tradition won't we? Only I don't intend that you shall be ridden to death by any congregation. It isn't the fashion now for the minister's wife to have to be the slave to the church. They don't even make calls on anybody except the ones they want for intimate friends. We'll see something of society, sweetheart, and go to some good concerts; and maybe get a trip abroad now and then. You don't realize what great things we're coming into. You won't know yourself five years from now. I'm not going to have you all worn out carrying soup to the sick and comforting the broken hearted, and running mite societies. You're *mine* you know. I shall need all the comforting you'll have time to give, and we'll have a maid to make the soup and a deaconess to visit the parishioners."

"But I should love to do that work, Dana. Don't talk that way. I've always said if I had been a man I would have been a minister."

"Well, you're not a man, thank fortune Lynn, and I don't approve of women ministers, so you'll have to be content to minister to my wants. Come, don't let's quarrel. Is that a cup custard that I see? Mother Brooke's cup custard as I live! What a feast! Lynn, was there ever a day so good as this one?"

Lynette tried to smile, handed out the wonders of the lunch basket, bit by bit, ate scarcely anything herself, and wondered what had gone wrong with her day. What did this vague uneasiness in her heart mean? Of course Dana was more or less joking, he always did, and all this talk meant nothing at all. Didn't she know him of old? He was earnestness itself, and this was only a glorified way of trying to show her he was going to take special care of her.

Yet after all when they had packed up the basket and picked up the bits of wax paper to leave the woods tidy as they had found it, she had a vague feeling of hurry, as if Dana's mind was not on the day. He had said nothing about the ring either. How often she had pictured the time to herself when he would bring it out of his pocket in its little velvet case, and place it upon her finger! He had told her it was to be the best diamond he could find, and though she had hushed his talk about it then she had pondered much in her heart all that he had spoken.

Yet the day was bright and it was to be longer. Doubtless he would wait till evening. There would be a moon. Perhaps he would wait till the shadows hid them out in the garden somewhere, although she had always thought of the ring in connection with this spot, their trysting place, where he as a boy of nineteen had spoken his first eager tempestuous words of love. How they had grown in her heart with her life through the years, till now she was waiting for their confirmation with a heart so full of answering love and exultation that it almost choked her to think about it as he talked on.

She was very quiet during the rest of the time that they stayed on the mountain, but he was so full of eager speech himself that he did not notice it. And when he looked at his watch and said impatiently that it was time to go, she got up with a smile, in a kind of daze of joy, for somehow the trouble had gone from her heart and she had got to the place where she could look up and wait and smile for the joy that was coming to her. Oh, he was wonderful! She looked at him with all her soul in her eyes as they stood up ready to go, and the late afternoon sun touched the crest of his dark hair and gave his face a statuesque look. What a wonderful minister he was going to make! How stunning he would look in the pulpit! But of course she must not think of that. It was his great spirit that she almost adored, his consecrated young spirit that was joyously giving up all the fine prospects he might have had in the world to devote his life to the ministry.

And then he took her in his arms, almost hungrily, she thought, and then fiercely, as if he could not get enough of her sweetness. He laid his lips on her hair, on her forehead, and she closed her eyes and dropped her face against his breast, feeling it was so good to be there at last in his strong arms. Yes, it was good as all her dreams had been. And at last his lips found hers, and it seemed as if all the promises of all the years of her young life had come to consummation now, in that one strong tender kiss.

And yet, when he finally freed her and they started down the mountain hand in hand, her cheeks rosy, her eyes downcast, there was something almost frightening in the thought of his embrace, it had been so strong and fierce, as if her whole being were submerged and changed into his. As if she might not be allowed to be her own self any more. What did it mean? Was it just life? Was life always like that? So startling?

She was pondering these things when they came to Round Hill a lovely eminence that rose in perfect symmetry between two higher hills, and burst upon one unexpectedly at a turn in the road.

Lynette remembered a time in her little girlhood when the hill had been covered with waving grain, green and velvety in spring, or golden like waves rippling in the autumn sunshine. But this day it was radiant with blue and white flowers, and fairly took her breath away as it burst upon her sight.

"Oh, look!" she said interrupting him in one of his seminary tales. "Did you ever see such a sight!"

They paused and stood before the miracle of bloom, half in awe.

The daisies had crept thickly over the lovely roundness of the hill which rose straight up before their vision. They covered it completely as with a fine white linen cloth, their golden centers making a shimmer like lights falling from above; and all through the daisies, in serried ranks, tall spikes of Blue Ruin had shot up in luxurious bloom, every little gray-green, rolled-up, leafy spike fluting out in the deep weird blue of its tubular corolla. They seemed like tall candles burning above the white cloth and lifting their blue flame to the blue sky above. It was a sight to take the breath away with beauty.

Dana took off his hat and stood, looking up.

"It is like a sacrament!" he said in the voice he used when he practiced pronouncing the benediction.

"It is like——" Lynette's voice had something hard and terrified in it. "It is like *Satan!*" she finished.

"What on earth do you mean, Lynette?" said Dana in a voice of reproof. He never called her by her full name unless he was displeased with her.

But she did not notice his displeasure. She was looking at the gorgeous display of beauty with sad eyes.

"Lucifer, fair as the morning!" she quoted. "It is terrible in its beauty to me. That Blue Ruin is a nettle you know, viper's weed. It chokes everything else out when it comes in. And daisies have the same nature too! Come, I can't bear it. It is too beautiful! It makes me think of Sin getting into the world, and spoiling all the good things of life! I can remember now how proud Grandfather was of his waving grain on Round Hill. And now Blue Ruin has spoiled all his work of the years!"

"What nonsense!" said Dana, speaking haughtily, harshly. "What utter bosh! That's some more of that ignorant little college, teaching you fanciful things like that! I really shall have to take you in hand I see. That belongs to the phraseology of a notorious class of ignorant literalists who think they know it all, and are making themselves ridiculous. Really, Lynette, I supposed you had more sense. We'll take a week off and sit down, while I give you a little of the exegesis we had in class. A good dose of notes out of my class notebooks will get that folly out of you. Meantime oblige me by leaving his majesty the devil out of the conversation." He finished half lightly, for glancing down he saw that her eyes were full of tears.

"There, Lynn, don't take things too seriously," he coaxed snatching her hand and drawing it within his arm. "You are tired. I let you walk too far. We'll have the car tomorrow. Come forget it. Everything will come all right and you'll get adjusted to things. You are not to blame, it's just the old-fashioned ideas you have been taught, but I'll change all that. I'll tell you all the modern ways. You're an unusually bright woman, Lynn, and must understand before you can follow. Most women don't bother themselves at all about theology but you have a mind that is worthy of being taught. It is a great pity that you couldn't have had a worthwhile college. I'd have liked to have had you study theology with some of my professors in the seminary. You certainly would have enjoyed it. They were keen men, broad-minded, with a vision of the future. They lost no time in sweeping the cobwebs of the ages out of my brain. I declare, I believe you could even have enjoyed Greek and Hebrew! Come, Lynn, be yourself and smile. It isn't like you to be in the sulks."

Lynette looked up almost sadly. She wondered what he would think if she were to tell him? But this was no time to disclose a secret she had been keeping for four years to surprise him.

"I'm not sulky," she said gravely. "I'm just astonished. Startled perhaps. You talk so strangely. You do not seem like yourself. It hurts to have you talk that way."

"That's natural," sympathized Dana somewhat loftily. "Everything changes as we grow older. We can't be children always you know. I confess I was somewhat startled myself when I first went to college and found out how many wrong notions I had acquired. But it will all seem perfectly harmonious when you get adjusted to the new order, my dear, and it's really much more beautiful and free. It gives one a chance for individual thinking along broad lines without being hampered by so many 'thou-shalt-nots'."

"I don't quite think I understand you," said Lynette in a voice that was cool, almost stern with apprehension.

"Don't try," said Dana lightly. "Let's put it aside for today. We've just a few minutes left before we get home. Let's enjoy every minute of it. Hasn't this been a perfect day? Look at the valley now with that broad band of low sunlight across it. That brings out your metal embroidery in fine shape, doesn't it?"

Lynette lifted unseeing eyes to the gorgeous valley but she was not thinking about the landscape. There were things that Dana had said that did not seem to ring true to his old convictions. Had Dana changed? She was weighing his words carefully to see if haply she might have misunderstood him.

Dana talked on volubly, but Lynette walked the rest of the way home almost in silence with downcast troubled eyes. There seemed somehow to have been a great many things said that day that were disturbing. Or was it purely her imagination? Yet he had been critical, of her college, herself, and her way of thinking. Was she perhaps growing conceited that it hurt her to be criticized?

The long afternoon shadows were beginning to lay gray fingers over the bright meadows and draw shy veils of mystery across the more distant mountains, as they came in sight of town. In the end they had to hurry. Dana left her a block from her home and started on a run, for it was getting near train time, and he had to go to the garage for the car before he could go to the station.

Lynette, lingering, walking slowly with troubled mien, tried to shake off the feeling of depression that hung upon her like a weight. How foolish of her to let such thoughts take possession of her! It was just because she was so wrought up about getting home and being with Dana again. Tonight they would have a good talk and clear all the trouble up. Dana was all right. Of course he had not changed! Hadn't she known him for years? Dana couldn't change!

But her mother was waiting on the porch! She must have seen Dana go by and would be wondering what was the matter, and where she was. She hastened her steps and summoned a smile. Her mother must not see that she was upset. Mother was always so keen to read right through her and pick out what was in her heart, sometimes when she didn't even know it was there herself.

"Dana had to go to the station to meet some tiresome visitors for his Aunt Justine," she explained as she came up the walk. "Oh, yes, he's coming back to supper. I'm glad I got home so soon. Now I'll have time to make the biscuits for you. No, I'm not a bit tired. I'll love to make them! You lie down in the hammock and rest. I just know you've been on your feet all day. You always do on birthdays. Oh, yes, I've had a wonderful time you dear little mother! And where is Grandmother? I haven't had my birthday kiss from her yet. And Elim! Did he go fishing? I'm afraid he was disappointed. I promised him a long time ago and didn't realize."

She passed lightly in at the porch door and her mother looked after her yearningly. Was there a shadow in her girl's eyes?

Well, but there was *no ring* on her girl's finger—— Not *yet!*

IV

Justine Whipple stood fuming at the east window of the big old sitting-room, anxiously staring up at the street, her old-fashioned hunter's case watch open in her hand. She seemed like a coffee pot about to boil over. In fact she had boiled over several times in the last five minutes. Grandma Whipple was enjoying it in her corner, her eyes twinkling, as she set a patch neatly by the thread under a thin place in one of the everyday tablecloths.

"There is just five minutes left!" declared Justine. "No, I'm mistaken, only four and a half. If he doesn't come then I shall call up a taxi and go for them myself! It seems outrageous that I can't depend on my own nephew for a little thing like that, and all because of a silly girl."

"He isn't your own nephew!" broke in Amelia furiously, arriving at that moment from above stairs where she had been powdering her red face and shiny nose with some powder she had bought a few days ago after prolonged study of the advertisements in her fashion magazine. She was a little nervous about appearing below stairs with it on for Grandma Whipple's eyes were sharp and her tongue was sharper, but Justine's words lashed away her shyness, and she rushed to the fray in defense of her son.

"He isn't even your own *cousin!*" she added viciously. "It's a pity you wouldn't remember that! He has no obligation whatever to come home from anything he

36

wishes to do, silly or not, to take his own car which he had washed and had to pay for, at *your request*, to go after *your* company! But he said he would do it, and he will! He never failed to keep his word, did he? Answer me that! Did you ever know him to fail to be on time, when he promised? You know that's one of his almost failings, to be exactly on time and no more. He says it's a sin to waste time unnecessarily!"

"H'm!" sniffed Justine. "A sin! When he's been wasting a whole day dawdling after a girl in the woods!"

"And you want him to go dawdling after another!" said his mother with a pin between her lips while she energetically reached back of her ample waist for the belt of her clean apron which she was preparing to pin over her best black and white voile dress. "Oh, you're the most consistent person I know! And he *ought* to be late just to punish you for not trusting him. Did you ever find him untrustworthy? Answer me that!"

"Well, yes, I did!" declared Justine angrily facing about toward Amelia with fire in her eye. "Yes, I certainly did!"

"You *did?*" roared Dana's mother turning almost white with rage.

"*I did!*"

"When?"

"Once when I gave him a letter to mail. He carried it in his sweater pocket for a whole week, and wore it all out so I had to rewrite it. It was an important letter too!"

"Humph!" sniffed Amelia with a flirt of her head turning toward the dining table and flinging the clean cloth deftly over the table pad as if the conversation had become too trivial to be worthy of her further attention. "Ten years ago! Dana was nothing but a child then. You never will forget that. You do hold grudges a long time, don't you? Holding a grudge against a child! And I remember that letter. I found it myself in his pocket when I went to mend the sweater. It was some ridiculous answer to a fake ad, something about removing wrinkles and making you look young again. Important! Fool nonsense! There comes Dana now! I *knew* he would be here on time!"

"Well, he's half a minute behind," said Justine severely, consulting the watch, "and he isn't here yet! Besides he's got to walk down to the garage after the car. I doubt if he can make it. He better phone for a cab."

"Justine, you certainly are the most aggravating person alive! What's half a minute? Your watch is probably fast anyway. You always keep it that way."

"A half a minute is a long time when one has to wait on a strange platform in a strange city," whined Justine petulantly. "And just look at Dana! He'll have to change his clothes. He can't wear a sweater and a soft collar to meet my friends from New York! And the creases are all out of his trousers! I don't see how he is going to make that train in time! And he'll have to wash! He looks a mess!"

"For pity's sake do shut up!" said Amelia riled beyond further endurance. "If he hears you he won't go at all, and then where will you be?"

"You don't seem to realize that it is almost time for the train to be coming in now, Amelia——!"

But Amelia had slammed out into the kitchen and was slatting pots and pans around in a manner that showed she would stand no more nonsense.

The old lady in her arm-chair cackled. She knew that Justine would not dare resent that cackle, for was not Justine expecting company who would perhaps stay the whole summer? And the small sum they were to pay for board would by no means cover the price of their presence in the house. The old lady wondered under her grim smile why she had told Justine she might bring them there anyway? Had it been mere pity for her lonely dependent, or a desire to stir up her daughter-in-law to further good works. She was not sure. At any rate, the visit ought to be good for a little amusement for herself, and there had been precious little of that coming her way for many a long year, especially since she had been crippled.

Deep down in her heart perhaps the old lady had

longed for the voice of a child in the house. "Her little girl," had been the vague way that Justine had spoken of the offspring of her old friend. But what was this that Amelia had said about Justine wanting Dana to dawdle around after another girl? Was the child grown up? Had Amelia been finding out things?

"Justine, how old is that child that's coming?" she suddenly asked, so crisply that Justine started and almost dropped her watch.

She carefully snapped it shut after a final squint at the second hand that she might give Dana the benefit of the last quarter of a second, and then looked up.

"Why, I'm not just sure," she answered nervously. "Excuse me, Grandma, I must let Dana know the time. He can't realize——"

"Nonsense!" said the old lady with annoyance. "Dana has a watch and you may be sure he thinks it's right. Come back here and tell me about that child! I ought to have asked you before!"

But Justine was off down the flower-bordered flagging to meet Dana.

"Oh, Dana, deah," she called eagerly, in the ingratiating tone she affected when she wished to show her superior culture.

They came in together a moment later, Dana loftily and leisurely, Justine talking vivaciously:

"And I told her to weah a white flowah in her buttonhole," she said with an affected giggle, "so you would know her at once. I thought it would be so awkward for you both. And you're sure you won't have any difficulty about getting the trunks up at once? She'll want to dress for dinnah. You know they always dress for dinnah in New Yawk. Dana, deah, you're a little mussed, did you know it? Would you like me to get you a whisk broom? There's dust on the cuff of your trouser, deah. Where have you been? You must have been sitting on the ground. Are you suah it was quite dry?"

"Yer Granny!" ejaculated the old lady half under her breath. "Justine, stop worrying Dana and come here! I want to know how old that child is?"

"Oh, Grandma!" giggled Justine nervously, "I really

don't know. She'll be here in a few minutes and you can see for yourself. Let me see, when did I come heah, what yeah? It was the yeah, no two yeahs after that, that Ella Smith was married. No—I don't really know just when it was. I can run up and look over my file of letters if you must know, Grandma," indulgently, with an anxious eye on the clock.

"Yer Granny!" said the old lady quite loud this time. "You've got something up your sleeve. Justine, I don't know what it is, but you lick your lips like a cat that had just been tasting the cream. I've always noticed that you have something up your sleeve, Justine, when your mouth gets that sleek look. But whatever it is it'll come out soon enough I suppose. Let well enough alone. Aren't you going to help Amelia in the 'kitchen? She sounds as if she had just broken the stove down and was trying to set it up. For mercy's sake go, and stop that clatter!"

Justine gave a furtive look at Grandma as she started toward the door.

"You're being unkind to me, Grandma," she said in her humbly gentle tone that always riled the old lady. "But it doesn't mattah. I'll try to bear it sweetly. Amelia, deah, is there anything that I can do to help down heah? What's the mattah? Have you got behind in the dinnah?"

"No I haven't got behind in the 'dinnah,' nor anything else, but I'd like to get behind *you* and find out what you're up to now," said the irate mother. "There's nothing the *mattah*, and you needn't come around *heah* calling me *deah!* Go on up stairs and keep out from under foot, for pity's sake, till the dinner's on the table. You make me *sick!*"

Justine vanished up the back stairs, shedding a bitter tear vindictively as she closed the door with a gentle emphasis. She was anxious to find out if Dana had left yet, and whether he had changed his clothes before he went. This trying to have company in a house that was not your own was difficult business but Justine had always felt that right made might, and she meant to have everything right for her friends. If things went the way she hoped—— But she must not even think about that.

Amelia slatted the last pan into place and came back to the dining-room.

"Amelia, how old is that child that's coming?" asked Madame Whipple.

"I'm sure I don't know," said Amelia angrily. "She's no child though, I can tell you that, if she *has* got bobbed hair and wears her skirts up to her knees."

"How do you know that, Amelia?"

"Well, because I saw her photograph, if you must know. It was lying on Justine's bureau when I stepped in to put the clean clothes on her bed. It said underneath it, 'This is the dear child's latest picture, just a snapshot, but it will help you to recognize us at the train.'"

"H'm!" said Madame Whipple with a grim twinkle. "You must have good eyesight to read all that across the room."

"I had to go over to pick up some papers that had blown down into the waste basket when I opened the door. The window was open and it made a draught. I was afraid something Justine wanted to keep would be thrown away if I didn't rescue them. You can believe that or not as you like, but it's *true*. I may have a bad temper but I don't pry into even my enemy's private affairs."

"Oh, I never said you did," said Grandma twinkling. "But Amelia, did you notice whether she was good looking?"

"I'm sure I didn't look to see!" said Amelia offendedly. "Do you want the best napkins used, or the second best?"

"Well, I suppose, since Justine's been to so much trouble, you might use the best ones just for once. Where are you going to seat her? Next Dana, or opposite?"

"I'm sure I hadn't thought," said Dana's mother looking more and more like a thunder cloud.

"If you put her beside him he can't see her quite so well as across. You might wait to see if she's good looking," teased Grandma.

Amelia cast her a withering glance and slammed out into the kitchen. It beat all how keen Grandma was! What one thought in one's secret chamber, Grandma Whipple snatched out and shouted from the housetop. There really was not a flicker of an idea safe from her eagle clutch. Amelia's big hot unhappy body quivered as from a chastisement, as she jerked the potato pot over to one side where it could not boil so hard, and turned down the gas under the peas. Things were getting done almost too fast, and she felt all sore and hot around her eyes and throat as if she would like to put her head down and cry hard. Then Grandma's voice crooned out:

"Amelia!"

Amelia dabbed her eyes hastily with the corner of her apron and put her head in at the door.

"Did you call, Mother?" Her voice had an annoyed tone.

"Yes," said the old lady with alacrity, "I forgot to tell you there's some flour on your face. Better wipe it off before the company comes. They might get an idea you're worldly."

Amelia shut the door sharply, but even through the heavy wood she thought she heard the old lady's cracked cackle.

Amelia went to the window and leaned her hot forehead against the frame, letting the afternoon breeze fan her wet, tired eyes and brow. She cast a wistful glance up the road to the old gray house standing back from the street behind tall elm trees. Was that Lynette sitting on the porch, or her mother? Lynette never taunted like that. She always had a pleasant smile of greeting, and never seemed to be trying to say mean things, and get the better of people. Perhaps, after all, there might be a day coming when she would have a refuge, and smiles instead of hard words. She drew a deep sigh and turned back to her cooking, thinking for the thousandth time that she had never expected such a life when she left a good home and got married. What fools girls were to leave home! Here she was the slave of her mother-in-law, and bound to take what was given her, because she had no other place to go! Would it always be this way? Would life never hold any of the bright dreams she had had when she was young? Would it be just this dull heavy existence full of work, and no love or joy, on to the end, and the grave?

Other people lived in their children. She had heard them say so. And she had always supposed that when Dana got old enough to earn a living she would go and live with him and they would have a servant and she would be a lady at last. But there was Lynette! Dana wouldn't be hers! He would belong to Lynette. She could see that plain as day. In fact she had been seeing it for three or four years back, and hoping against hope that perhaps her son would have a little time for her before he got married. But now since he had come home this last time he had made her realize most forcefully that he had no such idea in mind.

She could see most plainly that he considered her an old woman, quite out of date, and not at all fit to be presented to a congregation as a permanent head of the minister's home. Indeed he had spoken quite openly about the near approach of the time when he would be going away "for good," and made suggestions to his grandmother about several fine old pieces of furniture that he would like to take with him, adding carelessly, "You and mother won't need them when I am gone. The house is stuffed full to overflowing now."

There had not been time for the hard-worked woman to stop to brood over this since it happened, for she had been rushed to death getting ready for Justine's company, but it had stayed in her heart like a poisoned barb, and festered. Now, as she leaned her hot forehead against the cool window pane she seemed to be pressing against the poisoned throb of it, and the sting drove into her soul like a keen hot instrument of torture.

Oh, of course Lynette was well enough, pretty and well connected, and sweet and pleasant to her. She had no complaint to make about the way she had always treated her, but one could see it was only for Dana's sake. Of course she had no love for her. She was not her kind. And never would she consent to go and live in a home with Lynette, not with Lynette as housekeeper. That was not to be borne. If the children would consent to let her be housekeeper and they board with her something might work out, she doubted it. But they never would of course. Every girl wanted her own domain, and to be the boss of it. Well, she would *never* go to live with them, even if Dana got around to want it, which her heart told her he never would. Why, Lynette had been taught to wash dishes with two pans, one for washing and one for rinsing! Such folly! A perfect waste of time and material to say nothing of hot water. A great deal better to pile them in the sink after the washing and pour a little hot water over them. Lynette said her grandmother had taught her that the dishes did not get thoroughly rinsed unless they were entirely immersed in water. H'mph! The Whipple dishes were just as clean as anybody's dishes, and as smooth and shiny. And she never used a rinsing pan. That was the difference between the Whipples and Brookes anyway, the Brookes thought they were too good for other folks. They thought she didn't wash dishes clean. They thought she was *dirty*.

Her eyes snapped and she lifted her tired head fiercely from the window pane, her strength returning with her anger, the tears which but the moment before had been blinding her scorching dry with the heat of her indignation. No, she would never go to live with Dana as a dependent. But oh, if she could just get away from Justine! Justine was the thorn in her flesh which pricked and scratched continually. Oh, Life, life, life! What a farce it was! Trouble everywhere one looked. No comfort even in one's own children. The minute you got them raised they turned away from you.

And now here was this other girl coming upon the scene! No telling what complications this might bring about. There might be worse things in life than even to have Lynette as a daughter-in-law, dish-pans and all! Strange Grandma didn't think of that. But then she didn't know the girl was grown up. That was all a piece of Justine's slyness. It would serve Grandma right if the girl made trouble.

Grimly Amelia went back to her cooking, her lips set, her heart heavy. The dinner had to be got whatever came, and one couldn't live always, that was some comfort. Though heaven would have to be pretty nice to make up for all one went through here.

Amelia had an inherited belief in a life hereafter, not an active one, which she kept put away in her thoughts somewhere against the day of her departure from this life. It could not be said to be a bright and shining hope. It was merely a last vague resort. It seemed necessary for the mother of a prospective minister of the gospel to have this much. It wouldn't be decent not to. But it could not be said to be a comfort and stay to her soul.

Then suddenly the peas began to boil dry, it was time for the biscuits to go into the oven, the potatoes must be mashed, and the gravy made. What difference did it make whether life was worth living or not? The dinner must be brought to its usual perfect climax. Justine was coming down the front stairs. In a moment more she would dash into the kitchen with her obnoxious offers of help again, and she would see that Amelia had been crying.

Amelia seized the potato pot and poured the potatoes hastily through the colander. The rising steam would hide her eyes. Justine would think it was the steam that made her eyes red. Justine wasn't as keen as Grandma. Think of Grandma noticing that little bit of powder!

Amelia dashed her hand hastily over her eyes again to make sure there were no taletale drops on her lashes. Was that Dana's car turning in at the drive?

Now, what would that other girl be like? Everything depended upon that.

V

THE train was within a mile of the station, and Ella Smith and her daughter were preparing to leave it.

"We're going through into the parlor car and get out from there," announced the daughter as if she were conductor of the expedition.

"No," said the mother, "that's silly. I don't like to walk in a moving train."

"Well, you're going to walk in this one, Ella," said the daughter impudently. "It's bad enough to have to ride in a common car without having people see you did it. Come on, Ella, pick up your things. It's time we were getting started."

"Now, look here, Jessie, that's another thing I've been going to speak to you about. You've simply got to stop calling me Ella. It's disrespectful, and I won't have it. It was all right at home just for fun, where everybody knew us, but now we're going among strangers, and Miss Whipple would be horrified. I want you to promise me, Jessie——"

"Promise nothing!" said the daughter. "It's none of her business what I call my mother. If she's such an antiquated jane that she doesn't know everybody is doing it now it's time she learned. It's you that have got to cut calling me Jessie. I won't have it, do you hear? You promised you wouldn't do it another time. And you've called me Jessie half a dozen times in the last five minutes. I'm Jessie Belle from now on, and you're Ella. Get me? It won't take me two minutes to jump back on

this train and go to New York or some other place I
like if you go to getting funny. I may stay in this dump
if everything goes right for a while but I certainly won't
if it don't. Get that? I won't stick around a week even if
you call me Jessie once. I'm not going to arrive there
and be tagged with that old-fashioned name. It's Jessie
Belle or nothing."

"Well Jessie—I mean, Jessie Belle—— It's awfully
hard to remember Jessie when I've called you that all
your life, but—Jessie Belle, I'll call you Jessie Belle if
you will stop calling me Ella. It really isn't seemly, Jessie—I mean Jessie Belle——"

"Aw, cut that! It's Ella or nothing. I won't stick
around at all and go around saying 'Momma' the way
you want me to. It simply isn't being done. If you can't
be a good sport like an up-to-date mother I'll make my
own life. I've told you that before. And you've got to
improve on that Jessie business, or you won't find me
when the train moves on at all. You get in a Jessie
twice for every time you say it right. You've got to
think of me as Jessie Belle. Say it over and over to
yourself while we're getting off and then you'll be able
to manage it naturally. I thought I had you trained.
Come, Ella, the train's slowing down. You take that old
bag and I'll take the new one. Get a hustle on. Follow
me, and don't you dare let that young man know we
rode in the common car."

"Oh, but, Jessie Belle," said Ella Smith dubiously,
rising and trying to pull down the heavy bag from the
rack overhead.

"That's the stuff, Ella, keep her up!" said Jessie
Belle swinging jauntily up the aisle with the new bag
and boldly slamming the door open. "Get through this
door and into the parlor car quick before anybody sees
us. We're going clear through and get off the other
end. See? And we're going to give the porter our bags
to carry. I've got a quarter all ready to give him. Don't
you make any fuss now."

"But Jessie—Jessie Belle—why waste a whole quarter for that? It's only a minute or two more, and we can
just as well carry them ourselves. The young man will

likely take them for us. Here, give me yours if it's heavy. I can manage them both."

"For mercy's sake, Ella, don't you see it means everything to make a good impression at the start? Do you want him to *see* we had to carry our own baggage? Do you want him to *know* you're so hard up you couldn't even spare a quarter for the porter?"

"But Jessie! Belle! wouldn't a dime do well enough? I don't know where we're going to get any more money after this is gone."

"Hush, Ella, people will hear you. Hurry. The train is stopping! Let me manage this business. You're a back number. One would think you'd lived in the country all your life instead of New York. Buck up now and get down to the other door quick! You don't want to get carried on do you?"

Ella Smith came puffing laboriously down the aisle after her daughter, bowling from one parlor chair to the next with regular spasmodic lurches, apologizing first one side and then another, finally bringing up with an elaborate apology to an empty chair at the end of the line, and drawn up with a jerk by Jessie Belle's restraining hand.

"Cut it Ella! You've lost your head!"

"But Jessie," gasped the excited mother, "I mean Belle, we weren't brought up to deceive. All this about your name—and pretending we've been travelling in the parlor car! Jessie! Belle! I don't think it is really right to change your name this way. You weren't baptized Belle, you were baptized Barbour. Jessie Barbour Smith! I don't feel we ought to go on with this. Your father would——"

"Cut it, Ella. Dad's dead and he's nothing to say about it, and I *prefer* Belle to Barbour. Besides, you burned your bridges behind you when you wrote Miss Whipple my name was Jessie Belle and now you've got to live up to it. Here we are! Now, you remember, I mean what I say. I'll clear out if you go to Jessying me. There! That must be the car just driving up. Gee! He's good looking! Say Ella I'm crazy about him already!"

"Now look here, Jessie! I mean Belle!" said the

mother pulling at her daughter's sleeve. "You mustn't talk that way. That young man is engaged! You know Justine Whipple wrote me he was engaged! It isn't decent——"

"Applesauce! Ella. What's that to me?" trilled Jessie Belle joyously, "just a little more exciting that's all, Ella. Come on! Give the porter your bag!"

Ella Smith got herself down the steps of the parlor car dubiously, and stood like a nice bewildered old hen whose one pretty chicken had suddenly become a wild duckling.

She looked about her with troubled eyes, trying to find her old friend Justine Whipple, bewildered with the new scenes, anxious and panic stricken about the outcome of this visit. The bustle and noise of the departing train held her on the platform where she had first stepped off, and she glanced back to the fast moving car where she had been sitting a few short moments before with a wild longing to jump on its steps and get back to her home again, only there was no home to go to any more.

The last car swept past her. She turned to find her daughter and beheld her slim as a match in her little black satin sheath with its deep blue facings, silhouetted against a background of taxis and automobiles shaking hands most intimately with an attractive young man in a dark blue suit, his panama hat crushed carelessly in his shapely hand. With a stranger foreboding she went toward them, wondering what her wild girl was going to do next? Hoping it would not end in some mortifying experience. It had been that way ever since Jessie was born,—Jessie Belle she corrected herself in her mind—she had been wondering what she would do next—what wouldn't she do?—and feeling utterly inadequate to cope with it. She kept saying, "Oh, if her father had just lived, it wouldn't have been this way! He knew how to control her!"

But the repetition of this happy reflection, however true it might have been, was unfortunately like beating against the wind. It had no effect whatever on Jessie Belle. She continued to go airily on her wilful way.

It was Jessie Belle who had insisted upon their selling the home her father had provided for them in a little quiet New England village, and going to New York to live in a flat that she might have her voice trained. Someone, a summer visitor perhaps, had carelessly told her she had a voice and she rested not day or night after that until she got her mother to go to New York.

And now, when like that other poor soul in a far country, they had spent all, and the interest they had thought was for all eternity most unexpectedly gave out because the principal had been spent, Ella Smith had appealed in a panic to her old school friend Justine Whipple. Even in their dire extremity Jessie Belle had been most trying, weeping hysterically at the idea of leaving New York, berating her mother for mismanagement, threatening to go her own way and find a job at the movies, threatening all sorts of things that had not been considered respectable in the little New England town where Ella Smith had been brought up. It was only when Justine Whipple had casually mentioned Dana, that the girl had at last evinced an interest in the gushing invitation to come to the Whipple house for the summer. And here they were! And there was the young man! And what would Jessie—Jessie Belle—do next? Her mother trembled and went forward dazedly to meet him.

"This is Mrs. Smith?" asked Dana politely with his best parish-call manner.

"Yes, that's my Ella," chimed in the girl, "and I'm Jessie Belle. You are Dana, aren't you? I thought so. Your aunt described you so perfectly that I should have known you if I had met you on Fifth Avenue. She said there wasn't another like you anywhere, and I guess she was right."

She looked at him with a flattering flutter of her dark, curly lashes, and swept him a dimple from the corner of her mouth which managed to convey a sense of deep admiration, and flitted so quickly that he wondered if it had really been there or he had only imagined it. He had never made a study of dimples. He looked at her several times as they progressed to the car to see if it would come again, but Jessie Belle knew how to hold her charms in reserve.

"Is this your car? Oh, how adorable! It's new isn't it? I'm crazy about that make of car. Say, you'll teach me to drive, won't you? I'm wild to learn. I've had no chance you know, being in New York studying so hard. It really isn't any pleasure of course motoring in the city, and we never had time to get out very far. I've been doing a lot of serious work you know. But Dad was going to buy a car just before he died, and we somehow haven't had the heart to get one since. Of course we'll get one soon though. May I sit in the front with you? I'll watch and get my first lesson. Ella, you sit back with the bags."

She waved her hand to her mother imperiously, and Ella climbed in with deeper foreboding than ever. A car! She was afraid of automobiles, and Jessie—no Jessie Belle, she must remember that—was so head-strong. Oh dear!

Jessie Belle was rattling on, and Dana, in the intervals of avoiding traffic, was watching to see if there had really been a dimple.

"They said you were a theological student. Is that really true? I can't imagine it. You don't look a bit gloomy. Don't you hate it? All those stuffy old subjects about dying and being good and all that? I should think you would have chosen something more—well —up to date, you know. People don't believe those old things any more. Why didn't you learn to fly, and be an explorer? That's all the rage now. You're much too nice looking to be wasted making long-faced prayers."

Dana gave her an indulgent smile.

"What do you know about such things, Kitten? You don't look as if you had ever spent time even thinking about it."

She swept him an upward coy glance from under her gorgeous lashes, and the dimple came out and flitted back like a sprite.

"Oh, but I have," she said coquettishly, her highly il-luminated lips pouted out like a bright red cherry, with the dimple lurking at one corner, "I thought about it a great deal after your aunt's letter came. It seemed so perfectly awful for a perfectly good young man, a really fine peach of a fella, to throw himself away preaching to a lot of folks who never listen and don't want to hear him anyway. I just felt sorry for you. And I thought it was going to be perfectly horrid to be here all summer long and the only man on the landscape a preacher. Oh, my soul! I couldn't see it at all!"

Her laugh rang out like a chime of silver bells and the dimple flashed full at him and stayed for a whole second. It was simply breath-taking; he had never seen anything so pretty in his life. He almost ran full into an old gentleman driving a Ford coupé, and righted himself only to grind into the fender of a shiny new car driven by a woman who frowned deeply at him and gave back a full line of contempt for his driving. But Jessie Belle's laughter rang out and he got himself into the road once more and hurried on, angry for once with himself, for losing his head. A pretty child, just a pretty child of course, but a really bewitching one! Lynette would be charmed with her. He must take her over at once and get them acquainted. It was going to be quite amusing having her in the house all summer, instead of a nuisance as he had expected. What ridiculous ideas she must have about religion. It would be interesting to set her straight. A good mission to begin on. But he must let her see that her straightlaced idea of a minister was all wrong. Ministers were not like that nowadays.

Ella Smith in the back seat drew in her breath sharply. This was a new view of her daring daughter. In New York Jessie Belle had kept her associates a good deal to herself. When she brought any of her fellow students home for an evening's frolic she had made her mother spend the evening with the woman in the neighboring flat. Ella Smith had no idea that her daughter could talk so boldly to a strange young man. And then that lie about her father's going to get an automobile before he died! How terrible for Jessie to talk like that. She hadn't known that her child would really tell a falsehood. Perhaps she had been joking. Surely she was only joking.

"There's the house!" announced Dana as they rounded the curve in the road and brought into view the rambling white house in its thick coat of paint and green blinds. The nasturtiums made a bright border to the path from the gate, shimmering in the last rays of the setting sun.

"Oh, isn't it darling!" shouted the radiant Jessie Belle, to her mother's deep relief. "I know it's going to be perfectly gorgeous! But I'm going to be terribly homesick for the first day or two, I know I shall. All those dark old mountains off there that you can't get away from night or day, and that great stretch of emptiness down there. You call that a valley don't you? Why don't they build it up? It looks too empty. Say, you'll take me to a picture tonight, won't you, just so I'll feel at home? I shall die of homesickness if you don't make me have a good time the first night. I'm always that way. If I don't like a place at the start I never do. You'll take me somewhere, won't you? That's a darling!" she coaxed making a cupid's bow out of her adorable vermilion lips. It was bad taste of course, painting lips, immoral and all that, Dana reflected, but she was such a child. And why had he never realized how attractive it was in a smile?

"Jessie!" flung forth Ella Smith from frightened shocked lips, "Belle!" she added feebly, as her daughter gave an upward tilt to her pretty pointed chin, but it was futile. The two in the front seat had not even heard. Ella Smith was sick at heart, and cast a backward glance, and a fearful look at the road as it vanished behind them. If only she could get out unseen, and run somewhere and hide. What should she do with her child?

But it was plain that neither of the two young people even remembered her presence. It did not matter what she did.

"Are you going to take me?" urged the girl. "Say you will quick or I'll jump right out over the wheel and go back to the station." She was pouting now, adorably, and the young theologue looked down at her amusedly.

"What a child you are," he said indulgently.

"But will you?" she insisted eagerly.

"Well, sometime soon. I'm afraid not tonight. I have another engagement."

"Oh, bother the engagement! That's just what I was afraid of. You'd be stuffy. You'd always be harping on duty and trying to preach a sermon to me. Well, if you don't go tonight I'll know you don't like me."

Her brows drew down, her lips pouted stormily, and her eyes filled with what seemed like almost tears. He had a strange feeling that she was a little child whom he had hurt and he ought to gather her into his arms and kiss her.

"I'm sorry," he said rousing to please her. "It was a previous engagement you know. I couldn't very well break it."

"You don't like me!" drooped Jessie Belle with fatigue in her tired pretty face. "Well, you're only a theological student after all of course—— But if you did like me you'd make a way to take me somewhere when I ask you. I'm your guest, you know. It would be quite natural for you to have a duty toward me the first night I'm here. Oh, you could find an excuse if you just wanted to!"

"Jessie!" called out Ella Smith again in horror, but perceived she had not been heard above the purring of the motor.

Jessie Belle turned the soft contour of her profile toward Dana and swallowed hard with her slim white throat, and set her little pointed chin very firmly with a tip tilt to it; not another word did she say until Dana leaned over and spoke:

"I'll try to fix it somehow to take you along," he said gently, as one speaks to a little child. "Of course as a guest in our house I have a duty toward you, and if you want it so much I guess I can fix it somehow."

"Now you're a darling again!" murmured Jessie Belle turning the full flash of her dimpled smile at him. "I knew you weren't a dub. I could tell it the minute I laid eyes on you. Oh, is all that your yard? Why don't we make a tennis court? I used to play before I went to New York. You play, don't you? I've got some darling

sports things. We can, can't we? Say we can. I know
your mother won't mind."

Dana had a vision of Grandmother Whipple's face at
the mention of turning her staid front lawn into a tennis
court but he murmured, "Well, we'll see. Now, here we
are. Mrs. Smith, let me open that door." And in a moment more Justine Whipple came ouf in her orchid
voile and pale ribbons and kissed her guests effusively,
and Dana was free to drive on to the garage.

"Now I'm in a pretty kettle of fish," he told himself
disgustedly, "How'm I going to get out of taking that
kid along with us tonight? What'll Lynette think of it?
In fact, I don't believe Lynette will want to go to the
movies. She doesn't like them much. What a mess! I'd
like to strangle Aunt Justine, getting me into all this!"

And then came Aunt Justine herself hurrying along
in the sunset with her unaccustomed orchid ribbons all
a flutter, and her face shining like a pleased child.

"Dana, will you please come upstairs right away and
open Jessie Belle's suitcase? Something has happened
to the lock. I think she's broken the key in it or something and she can't get it open to dress for dinner. And
your mother says will you please hurry right in, she
wants to tell you how to serve the chicken."

Aunt Justine poised like an old robin in the doorway
of the garage and then turned to flee before her nephew
could object, but he roared after her:

"Serve! Serve! What does she mean? I'm going out
to dinner. I was invited to Lynette's. You knew that!
Mother knew that! I can't *possibly* be at the table to
night."

"Now Dana," said Aunt Justine turning upon him a
woebegone face, "you wouldn't desert me like that the
first night my company was here! You *wouldn't*, I
know you wouldn't! I couldn't think it of you. Why,
what will they think of you, going off like that? The
only man in the family. And a young girl here too."

She pronounced it as though it was a young "gull."

"Well, I can't possibly help it, Aunt Justine. You'll
have to be reasonable. You can see for yourself that
Lynette would be pretty sore. I had to cut my day short

as it was to go to the station for you, and you ought to be able to explain my absence."

"Oh, but Dana, I can't! I can't! Really I can't! You really must help me out this once. I won't ask it again, and of course Lynette would understand. I'll telephone over and explain to her myself. That'll fix it all right. I'll make it perfectly fine with her. You'll see," and she turned as if to go into the house at once and do it.

"Oh Gosh!" said Dana now thoroughly aroused. "No, don't you speak to Lynn. Leave that to me. I'll have to stay I suppose, but I wish you and your company were——"

But Aunt Justine did not stay to hear. She started back to the house and Dana looked up to see Jessie Belle standing in the doorway.

"I've come down to tell you you needn't bother to come up. I managed the lock myself, and your mother says dinner is on the table. Are you going to take me in?"

Jessie Belle stood in the glow of the last rays of the setting sun like a vivid little picture, poised slenderly in a bright blue satin scrap of a frock, with her long, slim, pink silk legs, and her long, slim, pink, bare arms, looking more like a child than ever. A shingled bob, with a few odds and ends of lock curling up adorably like her lashes, set off her white, white skin, and her red, red lips so temptingly pouted.

Dana, strangely stirred, closed the garage door and came, and made no demur when Jessie Belle slipped her soft pink arm within his, and walked beside him confidingly, looking up into his face. Somehow it surprised Dana that they had so quickly got so intimately acquainted. It was just because she was a child, nothing but a kid of course, a very charming kid. But how the deuce was he to explain things to Lynette?

VI

Lynette was singing about the kitchen again, perhaps a little more quietly, with not quite so gay a lilt in her voice, yet much of the sadness had disappeared. Here in the dear home kitchen, with its clean yellow floor, newly painted for her home coming, its white oilcloth tables, and its gracious appointments for work, nothing could seem quite sorrowful. Forebodings fled when she went about the familiar task of making biscuits. The feel of the flour and golden butter as she worked them together in the big mixing bowl was good again. She drew a breath of gladness that school days were over at last! She was back where such pleasant homely tasks were possible. And these must be the best biscuits she had ever made. She would show them all that she had not lost her skill in the months of her absence.

She smiled dreamily as she measured the water, ice cold from the spring in the back yard, and stirred her batter daintily with a silver knife, touching it lightly as if she were weaving a charm over it. Was not the evening before her? Was not Dana coming back in a few minutes now, and they two would be together in the old surroundings? They could talk then, real communion of soul, such as they used to have in the early days of their acquaintance, when the thoughts of each answered to the other. Why, half of the charm of their companionship had been in their absolute agreement about everything!

Those things that Dana had said that afternoon were

a kind of pose, of course that would wear off with his life at home. Probably every young college man got that way, that is in most of the colleges. If Dana only knew how wonderful the spirit in her college had been. She would wait until his prejudices had worn off, till they had been together long enough for him to see that she had gained real knowledge and culture in the college of her choice. But not now, he was not ready for it yet. She would bide her time. Let him get the mists from his own university out of his vision. Let the sky and the trees and the mountains do their work in his soul; wait till he got back to the simple vision of God he had held when he went away. Then she could make him understand. It would not take long. Dana was real. Oh, he could not be deceived by the talk of the day! And Dana loved her. She caught her breath at thought of his almost fierce caress, and her cheeks glowed as she slipped the bright aluminum pan of puffy biscuits into the oven and closed the door carefully. Then the lilt came back to her voice, and the shine to her eyes. How foolish she had been to think Dana was changed! And in a few minutes he would be here, and they would have the whole long twilight and evening to smooth the misunderstandings away.

It was perhaps five minutes after that conclusion that the telephone rang.

Mother Brooke was setting the table.

There was the best tablecloth, and the napkins were the ones that Lynette had initialed the last time she was home for a holiday. There were roses, too. Grandmother Rutherford had sent for those. She had been very particular about the shade of pink like the color of Lynette's cheeks, she told Elim when he went down to order them.

Lynette did not know it but the ice cream was in molds, a lovely pink rose, a luscious pear, an apple, a peach, and a little white lamb with a pink ribbon around its neck. The new caterer was making a feature of these, and it pleased Lynette's mother to have something new for a surprise.

The birthday cake stood on the sideboard ready, its

pink candles all set for lighting. It looked like a fairy cake in its glistening white frosting, four layers thick, and every layer lying deep in creamy custard, the kind of cake that Lynette best loved. Nobody could quite make cream custard cake like Lynette's mother, delicate as a feather, luscious with the cream filling, so that it would melt in your mouth, crisply sheathed in the perfect frosting that never got too stiff, nor refused to set. It was perfect birthday cake, reminder of others of the years that had preceded it. There was nothing lacking to make that birthday table the most beautiful birthday table that any beloved daughter ever had.

Moreover, there was roasted chicken in the oven, just turning the right shade of brown, and sending forth savory odors from its stuffing every time the oven was opened. There were potatoes almost ready, and crisp spinach and new peas as green as if they were still on the vines, hoping themselves done in the bright aluminum kettle, and little new beets in another kettle, ripe for the slicing into butter and pepper and salt. Oh, it was a good dinner, and it was almost ready to be eaten.

Lynette went to the telephone. It was good to be home and answer the phone again. It might be almost anything. She had been away from a home telephone long enough to get the thrill of answering one again.

Lynette's mother arose from the front porch with sudden premonition. Elim had not come home yet and he had promised to be back in time to get cleaned up.

Lynette's grandmother, catching the excietment of the hour, unlatched her door and listened, feeling there might be something new and pleasant; mainly perhaps just to hear Lynette's voice again with its dear lilt, answering.

The two listeners paused in their two doorways, trying to seem not to listen, yet holding their breath to catch the words. Dana's voice. Ah! Lynette's mother relaxed. It was not Elim then. But why should Dana telephone when he was coming right over? It must be the train was late and he was going to have to wait for it. He was probably down at the station now. That meant that the dinner would not be so good as if it were served on the minute. She must go and turn down the gas of the oven. The chicken would get too brown.

But Dana's voice was clear and penetrating. He could be heard across the dining-room distinctly:

"I'm in a jam, Lynn, I can't come to supper tonight. I find they expect me to stay at home. I'm sorry to disappoint you but there's lots of days ahead of us."

Then Lynette's voice in dismay:

"Oh, Dana! But didn't you explain to them? Didn't you tell your mother beforehand that you were invited here?" There were almost tears in the sound of Lynette's voice, the lilt all gone.

"Why, I don't know that I did, Lynn. It never occurred to me. I never tell her where I'm going. I just go. I had no idea they had counted on me here, but they do, so that's that."

"But Dana, couldn't you explain to them now? Surely your mother would understand and excuse you!"

"Understand?" rumbled Dana sharply. "What is there to understand? What is there to explain? Mother knows I'm over at your house for meals more than half of the time anyway. She certainly wouldn't understand why this occasion was any different from any other. Why, Lynn, have you got anything special for supper? Won't it keep till tomorrow?"

Lynette was struggling with her voice. It wanted to flicker and wobble like a disappointed child's.

"Ice cream won't keep," she managed to say with a little hysterical giggle.

"Ice cream? Oh, well, eat it up. There's plenty more to be had at the drug store, or I might manage to run away and eat my share later in the evening, but no, I forgot. I've promised to do something else. Miss Smith wants to go and see a picture tonight. I told her we'd take her. We'll be up for you early, so there'll be plenty of time to get good seats. They say the new theatre is crowded always for the first showing."

But Lynette's voice faltered into this explanation.

"Miss Smith?" she asked in a puzzled tone, "Why, who——?"

"Yes, Mrs. Smith's daughter," explained Dana with

a sound of impatience in his voice. "You know I told you I was going to the station to meet them."

"But I don't understand, Dana, you said she was a little girl."

"Oh, no I didn't. I said it was a child, but it seems I didn't understand. She is a young girl, about your own age. We must help her to have a good time, Lynn. She is deadly homesick. We must show her some good times. You'll like her, Lynn."

Somehow there was something in Dana's voice that gave the impression of Miss Smith standing near the telephone. The listening grandmother and mother sensed it too perhaps more in the stiffening of Lynette's voice than in actually hearing anything.

"You'll be ready by seven, won't you, Lynn?" came Dana's voice hurriedly as if he wished to forestall anything Lynette might be going to say.

There was a distinct silence at Lynette's end of the wire.

"Lynn! Where are you? Hello! Hello! Didn't you hear me, Lynn? You'll be ready at seven, won't you?"

Lynette's voice was cool, deliberate, kindly, but aloof.

"Why, no, Dana, I scarcely think I can," she answered.

"Why, why not, Lynn? You surely have plenty of time to eat your supper, ice cream and all. If it isn't ready come on down here and eat. We can't afford to hang around, Lynn. I just telephoned up and they won't reserve seats. You have to get there early for any chance at all. And Miss Smith is very anxious to see this special picture. She says it's all the rage in New York and she hasn't seen it yet."

"Well, don't wait for me," said Lynette still coolly, "I don't think I'll go tonight."

"Not go! Why Lynn, that's absurd. Of course you'll go! It isn't like you to act pettish, just because I can't come to supper. Tomorrow night will be just as good as tonight won't it?"

"Why, yes, of course, if you feel that way," answered Lynette with a forced gaiety, "but Dana, I think I'll be excused. I believe I'm tired. I don't think I'd care to go. And besides, I couldn't think of going away again tonight when I've been away all day. Mother and Grandmother and Elim——"

"Nonsense!" broke in Dana. "You'll go of course."

"No," said Lynette decidedly, "I'm not going, Dana. Don't waste time coming after me. I really don't care to go."

"Is that some of the nonsense they taught you at that fool college?" asked Dana roughly.

There was another distinct silence during which Mother Brooke's heart beat hard with indignation. She had often regretted Dana's quick temper, but she had never heard him speak so rudely to Lynette before.

"I—beg your pardon?" said Lynette at last, as if she had not quite understood. There was a gentle rebuke in her tone.

Dana laughed.

"Well, you've got so many antiquated notions out there, that I didn't know but you had cut moving pictures as an act of grace."

Lynette did not answer. It did not seem to her that she could answer.

"Lynn!" shouted Dana impatiently, while Aunt Justine at his elbow told him that everything was on the table and he really must come at once. Lynette could hear her distinctly.

Dana joggled the instrument angrily:

"Lynn! Lynn! Where are you? You certainly haven't hung up, have you?"

"No," said Lynette gravely.

"Well, then, why don't you answer me?"

"I thought I had, Dana."

"Well you didn't. I want your word that you'll hurry and be ready by seven."

"I told you no, Dana. Please don't come after me. I'm not going tonight."

"Well, that's foolishness. I suppose you want to be coaxed. It isn't like you to act this way about something I can't help, Lynn. But I haven't time to talk about it now. I'll be there in a few minutes, and I want you to be ready to go with us." There was command in his voice, and the assurance that he would be obeyed.

Lynette opened her firm little mouth to reply, but this time Dana had hung up.

Lynette lingered for a moment with the receiver in her hand, a look of bewildered pain on her face. Her mother glancing in from the kitchen door was reminded with a pang of the same look on her little girl's face years ago when a little playmate had slapped her in the face. The mother heart was filled with fury at the lover who could speak so to her daughter, yet there leaped behind it an exultant thrill. Could it be that she was glad to have Dana show up unpleasantly? What was the matter with her today anyway? Ugly fierce impulses seemed striving within her soul, primitive emotions that would not be downed. But to have Dana speak in that tone to her pearl of a girl! To have him lightly put aside the invitation to her birthday dinner, and say it was not different from any other day! Oh, she would like a chance to tell Dana just what she thought of him!

Lynette hung up the receiver and came slowly back to the dining-room, a blank look upon her face.

Mrs. Brooke began to cut bread furiously, forgetting entirely about the buscuits. She cut enough for twice her family. Her lips were set in a thin hard line.

"Mother, has Elim come yet?" Lynette's voice rang out in a sharp gaiety that her mother fancied hid a sob.

"He's just coming in the back door!" called back the mother with a false cheeriness in her own voice.

"Well, then we can have dinner right away," said Lynette. "Dana can't come. They've pre-empted him at home. He says he can't get away tonight on account of the company."

"Dana can't come?" said Mrs. Brooke apparently as much astonished as if she had not heard the whole dialogue, "Why, Lynette?"

"It's all right!" said Lynette bravely. "I'll just run up and change my dress, and I'll be right down. Elim'll be hungry. We needn't wait!" Lynette vanished up the back stairs, and Grandma Rutherford's door closed softly with an indignant click.

Mrs. Brooke stood with the bread knife poised and thought unutterable things. She turned around, the bread knife still in her hand, and looked out of the pantry window, down toward the Whipple house.

Over across the dining-room, in Grandmother Rutherford's room, Grandmother Rutherford stood softly at her own window, and looked with aristocratic indignation off down over the Whipple house and toward the eternal hills.

Up in her own room Lynette Brooke stood at her window flooded with the sunset glow, and looked through blinding tears with unseeing eyes at the Whipple house down the road.

Just at that moment Elim entered the kitchen door and crossed to the pantry.

"S'th' matter, Muth? You look as mad as a hatter!"

"I'm just——" Mrs. Brooke paused for an adequate word. "I'm just being a little *indignant*."

"S'th'matter, Muth, did that poor fish stand Lynn up?"

"Why, Elim, how did you know?" asked his mother surprised out of the feeble rebuke she had started to administer.

"Gosh!" said Elim hotly, "I saw him down at the station just now letting a regular baby doll put it all over on him. He was bringing her up in his car and he came mighty near smashing into Jabe Winslow's truck, looking at her. If Jabe hadn't nearly climbed a telegraph pole just in the nick of time there wouldn't have been any baby doll, nor any Dana either. Call that driving? Gosh he makes me sick. He oughtn't to be allowed on the road. I'd like to take him down by the creek and wallop him till he couldn't swing those graceful Whipple arms above his shoulder, nor lope along the highway with that look-at-me smirk. I'd like to give one of his lovely eyes a good black and blue swelling. I could do it too. He's as soft as putty. Always thought himself too good to keep in training. He makes me tired. He's a pain in the neck. I don't see what my sister ever saw in him anyway. Why, he can't even pitch a ball straight. He pitches exactly like a guyrrrl. Gosh!"

"Hush, Elim! Lynnie'll hear you! Don't make her feel bad. I guess she feels pretty bad now. She had everything fixed so prettily on the table, and she's been counting on his coming. Don't let her see you know it."

"Well, why'n't she get a *real man* then? Why'd she take up with that poor fish? Say, is she going to stand for him standing her up like that? Staying home just cause another girl has come, when it's her birthday and all?"

"Hush, Elim! You mustn't let her hear you! I don't believe Dana knew it was her birthday. He's probably forgotten——"

"Aw! Now you try to take up for him, Muth. Whaddaya wantta do that for? Know? He knows all right. Hasn't he been keeping her birthday parties for years, ever since I was a little kid? Keen on em, too, coming here and eating up half her birthday cake, and bringing her some good-for-nothing present that didn't cost more'n fifty cents or so, and flowers he picked in the woods!—aw bah! He's a pain! He may have forgotten, but don't tell me he didn't *know*. I'm too wise for that. That baby had something else he wanted to do, Muth, and don't you forget it, or he'd a come. He's too fond of your cooking."

"Elim, you must hush. Lynnie will——"

And just then from the dining-room came Lynette's voice, cheerful, brave and almost natural.

"Where are you all? Why don't we have dinner at once, Mother? I'm starved and of course Elim is. Come buddy, get your hands washed and help dish up. Isn't it going to be great having a real birthday together again, just ourselves?"

Elim looked at his sister with a relieved sigh and stamped off to wash his hands.

"Isn't she the little old sport, though," he said softly to himself while he combed his rough curls, and smudged off his face and hands. "I'll bet on my sister every time. She shan't marry that poor stiff if I have to wallop him within an inch of his life to keep her from it. She's too good."

Mother Brooke looked at her child and marveled.

There were marks of tears on Lynette's face, sudden fierce hot tears, the kind little Lynnie used to shed when all her child world went utterly wrong and she couldn't set it right, but there was a firm little set to her lips that gave a white radiance about them, and patrician tilt to her chin that reminded one of her Grandmother Rutherford. Lynette was not going to be utterly crushed by Dana's defection. She was going to carry the evening through with smiles. There might be storms and tears and anger afterward in the seclusion of her dark room, but she was not going to spoil the celebration for the family. Dear Lynette! She was wearing a little turquoise blue crêpe frock, and she looked heavenly to her mother, with the touch of sunset glow on her golden hair. The precious child! Her pearl of a girl! She had worn her grand new dress just for them!

Grandmother Rutherford came out of her room bravely garbed in soft gray silk with foamy white ruffles at throat and wrists, and the old cameo pin at her neck, that looked for all the world like a cutting in precious stone of her own exquisite face.

"It's so nice to have just us here, Lynnie," she said as she settled into her high-backed chair with Elim pushing her up to the table. "I've sort of wanted to have us all together without anybody else, just for once. It's so nice and cozy, like old times, Lynnie. Not even Dana to feel like company. Now he's a minister it somehow seems as if he was a stranger. I'm glad he isn't here just for tonight."

"Well, then, I'm glad too, Grandmother," said Lynette playing up to the occasion courageously. "Let's have a real time this evening. Just *us!*"

A light of admiration sprang into Elim's eyes, and Mother Brooke smiled tenderly, though in her heart she knew what pain these smiles were costing her beloved girl. She could see a little white rim of suffering around her Lynnie's delicate lips, and a shadow in the

dear blue eyes. He wasn't worth it! Oh, he wasn't
worth a shadow in such eyes, she thought, Mother-like.

Elim carved the chicken without a murmur, and Lynette served potatoes and spinach and peas, and passed
biscuits and jelly and preserves, and glowed over the
roses, and the tissue paper packages she found beside
her plate, and was duly surprised by the ice cream in
molds, ate two of them in fact, a rose and a lamb, and
joked with Elim merrily, until the spirit of depression
was exorcised, and it seemed almost as gay as in the
dear old carefree days.

"Gee!" said Elim, "Isn't this great? I wish we were
always just us. Say, Lynn, don't forget we're going fishing together tomorrow *all day*. Nobody else along. Get
me? I got lots of new places to show you, and there's a
thrush's nest right where you can look into it from a big
rock and watch——"

It was just then that the telephone rang, and Lynette
went white and severe around her lips and started to
her feet.

"Let me go dear," said her mother suddenly rising to
her feet, "I think that is for me. I'll answer it," and Lynette sank limply back into her chair, a sudden pained
hush upon her.

VII

THEY were sitting down to supper at the Whipple house.

Amelia Whipple with a smudge of powder still adhering to one side of her nose, and the rest of her face hot and steamy from the kitchen and the last minute dishing up. A long grizzled lock of hair that had escaped from its pinning waved over one eye in spite of her efforts to push it back with her tired moist hands. She did not present the impressive appearance which she had hoped to show to the guests from New York. Moreover she was disturbed by the snatches of telephone conversation which she had overheard as she went back and forth through the pantry swing door to the dining-room. The telephone was located in a little back hall that opened off the pantry and constituted a sort of semi-privacy. But Amelia was keen enough to sense what was going on. She knew that Dana had been invited to take dinner with Lynette. She did not like it that this other girl had kept him at home. Little as she really desired Lynette for a daughter-in-law she liked this other girl less, just on general principles. Was she not a girl of Justine Whipple's selection? That was enough for Amelia. She hated her even before she saw her.

"Dinnah is sehved!" announced Justine at the top of the front stairs, tapping lightly on the guest room door. Her voice floated jubilantly down the stairs and made the old lady cackle with dry laughter.

Amelia walked heavily to the hall door as the guest descended and in a grim voice announced clearly:

"Supper is ready!"

The old lady looked up with a twinkle in her eye. It began to look as if life was going to be interesting.

Dana helped his grandmother to the head of the table, although his mother always did the serving from her seat just at the right of her mother-in-law. The old lady kept an eye and hand thus on everything, just as if she were able to be about like other people.

Ella Smith entered the dining-room deprecatingly. She had a feeling that already her child needed apology. She regarded Jessie Belle with a sort of fascinated horror.

Jessie Belle looked startlingly out of place in the old-fashioned room, with her high heels, her entirely bare arms, and her vivid, painted lips.

She made the initial mistake of ignoring the old lady, merely tossing her a scornful nod when she was elaborately presented by Justine, and turning at once to Dana with some light remark, as if he and she were the only two people really in the room.

The old lady's keen little black eyes took her all in, cosmetics, nude stockings, bare knees, short skirt, and long earrings, and when they were well seated she held up the ceremony of grace just as Dana was about to bow an embarrassed head.

"Dana, I wish you would go to the top drawer of my bureau and bring me my black and white knit shawl."

Dana looked up in astonishment, but arose at once, went to the parlor bedroom which had always been Madame Whipple's and brought the shawl.

There was a moment's embarrassed silence while he was gone, which the old lady did not break by explanation. Amelia used it to cast an anxious eye over the table and make sure she had forgotten nothing. Justine tried to fill it with an apologetic smile at her guests. Jessie Belle was taking a frank inventory of the meal.

Dana came with the shawl and was about wrap it around his grandmother's shoulders, when she waved him away imperatively:

"It's not for me," she said ungraciously. "Put it on her," and she waved her hand toward Jessie Belle. "She needs it. The evening's getting cool."

"Why, Grandma *deah!*" gasped Justine anxiously, casting a deprecating glance at Jessie Belle.

Dana stood awkwardly holding the hideous knit shawl and looking perplexedly from his grandmother to the girl.

"Put it on yourself, boy," giggled Jessie Belle. "I pass. I'm roasted to a frazzle now. Nobody could ever drag a shawl on me, could they, Ella?"

Ella Smith shrank and shivered and tried to look as if her offspring were addressing someone else.

Amelia came to the rescue crustily:

"Sit down, Dana, and let's get this meal started. Everything's getting cold."

Dana tossed the old shawl to a chair and went to his place, mumbled a grace and unfolded his napkin angrily. He flashed a glance of contempt at his grandmother who returned it with a twinkle of grim humor, but said nothing.

Amelia had solved the problem of placing her guests by seating Jessie Belle at Madame Whipple's left, Dana at the foot of the table with Ella Smith beside him, and Justine at his right and next to herself. She thought by this bit of diplomacy to separate her son as far as possible from this obnoxious girl. Amelia Whipple had suddenly begun to feel that Lynette Brooke was a wonderful girl, the finest girl she knew. It seemed to her that she had always felt so. This girl with the fanciful name had ignored her so utterly from the first moment of meeting that it seemed to Amelia she had made no more impression upon her than if she had been a ghost.

But Amelia's plan to separate the girl from her son did not work. For all Jessie Belle cared they might have been seated side by side on a lone hillside. She carried on a rapid banter of words with Dana in a loud voice interspersed with much laughter and interesting phrases of speech which were most amazing to Amelia, and to Grandma Whipple, a rare treat. Grandma sat in slience grimly eating her dinner while the banter was going on, biding her time.

At last there came a silence and Grandma leaned over pleasantly toward Jessie Belle, and in a good clear voice said:

"Can you reach me the biscuits, Jezebel?"

Jessie Belle turned and gave her a stare.

"Oh, Grandma!" corrected the horrified Justine.

"Her name is Jessie, Belle. You misunderstood me."

"I understood perfectly, Justine. Will you please pass me the biscuits, Jezebel?"

Jessie Belle laughed and passed the biscuits.

"Why, of course I will, Grandma. What a gorgeous way to pronounce my name. I never thought of it before. Wouldn't the girls simply shout if they heard it! I believe I'll adopt it. It's quite original. None of the girls have a dashing name like that. They'd call me Jez of course. I believe I will. Ella, you better start in calling me Jez at once. I mean it, I really do. I'll write to Eve tonight and make them address my letters that way. Miss Jezebel Barbour Smith. How'll that please you, Ella? If I stick the Barbour in it'll be a go with you I know. Oh, boy! I gotta name for sure now. Dana, you're to call me Jez from now on, see?"

"Jessie!" burst forth the horrified Ella Smith, "Belle, I mean," she added hurriedly. "You really are the limit! I hope you'll all excuse her," she cast a deprecating glance around the table, "Jessie Belle's a great joker. That's why she calls me Ella. We're always such good chums you know," she finished lamely.

"Yes, we are not!" chimed in Jessie Belle like a chant. Lifting daintily manicured fingers tinted and polished to the last degree and serveral times beringed, she blew a most offensive little kiss in her mother's direction, with an after twist like the curve of a tennis ball in a good skillful cut that drifted it over to Dana's direction where it turned up having lost its offense.

Amelia fairly snorted and was sure she heard Grandma cackling under her breath, though her face was perfectly impassive.

"Oh, Jessie Belle!" giggled Justine spatting her hands together childishly. "How funny you are! That was perfectly delicious! Oh, we are going to enjoy you so much!"

Amelia suddenly shoved her chair back with a harsh grating sound and went with heavy footsteps into the kitchen for more cream. Even her back was eloquent of her feelings, but Justine was fairly launched now, and carried on a byplay of fulsome flattery, while Jessie Belle gaily took the lead in the conversation, addressing it mainly to Dana who was frowningly eating his dinner and saying little. He was in one of his worst moods, and was out of sorts with his whole world. It was like him to feel that this giddy little girl who had caused all the trouble was being martyred by them all, and to blame his family for the way they were treating her. Dana was angry with Lynette for being hurt, angry with his grandmother for being a hornet driving in her sting wherever it pleased her, angry with his mother for being so ungracious, and angry with Justine for being a fool. He was beginning to feel that out of them all only he and Jessie Belle had good sense. He tried to soothe this uneasiness about Lynette by realizing his own superiority. That really helped a lot.

So Dana gave himself over to bantering with Jessie Belle, and got what Jessie Belle herself would have called "quite a little kick," out of showing his family how well he understood her jazzy slang, and how neatly he could reply in what he knew must be to them almost an unknown tongue. He felt that they were saying, "Behold, how this our great scholar and theologian can stoop to understand the simplest foolishness and be at home in any atmosphere!" He felt that this was one of the attributes of a good minister, that he should be able to adapt himself to anyone, high or low. It was like Paul, the great preacher, who when in Rome did as the Romans—no, how was that? Oh, "all things to all men," of course that was the quotation, and Dana swelled on to a more comfortable position with regard to himself.

Of course Lynette would have gotten over her huff by the time they reached her house, and be ready. He knew Lynn. It was not like her to be rude and pettish especially when there were strangers by. She would go, and be as sweet as usual, and by the time the evening was over she would smile and they would plan to go somewhere tomorrow, and it would all be forgotten. It was a little tough on Lynette of course, his not being able to go to her house to supper when she had planned it so long beforehand. Lynette was sort of sentimental about things like that, keeping days and things, but then, she must learn not to be childish, and really this was nothing special, just a chance invitation given some two or was it three years before when they were both little more than children. They were grown up now and Lynn really must put away childish things and be a woman. Oh, well, he would explain this all carefully to her tomorrow, and she would see, just as she had sweetly yielded that afternoon when he had gone into details. Of course she ought to take his word for it without the details. But she would grow to that.

So Dana put his uneasiness aside and entered into Jessie Belle's talk with a gaiety that made his Aunt Justine flush all over her pasty face with an elderly pleasure, and cast a furtive triumphant glance in Amelia's direction; and made Amelia set the coffe cups down in their saucers with a sharp little click, when she handed them around, and shut her lips hard, and resolve to invite Lynette over to spend the afternoon and take dinner the very next day. Let Lynette come and fight this battle, she herself was unfitted to cope with this hateful little painted creature, but Lynette could. She would go over wholesale to Lynette. What a fool she had been to think Lynette wasn't good enough for Dana. Why, she hadn't ever known there *were* fools of girls in the world like this one!

Grandma Whipple sat and ate her biscuits, bite by bite, buttering them thoroughly and thoughtfully with her palsied hand, and sometimes lifting a knowing eye in which crouched a wicked little twinkle, to glance furtively round the table. But she said no more. Only Amelia fancied she heard a breath of cackling laughter now and then from the grim lips as the talk went on.

It developed at length from Jessie Belle's banter that Dana and she were going to a picture that evening, and Justine lifted her large limpid eyes to Dana's face and said in her most Bostonian accents:

"How lovely of you Dana, deah! So thoughtful!" Dana wanted to slap her.

Dana would have liked to slap Jessie Belle also. Why didn't she know enough to keep still about things? He must make her understand that it wasn't wise to let his family know everything if she wanted to have a comfortable time. Now they would raise the roof at his going off to a picture show. His mother and grandmother disapproved of the movies. They had read a great deal against them in their church paper. They thought Grandfather Whipple would not have gone to them if he had been living. Now there would be a family row! Dana hated family rows. He avoided them on every possible occasion. If he could not avoid them he faced about and made a worse one on his own account which stopped the first one instantly. He really could make a pretty bad row all by himself when he tried. But one didn't wish to do that when there were strangers by if it could be avoided. He watched his mother anxiously under his lashes. Dana's lashes were very long and black. They swept low when he arranged them for ambush, giving him an aspect of a formidable personage who was not to be lightly approached.

But Dana's mother was not afraid of him tonight. "Isn't Lynette going?" she asked sharply, speaking for the first time since she had ordered him into his seat.

Dana lifted reproachful eyes and answered haughtily:

"Certainly, Mother. We're going up for her at once. I told her to be ready at seven."

Justine looked anxiously toward Jessie Belle, and Jessie Belle showed the gleam of her little pointed teeth behind her carmine lips, and gave a twisted toss of her chin, with an almost imperceptible lifting of eyebrows and shoulders. Was Jessie Belle trying to let Justine know that she would be equal to any Lynette on the calendar? That she would show Lynette "where to get off?" Was that the phrase they used? Justine was tremendously flattered and delighted.

"Oh, Jessie Belle, you are delicious," she gurgled into her napkin, and Jessie Belle half closed one eye and stuck out her lips in a little face toward Dana again, till Justine almost choked laughing at her.

"Perfectly delicious," she gurgled.

Dana turned and dealt her an extinguishing look which quieted her for the moment, but her spirit rose joyously with the sense that there had been a comraderie established between this girl and herself. Jessie Belle understood just how she felt about Lynette and Dana, and Jessie Belle would take a hand at things from now on.

But Dana's mother could not let things go so loosely. She gathered up her courage to protest:

"But Dana, I thought you didn't care for moving pictures. I thought you felt it was not fitting for a——"

But Dana interrupted her hurriedly with a frown:

"You certainly misunderstood me, Mother. I merely said a student had no time for such amusement. I see no harm—of course it depends on the picture—but I see no harm in a little relaxation now and then. Mother, could we have our dessert now? It is getting late and we really ought to be on our way in ten minutes at the latest."

Amelia arose with a pained look on her face and began to remove the plates. She did this with quietness and a skilled technique that made it seem as if the dishes were moving off of themselves without the exertion of anyone. Amelia knew how to do it with the least possible effort. She never made an unnecessary move, and accomplished the maximum with each motion.

Amelia served the dessert in silence. It was strawberry shortcake, the old-fashioned kind made of flaky biscuit dough, split, buttered, and filled with the great luscious strawberries that grow in New York state, with the tang of the long cold winters in their spicy flavor. There were more berries on the top, with powdered sugar, and a big bowl of whipped cream to put over it. Jessie Belle exclaimed with pleasure:

"Oh, boy! Lead me to it! Say, Ella, I'm glad I came. How about you?"

Amelia set her plate down grimly without a word. How she was going to stand this girl for a whole long summer she didn't see. There was a choking sensation of tears in her throat as she turned to give Dana his shortcake. Why didn't her boy, descendant of the great Whipple grandfather, see that girl was not his equal? How could Dana be so blind?

But then, of course Dana had to be polite to guests in the house, or at least of course he thought he had to, though he needn't have gone quite so far with it. He might have made her understand that he had an engagement. She herself would see by tomorrow at least that the girl knew that Dana was as good as engaged. It must have been the girl's fault of course. Girls were that way in these days—all but Lynette. And Dana was so attractive of course. She couldn't be blamed for wanting him to show her attention. Probably it wasn't Dana's fault at all. Probably by tomorrow he would fix things up so that she wouldn't bother him. Probably Lynette would regulate it all when she got to see how things were. Of course Dana wasn't to blame. So she tried to explain to her tired heart, while she minced at a bit of shortcake and pretended to be finishing her supper.

Then she had to see her boy go off into the evening glow with that girl! It made her furious!

Just as they had watched Dana in the morning go off with Lynette, so they watched these two now, Grandma and Amelia and Justine, Amelia hovering back in the shadows with a pile of dessert plates in one hand and a bunch of forks in the other, her eyes full of smoldering fires, and unshed tears. Ella Smith had run down to the gate to give Jessie Belle a gauzy scarf shot through with rainbow spangles which her daughter had demanded to be found for her, and the three were alone for the moment.

Small and slim with her sleek little dark head almost up to Dana's shoulder, her bare arm linked in Dana's intimately, her curly lashed eyes turned up to his confidingly, her red lips pouted out teasingly with elusive dimple flickering in and out, with her short blue skirts, and her long slim legs, in nude-colored stockings, her shining patent leather heels twinkling, Jessie Belle looked like an abnormal child hanging on Dana's arm, as they walked away in the sunset glow up the hill toward Lynette's house.

"Jez-e-bell" murmured Grandma Whipple half under her breath as if she were chanting a line of an imprecatory psalm.

"Oh, Grandma! How quaint you are!" burbled Justine from behind her chair in the shadow of the room. "But isn't she a darling? Doesn't she look just like a lovely flower? I think she's like a flower!"

"Yes," said Grandma, "Blue Ruin!" and her keen old eyes sought the smoky blue of the distant hill across the valley.

VIII

THE Brooke telephone was on a little table in the front hall close to the coat closet. The cord of the telephone was long enough to reach into the closet and when anyone wished to carry on a private conversation or shut out the noises of the house it was easy to step inside this coat closet and secure a private booth. Mrs. Brooke had stepped into the closet with the telephone almost as soon as she began talking, so that the three who waited at the dining-room table could get no clue to whom she was talking.

Lynette made no further pretense eating. She sat with tense expression, her hands clasping each other tightly in her lap. Could that be Dana? And what was her mother saying to him? Surely she could be trusted not to tell Dana anything about this being her birthday! Lynette's proud, sensitive nature shrank unutterably from having Dana know, now that he had stayed away and forgotten. Her mother must not beg him to come. She simply must not. Almost Lynette started up again to go and warn her mother, and then thought better of it and forced herself to relax. But the thought was beating itself over and over again in her brain, Dana had forgotten the birthday which he had known and kept scrupulously for years. He had forgotten their unspoken tryst to which she had invited him two years before. He could stay away just to be polite to a stranger. Even if his aunt Justine had insisted, Dana well knew how to have his own way and Dana would never

have been persuaded to stay if he had wanted to come,
if he had felt that this was more important. It followed
then that Dana had not been impressed with the importance of the day, had not cared more than anything else
to come to her. He could not have been looking forward to it through the years as she had been. There
was tragedy written in Lynette's face though she did
not know it.

Grandmother Rutherford sat pretending to eat the
last bit of her ice cream, which she had decided before
her daughter went to the telephone was a little more
than would be good for her. But she could not bear to
have Lynnie think she was sitting there watching her.

Elim, boylike was devouring his third piece of cake
and a second ice cream mold in the shape of a great
pink peach with a green leaf. His brows were drawn in
a heavy frown, but he seemed to be wholly intent on
his ice cream.

Suddenly with keener hearing than the rest, or perhaps just boy instinct, he felt that someone was coming
in the gate. He lifted his eyes and glanced out the window.

"Oh, gee;" he said angrily, "there comes Dana! Now
I suppose he'll order you off somehwere, or else stay
here, and all the good times will be over. Gee, I think
we might have you a little while Lynn. You've been
away for ages, and we're your *own folks*. I don't see
what that guy has to be around here all the time for anyway. Who's he got with him? That blue-eyed baby
doll! Now they'll come walking right in here. Dana
never did have any manners, and they'll eat up all the
rest of the cake and ice cream. Gee. I'm goin' to beat it
while the going is good."

He shoved his chair back sharply, but Lynette laid a
detaining hand quickly on his arm, a glint like steel
suddenly coming into her sweet eyes, her delicate lips
set in a kind of frozen beauty:

"No, Elim, sit still," she said imperatively. "Nobody is coming here and I'm not going away anywhere.
I'll go out and send them off. I told Dana I couldn't go
out tonight. He had no right to come over after what I

said. Wait, I'll go out and tell him! Don't you go off!
I'll be back in just a minute."

Lynette went out of the dining-room quickly, closing
the door behind her with a decisive click. They could
hear her cross the hall and step out the front door.

Elim looked up with a troubled frown and met an
answering look of understanding from his grandmother's eyes. He made a bitter grimace:

"Gee, Gramma, I hate that guy!"

"I don't know as that will do any good, Elim," she
twinkled.

"Well, she's too fine a girl! She's——! She——! He——!"
he stumbled incoherently.

"Yes, I know," sighed his grandmother looking suddenly very tired and feeble. "But I don't know that hat-
ing will do any good. I think praying would be more
effective, don't you?"

"Go to it, Gramma, I'm with you," he responded
heartily. "Say, is there another piece of that cake cut?
Gee, it's good! I been holla all the afternoon."

The front piazza was flooded with rosy light from the
sunset, and Lynette looked like some delicate vision as
she came out in her little blue frock. The light touched
her soft hair and brought out the gold, and the blue of
the dress brought out the pink in her cheeks. She was
exquisite as she stood there awaiting them. Jessie Belle
looked up and stared rudely. She had not counted on
anything as chic and lovely as this. Justine Whipple had
written about Lynette, "She's just a sweet little country
girl you know," and Jessie Belle had whetted her weap-
ons accordingly. But this girl was different, unusual,
sophisticated in a way that Jessie Belle neither understood nor admired, but secretly feared.

Dana looked up as Lynette came out, with an exclamation of admiration, and the frown he had been wearing since his telephone conversation smoothed away.
Ah, here was his own Lynn, lovelier than he had ever
seen her!

"Oh, you're all ready, aren't you?" he exclaimed
with relief in his tone. "That's good, we haven't any too
much time to spare. We're going to walk. It would be

practically impossible to find a place to park the car near the theatre you know, and Miss Smith wanted to see the town. Lynn, this is Miss Smith. You two girls ought to be good friends this summer."

Jessie Belle glanced up with abrupt insolence in the sweep of her lashes. She merely tilted her chin disagreeably and lifted her plucked eyebrows a trifle, without smiling.

Lynette acknowledged the introduction gravely, almost casually, and turned back to Dana:

"I'm sorry you wasted your time coming after me, Dana," she said almost haughtily. "I thought I made it quite plain to you that I was not going."

"Nonsense, Lynn. Why aren't you? We aren't going to take no for an answer. I want you to go. Isn't that enough?"

Dana flashed her one of his imperious compelling smiles that she was wont to answer with a yielding one, but her eyes were still grave as she replied:

"Not tonight. It's of no use to discuss it, Dana. I wouldn't leave Mother and Grandmother tonight for —anything!" she finished.

Dana gave her a vexed look, and was about to present other arguments when Jessie Belle slid her hand into his arm and began to pull him.

"Come on Dana. We can't stand here all night. If she won't go there's no use in our losing our seats. I want to see that picture!"

"Yes, go," said Lynette with dignity.

"Well, I certainly don't understand you, Lynn," said the young man haughtily, "but if you're in that mood it would be unpleasant to have further words about it of course. I'll see you tomorrow sometime and meantime I don't in the least like the way you've acted!"

Then he suffered himself to be led away, arm in arm with that giddy, painted child! It was incredible! Dana Whipple! Her Dana! And never a word that he was sorry not to have been at her birthday party. He didn't know it was her birthday! Dana had forgotten!

She had not let herself believe it before, but now she let the sorrowful truth roll over her, as she stood in the golden light in her forget-me-not robes watching her loved one walk away into the sunset. One arm was lifted, her hand shading her eyes, the evening breeze fluttering the sheer ruffle at her wrist and billowing the transparent sleeve and showing the round firm arm with its pretty curves. She was a vision to make one glad. Dana looked back furtively and saw her, secretly rejoicing in her beauty, fiercely angry in his heart that she had not shown herself his slave before this other girl. She had humiliated him by not obeying his wish, and she must be made to suffer for it. He could not let her get in the habit of taking the upper hand. Women were that way when they got started. He must make it very plain to her that his word was law. Strange what had got into Lynn! She never acted that way before. Was she jealous? Well, perhaps a little jealousy might do her good. She had had his devotion so many years that she was getting to take it for granted, and really a man, especially a minister, must be the head of his own household.

So he walked away with the painted child upon his arm, into the sunset, planning how he would humiliate Lynette, planning not to go over the first thing in the morning as he had intended. He would take Jessie Belle out for a ride perhaps, and drive past the door where Lynn could see him. Then late in the afternoon, when she had given up expecting him, he would run over and have it out with her. By that time she would be sorry and ashamed, and after a salutary lecture, and due repentance on her part, he would forgive her. It would be delicious comforting her. Perhaps there would be tears in her eyes. Though Lynn was not given to tears. But he would kiss her eyelids. If there were tears he would kiss them away—and——

These thoughts were pleasant as an undertone of accompaniment to Jessie Belle's chatter, but they suddenly arrived at the door of the theatre and Jessie Belle asserted herself.

There were tears in Lynette's eyes as she stood in the sunset glow and watched the two walk out the gate. She was trying to understand the feeling that possessed her soul. Was it possible that she was jealous of that common little painted girl with the long earrings and the jazzy manner? She who had trusted Dana all these years when they were apart?

But such a girl! How could he stand her? He really seemed amused with her. Still, of course he had to be polite to a stranger in his home. Yet, did he? By any code did he have to forget her on this day of all days? He had come after her at last of course, but he had not seemed to recognize what he had omitted. He had brought no apology for slighting her invitation, only annoyance with her that she had seemed to expect him to come.

Well, probably she was tired and overwrought. She had counted too much on this special day. It was childish in her of course. She must learn to control her feelings, and not to be super-sensitive. Didn't Dana say something like that this afternoon? Somehow there seemed to have been a great many things that Dana said that were different from what she had expected, things that hurt. Perhaps she was becoming morbid. She would go in and try to make her family have a good time at least. They should not suspect that she was hurt to the soul. Never!

She went into the house, head up, smiling. A forced smile, but a smile. There were no tears in her eyes now. This thing was largely a matter of pride perhaps, or self-control. She would put it aside, and never should Dana suspect how she had been hurt by his easy willingness to stay away from her birthday supper. Some day probably it would all be explained, and the hurt healed, but until then head up, eyes bright, a smile!

But oh, she thought as she turned the knob of the dining-room door, if she only, *only* could get away and hide, far, far, far away till that terrible cheap little girl was gone! It was so humiliating to have her see Dana in that mood. She had so openly gloated over her. But that was pride too.

She opened the door and went in, a merry sentence about the gift her mother had given her upon her lips, but she noticed that her mother was still absent from the table, and the other two were sitting back obviously waiting for something.

"Why, where is Mother?" she asked surprised. "Not gossiping with the neighbors on the phone yet surely! What is it, the Mite Society, or the New Library reception? Elim, go motion to her to hurry up. We want to get to playing some games or something before Grandmother has to go to bed. I've brought two or three new things home that I want us to try. They're good fun and I think you will like them. Go get her, Elim, rescue her from her friends."

"I think it's long distance, Lynn," said her brother eyeing her gravely, turned suddenly thoughtful now that she had really sent the favored Dana away with another girl.

"Long distance! Why, who could it be, now I'm home?" laughed Lynette.

Elim shrugged his shoulders:

"Search me! Might be Uncle Ream, mightn't it?" he suggested.

"I only know 'twas long distance because of the long rings. They always do that when it's far off you know. Muth had some trouble getting connection. She had to wait."

Lynette gave her brother a startled look.

"I hope nothing's the matter, nobody sick or anything. They are sailing day after tomorrow you know."

Mrs. Brooke opened the door and came in then, looking flurried and excited, a bright spot of pink on either cheek.

"That was your Aunt Hilda," she said looking searchingly at her daughter. "Didn't Dana come in, Lynette? Didn't you ask him in for some cake and cream? There are several more molds in the freezer."

"No, Dana didn't come in. No, I didn't ask him, Mother. We're going to have a whole evening to ourselves for this once. What in the world did Aunt Hilda want? Why she wrote you a farewell letter and sent it by me. I hope you told her I delivered it. Mother, they aren't any of them sick are they?"

"No, they are not sick," said Mrs. Brooke breaking

off a bit of cake from her untouched slice and crumbling it absently as if to delay what she had to say. "No, there's nothing the matter with them. But Cousin Marta Hamilton who was to occupy half the stateroom with your cousin Dorothy is not going. She's had a telegram from her brother-in-law out west that her sister is very low with pneumonia, and she is needed to come and look after the children. She left on the six o'clock train tonight, and now that throws everything out, for Hilda simply won't hear to Dorothy's being in a cabin by herself, or with any stranger, and they've tried everybody they can think of and nobody can go. Lynette, your uncle Reamer is determined that you shall go. He thinks you ought to. He says it will be an experience that will last you your whole life, and you may never have another opportunity to go. He seems to think your father would have wanted you to have the advantages of travel. He is very insistent, and I don't know but he is right. Lynnie, I don't know but we ought to reconsider. Anyhow I promised we would think it over and let them know at half-past ten when they will call up again."

"How ridiculous!" said Lynette sharply. "They're sailing day after tomorrow, and I haven't a thing ready. Aunt Hilda and Dorothy have been preparing for six months." There was finality and a certain amount of satisfaction in her tone.

"Your aunt says you won't need to bother about anything. Just bring two or three dresses to wear on the voyage. She will see that you have all the little extras. Cousin Marta has left her steamer trunk and a lot of little traveling necessities for whoever takes her place, and the rest you can buy abroad when you need it."

"Well, it's not to be thought of, of course," said Lynette almost crossly. "You know what you said about my being home this summer. I'm going to stay here. And besides I promised to go fishing tomorrow with Elim," she finished with a smile at her brother.

"Aw, gee, Lynn. You 'spose I'd let you stay home from a trip like that to go fishing 'ith me? I think you oughtta go, Lynn. I sure do! Why, a trip like that!

Why, gee! You could get me some specimens of things, and write wonderful letters! Why good-night, Lynn, there'll be fish when you get back! And besides," he added bitterly, "if you stayed home you'd just trail off with that Dana Whipple. You wouldn't be much good to any of us."

This was intended for a joke, but there was a bitter tang to it that made Lynette look at him reproachfully.

"And your aunt says," spoke up Mrs. Brooke again, "that she wants you on Dorothy's account. She said she wanted to put it up to your conscience. They're really worried about Dorothy. She has been off to that school and got all sorts of queer notions, and she's depending on you to help her get a different viewpoint on life."

"Well," said Lynette, "I think my duty is at home, I haven't seen Grandmother for ages."

"Lynnie," said Grandmother Rutherford, "if it's for my sake, I think you ought to go. I'd take great pleasure in reading your letters from all those wonderful places, and it wouldn't be so long. A year goes fast."

"But—" said Lynette with troubled brow, "Mother?"

"Yes," said the mother studying her girl's clouded face, "yes. Lynnie, I realize you must look at this matter from every side before you decide. Would you want to—I mean would you feel that you had to consult with Dana before you made your decision. Because Elim could run down to Whipples', or we could phone for him."

"No!" said Lynette sharply again, "Dana has nothing to do with it! This is something I have to decide for myself. Besides, Dana thinks I'm a fool not to go. He told me so this afternoon."

There was silence in the room while the three listeners took in this thought and turned it over. Then the old lady leaned forward with her dear, beautiful, cameo smile.

"Lynnie," she said, "I think it would be beautiful. I want you to go. You've never been anywhere much but college and here, and a trip to New York now and then. It's time you saw the world a little before you settle down. And Lynnie, there's a little money I'd put aside. I meant to give it to you when you got married, but I'd rather give it to you now. I want you to take it and use it on whatever you find over there you think is worth bringing home. I want you to get some real pretty clothes for one thing. I've always heard they were cheaper there than here. And some pictures, and curious things, and pretty things. I think I'd enjoy seeing what you got with it.

"Then you'd have some money of your own back of you, in case it wasn't always pleasant to be dependent on others."

"Oh, you dear Grandmother!" said Lynette, and now her eyes were really filled with tears. "I couldn't, *couldn't* go and leave you all," she said, throwing her arms around her grandmother's neck and kissing her.

"Oh gee! You gotta go of course, Lynn," said Elim earnestly. "Why Lynn, it'll be just like us all going to have you go. You always make things so real when you tell 'em. Say, if you get to Jerusalem there's a fella at school has an uncle out there, had a land syndicate or something, I forget what, but he says it's great. Says they gotta railroad and a lotta things. Say, I'll let you take my new camera with you and you can take pictures of everything and then we'll know it's real."

And so they talked on forgoetting that the table had not been cleared nor the dishes washed, forgetting that there was more ice cream in the freezer at the back door, and that it was long after Grandmother Rutherford's bed time. They talked and talked but they did not mention Dana. But all the time Lynette was thinking of him, feeling the hurt in her heart that he had forgotten her birthday, crying out against his criticism of her that day, bleeding in her soul for the tryst he had forgotten, and her dreams that had not come true. Yes, there was no denying that in her present state of mind she would like to go abroad, run away tonight if that might be and leave no trace behind her for a little while till Dana had come back to himself. She never doubted but that Dana would come back to himself.

And then, before any absolute decision had been

reached the telephone rang out sharply and insistently.

"There they are, kid; go to it!" sang out Elim. "Let me answer. I'll tell 'em you're going!"

"Oh, but I *can't,* Mother," said Lynette looking toward her mother in a kind of panic.

"Certainly you can, Lynnie. It's all perfectly all right, child. I'll go talk to your aunt."

Lynette could hear her mother's voice.

"Hello. Yes, this is Mrs. Brooke. Yes, Hilda, yes, this is Mary. Yes, I think we've about persuaded her. Here, Lynnie, come and talk to your aunt yourself."

And Lynette walked slowly out to the telephone. When she came back she was committed to the trip.

They did some rapid planning after that, and then sent each other off to bed. But when Lynette took off the little blue dress that she had made with so many hopes and dreams for the wearing on this momentous day, and folded it to be put into her suitcase instead of hanging in her closet, her lips quivered, and she said aloud:

"Oh, oh, *oh!* How *can* I ever go away with things all in such a mess?"

IX

DANA WHIPPLE, having dismissed the annoyances of the moment for settlement late the next afternoon, really began to enjoy himself. He had not been at a motion picture show for four or five years, and it seemed a pleasant enough diversion, with Jessie Belle by his side to chatter away, regardless of the black looks that were turned in her direction, and the pointed remarks about people who couldn't keep their mouths shut. Who cared what the neighbors in the dark said?

Dana was thoroughly entertained. Jessie Belle was an entirely new type to him. He told himself that it would be good experience, getting to know her point of view. A minister needed to know all classes of people.

He told her the picture was rotten. Some parts were exceedingly silly, sentimental he called it.

Lynette was sentimental. There it was again, always getting around to Lynette!

He tried to argue with Jessie Belle about the picture. He called it vapid, and she said she didn't care, it was amusing, and what else did one want in an evening's entertainment? He found she was past master at sliding out of a corner. Just a silly, pretty child without a brain in her head, he told himself. What could you expect? But she was good fun and a relaxation after the strenuous exertion of his last year in seminary. He amused himself by trying to tell her what life in the seminary was like, and laughed over her clever scorn at young men who buried themselves in such a place for four whole years out of the best time of their life.

Occasionally an uncomfortable memory of Lynette's parting glance, that wide-eyed look of hurt surprise and withdrawal, pierced him like a thorn in tender flesh, but he told himself that it was best so. It really had to come to a showdown between Lynette and himself and it might just as well be now as later. Lynette had been getting notions in her head in that backwoods college, and they must be got out of her before it was too late.

Now and then he found himself remembering the vision of Lynette as she stood in the shimmering gold of the setting sun with that sea-blue dress fluttering softly about her, and the roundness of her white arm showing through the sheer sleeve—the long blue modest sleeve with its little frill around the white wrist, that seemed so perfectly a part of Lynette and gave her such an astonishing air of distinction. Lynette was not sophisticated of course, but there was something satisfyingly distinct about her. And she could learn! When he got her to New York he would mold her. She would make a wonderful woman, a truly beautiful woman. It gave him a distinctly pleasant thrill to think of her as she had stood there on the porch, and to realize that she belonged to him, like a perfect flower ready to pick, a ripe peach only awaiting his hand stretched forth to take it to himself. He had waited long, but the time was close at hand now. Of course, though, there were things that he must teach her, and there was no time like the present to begin. The little unpleasantness was annoying, but perhaps the wisest thing for the end in view that could have happened.

With this conclusion he gave himself over to the unusual relaxation of the moment and the study of this unique and amusing child. Of course he did not approve of her, but as it was his duty to amuse her for the evening, why not get as much amusement out of it himself as possible, and also make a character study of her incidentally for the help of his future ministry?

So Jessie Belle chattered on through the romance

that was flung upon the screen. Then, suddenly, the scene changed. Entered the villain with a concealed weapon, the audience of course being acquainted with the place of its concealment. Came on a storm, with wind and rain and hail and thunder. Lightning flashed, and the musicians helped out with plenty of noise and the roll of a drum at the critical moment.

Fire broke out in the building where the heroine had taken refuge, and she appeared at a window in terror, robed in frail garments of the night. The hero attempted rescue, fell amid smoke and blazing timbers, and was shown as one lifeless lying upon a litter. The moment was crucial.

Jessie Belle gave one great gasp and cringed to her escort's side, gripping Dana's arm fiercely, and hiding her face on his shoulder. He could feel her lithe, warm, little body quiver with each flash of lightning, each tinny roll of thunder. It was all very real to Jessie Belle. Or was it? But Dana was filled with deep pity for her pretty helpless fright. He reached his hand and gathered hers in a close, warm grasp, and felt her quick fingers answer his clasp, felt her bury her face closer against his arm, and shiver once more.

Then the voice of a woman behind him smote against his consciousness. He thought he heard his own name hissed in a malicious whisper. Shades of all the theological Whipples appeared in the darkness and groped for his reputation. He drew his hand away sharply. The perfume that clung about her sickened him. What was he doing? Giving evil eyes a chance to gossip. Of course this was only a pretty, frightened child, taking comfort from his presence, but the people around him couldn't know that. He drew himself up, and shoved her gently away into an upright position.

"That's silly, Jessie Belle," he said, trying to make his voice sound severe. "This is only a picture!"

"I can't help it," she gasped, shivering. "It's so real!" and ducked her face again into his unwilling shoulder.

Annoyed he gave a hasty glance about. After all

there was something pleasant in being a refuge for a frightened child. He lifted her face gently and straightened her up:

"Jessie Belle," he whispered in a tone that was intended to convey comfort, "you mustn't feel that way! You really must'nt! People will see us! And look! The storm is over! The fire is out! There comes the moon! And now—see, there is going to be a wedding!"

Jessie Belle sat up and wiped her eyes.

"Nobody minds what anybody else does at the movies you know," she informed him gaily.

He sat out the remainder of the picture unseeing. His face was burning with annoyance. He was painfully conscious of the two women behind him. They were whispering behind their hands:

"His grandmother . . ." he could hear, and ". . . always intended him to be . . ." and then a low mumble which the music covered, in the interval of which there came out another phrase:

"Yes, his grandfather was quite well known. But things ain't what they useta be you know. You can't expect much even from preachers."

All the way home he felt the hot waves of fury burning in his cheeks. Nobody had ever dared to say things against his character before. Of course there was a possibility that they had not been talking about him this time. But it sounded very much as if this silly girl had compromised him. He was inclined to be short with her as they walked along with the multitude.

Jessie Belle did not mind. She pretended to be tired. She yawned, hung upon his arm, looked up into his face pertly, and called him "Mr. Theological" and "Mr. Long-Face," and asked him if life wasn't an awful bore to him, and how he got that way.

Her gay little chatter eventually smoothed away his annoyance and by the time he had reached his own door and looked off up the hill a few rods to the old Brooke house in the moonlight, as had been his custom for years to look just before entering his home, he had ceased to be annoyed with Jessie Belle. He had somehow got it arranged around in his mind that everything that had happened had been the fault of Lynette. If Lynette had been along it could not have happened. Well, perhaps he was right. It undoubtedly would not have happened just as it did if Lynette had been with them. But Lynette was not along. It was hardly thinkable that she would have been.

Jessie Belle paused on the upper step, pirouetted, plucked a spray from the syringa bush that grew by the porch, brushed it lightly over Dana's face and said:

"Thanks, boy, for the buggy ride! I've had an awfully nice time, and you're not nearly so bad as I feared. With training you wouldn't be half bad. What are we going to do tomorrow?"

In half a minute more Dana followed her into the house committed to a ride out to the Mohawk trail the first thing in the morning.

That would lead him straight past Lynette's door, and now that he had promised he felt just the least bit uncomfortable. After all, perhaps he would ask Lynette to go with them. Why not? It would save gossip. And besides, he didn't want to carry things too far. He would see how he felt about it in the morning. The Mohawk trail had always seemed to belong especially to Lynette. It was almost a breach of loyalty for him to take a stranger there without Lynette. Still——

It was late when the Whipples at last retired for the night. Jessie Belle brought down a sheaf of photographs to show to Dana. They were mostly pictures of herself in various poses. There was Jessie Belle in evening dress "at one of the monthly receptions of our music school" as she explained; Jessie Belle in sports costume snapped on a public park tennis court; Jessie Belle in a one-piece swimming suit standing a-tiptoe at the very end of a diving board, her arms extended, a cherubic smile on her baby face. Justine Whipple gasped and blushed and giggled, "Oh, Jessie Belle!" when she saw this.

There was Jessie Belle at Coney Island; Jessie Belle on Fifth Avenue, and Jessie Belle in Central Park feeding the squirrels. Lastly there was Jessie Belle dressed for "the Recital." She did not state who did the reciting, the supposition being that the affair was given entirely for the purpose of bringing to the notice of an eager public, the marvelous development of Jessie Belle's voice. The fact being that Jessie Belle in all the glory of apricot silk straps, a rose, a brief skirt, and briefer bodice had occupied the back row of seats assigned to the freshman class during the entire evening.

But Jessie Belle shone now in the reflected glory of the laurels of her fellow students, and Justine Whipple drank it all in, and flashed and smiled and giggled, "Oh, Jessie Belle! How *wondahfull!*" Amelia in the background sniffed and watched her son jealously. Grandma Whipple twinkled wickedly, and Ella Smith cringed wondering how she came to have such a child.

Nevertheless Jessie Belle had made her impression on them all, and on none more than Dana. Dana knew New York. He had stood many a time just where Jessie Belle's picture showed her standing on Fifth Avenue. He could not help noting her slender chic lines, and her daring attitudes. There was something about Jessie Belle that swept him off his feet in spite of his resolve not to be interested in her. Of course she was only a child. And Dana found himself looking interestedly at the pictures, and feeling as if he had known her a long, long time.

And when the evening finally was over and Jessie Belle, about to mount the steps, made a graceful curtsy and blew him a daring little kiss, he smiled with a flattered self-satisfaction. After all, it was something to be able to interest a gay little butterfly like that. It showed he had ability. He was a "mixer." He would be a success as a public man. He could win the masses when he set himself, without half trying.

On the whole Dana lay down to sleep with a deep sense of satisfaction, and an exalted idea of his own worth and the real honor he was doing to the profession to which he had condescended to dedicate his life. He felt that it had been good for him to come into contact with this exceedingly up-to-date young woman. It was like a strong tonic, a challenge to his manhood. What a thing it would be to win a gay butterfly like this one to settle down and do some good in the world. What a power her beauty would be if put to win people to work for the church for instance. His last waking thought was a memory of her large blue-black eyes looking deep into his, pleading to have her way. Yes, she certainly was a winner! If she chose she could get great sums of money, for instance, out of really worldly people. That would be a wonderful help to the cause of righteousness. He must present that idea to Lynette tomorrow, and make her see that it was essential to win Jessie Belle and set her to work for good causes, uplift work and the like. That would be a worthy object for his summer work, and there was no denying that the prospect was not an unpleasant one.

Downstairs in the parlor bedroom Amelia was helping Grandma Whipple to bed. Her lips were set, her brow was furrowed, and her large face was damp with perspiration and weariness.

"Amelia," said Grandma grimly, as she let herself be eased down into the feather bed, "I think there's a snake in the grass. Do you know it?"

"Yes," snapped Amelia bitterly, "there is! And I didn't let it in either!"

"No!" cackled the old lady amusedly. "But you brought up your boy, and if you didn't teach him to look out for snakes, and know them when he saw them, is that my fault? Snakes are snakes wherever you meet them, at home or abroad. All I'm saying is, watch out it doesn't sting you. If Dana can't look out for himself by this time he deserves to be stung, and he better find out what kind of a man he is before he puts on his great-grandfather Whipple's mantle. Stolen mantles may cover a multitude of sins but they don't always fit, and everybody isn't ever deceived. I'm telling you."

"What's the use of telling me!" blazed the weary Amelia. "You let her come here! You and Justine! I'll have to bear the consequences as I always do."

"Well," said Grandma with a kind of grim relish of

her daughter-in-law's evident discomfiture, "maybe it won't be so bad after all. Maybe you'll like her. I don't know what kind of a girl you do like, anyway. You never liked Lynette Brooke. You've got a chance to look over the other kind now."

Amelia turned a quick suspicious glance at her tyrant. Was it possible that Grandma had a threefold reason for allowing this invasion of the household?

"Mother, did you know that girl was grown up when you let her come here?" she blazed again.

"Well, I kind of wondered," said the old lady amusedly. "I remember when Justine announced the birth of a girl child some years back. But that's neither here nor there, Amelia. How long have you know that girl was grown up?"

"Only since yesterday," said Amelia with a kind of rasp in her voice that sounded like a hidden sob. "But what difference does it make? She's here and you brought her. I hope you enjoy it. Do you want the east window open or shut?"

"Shut!" said Grandma. "I feel a draught. And Amelia, you don't need to bother to have hot cakes for breakfast. I heard Justine tell you to. But it isn't necessary. That girl's a pig and doesn't need any encouragement to eat. If I was you I'd invite Lynette Brooke over to dinner tomorrow night and have a birthday cake. It was Lynette's birthday today though nobody seems to have remembered it. But you can do as you like. It's nothing to me. Perhaps you'll think it's too much work. Draw up that blanket a little higher, won't you? My lame shoulder's cold. Did you wind the clock and put the cat out? Well, you can do as you like about Lynette, that's all." And the old lady turned over and closed her eyes.

Amelia gave her a keen, dismayed glance and departed.

So it was Lynette's birthday and Dana had not gone! Strange they forgot it. Did that cat of Justine remember it? Of course she did! Justine always knew dates and festivals. Justine had the meanest little ways of digging her velvet claws into people. Did Dana know? What was the matter with the whole universe? What was the use of trying to live? Day after day, and each one worse than the last. Thorn in the flesh and fly in the ointment! Vanity of vanities! What profited it for a man to give his life to preaching the gospel anyway to a lot of sinful headstrong people? Nobody would do as he preached. Why was the earth, and why were men and women born to suffer in it? The old question since the beginning of the world, that every suffering, disappointed sinner has asked himself again and again.

Amelia Whipple fell into a heavy sleep the minute her head touched the pillow, even while her burdened mind and her prayerless heart were propounding such questions to her hopeless self.

Justine Whipple, in her little room, which faced up toward the Brooke house, turned out her light and knelt for her smug bleak prayer. Then she drew up the shade and opened the window, casting a catty glance of triumph in the dark to Lynette's window which she could see through the branches of the elm tree, still lighted up.

Strange what was keeping Lynette up so late. The Brookes kept early hours. Well, at least that girl didn't get Dana for the evening. And she saw at last that there were other girls in the world for Dana as well as herself. Now, perhaps she wouldn't be so sure of herself, with her haughty grandmother, and her exclusive mother, and her utter ignoring of Dana's relations. Thought she could have Dana all to herself the rest of the summer, didn't she? Well, let her find out. Jessie Belle understood the situation thoroughly and was going to be fully equal to the occasion. It was going to be as rare as a play to watch developments.

Justine crept primly into her bed and lay down watching the steady glare of light from Lynette's window far into the night, beneath her thick, blunt lashes. It was going to be good to have Lynette put in her place at last.

Justine had never forgiven Lynette for taking Dana away, times without number, ever since he was a small boy, when she, Justine, had planned to use him in some other way. But more than that, deeper than any little grudge, Justine could not forgive Lynette for being young and beautiful, and beloved on every hand. Justine had never been beloved, nor beautiful. Why should she have to watch another have the things for which she had always longed and to which she could never attain?

X

THE Brookes were astir with the first morning light.

Mother Brooke had breakfast on the table when Lynette came down. There were her favorite gems, and an omelette as light as a feather. But Lynette ate scarcely a mouthful. It seemed to her that every particle she tried to swallow choked her, though outwardly she maintained a degree of calm, and even a touch of gaiety.

Elim was glum and unnaturally serious. He fell to advising his sister as though he were a man, widely traveled.

"You wantta look out they don't cheatya over there, kid," he addressed her pompously as one suddenly assuming responsibility toward her. "And tips! They take the very eye teeth outta ya. You wantta have plenty change er ya can't get anywhere. Tom's uncle hadta——"

Lynette smiled mischievously at him.

"You write it all out for me, Elim," she said tenderly, with a lingering wistful look at her brother. "Write me a volume of advice and send it down by tonight's mail. It'll get the boat before it sails and I'll have something to read on board. You know you and I have got to keep up this summer by writing a lot to each other to make up for all that fishing we're missing."

Elim grinned and then choked over his graham gem, and retired precipitately to the kitchen to get his voice once more.

There were tears in the eyes of the others as they looked bravely at one another behind smiles.

But it was the dear grandmother who was the most courageous of them all. She said the quaintest things to make them laugh, and was constantly fluttering out of her chair and into her room to return with some little offering for the journey.

Once it was a pile of sweet, transparent handkerchiefs all marked with tiny little initials. She had sat up half the night to mark them. They were frail as cobwebs and faint with lavender and violet, and some of them yellow with age. Lynette took them tenderly and flung her warm young arms about the frail old lady with the tears springing anew to her eyes:

"Grandmother! Your lovely hankies! How I've always loved them! That's the one you let me take to my first birthday party. And the one with the butterfly is the one you bound around my head when I fell down stairs. The for-get-me-not one you let me carry to Aunt Lute's wedding. And the one with the little lace corner you pinned around my doll the day Mother had to go to the hospital. Oh, you dear! How can I dare to take such precious things with me?"

"That's all right, Lynnie. I've been saving them all my life for just this time. Why, don't you know it's almost like going myself to send my handkerchiefs."

So they lifted one another's burden and strain, and made the way of going glad for the girl they loved, until it almost broke her heart to leave them. Nothing had ever seemed so dear as her home, in the morning sunlight, the breakfast table ready to clear off, the dishes to wash, and Elim's lines and poles outside the kitchen door waiting to go fishing. For an instant, as she rose from the table, it seemed to her that nothing could ever drag her away. She would telephone that she could not come. She would stay at home, and wash dishes with Mother, and read to Grandmother, and go fishing with Elim. Dana wasn't even in the picture. It was just the dearness of home and her own folks. And she was leaving them, for what? Suppose she didn't ever have a chance to see the world again. Well, what of it? It couldn't be any better than just this precious piece of the world. Her world.

Every line of her little figure suddenly sagged, every feature of her expressive face faltered. Her grandmother saw it, and began to pray. Her mother saw it and rose to action. Lynette must not hold back now. God had sent this way out of a critical situation. Lynette must have time to save her from making what might be a grave mistake in her life.

"Lynnie," she said suddenly grave, "aren't you going to—that is, why don't you—I mean, I would if I were you. I think you should call up and at least—well—*tell* Dana, or say good-by or something!"

Lynette faced about with a startled look, all her hesitation gone, strength, and decision, albeit perplexity, in her glance.

"I wonder!" she said as if she were thinking aloud. "I'm not sure I should."

"Well, I think your long friendship merits at least so much courtesy. You will feel better afterward if you have done it. It will look—well—less like running away." She was about to add "pettishly" but changed her mind.

Lynette, wide eyed and thoughtful, answered with slowly hesitant lips:

"He—has no right to expect——"

"No, of course not!" answered her mother with a sharp relief in her voice. "But it would be courteous. He cannot complain if you have been perfectly courteous. And you can make it quite casual."

"Yes," said Lynette, and with head up marched quickly out of the hall to the telephone.

They heard her call the old familiar number, with a clear almost haughty voice. A moment more they heard Justine Whipple's Uriah-Heepish whine, as Lynette had once called Miss Whipple's telephone voice.

Lynette asked if she might speak to Dana. Her voice was purely haughty now, almost business like.

"Why, I'll see if he can come—unless—perhaps you might give me the message," drawled Justine Whipple slyly. "You see Dana and Jessie Belle are getting ready to drive to the Mohawk trail this morning, and——"

The truth was that neither Dana nor her young guest were as yet awake.

"I see," said Lynette coldly cheery. "Well, it's of no consequence at all, Miss Justine. No, don't bother. It'll do next time I see him. No, it's not important. Goodby!" and Lynette hung up sharply and came back into the dining-room, head up, cheeks blazing, eyes bright like steel blades.

"He's not there just now," she stated coolly. "I'll leave a note."

She stepped to the little dining-room desk where her mother kept her bills and check book, and tearing off a slip of paper from a pad that lay there she wrote quickly:

> I've changed my mind and am going to Europe in search of poise. Hope you have a pleasant summer,
>
>> Hastily,
>> Lynette.

She slipped it in an envelope, sealed it and addressed it to Dana.

"There, Elim can leave that at the house as he goes by on his way home this morning," she said carelessly. "Grandmother, would you mind asking him if he has remembered it?"

Elim had gone down the road to borrow Hiram Scarlett's Ford to take Lynette and her mother to the train. He came driving up to the door with a swagger, as if he had just purchased a five thousand dollar car.

"Now, girls, don't you worry about us tonight!" said Grandmother. "Elim and I will be perfectly all right. We're going to play checkers till eight o'clock, and then read for an hour and then go to bed, and Elim is going to sleep on the living-room couch, close by my door, so you just have a good time, and don't think of us once. We're going to have 'the time of our life.' Isn't that the way you say it, Elim?"

"You said it!" responded Elim heartily. "I'll bet on you every time, Gramma. Say, you know you promised you wouldn't wash those dishes till I got back to help.

No fair if you do. I shan't keep any of my promises unless you do. See?"

"Sure!" responded the old lady with such a perfect imitation of Elim's way of saying it that they all went off into gales of laughter, and the old lady, putting her frail white hands with their soft, white frilly wrists comically on her slender hips said gaily:

"Gee, but we're all going to have a good time!"

And so they went away on a ripple of laughter, that might have been tears if it had not been for the old lady's courage. The echo of the laughter rippled down the road, and perhaps a wave of it wafted into the windows of the Whipple house and made Dana stir uneasily in his morning dreams, and start awake with the sensation of something pleasant and beloved passing by. Then sleep closed in once more, and the old Ford passed on, without a lifted eyelash from Lynette, or her mother who was conspicuously arranging the scarf about her neck. And though Justine Whipple, whose eagle eye had espied the Ford, and watched it spitefully from afar, studied its brief passage eagerly, she could not make out who was in the back seat, nor how many, nor what for. It was most annoying.

Elim drove the Ford back to its home by the valley road which was two miles around but had the double advantage of giving him a longer ride, and of not passing the Whipple house. Dana's letter was safely buttoned into the inner pocket of Elim's coat. There was time enough for that he figured, even if Lynette had asked him to be very sure to deliver it at once. Well, he would, the first "at once" he had. He returned the Ford to its owner and slipped across lots home, deciding to see how his grandmother was getting on, and help her do the dishes before he went down to Whipple's. He loathed going to Whipple's. He had once strung a line across the sidewalk in his younger days, and had the misfortune to bring Justine Whipple sharply to the sidewalk with a turned ankle. Her remarks on that occasion had not endeared her to Elim Brooke, She had told him plainly what she considered him, and left no doubt in his mind as to her opinion of his family and his upbringing. Elim bore her no grudge personally, because he knew that there was truth in what she had said, but his family were a different matter, and the grudge he bore her for them grew with his years.

All the time he was wiping dishes with Grandmother Rutherford, and talking gaily of the great times they would have reading Lynette's letters, Elim was trying to think how he could put off delivering that letter until Justine went out, say, down to the post office, which she often did of a morning. It would be much easier to deliver it when Dana's mother was at home alone to receive it. He didn't mind Dana's mother, much, although he considered her far inferior to his own mother, and he resented the idea that she might some day be related to his sister.

Neither did he relish handing Lynette's letter to Dana himself, especially if that "egg of a flapper" as he called the visitor at Whipple's, were present. It seemed a humiliation for Lynette to have to tell Dana she was going away.

But while Elim polished glasses and silver, and knit his brows over how to avoid his duty and yet remain loyal to his sister, he heard a car go by, and hastened to the window in time to see Dana in his new car going up the road with the despised visitor by his side, smiling up into his willing face.

Elim frowned blackly, as he polished the plates and put them away elaborately in the china closet. Now he had done it! He had promised to deliver that letter at once, and Dana had gone away, probably for the morning. All indications pointed toward a picnic. His quick eye had noted the willow handle of a basket in the back seat, and the nickel top of a thermos bottle.

"Oh, bah!" he said under his breath as he thought how Lynette had gone out as bravely with her lunch basket the day before. *His sister*, and a girl with paint on her face! One one day and the other the next! All the same to Dana! "Gee, I'd like to wallop him! Gee, I'm glad she's gone!"

But there was the letter, and there was his promise, and boy though he was he had been brought up on the

Brooke conscience. He was bright enough too, to see what Lynette must have had in mind, that if the letter were delivered at once, and Dana should *want* to do so, there was ample time for him to take the next train down to New York and persuade the lady of his heart —if she really was that—to give up her trip and return with him. Or at least to say good-by, and to apologize for his conduct of the evening before.

"But he donno he even did that!" soliloquized the dish wiper. "The poor fish! *He* donno she even *had* a birthday!"

When the dishes were all put away, Elim sauntered back into the kitchen where his grandmother was fussing around the stove.

"Gee, Gramma! I gotta get that letter down ta Whipple's!" he said. "You stick around on the porch and read the newspaper till I get back, willya?"

Elim slipped away and took his bicycle around the house, across the field and through the fence, and was off like a streak down the road toward the post office. A solution to his difficulty had presented itself to him. He would *post* the letter! There was plenty of time to get it into the eleven o'clock delivery, and it would be at the house when Dana returned. If Dana did not return until evening that was his look out, wasn't it? There would still be time for Dana to get to New York before the boat sailed *if he wanted to do so!*

Elim reached the post office and made sure his letter got into the morning sorting. Then he streaked it home again, and came nonchalantly in at the back door.

"Now, Gramma! What are you doing?" he protested loudly. "Muth said you'd be up to some stunts if I didn't look out. No sir, Gramma, you aren't cleanin' out that tin closet this time, not on yer life. Gimme that broom!"

"But Elim, I saw a mouse run under the door."

"Domakenydiffrunce!" contended Elim. "I'm here to look out fer things like that. You go int' the living-room. I'll ten' to the mouse."

So Elim manged to turn the interest away from the letter, and it was not till several hours later in the day that Grandmother Rutherford remembered it and asked him:

"Elim, did you remember to take that letter?"

"Sure!" said Elim readily enough. "Don't you remember you were killing a mouse when I got back?"

And she was not the kind of grandmother who asked him who he saw and what they said.

About two o'clock in the afternoon Mrs. Pettingill ran over with her sewing announcing her intention of staying till her folks came back on the five o'clock train, and Elim feeling Gramma was in good hands took his fishing rod and tin cans and wandered off for a while. He felt the need of a little relaxation after the strenuous day he had had. Not that he had done anything much. It was just the weight of the responsibility. Also, it had been a strain to keep an eye out for Dana's return. But now it was late enough so that it no longer mattered, for the letter must be already at the house awaiting him, and Elim felt that he would just as soon be away for a little while, in case Dana came over to find out more about Lynette. "Let Gramma handle him! Gramma was wise to the whole situation."

So with a free mind Elim went a fishing.

XI

JUSTINE WHIPPLE did not tell Dana that Lynette had called him up. She did not tell anyone that she had called. She would have enjoyed holding it over Amelia's head like a lash as one more evidence that Lynette ran after Dana, but she would hold that in reserve for a time when it had been forgotten that she had not reported the call. At least she could tell him later in the day if it became necessary to save her face. It was easy to say she had forgotten, or to pretend the call came after he left for the drive.

So Dana Whipple went away into the brilliant broidery of the June day, even as the day before, without an idea of the changes that were about to enter his well-planned life.

The morning was perfect. That always put him in a pleasant mood. He somehow always had the attitude that bad weather was intended as a personal affront to himself, and he made everybody around him uncomfortable, as if they were personally responsible.

But the day could not have been brighter. He felt no qualms that he was going in the same direction, and with the same eagerness, as he had gone the day before with the girl who was supposed to be going to be his wife some day. In fact there was a slight spice to this day in the fact that he was going without her, going with a distinctly different type of girl, and going on purpose to teach Lynette a much-needed lesson. And he meant to enjoy it while he was doing it. Of course he would be glad to get back to Lynn, and it gave him a sort of satisfaction to know that she was different from this brilliant, vapid creature by his side, but it was good to know that he could adapt himself to all kinds of girls. It flattered his pride that Jessie Belle seemed interested in him. He knew that he was good looking. Well, why not enjoy the day and sample this style of girl for an hour? She was only a child at most.

Nevertheless, so strong was habit, that he felt a great desire to put aside his anger with Lynette for not going with them the night before, and take her along on this drive. It seemed a pity for her not to go! And he had told Lynette they would take this ride together. In fact, hadn't he said something about taking a ride this very day?

And so keen was his desire to have Lynette go along, so proud his rememberance of her beauty as she had stood on the porch in the sunset, that had she been on the porch as they passed, or had any of the family been in sight, he would have hailed them and stopped for her.

But the house stood silent and unpeopled, with that "not at home look" about it. Somehow Lynette's silent rebuke of last night seemed to hover about its quiet, shut-up air. The front door was closed too. Surely they were up by this time! Half past nine! No, nearer ten! very likely Lynn was gone down to the village on an errand, or perhaps in the garden, or off with Elim. He really must do something about Elim. Lynn ought to make him understand that he could not treat him like an equal in public. Calling out as if he were a kid! And presuming an intimacy because of his sister's supposed relation. Not only was Elim's greeting a trifle previous, as no engagement had as yet been announced, but it was offensive in itself. Elim acted as if they had been playmates at least. Elim must learn a certain respect due to position too. But all that would come into the talk that he meant to have with Lynn that afternoon or evening

Out on the open road Jessie Belle pleaded to be taught to drive the car, and when they reached a rea-

sonably smooth stretch, where there would not be likely
to be much traffic, Dana changed seats with her and
began to teach her.

It was perhaps a miracle that they were not wrecked
that morning, for Dana was new at driving himself and
Jessie Belle was both hilarious and impulsive. They
wobbled about all over the road, and Jessie Belle did a
great deal of boisterous laughing over nothing, and
made a point of being frightened to death every few
minutes, and clinging to Dana in terror. This after the
first shock was rather amusing to Dana. Of course she
was only a child, he told himself, just a child with
charming confiding ways.

They stopped at a mountain top to look out over the
trail, and Jessie Belle here took occasion also to slip
her hand into Dana's arm and cling. She said the great
height, and the overwhelming space of valley and distance and mountains, frightened her and made her dizzy. She clung to him all the time they stood there gazing, but most of Jessie Belle's gazing was up into Dana
Whipple's face rather than off to the eternal hills.

Jessie Belle continued her clinging when they turned
about and went into the pavilion where spicy pillows of
pine needles, and Indian baskets, and arrow heads, and
souvenir postals were for sale, and where she made
Dana buy her one of every trinket she fancied by the
simple device of saying: "Oh, I do wish I had brought
my pocket book. I'd love to have that!"

Before they had finished with ginger ale and chocolate bars and souvenirs. Dana had spent several dollars.
He frowned as he put the change from a ten dollar bill
back into his pocket book and realized how very little
was left. Only a dollar and thirteen cents! And all for
foolishness! Why had he done it? And Dana had been
brought up to be exceedingly careful with money. No
member of the family under the eye of the indomitable
Madame Whipple could comforably be otherwise. It
troubled him not a little and made him silent and distraught as he conducted the elated child back to the
car.

They ate their lunch on the way back in one of the

lovely wooded retreats that Dana and Lynette had dis-
covered and grown fond of during the years of their
friendship. It was high above the world, with a view
off toward the valley, yet screened from the road by
tall pines, a little clear space floored with delicate moss-
es, and sheltered about almost like a room, with a great
smooth rock drifting out of the moss on the open side
for a table, and the air resinous with pines.

If any sense of disloyalty to the wonderful girl who
had come here on hikes with him all the years, and
been true and faithful to the friendship, entered into his
soul to make Dana uneasy, it was quickly dispelled by
his companion. For Jessie Belle was quick to read a
man's face. She knew just when to exercise her charms,
and just which kind of a charm to use. She had been
quick to note that he considered her a child. That then
was her rôle. A charming child! She even descended
to baby talk with a delicious little lisp, accompanied by
a drooping of her curly eyelashes and a lifting of her
limpid eyes at just the right moment. Jessie Belle's eyes
were not naturally limpid. They were hard and bold,
but hidden under those lashes, whose curl had been
carefully accentuated with a tiny iron that morning,
they acquired a limpidity which was not noticeably akin
to stupidity, artificiality, emptiness, and had quite an
effect on the unsuspecting Dana. A man brought up
under the direct influence of a girl like Lynette Brooke
is not naturally on the outlook for deceit in womankind.
Jessie Belle chattered on like a charming child. She related incidents of her musical life, largely fabricated of
course, or original with someone else. She told of esca-
pades in which she had played a prominent part, and
she made him laugh at things he would have preached
against. If her naïve frankness was surprising in one so
young, he rather prided himself that he was sufficiently
sophisticated not to be shocked at her. It would never
do to let a girl feel she had shocked anyone. So he
smiled at her questionable jokes, and let her think that
they did not bother him in the least, and she led him on
daringly. This was no long-faced divinity student, no
devoted lover absorbed in his lady, as she had been led

to suppose, no Galahad in high and holy armor. This was a mere man, and Jessie Belle thought she knew how to manage him.

When the lunch was ended she flung papers and boxes away down the cliff without a thought of the disfigurement of the place, and turning with a flirt of her brief blue skirts flung herself down on the moss close beside Dana, where he sat with his back to a tree amusedly watching her, and dreaming perhaps of the days when he would be a great city preacher with girls like this one perhaps, hanging on his every word. A wave of ambitious pride swept over him and lighted his eyes with pleasure, and Jessie Belle thought the look was all for herself. And, well, perhaps in a way it was. She was a type of adoring femininity of which he hoped one day to be the center. That she was a new type to him, and exceedingly lovely in her wild, flowerlike way to his eyes, made him more open perhaps to her power; a power that was as utterly unsuspected as a nettle might be in the stalk of some lovely bloom of the field. Dana was as unsuspecting as Adam in his garden with the serpent that afternoon. Life looked all rose color, a garden full of good things, and he the ruler of it all. It was coming near to the time for him to have it out with Lynette. That loomed a trifle unpleasantly in the offing. But it would soon be over and Lynette restored to favor. Then he and Lynette would take this charming child out together somewhere for the evening, a ride or the movies, or perhaps a concert if there was a good one. And Lynette would be all the more gracious for the rift there had been between them. He knew Lynette. Of course she would be ready to apologize by this time for her rudeness to his guest the night before. For Jessie Belle had by this time established herself in his mind as *his* guest.

And then, suddenly, Jessie Belle, with a lithe wriggle of her slim body, flung herself about, and backward, her lovely little head and shoulders lying across his arms, her eyes dancing up into his startled ones, her cherry carmine lips pouting in a a laugh half defiance, half daring:

"Oh, kiss me!" she cried childishly. "I'm getting lonesome. You're so silent and gloomy! Kiss me, quick, or I shall cry!"

Dana stared amazedly at her, the color flaming into his face, and saw his arms close about her, felt his own lips drawn as if by a power without himself, stung into being partly by that challenge, partly by the power of her own tempting beauty.

Was the serpent, perchance, lurking behind the stately pine tree against which they sat, watching, whispering, "Thou shalt not surely die!"

With a sudden impulse he caught her close and kissed her, half fiercely, once, and again. Then as if the touch of her lips had brought him to himself and let loose a flood of shame upon him he sprang up, flinging her from him. The cry of dismay which came involuntarily to his lips for what he had done, changed even as it left him into a half-ashamed laugh, and then another laugh as if he were adjusting himself back into the world of convention and tradition once more.

"You crazy child!" he said and tried to pass it off as a bit of fun, the while his stainless reputation toppled before his dizzy mortified eyes. He had not thought that he would do a thing like that. Not even with such provocation. Of course, she was *only* a *child*. A kiss like that meant nothing. She did not expect it to mean anything. Her very challenge told that. She was only trying him out to see if he was a good sport. But he ought not to have done it.

Yet there was within him a strange menacing satisfaction in the fact that he had. He stared at Jessie Belle, that forced laughter still upon his lips, and saw a new light in her eyes, a fierce, wild gleam of triumph which only added to the subtle charm of what seemed now almost unearthly loveliness. There flashed through his mind the hillside that he and Lynette had seen the day before, spread with its white cloth of daisies, and lighted by the tall spikes of blue flowers, an almost unearthly radiance upon their fairy scalloped bells, tolling the slender whiteness of their frail stamens in the breeze, even a stab somewhere of brilliant carmine in the tiny closed bud. Was Jessie Belle like that? A holy sacrament he had compared it to. Had Lynette been right? Was there something Satanic in its beauty?

Even as the thought hovered in his mind he felt her eyes upon him now with more than challenge in their daring triumph. It was almost as if suddenly she held a power over him, a whip lash in her pretty hand, and the ancient Whipple reputation stood tottering on its foundation. Had he, Dana Whipple, the cynosure of all eyes in the home town, and also in the seminary, descendent of the great and good advocate of purity and righteousness, had he suddenly done a thing of which to be ashamed?

He tried to shake it off. Tried to face those big blue wistful, devilish eyes of her and show her that it was not so, that he had not yielded to her power, that he had done nothing of which he was ashamed, that she had no triumph to rejoice over, no whip lash over him. He tried to consider her lightly, and his act as nothing. But he could not face her eyes without yielding to them, and so he wavered into that embarrassed laugh and stooped to flick the dead grass from the cuff of his trouser leg.

"An unspeakable child!" He repeated with another forced embarrassed laugh.

But she answered in a low meaningful tone that held a startling amount of menace for his hitherto satisfied soul:

"You know I am not a child, Dana! You knew it when you kissed me!"

The moment was fraught with intensity. The perspiration suddenly sprang in little beads to Dana's forehead, and he grew white to the lips, because there was deeper challenge now in the girl who stood there in her smoky blue dress, with the afternoon sunshine drifting down upon her black bobbed wave, her cream and rose complexion, her lovely impish eyes, her beckoning carmine lips. And then, she lifted her slim white arms and held them out, her head on one side, her eyes daring him to come and kiss her again. She knew she was lovely, she even let the wickedness show like a charm of jewels in her eyes.

'Twas such a little thing that brought him to his senses! The snapping of a twig behind him. He had not stirred—not yet. Had the God of his grandfather sent an angel to protect him? He froze into sudden attention.

Jessie Belle, quick to catch a changing mood flashed out her white hands, as if that was all she had meant in the first place, almost as if it had been a continuous movement, caught Dana's hands and whirled him off his balance into a circle.

"Come, let's dance!" she said. "I'm dying to dance. Let's do the Charleston. Don't you know how, you great big nice boob? Well, follow me, just let yourself go—I'll guide you——"

But Jessie Belle had overdone her part. Dana's dignity was at stake. Never in his life had he allowed himself to be made ridiculous. And—there was that snapped twig.

He wrenched himself free and faced about, still struggling with various emotions, and there, standing imperturbable in the entrance of the wooded amphitheatre, his cap on the back of his head, his hair on end, his face smudged, his fishing rod over his shoulder, a string of fish in one hand, and an inscrutable look in his dark, smoldering eyes, stood Elim Brooke.

The color rolled up over Dana's pale, patrician features, and fury blazed forth in his eyes. He opened his mouth to speak and closed it again. What was there to say? What could he say? How could he explain the situation without making it worse? He might tell Elim what he thought of him for spying on his actions, for being where he obviously was not wanted. But the woods were free, and why should Elim not come to that particular haunt if he chose? As a matter of fact it was Elim who had originally led Dana and Lynette to this lovely spot, for just below the big rock, reached by a circuitous and somewhat precipitous path, there was a point where one could drop a silent hook down into the cool, shadowed depths of the creek, and be pretty sure of getting a wily fish of no mean parts, if one knew how. There really was nothing to say to Elim on that score when he scanned the subject hastily.

And somehow Elim seemed to have grown and aged suddenly. He seemed to be grave and dignified, and to have attained a point of vantage which by right belonged to Dana. It galled him unbearably. He hated Elim with a new and savage quality which should have given him new light on himself.

Elim continued to stand there silently holding Dana with the power of his scornful boy's glance.

Jessie Belle for the instant was silent, startled, staring at the intruder belligerently, puzzled to understand why a mere boy's arrival had caused such a reaction in her companion.

"Oh!" said Elim at last, with a contempt in his voice that was beyond description. "It's *you,* is it, Dana? I—thought it was a couppla bums!"

But with the first word Dana's composure returned. He straightened his collar with a laugh, brushed a leaf from the sleeve of his immaculate coat, stooped and brushed more dust from the leg of his trousers, and arose to the occasion grandly:

"My soul! Elim! Is that you? I'm glad you've come. I've got a crazy child here that wants to dance, and she took me by surprise and whirled me off my balance. I'm getting too old and stiff to play games with children. Come on in and I'll introduce you. She's about your age, and you can play around together. Jessie Belle, this is——"

But Elim cast a withering glance at Jessie Belle, so full of disgust and scorn that he might as well have spit upon her, and advanced with a shrug into the shadowy arena, his back toward Jessie Belle, his eyes once more upon Dana:

"Thanks awfully, old man, but she's not my type. I like 'em real, not painted! Besides, I think too much of my mother! What's the matter with keepin' it up yerself? You were takin' to it fine. Shake a nasty foot, dontcha? I didn't know they taught the Charleston at

seminary. Must be great. Come on Spud, it's gettin'
late. We gotta get those fish home fer supper."

Spud Larkin appeared grinning in the offing, a tall
boy with a freckled countenance and fire-red hair. He
crossed the arena like a shadow and dropped down behind the rock after Elim as silently as an Indian. A
sudden portentous stillness drifted into the quiet retreat.

It seemed to Dana that life had suddenly gone upside
down and fastened him in a situation impossible for a
Whipple to tolerate. In swift procession the forces
which had gone to make up his life circled round him,
like stark, horrified ghosts, lifting hands of holy horror
at the position he had allowed himself to assume before
the world, for that it would presently be broadcasted to
the world with those two boys aware of it, he did not
doubt. There were the shades of all the Whipples' past,
his grandfather the great preacher in the lead, his father close behind, his tyrannical grandmother, his mother, Aunt Justine, and Lynette, with her white face and
sad eyes as he had seen her last standing on the porch
in the sunset. Lynette's mother! Lynette's patrician
grandmother! The whole gossiping, praying, prideful
village! Yes, and further than that. The Theological
Seminary! All the professors, and his fellow-students
whom he had so carefully and at such odds subdued to
his allegiance. The Church at large who had him in
view as a promising leader of things religious. The particular congregation upon which his immediate hopes
of the future were pinned.

They circled about him in quick questioning groups
to his excited imagination, and insisted upon his right-
ing the situation at the instant before it became forever
too late.

There were those two unspeakable devils down behind that stone, waiting undoubtedly, listening.

And how long had they been there before he discov-
ered them?

Cold chills crept down his spine. Cold beads of perspiration broke out upon his forehead. His throat grew

hot and dry. His eyes seemed to be balls of fire. He felt as if he were in an aeroplane high in a storm that had taken to diving into space of its own volition, and the engine had suddenly gone dead. He must do something at once or his great reputation would crash to the ground in utter destruction.

Presence of mind! Concentration! What were those things they taught in the seminary? He must right himself at once.

Clearing his throat and assuming a cheerful attitude he took out his watch dramatically.

"Great Scott! Jessie Belle, do you know what time it is, child?" he said in tone of declamation, audible he was sure even down to the fish in the cool pool below. "We've got to get right back. I must get off a telegram to one of my professors before six o'clock or I may lose a chance to preach in one of the best vacant churches in the East. Come on, pick up your duds and let's get to the car. We've wasted time enough playing games."

"What's eating you, Dana Whipple?" said an arrogant Jessie Belle, flashing her eyes and setting her painted lips in an ugly red gash as if she might have been Jezebel herself. "Aren't you going down and fight those dirty kids for what they said about me? I won't stand for being treated like that. No gentleman would stand for it."

"Nonsense, Jessie Belle, they're only a pair of ignorant kids. Don't be a fool. Come, you're only a child yourself. I've got to get back home. I have an engagement. I had no idea it was getting so late."

An evil look came into Jessie Belle's belashed eyes:

"You're a coward!" she said in the sophisticated tone of a girl of the slums. It seemed to transform her into a menace.

But Dana was intent upon the part he was acting, upon his well modulated laugh, and his distinctly pitched voice, a voice that could reach so easily to the people away back in the last seat under the galleries, and was even now echoing over the rock, and down to the fishing hole below.

"Thank you, Jessie Belle," he laughed lazily. "If compliments are being handed out I might call you several degrees of a child."

"You're afraid!" hissed Jessie Belle. "You're afraid of those boys!"

"Have it your own way," orated Dana Whipple wearily. "I'm going home. If you don't get down to the car at once you'll have to walk, for I've got to send that telegram."

After that the woods were silent, save for the snapping of a twig under a quick step now and then, a bird's note high in the branches, the soft plink of a pebble sliding into the water.

Dana had gone with great strides, down to the car without looking back. He had not even seen Jessie Belle's scorn of him. His very back was indignant as he disappeared between the branches. She stood sulkily, lowering, her wrath smoldering. He would come back! Of course he would come back. And she would *make* him go down and pitch those despicable boys into the water. That first one had been awfully good looking. Jessie Belle never could brook indifference in a good-looking man or boy. He must be punished and be made to take notice. This Elim whoever he was should be humbled till he groveled at her feet. And then perhaps she might take notice of him, for he *was* good looking. But it was up to Dana to do the humbling. Dana had been yellow. Dana had been afraid of him. She would humble Dana too. She had almost had him where she wanted him, and then that horrid boy had come. That was where the long-faced part of the theological student came in probably. He was a slave to his orders. He was afraid to be caught. But she could manage him. He would come back.

But Dana did not come back.

The spirit of the orthodox Whipples had been outraged. Dana was himself again. And presently she heard the snorting, the chug-chugging of the motor. Dana couldn't be going to leave her here? It wasn't thinkable! With those unspeakable loathsome boys!

She cast a hurried frightened eye about on the serene

cool shadows of the green retreat, that suddenly seemed so empty, so alone. Then she picked up her feet and ran in a panic. She ran until the car was in sight, and then she stopped and picked a handful of ferns, in full sight of the unseeing Dana she picked them, carefully, deliberately and emerged slowly, leisurely, as if she had been following him all the time. She presented a charming study in blues and greens, with all the air of a pretty peacock, stepping along; stately, unhurried, gorgeous, unaware of her escort's cold fury.

All the way back to town Dana was silent, furious, haughty, his mood growing more and more unpleasant.

But Jessie-Belle was apparently still unaware of his lack of sympathy. She began to sing, little trills at first, runs up and down the scale, a high note or two of an opera, which she had not been allowed to study yet because it was too difficult for her present development, a quaint little folk melody, a sad song, a bad song or two, with a sidewise, coy glance to see what effect it was having.

It only made Dana more cold and severe. His clerical Whipple profile was turned well away from her vision. As they passed the Brooke house he turned his head and searched it frowningly, forgetting apparently that she was along. It occurred to him that this whole trouble was Lynette's fault anyhow—began yesterday afternoon—Lynette's insisting he must come to her house to supper—so childish. Yes, it was all Lynette's fault, and Lynette had got to learn! He would go right over there and attend to it, just as soon as he had safely landed this unspeakable kid that he had been fool enough to try to show a good time to. Never again! It was the last time for him! He would go over and have it out with Lynette, and when she was sufficiently humble, he would stay to dinner, and then afterward perhaps he would have a chance to tell her all about the church that wanted to hear him preach and paid such a high salary and had complimented him so on his eloquence. His pride had been suffering severely for having had to keep this news from her so long. And it was all Lynette's fault.

XII

To LYNETTE's surprise Mrs. Brooke had taken seats in the parlor car. It was an expense that they usually felt they could easily forego, for the common cars were not apt to be overcrowded at that point on the line, and it was only four hours' ride. Why waste the money?

"But we're going to enjoy ourselves today, Lynnie," said her mother with a wistful smile, and Lynette felt the tears in her throat again as she saw the look in her mother's eyes. This ride was to be all the vacation her mother would have for many a long day. She must not break down. She must not let her mother see how almost frightened she was at what she seemed to be doing. She must just take it calmly, and make her mother have a happy time.

And after all, perhaps it was only a day's pleasant trip. Perhaps tonight or tomorrow night she would come back with her mother to the home town and the summer would go on as it had been planned. It seemed absurd, now she was really on the way, that it could be possible she was going away with so little preparation for so long, so far. Well, perhaps she wasn't. After all she had not fully promised. She had only agreed to come down and talk it over and let them persuade her to go if they could. She had held a reservation. And that reservation was all that saved her from pulling back at the last minute as they were stepping into the train, and saying:

"No, Mother, I can't go! I simply can't! It isn't right, and, anyway, *I won't!*"

But she could go back still, if she would. She wasn't out of the country. The decision was yet ahead of her.

How dear Elim looked as he lounged easily on the platform waving them out of sight with a grin, so casually. Just as if they were coming back to dinner. Well, perhaps—a word, a telegram,—Ah! Would Elim remember to deliver her letter at once? A frantic smothering sensation crowded in her throat. Oh, suppose he should forget! Suppose Dana didn't find out that she was going until she was gone! The boat out on the ocean, plowing unfathomable distances between them, that days and months would have to bridge with memories, and with bitterness, till she could come back, and they could talk together and it could all be explained. Why, *why* had she trusted to Elim? Why had she not sent for Dana and told him plainly what she was going to do and let him have a chance to stop her if he wanted to?

She had almost turned back to the platform at this thought, with some wild idea of still going back, perhaps waiting till a later train, and sending for Dana even yet; and then the vision of his riding out the Mohawk trail with that hateful little blue flapper by his side froze her suddenly into sense. No, she must go on! She must let Dana see what it would be to have her gone. Surely, when he knew, he would realize how hurt she had been by what he had said about her being foolish not to go. How it had stung her for him to take that other girl to the movies and refuse to come to her party, the party that had been planned two long years before. And then he would call her up. Or he would telegraph her frantically to return. It might be that even now the wires that ran between those telegraph posts were alive with a message for her, and it would be there before she reached her uncle's home.

But no! That could not be either! It was not half an hour since she had passed Dana's house. Elim could hardly have delivered the message. Why, she had not yet sat down in the train! How long it seemed since she mounted those steps from the platform!

It was just at that moment that she looked about her and realized that they were in the parlor car and that her mother had dropped into a chair and was motioning her to take the next one, and she came back to the surface and smiled, and roused herself to a semblance of happiness. Well, of course, but Dana would do something about it when he got the message. It wasn't like Dana not to. Why worry? He would come down to New York at once. He would of course. And they would talk it all out, and—she would likely come back with him to a happy summer. And then sometime he and she would save up and take this trip together. It would be that way of course.

And she talked brightly to her mother and pointed out things in the landscape, and grew almost garrulous.

But *would* he? Would Dana come? An undertone of uneasiness kept urging, while she was telling her mother some anecdote of college last days that she had not had time to write. Would this new Dana with his self-sufficiency, and his wholesale advise, and his high-handed scorn of her college, would he come after her? Would he perhaps rather expect her to return to him and accept a hearty scolding when she got there? As she thought back over the years, she wondered if perhaps that had not been her attitude ever since they had been friends, he the one to condemn, she the one to apologize and return to where he had waited, indifferent. Well, perhaps it was good that she was going. Yes, she had made a wise decision. At least she would be able to test him. People always ought to be sure of one another before they were married.

But she had thought she was sure. Well, of course she was. This was only an act in the play of life. The curtain would soon rise on the next, and Dana would be taking her back home again.

But would he?

So the undertone of reasoning went on, mile after mile, while she talked and smiled, and made the way bright, as she thought, for her mother.

But mothers are not easily deceived.

Mrs. Brooke watched the beloved eyes with the deep look of pain in them behind the smiles her daughter was forcing there, and at last she suddenly swung her chair about until their heads were quite near together, and then she said:

"Lynnie, dear, is it so very bad? If it is I don't think I am doing right to urge you to go."

Lynette stopped in the middle of a sentence about the college play on class day and looked at her mother like a sorrowful child.

"Oh, Mother! Have I been so glum as all that?" she said in dismay. "I wanted to make this a happy time."

"Yes, dear child, and so do I," answered the mother, "but there are some things that must be cleared out of the way first, or the hurt will last all the time you are gone. Tell me, dear, is it Dana you are grieved about?"

Lynette had turned her head quickly away from her mother's earnest gaze until only the sweet curve of cheek and chin were visible, white as chiseled marble. It was not like Lynette to be so white. The stab must have gone deep. The mother's eyes hungered over the sweet drooping figure in the chair next her, and a wordless prayer went up from her heart. Oh, how had she done wrong to let this thing go on so long! If it was really Dana—and it must be—what had he done? Would Lynnie tell her? Her heart yearned over her child. Perhaps after all she ought to go back home and work out her problem on the spot. Perhaps it was wrong to let her go away with this wound in her heart and expect her to forget. Perhaps—Oh, perhaps——! For hadn't they really been separated for nearly four years? And been together again only a day again? Wasn't she trying to meddle again with the ways of Providence? Or was she? Hadn't God perhaps put this into her heart to urge her daughter to go away? Hadn't He sent the invitation for just this time of need? Who, who was to show her what was right?

"Oh, guide me aright!" she prayed. "Guide my child!"

Then Lynette turned about, her clear troubled eyes looking straight into her mother's.

"I suppose it is, Mother, although I feel bad about leaving you all again, too; and when I had just got back. But I'm really worried—well, about Dana. I don't know what to think."

The mother watched her daughter guardedly, and did not answer at once. Finally, quite quietly, she asked:

"In what way, Lynnie? Do you mean that you think he does not care any more, as he did?"

The answer came deliberately:

"Oh, no! At least—No. I'm sure he cares!" and a flood of color stole slowly into her white cheeks and receded again, leaving them seemingly whiter than before, as she recalled Dana's almost fierce embrace on the mountain side.

"That is——!" she began lamely.

Mrs. Brooke waited, watching the dear face hungrily, yearningly.

"Well, Mother," said Lynette looking up again with a little dismayed smile, "I don't seem to be getting on very well, do I? But it is kind of intangible. I don't know just what it is that troubles me."

The mother smiled a warm understanding, and asked: "Is it that girl, Lynnie?"

"Oh, no!" said Lynette quickly, "at least——" she hesitated again.

"You mean," said her mother, "that if everything else had been right you wouldn't have thought anything about Dana's bringing another girl up to go with you? You mean that circumstances might arise anywhere that would make such a happening necessary. She was a guest in his mother's home. You mean that if Dana hadn't been so seemingly indifferent to your birthday dinner, and so careless about your wishes you would have thought nothing of it?"

"Perhaps," said the girl, her eyes downcast now.

"But you know dear, there was excuse for him. You know how unpleasant his Aunt Justine can make it for him if he doesn't accede to her wishes. He perhaps

erred in being impatient when you tried to urge him,
but he might not have fully understood the importance
of it to you."

Lynette flashed her mother a look of gratitude, but
the cloud of doubt settled again into her eyes the instant it had passed.

"Yes, he did, Mother. He understood perfectly before we left the woods. And—it was my birthday. He
has always remembered my birthday." Her lips showed
the least tendency to tremble.

"But men do forget, Lynnie. They do—I guess
they're made that way, most of them—all but your
father, he never did. But you mustn't lay it up too
much against him. They do forget."

Mrs. Brooke was looking down into her own lap
now, fumbling with the button of her glove, trying to
hide the indignation that came into her eyes at sight
of the hurt her daughter had received.

"Yes," said Lynette slowly, "I know. I guess there
aren't any like Father—not nowadays. Only Elim. I
hope he'll not be like the rest of them."

"I hope not," echoed the mother fervently. "We
must see that he isn't. We must not spoil him. I guess
that's the matter sometimes. The mothers and grand-
mothers and sisters spoil them."

Lynette's face was tender.

"Elim is a darling," she said tenderly. "I wish so
much I could go back and do yesterday over. I should
have gone fishing with Elim in the morning and stayed
with you and Grandmother in the afternoon. If I had
only known how quickly I was to go away again I certainly would."

The mother was watching her keenly now, anxiously.

"You—didn't have a happy time yesterday, Lynnie?"

"Oh, yes!" she answered half sorrowfully. "Yes, and
no. I don't really know what to think. That's why I
wanted so to have Dana come last night to wipe away
some of the impressions I'm afraid I imagined. Dana
seemed somehow changed. I'm not sure—Oh, I don't
know what I think! He did seem changed in some
ways."

"In what ways, dear?" the voice was quiet, restful, not in the least prying. It was the mother-tone that had always invited confidence. Lynette put her head back on the seat and prepared to bare her soul. She drew a breath of relief as if she was glad to share her burden with her mother.

"Well, I'm not sure, Mother. Perhaps I'm crazy. Perhaps I only imagine it. When I try to think of telling it, it seems so small in me."

"Well, better talk about it then and that may dispel the imaginings. Do you mean that Dana wants to withdraw from the sort of semi-engagement that existed between you?"

"No, Mother," said Lynette quickly. "No, he talked continually about what we are going to do together and what he wants me to be and do, only—there is a difference. It seems almost conceited of me, and perhaps it is only my pride that is hurt, but somehow he doesn't seem to treat me with the same—I hardly know what word to use. I would say 'reverence' only that does not seem a word for a mortal to use about herself. But it really fits. You know he used almost to frighten me he was so reverential toward me, used to lift the hem of my dress and kiss it, and all that. Of course I laughed at him, and called him romantic, but somehow yesterday he seemed so much the opposite way—I guess I'm just a baby, and haven't grown up yet."

"No!" said Mrs. Brooke sharply. "No. Never get that idea in your head. You're beautifully and sweetly grown up. Your mother knows. Put that out of the question entirely. But tell me, Lynnie, what do you mean by saying he acted in the opposite way?"

"Why, he seemed so critical of me."

"Critical! Of *you*? What can you mean? How?" She could scarcely believe it possible. Dana had always been so worshipful of her girl.

"Well, of my hair for one thing. He said when we went to a big city church I would have to bob my hair. Mother, he thinks I'm unsophisticated."

"I should hope you were!" said the mother haughtily settling back in her chair with an indignant look about her firm lips. "With the present-day meaning of sophistication, I *should hope you were!* Thank God you are, my little girl!"

"He said I ought to go to Europe to learn poise. He seems to think that is more important than any other quality in a minister's wife. He blames my lack of poise to my college. Mother, he said horrid things about the college, he laughed at it several times. And he talked strangely about the Bible too, and about things that he used to think exactly the opposite about. Oh, Mother! I don't know. Perhaps I was just excited and got things all twisted up. Perhaps I ought to go back and talk it out with him, and let him see what he has made me feel."

"But I don't understand dear; haven't you made it clear, that you chose that college because of its Christian standing? Because your father thought highly of it, and wished you to go there, and because there were certain advantages there which could not be had in any other place that we knew of? Haven't you ever explained about it to Dana?"

"Oh, yes, Mother, I told him all about it several years ago. He knew. And he thought it was fine then. I tell you he has different ideas now, and I'm afraid has acquired a set of new ideals."

Mrs. Brooke was gravely silent for a moment and Lynette went on:

"I had a feeling that he would sneer at whatever I told him. Why some of the simplest things I said seemed to bring a look of scorn on his face."

"But didn't you tell him what you had been studying there? How you have been taking up the Greek and Hebrew in order to fit yourself to be a more perfect helper for him?"

"No, Mother," said Lynette sadly, "I couldn't tell him. I was afraid he would be angry. He said so decidedly that he did not intend that I was to be a minister's wife. That it wasn't the fashion any more for the minister's wife to feel that she was hired along with her husband. That he wanted his wife to have social duties, and devote herself to him, and not to the congregation, that they had deaconesses for such things now, and a minister's wife nowadays was just as free as any other woman to go into society, and attend plays and hear good music and have a good time. She was the minister's *wife*, not the minister. And he intimated that I would need poise more than anything else in the world to occupy a position like that."

"Lynnie! You don't mean that Dana said things like that!"

"Yes, Mother, he did, although he didn't say it very disagreeably, you know. He was nice and pleasant about it, that is if I didn't take issue with him. And then when I did he blamed it on my poor training in a little backwoods college. I couldn't tell him anything about the college. Of course he showed he hadn't the least idea what a really wonderful place it is. And anyway, I had no chance to talk much. He was full of all the wonderful things that have happened to him. Mother, he has really taken high rank in scholarship, and brought himself to the notice of his professors in an unusual way. I couldn't help but be proud of him for that of course. They say he is very eloquent—he showed me some letters from his professors—they say wonderful things about his attainments, and his promise, he has preached in some very prominent pulpits, and been asked to consider coming back to them. And he seems so full of what he has done and so determined to have a big city charge right off at the start that it troubles me terribly."

"He would!" said Mrs. Brooke, with a tragic look in her eyes, and quite as if she were thinking out loud without intention.

"Mother, he didn't used to be conceited," said Lynette on quick defense. "I don't think he really is now. He was only telling *me!*"

"And what are you?" said her mother. "Someone to adore him, and to humbly wait upon his will, to be an ornament to his life, and to do his will and glorify his career!" Her voice was almost hard as she uttered the words and her eyes were out of the window on the fast hurrying fields and woods they were passing.

"Oh, Mother!" cried Lynette in distress. "Did you always feel that way about Dana? Then I am doing wrong, I am being disloyal to him to talk about this to you." There were almost tears in her eyes.

"No," said her mother, "don't imagine I am against Dana. In a way I have been as fond of him as you have, but I have always seen shadows of these things in him, but I have sometimes been deeply troubled that I allowed such an early intimacy between you before either of you had really formed your characters, or before your judgment was mature. And now if Dana is any of these things we must know it before it is too late and do something about it."

"Do something about it?" asked Lynette in dazed alarm. "What could we do? What do you mean? I couldn't do anything against Dana. Mother I love Dana."

"Yes, I suppose you do, Lynnie, at least you think you do. But if Dana didn't fully love you, at least more than himself, more than his own career, why you would be the most miserable person on earth when you found it out, and I for one don't want to give you to him until I am sure about it."

"Oh, Mother, there is nothing like that," said Lynette, eagerly trying to defend him now. "Why, Mother ——" and her cheeks flushed softly, "he was—very loving."

"Oh, those things! Yes," said Mrs. Brooke almost impatiently. "Lynnie, don't you know you are a beautiful girl? He would love you that way of course. I never questioned it. You can hold your head up with the prettiest girls in the world, even if you haven't bobbed your hair. And I'm not saying that because I'm your mother either. Other people have said it to me about you, people of the world who have seen much beauty and know. And the most beautiful part about it is that you don't seem to know it yourself. I've never talked this way to you before, and it isn't likely I will again, because I don't believe in making much of earthly beauty. But it's time you understood that the good looks that God has given you have a certain kind of wordly draw-

ing power, and you must not overestimate the worth of
the love people give you because of your beautiful face
and perfect body. Maybe I ought to have told you this
before. The world is especially full of people today who
live in the flesh, and every girl ought to understand
that, and use her judgment accordingly, not suspiciously of course, but wisely, unprejudicedly, not letting the
things of the flesh have undue weight. Those things of
course count for something, but we must not let anything get out of proportion in our scheme of life. Lynnie, the things of the flesh are only one third of our
earthly being. They must have their due proportion,
but they must never get the ascendency. They must be
considered, of course, and a marriage without physical
attraction is not likely to be a happy one, but it is not
all. If Dana merely loves you for your beauty, because
he loves to look at you and touch you, where will his
love be when you are old, and your beauty is gone, or
when you are wasted with sickness perhaps? No, child,
you can't judge whether he loves you *just* from that.
There has got to be an agreement of the mind and spirit too, or there will be trouble. And from what you
have said, I'm afraid that both his mind and spirit are
finding disagreements in your mind and spirit. Isn't that
what you mean, child?"

Lynette was looking with troubled eyes from the
window and did not answer at once.

"Now, Lynnie dear," went on her mother, earnestly,
"I can't bear to seem to be raking over your heart. You
must decide this matter for yourself. But I can't help
feeling that if Dana has the real thing in his heart for
you he will come down to New York on the next train
and talk it over with you, and all the troubles can be
straightened out. And if he hasn't—well, you want to
know it, don't you dear, before things go any further?"

Lynette with her eyes full of unshed tears nodded.
Her voice was too full of tears to let her speak. She
only held her lips from trembling by main force.

Anxiously her mother leaned forward and spoke in a
low sweet voice:

"Little girl, you know this isn't all up to you. It's

God's plan, whatever it is that is coming to you, and if you yield yourself fully to Him, He will lead you into the light, and—yes, into the brightness too, in His own good time. You believe that, don't you, Lynnie?"

"Yes, Mother," smiled the girl through her tears. "You taught me to believe that when I was a very little girl and it has helped me through a lot of hard places already. It seems as if this one is the hardest that ever has come, but I'm game, Mother! I want God to do what He wants with my life. I know it's the only possible way of happiness, even though it does look black."

She smiled again, and her mother squeezed her hand and said with a tremble in her own voice:

"Bless you, darling child! There never was such a girl as you are. I'm positive of that! Elim would say you are a good little sport, and he's about right. I'm not sure but your grandmother would express it in those very words too, if she were here." And they both broke into a ripple of soft laughter over the memory of the dear little fragile sport of a grandmother jauntily saying she was about to have "the time of her life" while they were gone.

The laughter broke the solemnity of the occasion somewhat, and gave Lynette control of herself once more.

"Now, Lynnie," said her mother, "it may be that you have a hard way ahead of you, but it will end in brightness if you keep your trust. So don't be downhearted. If Dana really loves you better than himself it's bound to come out. Your being away from him for a little while isn't going to hurt it a particle. You know it may be that it will do him a lot of good to be unahppy for a while. Oh, yes, he'll be unhappy if he really loves you, even if he does have that little flapper child to go around with. No, don't tell me you think maybe you ought to stay home and protect him from her, and save him from himself. He's not a child in leading strings and you can't hold him in your lap all your life. He's got to meet other flappers beside this one, probably has, and if he has the Lord in his heart and the real thing in his character they aren't going to hurt him. He isn't fit to be your husband unless he can stand a few tests. You've stood many of them for him, and his soul must be as true as yours or there'll be disaster sure. So put away your burdens and tears, darling girl, and bring out your smiles. You've put yourself in the Lord's keeping, well, then, _trust_ Him, and await His leading. If He sends Dana down after you, and you feel the Lord, not Dana, _the Lord_, mind you, is wanting you to stay, then you go back home with Dana and be happy all summer. But if the Lord says go to Europe a while and wait till He is ready to reveal the way ahead to you, why then you go to Europe and be happy, knowing that you are in the Lord's hands, and be of good cheer. Now, do you know, we're almost to New York? Wasn't that Yonkers we just passed? Get down the bags and straighten your hat and don't let even yourself suspect for this day at least, that you are afraid you ought not to have come. You'll be led. God has promised!"

Lynette leaned forward and took her mother's hand and pressed it against her hot eyelids, touching her lips to it tenderly and murmuring softly:

"You're the most wonderful little mother that any girl ever had!"

XIII

WITH small show of courtesy Dana Whipple landed Jessie Belle at home, shot his car into the garage, and strode up the road to the Brooke home. His eyes were on the ground as he went, as always when he was thinking deeply. He was trying to plan just how to impress Lynette with the feeling that he was very deeply and gravely offended at what she had done the night before, and in fact at her whole attitude toward him since his return.

She must be made to see that she had deprived herself of many interesting items of his career since they had last seen each other, that he would most certainly have informed her about fully if she had not shown such an attitude of questioning, answering back, almost seeming to poke fun at what he was saying. Really sacred things too, like the remark she made about teaching the heathen about sin. As if even heathen didn't know there was sin in the world without having to waste precious time talking about it! Oh, it was all wrong allowing Lynn to go to that fool college. He ought to have put his foot down earlier in the game. Her people would have taken his advise. Lynn would have managed it if he had insisted. What right had a man to insist upon ruling his family after he was gone from the earth? What right had Lynn's father to leave an embargo on going to any college she chose? The world changed and progressed and Lynn's father had not been very far-seeing not to realize that the little old col-

lege he thought so much of in his younger days would
have become a back number by the time his daughter
was ready to get her education.

Well, the damage had been done now, and it was his
place to repair it. He would have to be as patient as he
could, for she had evinced a certain amount of bull-
headedness yesterday which was very annoying, very
different from the sweet yielding little Lynn of high-
school days who thought everything he said was law
and gospel, and who looked to him to explain difficult
problems.

And here was he at home now from one of the most
renowned seats of learning in the country, in the whole
world perhaps, and fresh from the heart of theological
learning and research, and here was she, a little un-
taught child, who had been under ignorant, fanatical
teachers. Probably most of them women—old maids
—who had read mistaken writers of centuries past, and
still believed that Genesis was to be taken literally from
cover to cover; still believed there was a whale big
enough to have swallowed Jonah, and wise enough to
bring him up and land him at the right port at the right
moment. Here was Lynn, prating of theological questions, talking of sin and the devil as if he were a person,
and presuming to hold her wisdom on a par with his. It
was ridiculous. It was heart rending! To think he had
been trusting her to grow into the sweet pliable thing a
woman should be, with a broad mind, and strong spirit,
and an unlimited faith in her husband's judgment, and
here this ridiculous antique of a college had stepped in
and warped her mind and judgment, and put her
through some hardening process that was setting her
into narrow grooves. But he would put a stop to all
that. After he had broken through the false veneer of
ancient ideas, he would mellow her and mold her to
please himself, and she would be a splendid wife. Yes,
she would be one to grace any position no matter how
much in the public eye she might be placed.

As he turned in at the Brooke hedge he was already
dreaming of honors that would be thrust upon him, of
lectures he would be asked to give here and there, of

noble pulpits he would be asked to fill, of corner stones
he would have to lay, and commencement addresses he
would make, of high offices in his denomination to
which he would be elected. And Lynette as his wife
would be a great lady, chosen for president of this club
and that, asked to be a patroness for charitable affairs,
heading the denominational gatherings of women, as a
matter of course, gracing his home, and even gaining a
reputation herself for her small and select social affairs. Of course it was absolutely necessary, however,
that she get rid of some of her narrow-mindedness if
she were to rise in such a broad and phenomenal way
to be a lady of influence and take New York by storm.

All this Dana planned between the entrance to the
hedge and the front door of the house. Then he lifted
up his handsome head, and looked about him, and behold the door was shut!

Late afternoon of a warm spring day, and the front
door of the Brooke house closed! Unprecedented oc-
currence! It had always stood open afternoons in summer. What had happened? Was there intention in its
closing?

A further examination proved that the door was not
only shut but locked. Had they all gone away? But no,
Grandmother Rutherford scarcely ever left the house
nowadays except to go to church occasionally when
some neighbor stopped in a car to take her. There must
be someone at home.

He rang the bell, and it echoed through the house in
an empty way that almost startled him. He knocked
also to make sure, and the hollow sound of the empty
hall struck annoyingly on his already rasped nerves.
While he waited his excited mind suddenly flashed him
back to the scene in the woods, Jessie Belle asking him
to kiss her, a hot fire of mingled excitement and disgust
flashing through him, and Elim—Had Elim been there
then? Had Elim seen it *all?* Just what had he done anyway? Had he really kissed Jessie Belle? Bah! Only a
child of course, but *bah!* Why had he done it?

His cheek burned hot with the memory. It must be
the wind in his face all day that made his face so hot.

The blood was surging into his head too. It was really a hot day.

He took off his hat, mopped his forehead impatiently, and rang the bell again, a long, intermittent, impertinent ring, and followed it by another knock loud enough to waken the seven sleepers.

It must be that he was nervous. Those last few weeks of course had been strenuous. He ought to get away for a little and take a vacation. Say a run up to Maine, or out to the Pacific Coast, or at least to the seashore. Well, after he got this matter of Lynette fixed up and set her a task of reading to occupy her time he would see about it. Perhaps Grandmother Whipple would come across with the necessary cash if he presented the matter to her in a diplomatic manner.

He put an impatient finger on the bell once more, but just then he heard the key turn in the lock, in a slow grinding way, as if it were an effort, the door opened half hesitantly, and there stood Grandmother Rutherford, a little flustered from hurrying, a trifle excited at the thought of who it might be ringing the bell so insistently.

"Oh!" she said in a relieved tone, and then, "Oh!" with a trifle more of dignity. Then with perfect control and sweetness:

"Why, Dana, is that you? I haven't seen you since you came home. Come in. I hope you haven't had to wait long. You see I was down cellar looking for a mouse trap. We found a mouse in the tin closet. Elim said we'd have to get a new one, but I knew his mother had put the old one away down cellar, and I had just found it when I heard your ring."

The old lady had succeeded by this time in unfastening the hook of the screen door wherewith she had doubly barricaded herself.

"You see I'm all alone," she explained as Dana stepped in, hat in hand, and lifted his eyes to look for Lynette, impatient to begin her reconstruction.

"Alone?" he said surprised. "Alone!" he added in annoyance. Now he would have to wait.

"Yes, but please don't tell Elim. He thought Mrs.

Pettingill was going to stay till five o'clock or he wouldn't have gone off and left me. It's silly of course for them to feel that way and Mrs. Pettingill had said she would stay, so Elim thought I would be all right. But her husband came back sooner than she had expected and stopped here for her, and I just told her not to mind, I was perfectly all right, and you know Sam Pettingill never can bear to be crossed in anything. I knew he'd be cross if she didn't go right that minute. But it's very silly of course that I can't stay alone in broad daylight. I do feel better of course when the door is locked and then nobody can come in on me unaware and startle me, but really I'm as spry as I ever was, and can perfectly well stay alone."

"But why are you alone?" asked Dana as if it were some fault of her own for which she were accountable to him. "Where is Lynn? Where is Mrs. Brooke? Gone visiting?"

"Come and sit down," said Grandmother, motioning her hand toward the dining-room with her stately little formal gesture that was so characteristic of her. "No need to stand up and talk, and really I don't know but I am tired a little after poking around down cellar. There, I've got a cobweb on my sleeve, too, haven't I?

"Come in and sit down and I'll tell you all about it. It's nice to see you again, and have a little talk. You never did mind talking to old ladies you know. And wait, suppose I get you a piece of Lynnie's birthday cake. You always liked cake, and you didn't get any yet, did you? It's specially nice this time. Too bad you couldn't get over to Lynnie's party last night, but of course I suppose you couldn't help it!"

"Birthday cake!" said Dana stupidly, staring at the old lady. "Birthday cake!"

"Yes," said the old lady sweetly. "It was the nicest one Mary has made for years. You see Lynnie was especially anxious to have it the best birthday party she has ever had, because now she is through with school. And it was. Too bad you had to miss it, but of course— Well, they had the cunningest little ice creams. Flowers and peaches and pears and apples all made in

cream, and they were so lifelike. My what wonderful
things they do nowadays, don't they? To think of making the ice cream into pictures. Too bad it didn't keep.
We had some left over, but Elim finished it all at noon
today, and it was pretty soft then. I didn't care for it
myself."

All the time the old lady was busy getting out a
sprigged china plate from the latticed corner cupboard,
getting a silver knife from the ancient sideboard drawer, getting out the big half a cake from the closet in the
opposite corner, and cutting a generous slice of Lynette's birthday cake. Then hurrying out to the little re-
frigerator porch she returned with a glass of creamy
milk, talking all the while. Dana stood and stared at
her.

Such a dear little old lady, so aristocratic, so re-
served usually, and now turned suddenly garrulous. But
Dana had no thoughts to wonder at that. He stood
there dumb, stunned. Lynette's birthday! And he had
forgotten all about it!

All the pretty plans they had made together as boy
and girl, all the sweet ways of the girl he had loved so
long, came rushing back upon him in a tumult and ac-
cusing him.

And he was so unused to being accused. He could
hardly stand there and take it even from himself. So
this was why Lynette had been so sore, and had acted
so unnatural last night, had really been rude in a way
to Jessie Belle. It had been her birthday and she was
angry because he had forgotten it and had stayed away
from her party. Well, of course that was something,
and she would probably harp on it a long time. The
worst trouble with Lynette was that she was sentimental. Of course one's birthday was no different from any
other day if one just thought so, but he would make up
for that. He would take her down and get some ice
cream this evening and they would have a pleasant time
together. He would stay to supper. He would show Jessie Belle that he was done with her too. That was the
thing to do of course, even if she was staying at his
home. But really after all, Lynette was to blame. Of

course she was if she cared so doggone much about the birthday party she should have reminded him that it *was* her birthday. Lynette was so awfully proud. She expected him to remember every little detail of childhood and then was sore if he didn't. Of course he always had remembered it without her telling him, but after all, it wasn't a thing to make a lot of trouble about, and Lynette ought to know that.

Well, she would see that. She would be reasonable when he had explained how annoyed he was at Aunt Justine, and how his mind had been occupied with that invitation to preach in New York some time in August. He hadn't had a chance yet to tell her that. That would have impressed her all right of course, but he had been saving that for a choice bit at the end, and the end hadn't come. Well, it would come this evening.

He would just stay now, not even telephone home to say he wasn't coming, for if he did Justine Whipple would somehow manage to worm it out of him where he was and insist on his coming home for some absolutely necessary reason. He would stay and help the old lady get supper if that was what she was going to do, and Lynette would be mollified when she came in and found him setting the table just as he used to do when he was a kid in High School. Of course he didn't want to get in the habit of doing that for it would never be within the dignity of a minister to have to be always helping out with the housework, and he must begin right at first of course, but still, he would do it this once.

By the time the old lady came back with the foaming glass of milk he was feeling almost comfortable again, and quite himself.

"Well now, Grandma, this is just like you, to think to save some cake for me. I'll get a double dose, won't I? I'm going to stay to dinner you know. Yes, I promised Lynn. It was a terrible disappointment not to be able to get over last night of course, but I'm going to stay tonight. I was hoping—that is—Lynn's birthday present hasn't arrived yet. It ought to have been here yesterday of course, but it wasn't—I—— She——" He was growing embarrassed. On such occasions it was his habit to change the subject. It gave him an appearance of ease, and enabled him to pass many an uncomfortable situation with credit to himself. He changed the subject now:

"When did you say she would be here?"

Grandmother Rutherford looked at him keenly, but answered in her usual sweet tones:

"Why, that's quite uncertain. She wasn't sure when she went away. Mary of course will be back either tonight or tomorrow evening. I think myself she'll be likely to stay to see them off. It isn't every day one gets a chance to see friends off on a trip you know, and I told her not to worry, Elim and I would be quite all right."

"Oh, Mrs. Brooke has gone down to New York to see her sister-in-law off to Europe, has she? Lynette told me they were going."

"Yes. She hesitated about leaving me, but I told her it was almost like going myself to have her go and then come back and tell me all about it. Mary is a wonderful story teller. She can make you see just how they all look, and what they said, and even the way their dresses are made, and what they are taking along for the trip. Lynnie is like her that way too. Lynnie is very much like her mother in everything I think, don't you?"

Dana frowned. Mrs. Brooke was a very determined woman sometimes. He didn't know that he cared to think Lynette was entirely like her. So he changed the subject again:

"When did you say Lynn was coming back?"

He looked at his watch half impatiently.

"Well," said the grandmother, with a wicked little twinkle in her eyes, "she hated so to leave me when she'd just got home, that I told her I wouldn't be a bit surprised to see her coming back for supper."

"What?" said Dana with a startled look. "You don't mean you don't expect her back before supper? Was she expecting to stay some where? Why, I told her I'd be here for supper tonight!"

Was it possible that Lynn was daring to stand him

up when he had told her he would be here? Had she planned this for revenge? He had never thought Lynn was vengeful. If that was it—if it proved to be that she had planned to be away if he came—when he had said distinctly that he would be here—if she was trying to work any little tricks to get it back on him—why—he would stay away for *two weeks!* He couldn't have her putting anything like that over on him.

Grandma had gone to the door to pay the paper boy who had arrived at that moment, so he had opportunity to think it over before his hostess returned to answer.

"Why, she sent you word. I'm sure she sent you word," said Grandma sweetly. "Elim took the letter over just after they went. I saw him go."

"Oh!" said Dana blankly. "But I didn't go home. I had to be away all day—— Ahem! I was called out of town. I tried to get back sooner but it was impossible! I didn't even go into the house when I got back, just ran the car into the garage and came right up. Do you happen to know what message was in the letter?"

"Well, no, I don't, not definitely," said Grandma. "It wasn't a long letter. She hadn't but a minute to write, it was almost train time and her going was so unexpected. They just called her up while she was eating dinner. But of course it's all in the letter, and the letter must be down there at the house."

"Train?" said Dana puzzled. "Did she go on the train? What time did she go?"

"Why they went on the eight seventeen. It's an express you know and Aunt Hilda wanted them to get down as early as possible to help in the shopping."

"Do you mean that Lynn went to New York with her mother?" Dana's brow was clearing now. Then perhaps Lynette did not do this on purpose. There might of course be some explanation, some alleviating circumstances which the letter would explain. Probably someone was sick, or they needed her help. People were always so careless about putting burdens on their relatives when they got in a hurry. They likely wanted Lynette and her mother to close up the house for them after they were gone, or something like that. Mrs.

Brooke was always so kind and willing to help others. But Lynette!

"Did you say you thought Lynette would be home on the five o'clock train? I'll go get the car and run her home," he said rising with something of his old boyish friend-of-the-family air.

"Oh, no," said Grandmother Rutherford, "she won't be home on the five o'clock train. She—but perhaps you better read Lynnie's note first. Then you'll understand."

"But," said Dana puzzled at her manner, "you think she may be planning to stay and see them off?" His manner was almost glum now. And he had planned so nicely just what to say to her. It was hard to have to wait a whole day longer. She oughtn't to have gone without seeing him.

"But you don't understand," said Grandmother Rutherford serenely. "Lynnie has not gone to see them off, she is going with them to Europe. I thought she would have told you about it herself. But the letter will explain."

"Lynn has gone to Europe, you say? Why, that is impossible! She told me herself only yesterday afternoon that she had refused to go!" Dana's voice was dazed, irate, unbelieving.

"Yes, but they called up last night at dinner time. There was a vacant place. A member of the party could not go on account of illness. They insisted Lynnie should take the place. She hesitated on our account of course, but we overruled her. We felt she ought not to lose the opportunity. It is a pity you had not been here to talk it over with her. But it had to be decided right away of course. Won't you have another piece of cake?"

But Dana suddenly pushed back his chair and arose almost haughtily. He felt that he had been affronted. An old friend of Lynette's, a friend of the whole family, almost a member of it, sustaining almost a closer relation to Lynn than any they bore, and yet not told till after it was all decided! Lynn gone without a word! It was more than mortal man could accept.

"It's a pity Elim hadn't left your letter here," went on Grandmother Rutherford placidly. "If we'd only known you were coming he would."

Thus reminded the old Dana would have dashed off in a hurry after his letter, forgetting his hat, forgetting to say thank you, forgetting even to finish his cake.

The present Dana sat down again and ate slowly, silently, coldly, picking up every crumb. Taking the last swallow of milk. Giving a cold "No I thank you," when Grandmother Rutherford offered him more, and then arose composedly, gathered up his hat from the table, turned a chilly eye on his hostess, thanked her for the cake, and retired with dignity. He did not hasten his step, nor flicker an eyelash. He walked leisurely down the sidewalk just as he had walked many a time, but there was no swing in his stride this time, and no light in his eyes save the light of anger. He was furious, with a growing fury that was rapidly working itself up to white heat. He had been dealt an indignity! He, the star graduate of the Theological Seminary, the rising young preacher whose eloquence was to astonish the world, and *New York!*

And she had dared to go off to Europe without letting him know! She had done it for revenge! More and more their conversation of the day before took form and repeated itself in his brain. She had taken exception to what he had said about her college and gone off in a huff! A strange spirit for the girl whom he had chosen for his wife, whom *He Had Chosen!*

He stalked through the house without speaking to anyone. His Grandmother chuckled audibly as he mounted the stairs, and a flush of fury rose higher in his hard face.

The letter was lying on his bureau. If it had not been visible he would never have asked for it. No one in the house should suspect that he had not known Lynette was going. He sat down with it in his hand and contemplated the possibility of returning it to her unopened. That would be heroic treatment but perhaps it would bring her to her senses.

However, his own curiosity got the better of him and

he finally opened it, feeling sure that it would contain
something to relieve the strain, and make it possible for
him to go on blaming her a little more comfortably.

Then he unfolded the paper and read the brief message:

> I've changed my mind and am going to Europe
> in search of poise. Hope you have a pleasant sum-
> mer.
>
> > Hastily,
> > Lynette.

He read the words until they danced before his eyes
like little insects in the light, until they beat their way
into his angry brain, and pierced their meaning to his
soul. And gradually he sifted them and twisted them,
until he evolved a theory that satisfied his mood.

Ah! So that was it. Lynn was sore because he had
said she lacked poise. It was all a case of pride! That
showed how changed she was. In the old days she wel-
comed criticism and always set herself to make right
whatever he suggested. But now she wished to set herself up as perfect. Well, that was the natural tendency
in these days for all fanatics to think themselves perfect
and everybody else in the wrong. She had got that way
in college of course. Where else!

He sat there a while longer meditating on the letter,
and evolved further. Lynette had run away down to
New York because she was angry. She was not really
going to Europe. She would never dare carry it that far.
She expected him to come after her and bring her back.
That was what he would have done if she got what she
used to call "hurt" in the old days. But those days were
gone, and he was a grown man with a right to respect
and honor. She must learn that they were not children
now, and she must not run off like a cry baby and expect to be run after and petted. No sir! He would not
go after her! She might come back when she liked. He
would see whether she would really carry out her threat
or not. She never would. He remembered with a satisfied thrill the way she had looked at him yesterday af-

ternoon when she told him she would rather stay at home because he was going to be there too. Ah! Poppycock! She would never go to Europe. She just said that for effect!

And that dig about having a pleasant summer showed she had another grievance too. She was jealous of Jessie Belle!

Well, his lesson had worked then. She had seen them drive by in the morning. But no—Lynette had gone on the eight seventeen. She didn't get the idea of the drive to the Mohawk trail after all. But it was plain to be seen she was jealous of the other girl. Well, that was a good sign. She would come back all right, and probably before night. She might be even now coming in on the five o'clock train. But he, Dana, would not be there to meet her. She was not to have the fatted calf killed for her either, when she did return—not by him. She would have to eat humble pie before he would forgive her for this tantrum. How strange that Lynn, his Lynn, should have fallen to such a ruse to bring about her own way. Well, it was all her fault. He had nothing for which to blame himself.

He sat there glooming until the dinner bell rang, and he could hear Jessie Belle's chatter downstairs. Then he got up and swiftly and silently stole down the back stairs, out the back door, to the garage, and in a moment more was driving furiously off in the direction of the town. He did not intend to meet that girl again tonight.

And if Lynette came back on the five o'clock train and waited for him to come as he had promised, well —she would wait in vain. He would not be a party to any such childishness. He would let her know that he was a man now, and she had got to be a woman, and that the whole thing was her own fault.

XIV

Elim arrived home at exactly five minutes to five, and was dismayed to find that Mrs. Pettingill had departed.

"How long you bin alone, Gramma?" he asked anxiously.

"Oh, not long," said the old lady contentedly. She was still seeing the dazed look in Dana Whipple's eyes when she told him Lynette was going to Europe, and she didn't know whether she was more glad or more sorry about it. He was a well favored lad, and perhaps he would grow out of his conceit. Perhaps she was wrong in her feeling that Dana was not good enough for Lynnie. Dear little Lynnie!

"Well that Pettingill dame is a beaut, she is!" declared Elim angrily. "When I trust anything of mine to her again I'll know it! She said she'd stay till five an' I got here five minutes ahead. What got her?"

"Oh, her husband came along and she wanted to ride. I told her I was all right."

"You bet you did, Gramma! You'd lie down an' let 'em all walk over yah. Well, all I gotta say is, ef you wantta thing done you gotta do it yerself. Here's where I stick around now till Muth comes home. I'm not letting any more silly old dames take care a you. You're too precious."

"That's all right, Elim. I found the mouse trap. Don't you want to set it? We might catch that mouse before your mother gets home."

"Aw shucks! I'll leave Snipe sleep here tonight. He'll get him."

He opened the door and called his dog.

"Here, Snipe! Snipe! Mouse, Snipe, mouse! Catch him, Snipe. Mouse! Mouse! Good old fellow!"

Grandmother Rutherford turned away well satisfied and began to beat up some flannel cakes for Elim's supper. Elim loved flannel cakes and maple syrup.

"Gee, Gramma, goin' ta make flannel cakes? Say, that's the cat's whiskers! Want me ta put the griddle on ta heat? Goin' ta make hot syrup? Want me ta shave the maple sugar down?"

Elim went to the dining-room closet for the maple sugar, saw the cake plate on the table, saw the empty milk glass standing by it, saw the chair shoved back from the table, sniffed and looked wise. He went to the window and looked out down the road, stood and thought, and presently saw Dana's new car shoot out the Whipple driveway and down the road in hot haste. He watched it out of sight and then took the cake of maple sugar with him to the kitchen. He hunted out the kitchen board and the sharp knife and began to shave thin, smooth slices of maple sugar, like wide wafers, curl after curl of them rolling away from the knife. He cut enough sugar to make syrup for a dozen people.

"Say, Gramma, what time did Dana go home?" he asked casually, gathering up his sugar carefully from the board and putting every crumb into the saucepan ready for melting.

Grandmother Rutherford lifted a quick keen eye and searched her grandson's innocent face intent now on measuring the exact amount of water for the sugar, then she dropped her gaze and went back to beating eggs.

"Why, I guess about five minutes before you came in," she answered innocently. "He hadn't been home yet."

"He hadn't?" said Elim thoughtfully. "H'm!"

"I thought we might put another plate on for him," said Grandmother Rutherford tentatively. "I didn't know but he might come back after he read the letter. He might want to ask some more questions about Lynnie's going."

"He won't come back!" said Elim with conviction. "You c'n putta plate on if you wantta, but he won't come back!"

"What makes you think that?" asked Grandmother with interest, with a motion of her head almost like pricking up her ears.

"Cause, he's a mutt! That's why! The poor fish wouldn't humble his pride ta come enask about Lynnie ef it was his las' chance ta ever see her again. He's too stuck on hinself. Aw! He gives me a pain! I'm glad Lynnie's gone. Gramma he's a flat tire, that's what he is! I told ya before, but now I know, and don't ya forget what I told ya! Lynnie'll be glad she got away when she did. See if she isn't. Grandma, does this have ta boil any longer? It's gettin' thick. Gee, doesn't it smell good! I'm holla clear down to my toes. Say, Gramma, these fish are burning. Aren't they done? I'm glad you set the table in the kitchen, then I can help bake cakes. I like ta hear 'em sizzle! Gee, Gramma, but this is a good supper. I wish Muth an' Lynn were here, don't you? But I'm glad they aren't. Gee, ain't it great just us here havin' a good time?"

The Grandmother smiled her rare smile, but she did not ask questions, although she knew that something unusual was disturbing Elim. She was one of those wise ones who had learned to keep her mouth shut on trying occasions. She had her own reservations, and she respected other people's. That was why Elim trusted her and chummed with her, and why he often told her things he wouldn't even tell "the fellas."

But this was one of the occasions when he did not tell Grandmother. What had happened that afternoon would worry Grandmother Rutherford beyond words to describe. Grandmother Rutherford was aristocratic, and Grandmother Rutherford was religious. She would have thought that Dana had lowered himself to companion with that little cheap, painted girl, and she would have thought that he had let down very far in his principles to have done what Elim had seen him do. She would have felt the humiliation keenly for the family too, as well as on her granddaughter's account, and Elim did not mean she should find it out, at least not while she was under his charge, so he whistled instead of telling her, though he was bursting to explain his particular new grudge against the young man. New York was too near yet, and Lynnie not on board the ship. Who knew but Dana was already on his way to bring Lynnie back? He was perfectly capable of it, and of doing it with a high hand. And Lynnie might be just fool enough to give in and come. Girls were that way. They liked to be ordered around. Cave-man stuff!

Well, if his sister did anything like that he would tell her. He would tell her everything!

He wasn't sure but he ought to tell her anyway!

He contemplated the idea of calling her up on the telephone, now, before Dana could possibly get to New York, and telling her everything. Only there were so many prying females on the line he was positive it would be all over the neighborhood before morning. Perhaps it might be a good thing for Dana if it would get around, but the trouble was, Lynette was so mixed up with Dana that the one couldn't suffer without the other being dragged in. Good night! What was he to do? If only Muth was home. He'd tell her quick enough! Yes, Muth had better know at once.

But Elim in spite of his worries and responsibilities managed a good sized supper of delicate trout and fried potatoes, and many flannel cakes swimming in syrup and washed down by plenty of creamy milk.

After supper he helped wash up the dishes, but he took each dish with him to the dining-room china closet as he wiped it, and managed to keep a weather eye out toward the Whipple house, and a keen ear for the sound of Dana's car.

They carried out their program as Grandmother Rutherford had announced it. They played checkers until eight o'clock, and then they read aloud. At least Grandmother read aloud, and Elim sat where he could see the Whipple driveway through the window and listened. Listened both to the story that was being read, and for the car that did not come.

At nine o'clock they went to bed, Elim on the couch which he insisted on having so arranged that he could see out the window.

Grandmother went to bed and to sleep.

Elim went to bed and lay with his eyes wide open looking out the window and getting madder and madder.

Snipe went to sleep in the kitchen.

The mouse in the tin closet came out and peaceably nibbled away at the crumbs Snipe had left on his supper plate, without disturbing him, and then he went back to his work of gnawing a hole from the tin closet into the pantry where the bread box was kept, but Elim lay and thought.

The clock struck ten. It struck eleven. It struck twelve. It struck one! Still Dana's car had not come back. Could it be possible that Elim had missed it? He had been on the alert every minute since he had seen the car go away.

Had that flapper gone away with Dana? Gone to some party or show or something? No, for he had watched the lights in the house go out. Grandmother Whipple's room on the first floor, Dana's mother's room, Justine Whipple's, he knew them all, and the very last to go out was the guestroom in the second story front. He could see two figures distinctly moving about for some minutes before they pulled down the shade. No, the flapper had not gone with Dana. Dana must have gone to New York! Dana *must* have driven to New York!

Gee! What should he do?

Gee! He believed he'd slip out into the hall, and get the telephone in the closet and call Muth. Gramma was asleep, she wouldn't hear him. Muth oughtta know what Dana Whipple was. The old cats were all asleep now, nobody would be listening in. He believed he would call Muth.

And then, just as he was raised softly up on one elbow, and had begun to move one bare foot out to the carpet, carefully, so the old couch wouldn't creak, he heard the quick throbbing of an oncoming car, saw a long shaft of light come piercing up the road, and in a moment more Dana's car shot into the Whipple drive, and up to the garage. He heard the stopping of the engine; saw the lights of the car go out, and in a few minutes more got the twinkle of a light in Dana's room. Then he crept back under the covers, and lay down with a sigh. Dana hadn't gone to New York after all. But what had Dana done? And what would Dana do next?

What Dana did next was to come downstairs in the morning wearing his pleasantest manner and making himself most agreeable to everybody.

Justine looked at him suspiciously. Was he planning to go off with Lynette again today, and desert Jessie Belle? If he did most likely Jessie Belle would carry out her threat, which Ella Smith had confided to her during the gloomy evening while Dana was off scouring round the country with his ill temper, and leave for New York. Ella Smith was most anxious that Jessie Belle should be appeased. She went around with her eyebrows drawn up in anxiety, so nervous that she jumped if anybody spoke to her, and cast furtive frightened glances at her offspring. Grandma Whipple told Amelia she reminded her of a wet hen crossing the road in front of an automobile.

Justine also, had her own reasons for wishing Jessie Belle to remain. She wanted to take down Lynette, and show her that she didn't own Dana.

But Dana showed no signs of going off with Lynette. He didn't go out, he didn't call up, he didn't even look up the road toward the Brooke house.

The reason for it came out when Grandma Whipple reminded Amelia that she ought to call up and give the invitation if she expected Lynette to come to dinner that night. That was Grandma Whipple's way of giving a command.

Amelia opened her mouth to speak and then shut it again. She hadn't intended to ask Lynette to dinner. She had trouble enough without making any more, she thought. Besides, she wasn't altogether sure she wanted to bring Lynette into things yet.

But Dana looked up sharply as she rose to obey her orders:

"It isn't worth while to call," he said briefly, "Lynn's away just now," and went on talking with Jessie Belle about a restaurant in New York which he said was positively the best in the city, barring none. Jessie Belle dearly loved to show off her knowledge of New York, which she considered the center of the universe. So, in fact did Dana.

Justine pricked up her ears and tried to get in a question about Lynette's absence, but Dana managed to evade it, and hurried out to get the car. He had invited Ella Smith and her daughter to take a ride, and told Justine quite casually as he went out the door that she might come along too if she wished. He knew he would have to take her for a ride sometime and it might as well be over with. He whistled gaily as he went across the grass to the garage. Not that he felt light-hearted, just that he wanted to appear so. Besides, a whistle is penetrating. His had been known to reach as far as Lynette's open window in times past. And it just might happen that Lynette had come home on the midnight train, after all. If she had he wanted her to see that he was happy and paying no attention whatever to her whimsies. He had thoroughly convinced himself during the watches of the night that Lynette would return to her home not later than that evening, and he meant to give her three or four good long lonely days to recover from her escapade before he condescended to visit and forgive her. In the meantime he would play around with Jessie Belle. Not that he cared for any more of Jessie Belle's society. She was a vapid little devil! But one had to do something and meantime why not gain experience? Jessie Belle was in the line of education and experience. One had to have experience to preach well.

He had been strongly tempted to run down to New York last night in spite of all his common sense and indignation, and do the cave-man act, pick up Lynette bodily and carry her off back home. In fact he had actually gone nearly sixty miles on the way, but had finally been able to control his foolishness and turn back. It would only have meant an endless giving in to Lynette all the days of his life, and that was not to be thought of.

But now that morning was here, his sentiment or foolishness or whatever it was had fled. He was positive Lynette would be home during the day, and he went about as cheerfully as possible, filling in the time until he could with reasonable dignity go to her.

It was a radiant morning, and Jessie Belle looked more than ever like a blue flower.

In the house Ella Smith was fearfully protesting. She was afraid of automobiles, but more than that she was afraid of Jessie Belle. She wanted to stay quietly in her room and read and try to forget what that wild child of hers might do next. She wanted to shut her eyes and hide her head, and be comfortable a little longer before some kind of cataclysm arose that should destroy them all.

But Justine would not have it so. For one thing she knew Dana would never allow her to go along unless Ella went too, so she nagged her upstairs for her hat and coat, and nagged her quickly out to the car, and they started off, Ella Smith huddled miserably in a corner of the back seat, watching an approaching truck with eyes that fairly bulged with apprehension.

In her window in the dining-room, her trusty crutch at her side, sat Grandmother Whipple cackling out her rusty laughter at their expense.

"It only needs you, Amelia, to complete the party," she chuckled. "The wet hen is all in a flutter. She'd druther cross the street and get run over by one than ride in one and get scared to death. Why don't you go, Amelia, and let 'em have a little common sense aboard?"

Amelia cast a withering glance at her tormentor and stalked silently out to the kitchen with a pile of plates to be washed.

When she came back Grandmother Whipple chuckled out another sentence:

"You ought to have taken my advice last night and got in your invite to Lynette before she ran away. I must say she shows more sense than I thought she had, and she's got a good deal. Maybe she thinks 'give a man rope enough and he'll hang himself.' Anyhow she's gone! Know how long she's going to be away, Amelia? Just for the day, or longer? If I was you I'd go over and leave the invite for her. Maybe her mother'll telephone it to her and she'll come home. It would be a good scheme to have her here when they get back. I'd like to see that little devil's face when she sees her."

Amelia's lips set in a hard thin line, and she walked heavily about the table clattering the dishes together in stacks:

"No, I don't know anything about her plans," she said crossly, "and what's more I don't intend to invite her—ever—maybe! You've invited that huzzy here, now you can take the consequences. If that's the kind of a girl you want Dana to get mixed up with, with his prospects and all, why I suppose you'll have your way. You're financing him. I'm only his mother, not fit to wipe his shoes on, and poor at that! My hands are tied. I can't do a thing! But I won't be a party to bringing Lynette Brooke here on top of it. She wouldn't ever come again, I'm sure of that, with that painted brat making eyes at Dana, and smirking around and snubbing everybody else. Ellaing her own mother too! I declare it makes me sick! I don't know as I'll be able to get dinner I'm so disgusted!"

Grandma chuckled.

"Oh, Jezebel's all right in her place," she cackled, "A place for everything and everything in its place. She'll serve a purpose for a while. We'll see how it turns out."

"Well, her place isn't here, I'm sure of that!" snapped Amelia, "I wouldn't like to state where I think it is."

Grandma chuckled more than ever at that.

"You mean New York, I suppose. Amelia, I hope you don't mean anything worse than New York."

Amelia stalked offendedly to the kitchen, and from that shelter retorted:

"I don't make a practice of swearing, though you do try to turn everything against me."

Grandma cackled to herself a great many times that morning and along toward noon when Amelia came in to set the lunch table she said:

"Amelia, you're a good old soul, and I do torment you a lot, but haven't you ever figured out that there's sometimes sense behind what I do? Ever hear how they find out whether gold is real or not? They put it in the fire. That boy of yours needs a good hot test or two to take the dross out of him before he gets to be a great preacher and gets his head turned, or his grandfather Whipple will turn over in his grave and send down some kind of a curse on him. I've seen it coming. I didn't go to get this Jezebel in the house. I wasn't just sure what she might be. But since she wanted to come it kinda seemed providential. Now she's here let Dana take his test. If he ain't fit for the great work you an' I and his grandfather been tryin' for years to push him into, if he ain't strong enough to stand the test, he ain't fit for a preacher. There's more'n one Jezebel in the world, and he's bound to meet 'em. I guess you don't need to worry."

Amelia stood with her large capable hands resting on her hips, a desperate look on her face, while this speech was being delivered. Now she considered, with set resigned lips:

"All right," she said at last, "gimme that old Whipple breast pin of yours! I wantta put it in the fire and see if it's real!"

Grandma chuckled heartily, her eyes twinkling with appreciation.

"You're smart, Amelia!" she said. "Do you know that? You have times when you're real cute and amusing. Don't I smell those beets burning? You better look after 'em. I think I'll take a nap."

XV

THE train drew in to Grand Central Station, and Dorothy Reamer rushed at her aunt and cousin and fairly overwhelmed them in her delight.

"Oh, you precious dears!" she screamed, regardless of bystanders and curious passengers. "I knew you'd come! I knew it! I knew it! If you hadn't I was ready to jump overboard tomorrow with despondency. Come on, hurry up! Mother is in the car, and Daddy's waiting to get my telephone that it's all right before he has the passports changed. He's got it all fixed up so that Lynn can take Cousin Marta's. Now come on quick, for there's heaps and heaps to do before the stores close. Mother wants you to help her select some last things. Will you have to go up to the house first Aunt Mary? Are you tired? Sure? Well, the house is all swathed in covers of course and it looks like a ghost. We were planning to take lunch down town, and not go back till the shopping is all done. Are there any more bags? Here, porter! Take these out to the car!"

She overwhelmed them with her plans, and swept all thoughts of home and problems out of their minds. It was as if they had suddenly landed in another planet where the laws under which they had been living hitherto did not obtain.

The handsome car awaited them, and Aunt Hilda greeted them with joyful affection. Something cold and tremulous suddenly swept out of Lynette's heart, and life seemed to pulse on again. After all, there was a whole day before the ship sailed, and lots of things can happen in a day.

Who could help being interested in such a heaven-sent trip, and such a day of delightful shopping? There was an evening dress to be purchased, and a coat. Mother Brooke insisted on that. Lynette needed a new hat too, and since the fiat had gone forth that there was not much baggage to be taken across, she could indulge her taste a little more leniently in the things she had to purchase.

The morning became suddenly glad.

The day in the woods, theological differences, and little painted flappers became as a dream. Even her birthday was forgotten. What was one birthday more or less anyway. She was going out to see the world! Her heart grew suddenly light.

Lynette stepped off with Dorothy to get fitted to slippers and her mother looked after her with a sigh of relief. The smile she wore was Lynette's own dear happy one. Perhaps the hurt had not gone so deep yet. Or was the child counting too much on Dana's coming down tonight?

They separated for a while to expedite their shopping, and met at two o'clock for lunch.

"I just telephoned Dad's office and he says everything is fixed," announced Dorothy. "They didn't kick at anything, even the change in staterooms. Wasn't it lucky the corner one on the other side of you was vacant, Mother? Funny why Cousin Marta insisted on the other one away off at the other end of the boat. But I thought it was fun. I hate to be in leading strings, and now I suppose Mother will watch up every night to see what time you and I turn in, Lynn."

She made a comical wry face, and pounced on the menu card.

"I'm going to have lobster salad and café parfait," she announced defiantly, looking at her mother.

"Oh, Dorothy!" protested her mother, "I'm just sure you are going to get sick before we leave and hold up the whole expedition."

"Oh, rot!" said Dorothy inelegantly, "I never get sick. Lynette what are you going to have?"

Lynette came back from a glance around the big beautiful tea-room and gave attention to the menu, the happy smile still on her lips.

"Oh, anything," she said happily. "It all looks good to me. I think I'll take a tomato stuffed with chicken salad. I remember I had one of those here last winter when you brought me and it was delicious."

Then she lifted her eyes and suddenly saw a back and shoulders and a sleek black head that reminded her of Dana. It wasn't Dana. She knew that instantly, but her heart had had time to give a joyful leap, and her eyes to light themselves with a heavenly light, before they suddenly went dark again, and her heart gave a tug of disappointment. It wasn't Dana, but it brought Dana right there in the room with his back to her, and she had to sit and watch for him to turn his face—the face that was not Dana's—to prove to herself over again each time, that it was not really Dana, so like were his shoulders and his sleek head, and his long white tapering hands that he used with such grace. Even his movements seemed to be Dana, until he turned a hawklike face and frowned at the waiter.

Mother Brooke's watching eyes saw the cloud come over her girl's face, and following her glance knew instantly what was the matter. She had thought that Dana had come after her! Poor child! Poor little girl! The mother began to pray in her heart, a wordless prayer, leaving the issue with God.

Presently the man who looked like Dana got up, paid his bill, and left the room, and the restlessness died out of Lynette's eyes, but the light did not return. There was a wistful, anxious pucker around them like haunted eyes, which hurt her mother.

Aunt Hilda, however, created a digression by getting out her list and making the girls check off the things that were still remaining to be done.

"There's hair nets, and my blouse at the dressmaker's, and some aromatic ammonia. Don't forget those, Dorothy! And your father needs a couple more shirts.

Just call up the place where he always gets them and ask them to send them out special late this afternoon. Mary, I think Lynette won't need but one hat. Let everything go till we get to London or Paris. Did you say she has a black dress? Satin? Oh, that's perfectly all right. They're useful, one can get along with very few other dresses."

So the talk drifted back to the immediate preparations, but somehow they had lost their zest for Lynette. Her eyes were ever searching the throng around the tables, and her ear listening above the orchestra that was discoursing wonderful music, for the sound of a voice she knew and loved.

For now a strange thing had happened to Lynette. All the differences of the day before seemed to have vanished, and Dana had become a dream man once more, the lover of her childhood in whom was found no fault. She saw him with the eyes of her soul, a man who had made great attainments, and won great honors; a person who had a right to say what was what, and whose future was to be phenomenal. And now she began to wonder why she had felt she must go away, and to berate herself for having cared so much about a trifling birthday party, and to be restless for the time to come when they would go up to the house, because that would be the place to which Dana was coming if he came after her, or to which he would telephone or send a telegram in case he could not come. He could not find her down here in this throng.

But she was whirled away on the business of the hour again, and made to forget for a little, and to be interested in finding a little book to send back to the dear grandmother, and a special kind of fly in the sporting and athletic department for Elim's fishing. But that brought a pang too, for she was sending no message to Dana.

But now she must wait for Dana to make a move. It wrung her heart.

Night came, and the family dinner, sent in from a caterer's. It was all delightfully new and exciting, and Lynette entered into it gaily, for now she felt that at any minute Dana might call her up, or the door bell might ring and there be Dana, come to carry her home. What joy if he had! She would be ready to forgive him everything, she thought, if he felt that way about her, and really could not bear to have her go away. The undertone of these thoughts ran along with everything she said or did.

Until at last she awoke to the fact that it was half past eleven and Dana had not made a sign, and they were all going to bed.

Even on her pillow, with her eyes closed, she remembered that the telephone was just outside her door in the hall, and Dana might be driving down, and get in late; or perhaps he had had a flat tire or something, and he would telephone the house.

But no ring broke the silence of the sleeping house, and Lynette, worn out with the excitement of the day, slept too.

Only the mother, by her side, bearing the pain of her child's life testing, kept vigil, and prayed that all might be as God had appointed, and that her darling might be fully yielded to His will.

Morning dawned, and the glad hurry of the departure.

"Are you sure you put those slippers in my bag, Dorothy? Have you got plenty of handkerchiefs along, Lynette? Mary I wish you would take this shawl to your mother as a present from me. It looks just like her and she ought to have it. I always think of her in her pretty gray silk and white lace when I take this out of the drawer, and I simply never wear it myself. It's practically new. Dorothy, where are the boys? You'll have to see whether they have put in everything I laid out on their beds last night. Don't let them forget their pajamas. They are so careless! Lynnie, will you just see if that's the mail down at the door? I thought I heard the postman's ring."

And Lynette hurried down in one of her breathless moments of hope. There might be a letter! A special delivery letter! That was it! Perhaps somehow Elim had forgotten to deliver hers to Dana right away and he had written her at once that he was coming, or that she must wait for him, or something—in her desperation she didn't know what.

But there was no letter for her.

Slowly she came back and went on with her preparations, steeling her heart somehow to put Dana out of the question. He had not cared to even write her a farewell line.

Then out of the possibilities there leaped another pleasant one. Perhaps there would be flowers at the ship for her! Perhaps he would send her a message in that way, a wordless message, but still one that would make it possible for her to go on and carry out the trip as planned, and wait patiently until a letter could come across to tell her all that his flowers would promise. That would be it of course. Or—he *might* come down to see her off. He might have been detained till the last minute. Would it be wrong to go back if he asked her even as late as that? Would it be dishonorable toward her uncle and aunt? She wondered what her mother would think about that. She ought to be prepared for any possible contingency. There might not be time when it arose to consider a question like that. She would have to act, and she felt sure that unless she had steeled herself beforehand she could only trust herself to act from her heart, not from her head.

So she solaced herself with hope from moment to moment, hour after hour, till the time came at last to get into the car and be driven away down to the wharf. Then suddenly she realized that her mother was not going with her, and she turned to her with panic in her eyes.

"Oh, I can't go, Mother dear! I can't! It seems as though it would choke me to go. I must go back with you tonight. I must! I must!"

"But you won't, dear," said her mother folding her in her arms tenderly. "You are walking in the appointed way, and you are going to be led. You could not go back with dignity now, and all the arguments that you agreed to yesterday are just as true today. Trust your own decision and trust in God."

"Yes, I know," said Lynette, her eyes full of trouble yet.

"But Mother, if Dana comes to you, you will explain everything? You will not let him think I ran away in pique. You will not—oh, I don't know what I mean, but you understand, don't you mother?"

She clung to her mother's hand in almost tragic appeal and the mother did not fail her.

"It's all right, Lynnie, I understand, dear. And I'll say all that you want said if the time comes. You trust your heavenly Father!"

Then they came to the gang plank and stepped on board, and all was bustle and eager confusion. There was no further chance to talk alone to her mother, no spot to get away by one's self. Everybody was laughing and talking and crying and saying good-by. People were crowding into cabins with arms full of flowers, and exclaiming over the accommodations, and making feeble jokes and laughing very hard at them.

They went to their cabins and saw their baggage safely placed. They exclaimed as others had done over the convenience of the appointments and the skillful economy of space, over the big wardrobe and the chest of drawers, and the adorable little port hole of a window, and had their laugh and their joke about the two-story beds.

And there were flowers there, banks of them for Dorothy, and a lot for Aunt Hilda, but none for Lynette, though she went carefully over the cards while Dorothy was powdering her nose.

With a sinking heart she followed the rest on deck to watch the people.

They passed through the big cabin with its comfortable chairs and scattered tables, and great book case filled with enticing books of travel and art and history, and Lynette had a passing thought of how delightful all this would have been if she had not carried such a heavy heart. Then they went out on the upper deck where they could see the people arriving, and Lynette searched the throng in vain for Dana's tall shoulders, and well set head, with his soft panama hat pulled well over his eyes in what seemed such a distinguished way.

At last the gong sounded and the cry went out "All ashore!" It thrilled through Lynette's heart with a sick sore feeling that made her want to cling to her mother, hide her head in her neck, go home with her and never, never leave her any more.

But the clinging and the weeping and the good-by were over in a moment. The mother kept a brave face till the last, smiled, waved her hand, said "Remember!" and just as they were parting "Trust!" Then the second cry went out, and she was gone, down among the throng.

Lynette's eyes followed her. There she was, standing on the dock alone, except for the chauffeur who was to take her back to the Grand Central Station at once when the boat sailed. Her mother, down there alone! Why had she let her do it? Something keener than her love for Dana gripped her heart now. What was this unspeakably awful thing that she was about to do? Put the ocean between herself and all that she loved! For what? Why did she want to see the world? These thoughts beat their way through her excited brain, while she stood there and tried to smile, and shout maudlin nothings into the air as everybody else was doing, things that nobody could hear, nor answer.

Then Uncle Reamer came with little rolls of bright paper tapes and showed her how to snap them off into the air, toward the beloved one on the pier, and she tried her hand at this too, while yet in undertone her anxious heart was crying out for Dana, sick and sore because she could not see him anywhere, and the minutes were going, going. Oh, if it could just be over! If she were coming home instead of going out into the unknown!

There seemed an unconscionable delay. Something about a boat ahead of them that could not get out of the way till it was unloaded. And there they stood on tired feet, and tried eagerly to signal last messages that they had not thought of before, messages that did not matter anyway and could not be understood, and Lynette suffered a whole year's agony during that few minutes' wait. She studied her mother's face and saw the lines of care and age that had been graven on them since she went away last year, and she thought again of all the things she had planned to do for her and with her this summer, and now she was running away!

Over and over again!

But at last the gang plank was shoved off, and the stately vessel glided slowly out from its moorings, and sailed away.

Till the last minute Lynette studied the crowd, strained her eyes to recognize someone who came running down the dock, stretched her neck and stood on her toes till they ached to eagerly scan the dock, but Dana was not there!

And the mother, watching her child through eyes that were now filled with tears, had her own agony to fight out. She knew when the beloved eyes were looking over her head, hunting, hunting for a face that was not there, that *should* have been there! Ah! She understood, and wondered again if she ought to have encouraged the child to go.

And when the forward part of the vessel had passed too far to recognize her Lynnie, and she let her indifferent glance wander over the rest of the boat as it passed, taking in the whole length of deck with its struggling, shouting, almost frantic good-bys, picking out an individual now and then who was particularly noticeable, life suddenly seemed a ghastly thing to her, and she found herself pitying humanity as a whole. The boat seemed like a picture of life, and its separations. There sat an old lady close to the rail, her head decked out with some foolish youthful headgear, her face befloured, her gnarled hands gripping a great mass of the bright paper ribbons, her trophy from the fray. An old woman caring to snatch and keep a mess like that! And there at the stern alone, clinging to the rail and waving frantically, stood two fat youthful flappers, skirts very brief, hair the latest thing in boy bob, noses white as a marble statue, lashes darkened heavily, their painted lips stretched wide as any baby bawling, the tears rolling down their rouged cheeks. Crying

at the top of their lungs they were, and shouting, "G-
g-g-g-gd! B-b-b-by!"

They were the most laughable objects her eyes had
ever seen, yet she found herself suddenly weeping with
them. Weeping not alone on her own account that her
girl was going from her, and in trouble, but weeping for
the sorrow of the world. Sorrow that was going on every day, and yet did not seem to draw humanity any
nearer to the only possible source of help and comfort,
the heart of the Saviour of mankind.

She turned away, wiping her eyes, and signaled to
the chauffeur that she was ready to go. The ship was
out in the water now, mingling with the others like her,
and hard to distinguish any longer. Well, Lynnie was
gone, and safe for a while from the thing her mother
had feared.

And yet, the mother heart was heavy, for now the
burden of the girl's doubt had descended upon her and
she could not help continually wondering whether she
had done right to urge her to go.

"Well, I must just take the advice I gave her," she
said to herself as she settled back into the cushions of
the car. "I have done the best I knew how, and I must
just leave the rest to the Father. But now, I've got to go
home and face Dana!"

Lynette, standing alone at the rail of the vessel,
looked off to the rapidly disappearing shore, and kept
saying over and over to herself:

"He didn't come! He didn't come! Dana didn't care
to come! He didn't even write or phone or telegraph!"
Oh, it seemed as if she must plunge back in the waves,
swim to the shore, get home somehow and straighten
things out. It couldn't be that she and Dana had suddenly become separated this way! Oh, ghastly, ghastly
life! How was it to be borne?

And all about her was the unspeakable loveliness of
distance, water dancing in the sunlight, new and wonderful ships passing by. A future of delight before her.
Oh why could she not have had this before she went
home at all? Before her heart rest had been disturbed?
Why had it come, this wonderful opportunity that she

never dreamed would be hers, and come just when she could not enjoy it? Oh, if her heart could only be free from worry while she was gone!

Then she remembered her mother's words and she looked up to the blue expanse overhead and said softly under her breath, "Father, I'm going to try to trust, but you'll have to help me. I can't do it alone. Teach me what you want of me!"

XVI

ELIM had not got off his letter in time for the boat. He had been too much occupied the first night to even remember it. When he considered it the next morning he found that he felt embarrassed over the knowledge that had come to him. How could he write in gay vein to his sister with that maddening knowledge on his conscience. He had a feeling that it would glare between the lines and shout itself out to her as she read. And yet he must write, and he must somehow make her know what kind of a mutt that poor fish was.

So after lunch the next day, he took a pad and pencil, and wended his way to the woods while Mary Somers the washerwoman kept Grandmother Rutherford company, washing up the kitchen floor and detailing how her seven grandchildren had the whooping cough.

Humped on the moss beside his favorite stone Elim got out his knife, sharpened his pencil elaborately, and then sat and thought. He bit three beautiful points off before he got down to work at last. His brows were knit with perplexity and doubt, but his jaws were set with a grim determination.

Dear Kid: (it began)

Didn't get this off after all in time to make the ship. But I guess you didn't miss it. I had to keep the old sport from getting down in the mouth. I guess you know who I mean. Found her chasing a mouse in the tin cupboard when I got back from the station. Called Snipe in and I guess he finished him. Haven't heard anything more from him to date. Went fishing with Spud and caught a whole string. Gave him half. We had them for supper with flannel cakes and syrup. Some combination. You ought to have been here. You wouldn't believe it but it's darned lonesome since you left. Hope Muth gets home by night. I didn't leave the house alone when I went fishing, so don't worry. Old Petticoat said she'd stay till five o'clock. She didn't keep her word on account of her husband getting home and demanding her at once, but somebody else came. I guess you know what chump I mean. Sorry to hurt your feeling, but I don't like to spoil this nice paper with his name. He came straight from a ride, hadn't been home to get his letter, and Old Sport asked him in and gave him a piece of your birthday cake. Clever lady, what?

Say, Lynnie, I don't want to be mean, but for cat's sake, what do you see in that egg? I don't know if you like it or not, but I think you ought to know he isn't worth the parsnips. He's a sneak and a coward. He has a yellow streak a foot wide up his back. The truth is nothing in his young life, and as for his religion it's all bologny! I'm telling you! Take it from me, and forget him! He isn't worth the paper his name is written on, and I know what I'm saying. I'm your brother and I wouldn't say it if I didn't think a whole lot of you. Just call him a blank and think no more of it. Next time you pick one, pick a man! I'm saying it!

Say, Lynn, what about the pyramids? Heard anything of them yet? Don't forget to drop me a line written in front of it, and say, bring me a bag of sand from the desert, can't you? A square inch will do, and it won't cost anything. You can put it in your glove and they'll never catch on.

And say, Kid, pick me out something nice for

Muth, and for the Old Sport too. Make it snappy. I'm getting a job tomorrow down at Smith's garage, and I can pay around twenty-five bucks apiece by the time you get home, I guess, so go to it Kid!

There isn't much yet to say, but I guess there will be by next week, so long till then, Yours as ever,

Lim.

P.S. I forgot to say, *Don't you write to that sucker!* Not even if he writes, don't you answer! You wouldn't want to if you knew all. Take it from your brother who loves you. He's a flat tire! And some day good and soon you're going to find it out.

So long!

E.B.

With a sigh of relief he read the letter over, folded it and stuffed it into a pocket-worn envelope. That was done now and he could breathe easier. Now, if Lynnie wanted to throw herself away he had done his duty to her, and he'd wash his hands.

He decided to mail his letter at once before his mother got back. It would be better that way. Muth might object to worrying Lynnie that way, but a man had to decide those things himself now and then. A woman didn't always understand how doggone low down another man could be when he tried. Maybe he would tell Muth sometime, and maybe not, but anyhow he would run no risks with having the letter held up.

So he got his bicycle and sailed off to the post office, and when he came back Justine Whipple was waiting for him at the gate, a paper bag in her hand full of hot cookies that she had stolen form Amelia's new baking, set to cool in the back kitchen.

"Elim, I wish you'd take these up to your grandmother with my love," she called holding out the paper bag with an alluring odor of cinnamon and raisins.

Elim slowed down, looked suspiciously at the bag, and gave Miss Justine the "once over" as he called it.

"Your sister's away, isn't she?" she asked in tones of honeyed sweetness.

"Yep!" said Elim holding his bicycle by one toe touching the ground, wavering back and forth and eyeing her gravely, but making no attempt to take the cookies. What had the old girl got up her sleeve now, he wondered. She couldn't put anything across on him. He knew his onions!

"Oh, that's disappointing, isn't it, when she's just got back home! Is she going to be gone long?" cooed Justine.

"Yep!" said Elim succinctly.

"She *is?*" Justine gathered in the truth like a hungry person. "And did your mother go too?"

"Yep!"

"Oh! Why, then your Grandmother is all alone isn't she?"

"Nope."

"Oh, she isn't? She has someone staying with her, has she?"

"Yep."

"Oh—well, then it's all right. I was just going to suggest that I might come up and stay nights. But you say she has someone?"

"Yep." .

"Well," bridled Miss Justine, "of course. Well, that's very nice, and I've got company too. It would be hard for me to come just now, too. But I came out to say that I'm sending these cookies up to your grandmother. I thought she might enjoy them. She used to like my cookies." Justine never make a cooky in her life, but that made no difference in a case like this. She proffered the cookies as if they were pearls, with smiles. Elim accepted them reluctantly and held them with the tips of his thumb and finger as if they were a dead rat, but he did not relax his cold stare, nor thank her. He did not trust her. And he was impatient to be off.

"Where did your sister go?" she asked quite casually as she stepped back from the curb after forcing the cookies upon Elim.

"Oh, all around," said Elim casually. "She's traveling in Europe. Gub-by!" and he shot off around the house, leaving an astounded maiden lady standing tottering on the curbstone staring after him in dismay. Lynette gone to Europe!

She stood a moment looking after him, recovering her poise, and then, having adjusted what Grandmother Whipple called her cat-and-cream expression she went slowly, smilingly, home and sat down at the table where the family were already assembled.

"You're late, Justine!" snapped Grandma fixing her sharp little eyes upon her. Nothing ever escaped Grandma. She knew Justine was up to something.

"Yes," said Justine, accepting her plate from Amelia, "I was just talking to Elim Brooke. I thought Grandma Rutherford might need someone to stay with her, poor old soul! Mrs. Brooke and her daughter went away yesterday morning you know. I thought it might be my duty to run up and stay nights, but he says they have someone. Do you know who it is Dana? Elim didn't say, and he seemed in a hurry so I didn't detain him."

But Dana was suddenly busy giving Jessie Belle another lamb chop and seemed not to hear. Grandma kept her eyes on her plate thoughtfully and did not seem surprised. Amelia was standing behind Justine filling her glass with ice water, and Justine could not see the startled look in her eyes. Justine waited a minute and then raised her voice a trifle to make sure of attention.

"So it seems Lynette has gone to Europe!"

She flung the sentence into the conversation like a bomb and enjoyed the sensation it created immensely.

Dana was helping himself to more potatoes and feigned an indifference he was far from feeling.

"Isn't that something new?" pursued Justine persistently. "Did you know she was going, Dana?"

"She has been contemplating it for sometime, I believe," said Dana cooly, reaching for the butter plate and helping himself bountifully.

Then up spoke Amelia, stung into action by the superiority of Justine:

"It's a pity you hadn't decided to go along, Dana. I felt all along you should. What's a few summer engagements to preach when you have an opportunity to travel with people who are congenial?"

Grandma cackled her appreciation.

Dana flashed a look of surprise at his mother, but came across in fine shape:

"Well, Mother, duty is duty, and a promise is a promise. I gave my word I'd fill those pulpits, and I can't go back on it. This is a critical time in my career! Besides it takes money to go to Europe, and I ought to be saving up for the future."

"Oh, money!" said Amelia with a toss of her head. "What's money in a case like this? You knew I'd see that you had what you needed! I've got some saved up of my own!"

Justine looked up with a sneer in her eye and Grandma cackled again. Life was rare these days.

"Well, Mother, I didn't go," said Dana smiling. "I thought my duty was at home this summer," and he beamed upon the table with a self-righteous smile that was charming. Even Jessie Belle succumbed to it, and showed her dimple in admiration of him.

"It's not too late yet!" said his mother with a surprising show of initiation. "You could catch the next boat if you started tomorrow. I was reading about the sailings this afternoon in the paper. And you could telegraph tonight for reservations."

Dana looked startled, but went on eating his supper, steadily.

"I couldn't possibly do it, Mother. I've telegraphed that church I'd be there the third of August. It's all settled. Besides, I may run over in September, if Lynette stays so long. I don't know. Have another chop, Jessie Belle? They are awfully small ones. You must be hungry after your ride."

"Yes, Jezebel, eat 'em up!" piped up Grandma to the surprise of everybody. "Justine never eats a second one, and Amelia never has time to. Eat 'em up, Jezebel! No use having to put any away!"

"Oh, Mrs. Whipple, you're a scream!" giggled Jessie Belle. "Oh, I love the way you call me Jezebel, don't you, Ella? I thought I'd simply pass away the first time I heard it."

Ella Smith grew very red and tried to apologize for her child to Madame Whipple, but the old lady only grinned and went on drinking her tea.

Justine cast a dark look at Grandma, but smiled back sweetly at Jessie Belle.

"Yes, Jessie Belle, dear, take the chop. I don't think I care for a second one tonight, really."

Then she continued her pursuit of knowledge.

"How long does Lynette stay in Europe, Dana? Elim seemed to think she would be gone a long time?"

"Probably a year. It's a little uncertain," answered Dana glibly as if he knew all about it. "They may take in the Mediterranean trip if they winter in Italy. They are going to follow their own fancy after they get over there I believe." Dana still believed in his heart that Lynette would return that evening duly humbled, but time would take care of that.

"They? Who are they?" caught up Justine avidly. "Just Lynette and her mother?"

"No, her mother only went down to see her off. She went with relatives. Her uncle and aunt."

"Oh, that must be a very expensive trip. I wonder how Lynette can afford it. They never seemed very well off. Their house needs painting terribly!" Justine's lip curled bitterly as she said it. Amelia was on the defensive at once.

"People who don't put all their money in show and improvements have plenty left for traveling and luxuries. Besides, I've been told that Lynette's grandmother is very wealthy indeed. Someone told me the other day at the missionary meeting that Mrs. Rutherford pays the largest income tax in town."

Grandma cackled enjoyably.

"Is that so, Dana? You ought to know," asked Justine with her head on one side like a saucy bird.

"Well," said Dana preening himself somewhat, "I have no means of knowing her exact income of course, but she always seems to have plenty of money for any-

thing she wants to do. She is always giving Lynette
something nice. I believe it was she who sent her to college, which explains her choice of colleges I think. She
is old fashioned in her ideas you know, and Lynn
adores her, and humors her every whim, although I do
think in this case she should have taken her stand for
Wellesley or Vassar or some better known institution."

Dana was playing to the galleries, the gallery in this
case being Jessie Belle. Dana did love to make a show
of power. He loved to parade his opportunities and his
wealthy friends, and his advantages, even before this
foolish little scatter-brain.

"I wonder you didn't go down and see Lynette off
yourself, Dana!" cooed Justine attacking the subject
proper again. "It would have been so interesting. Something to remember. I just love to see people off. Why
didn't you go, Dana, deah?"

"Well, I did think of it quite seriously," said Dana
pleased to be still the center of interest, "in fact I almost started, but I decided there would be little pleasure about it. Just a big mob, and a long wait, and Lynette was going to be awfully busy shopping beforehand so there wouldn't have been much satisfaction."

"And is she going to write to you? Won't it be interesting to be having all sorts of foreign stamps coming to
the house?"

"I shall be hearing from her from time to time, of
course," answered Dana with a gratified smile, "and
perhaps if things shape up I might get over while she's
there. I can't tell!"

Dana shoved back his chair with finality and arose.

"How about another picture tonight, Jessie Belle? I
shan't have much time later on, but I might as well
amuse you while I can."

They watched them go, Justine with a smile of satisfaction, and a furtive triumph flung at Amelia. Ella
Smith, like a frightened hen whose duck was swimming. Amelia with a snort of baffled fury. The old lady
sat by her window far into the twilight, and looked out
across the mountains where the blue ruin grew like

smoke, and laughed softly to herself, until Amelia thought she should go insane.

As Jessie Belle and Dana went down the street arm in arm, a long fringed brilliant shawl of magenta silk hanging over Dana's arm, they passed Elim and his mother just coming home from the New York train in Scarlett's old Ford. Mrs. Brooke looked out and expected to speak, but Dana did not look up nor seem to see them, and Elim whistled, pointedly, with sharp stacato notes:

"I *wonder*—who's *kissing* her—*Now!*"

Mrs. Brooke watched them walking away into the twilight, and felt she had her answer to her prayer for guidance. She had been praying all the way home. She had not done wrong to urge Lynette to go abroad!

"Gee, Muth! I'd like to wallop that cuss!" broke forth Elim when they were almost home.

"Elim!"

"Well, I would, Muth. And don't the Bible say it's just as bad to wantta as to do it? Well, then, why can't I do it? It ain't any worse than what I *have* to do now, is it? And it would do Dana a whole lot of good! It would be an experience. Dana needs experience, Muth!"

"Elim, don't talk that way! It is terrible! What has Dana been doing to stir you up so? Anything new?"

"Aw! He's a rotten sucker! That's all! Wait till I tell ya. You stick around till Gramma goes ta bed. Ain't any need ta worry her with it. She's game all right but why worry her?"

So Mary Brooke "stuck around," and Elim told her, and after that she was doubly sure that she had been right in urging Lynette to go abroad.

But yet, she was troubled about Dana. Oughtn't she to do something for Dana, the friend of Lynette's childhood? Hadn't they a responsibility toward him? It is true he had acted most indifferently toward Lynette, but perhaps there had been something to excuse him. Still, what could she do but pray for Dana? And pray she did with a heart like lead, but a faith that laid him at the foot of the cross and asked for his salvation from self and sin. She did not pray that he might be made fit for her daughter to love. She did not feel that her wisdom was able to judge whether or not that was a right prayer. It was for God who knew the end from the beginning, and reads the human heart perfectly, to judge that. She must be content to let the matter lie in God's hand. And yet she prayed that Dana would be kept from utter ruin, and she prayed with a heart of love too.

And Dana, walking the ways of what he knew was temptation, and thinking himself strong to keep from falling, strong in his own fine character, strong with the education and culture he had acquired, strong in his pride of family and church, strong in the strength of what he expected to be some day, yet went and put himself in the way of death, and tried to enjoy it awhile just for the experience.

Nor was Mary Brooke's prayer that night wholly without immediate answer, for the silver screen flashed a story before Dana's indolent eyes, that should have been a warning to him, if anything can warn a man who is so wise in his own conceit. For God can make even the wrath of man to praise Him, and that night he must have used that picture to answer that prayer and send a warning to Dana Whipple's sleeping soul.

Grandma Whipple was not one to read her Bible much, but she asked for it that night, and studied over it awhile, flipping the leaves back and forth till she found what she wanted. She got out a pencil and paper from the little stand drawer by her side, and wrote with her rheumatic fingers a line or two.

Dana's big white college sweater lay on a chair not far away. She poked at it with her crutch while Amelia was out of the room, and Justine and Ella reading over in the parlor. She pinned the paper to the sweater, quite conspicuously, and hobbled over to a chair by the hall door, laying the sweater across it where Dana would be sure to see it and take it upstairs with him. Then she announced to Amelia that she was ready to go to bed, and she lay a long time under the blankets chuckling to herself at what she had done, what she was going to do perhaps, if things didn't come out the way they ought to.

"You're a smart woman, Amelia," she said by way of good night, "but you haven't enough git-up-and-git! You were real smart tonight several times, but you didn't keep it up. If I was as smart as you I'd never let that Jezebel woman get away with what she has set out for. Better go to bed and think that over. You didn't take my advice in time or you might have had Lynette here yet!"

After Amelia had shut Grandma's door she went over to the paper pinned on the sweater and read what Grandma had written there, but she did not dare to unpin the paper and throw the note away. Or perhaps she thought it wiser to let it alone. Anyway, she left it there. It might have been due just to her lack of "git-up-and-git."

The words that Grandma had written on the paper were these:

"He that walketh with wise men shall be wise: but a companion of fools shall be destroyed."

When Dana found it later in the evening and took it up to his room, he read and pondered over it for some time, with a frown. Now what could Grandma mean by that? For the old lady never did anything without a purpose, and that was unmistakably her writing. Was it in the nature of a threat or a promise? Dana went thoughtfully to bed, and spent some wakeful hours in profitable meditation. And yet, his eyes were so blinded by his own conceit, that he walked blandly back into danger the very next day.

XVII

LYNETTE was not left long to think her sad thoughts alone that afternoon. Dorothy came pouncing down upon her and carried her off to see the boat. Led her the lengths of the decks, up and down, through cabins and corridors until she felt lost and bewildered, but for the time her regrets and anxieties were put aside and she was just a girl, off for a good time with her cousin.

Dorothy was tall, and slim, with pretty features and a good-looking hair cut, rather boyish though it was. She was gay and a bit impertinent in her way, but it was such a pretty way, and she seemed so cocksure of herself that Lynette felt a sort of fascination in watching her. They had not been together for four years, except for the three days that she had spent in New York on her way home, and the fascination had not yet worn off. Dorothy was only seventeen, but she actually seemed older than Lynette, who was just twenty-one. Dorothy had assumed the position of mentor to her cousin at once.

"Now, we're going to our stateroom and unpack," she announced after they had made the rounds of the ship most thoroughly, located their deck chairs, and summed up the points of vantage generally.

"I haven't much to unpack," laughed Lynette. "I'm afraid I shall make a sorry companion for you, you bird of gorgeous plumage. I had a peep into your steamer trunk and suitcase before they went away and it certainly looked like a rainbow. I shall have to stay in the background till we get somewhere and I can get fitted out a little better."

"Indeed you won't, Lynnie dear," declared the vivacious Dorothy, "I got after Cousin Marta on the telephone and made her will you all her darling dodabs and sports clothes and evening dresses. She would have done it anyway if she had had time to think. She'll never wear them again. Her sister can't live. The doctor said so when she went out to California, only she rallied for a while, and they hoped she might live for a few years. But the telegram said she was sinking rapidly and Marta will go straight into mourning of course. When she comes out of mourning these tricks will be all out of date and she'll have to get new things. You might as well have them as her maid, anyway she has loads of money to buy more. Of course she's ages older than you, but that don't mean a thing these days, and Cousin Marta wears her skirts to the limit, so they won't be too long for you. I'm dying to see them on you. She's just your build and size. I know some of them will be just precious. Of course we may have to change something here or there, but that's nothing. The stewardess will help us. And evening dresses are easy to fix. Almost anything goes if it has a back and a front and a gold rose."

"Oh, but Dorothy! I couldn't wear your cousin's things. They would be much too gorgeous for me. Why, I wouldn't have any place to wear them either. Remember I'm only along in the background. I'm not going among people I know. Don't distress yourself about me. Don't try to dress me up to fit the picture. Let me stay in the background."

"Background nothing! You're my cousin, and you're going to stay so. We are going everywhere together and you've got to play up. Let's open Mart's steamer trunk and see what she sent. I do hope she put the silver and jade one in. It's a corker! We'll want that for the first night. You and I are going to dance the whole evening long and have the dandiest time! They have a wonderful orchestra on board and the floor is peachy. There are three men I know, and I'll let you have one of them for your special during the trip. He's rather wild, but he has nice eyes, and he can dance like an angel."

"Do angels dance?" asked Lynette amused, and then sobering down. "I'm sorry dear, but *I don't!* You must just make up your mind that I'm an older sister, a sort of country cousin who isn't in society and doesn't want to be. I'm very old fashioned you know."

"So's your old man!" said Dorothy gaily. "You're going to learn to dance! I'll begin to teach you right now!" and she caught up her cousin and whirled her about in the tiny space beside the trunk, till they both fell laughing into the berth, and Lynette's hair came tumbling down about her shoulders in a lovely golden mass.

"Oh, look at your gorgeous locks!" cried Dorothy. "Aren't you the bees' knees with all that top knot! I thought of growing mine but it would take so long, and look so scraggy that I gave it up. I hate to be a fright while it's growing. Get up now and try the step again. It won't take you long to learn."

"No, dear!" said Lynette quite firmly. "You'll have to make up your mind that dancing is one of the things I don't do. I don't want to argue about it, and I'm not going to try to make you think as I do about it, but I just don't do it. I went over that question four years ago, the first time it had ever really come to my notice as something to be decided, because as a matter of course I had never done it before. I decided that it wasn't a good thing, not for me anyway, nor for what I have planned to do in life, and so I just settled the question once for all. I'm sorry if I disappoint you, but there are some things I can't yield and this is one of them."

"Oh hen!" said Dorothy disappointedly. "But you'll get over that when you've been out in the world a little while. I suppose I'll just have to wait. Mamma said you'd have ideas of your own, but you're nice anyhow. Come on, let's have a smoke! I'm almost ready to pass away. I haven't smoked all the morning because Mamma kept sticking around and she makes such a fuss!"

Lynette faced about aghast. Her cousin!

"But Dorothy! You *don't smoke!*"

"Sure I do! Been smoking ever since I went to boarding school. Wouldn't be in it if I didn't. All the girls smoke. Where've you been that you didn't know that?"

"I've been in a place where no one does," said Lynette with a wistful look in her eyes, and a sudden yearning for the safe sane halls of her alma mater. "But Dorothy, we might as well talk it out now as ever, and then if you don't want to go around with me why that's up to you. I don't smoke, and I don't believe in it! In fact I hate it! But that's neither here nor there. If I *didn't* hate it I wouldn't do it because of what my mother and my dear little grandmother would think of me. I can't see how you can go against your mother's wish even if you haven't any ideas of your own against it."

"Oh, bologny!" said Dorothy casting herself down upon the pillows and kicking a hat box off the foot of the berth. "You don't *have* to mind your mother! That's an antiquated theory. It's all been shown up! Haven't you ever found that out? Why your father and your mother aren't really any better than you are! They haven't any right to say what you will do or what you won't do just because they've been here longer than you have! Everybody is born free and equal, and everybody has a right to order his own life as he pleases! I please to smoke. Why should my mother interfere, merely because she's my mother? She loves me because she is in the habit of having me around of course, and I'm fond of her, but I'm not going to be hampered and hindered by her. She has no right whatever to order me round."

"Dorothy!" said Lynette standing up and facing her cousin, "I can't listen to such terrible talk any longer. I'll go out in the cabin there and sit in a chair all night, but I won't stay here and listen to you dishonor your father and mother! Do you know what the Bible says about honoring your father and mother? Don't you know it is one of God's commands?"

"Poppycock! More bologny! People don't believe in

a God any more, and the Bible is an antiquated book! Why should I try to obey some stuffy old commands?"

"The fool hath said in his heart there is no God!"

Lynette quoted it quietly, almost without knowing she was speaking aloud but Dorothy caught up the words:

"Oh, yes, I'm a little fool, I suppose, but don't preach at me for pity's sake. I'm dying for a smoke, that's all. I'll be all right when I have it, and I'm going to take it! If you don't like it you can go outside," and she sprang up and took out her cigarette case.

Lynette quietly opened the door and went out. She felt suddenly alone and old, and wondered again why she had ever thought she could come? It wasn't a place for her. And here she was in a discussion with her cousin right off at the start! How was life going to be possible together if that was the state of the case? Had she done wrong? Should she have avoided the issue? Such had not been her training, but would that have been being wise as a serpent and harmless as a dove?

No, she couldn't listen to Dorothy calling her mother and her Bible and her God in question! Aunt Hilda had wanted her to be an influence for good in Dorothy's life, and surely she shouldn't pass such things over lightly. Yet was there anything else she could have done or said? Had she been wrong in being so outspoken?

She wandered off to a far corner of the deck where few people were about and where she could stand by the railing and look off at the wide glittering sea upon which they were gliding along so smoothly it seemed as if they were on wheels.

Problems, problems, on land or sea! Was the fault her own? Had she grown narrow? Had she grown sharp and argumentative? Perhaps Dana had seen that in her too. Perhaps he had had reason to feel she was as much changed as she felt him to be. She must pray for sweetness and strength. She must keep quiet and let the Lord lead her. She must not grow narrow or critical or hard. She must not try to impose her own beliefs on others and make herself disagreeable of course. But she *must*

not yield an iota of what she believed to be right, nor
lower her own standard in any degree! That was settled! For the rest she was here, and must stay for a
time at least, and her business was to witness. That was
all, just witness, witness for the right, not preach. Let
everybody see what Christ could do with a surrendered
soul. She could leave the rest with God. She need not
worry whether she was accomplishing anything or not.
She did not have to accomplish. That was God's part.
She was just a witness!

She did not know what a pleasant picture she made
as she stood with her hand on the rail, her soft hair
blown a little about her face, her simple dark blue tailored
dress that was neither too short nor too tight and
yet was lovely in its outline, her slim silken ankles
braced against the breeze. Yet off across a pile of
steamer chairs a young man who had seen her when
they first came on board was watching her, and was
hoping he might meet her. She looked like a girl who
would be worth meeting. There were not many like that
in the world any more. He doubted if this one would be
what she seemed if he knew her better. Perhaps it
would be better not to know, just watch her from afar
and have the pleasure of thinking she was as lovely in
her character as in her face. Very likely she was like all
the rest, though, for there came that other girl again,
the tall one with the boyish hair and form, and the
pouting discontented lips that were too hideously red
—the girl that took her away before. She was putting
her arm around her now, and drawing her away with
her again. It was just as well! They were probably all
alike. Some hours ago when they first came on board
he had seen the tall one out behind a pile of life pre-
servers puffing away at a cigarette with frantic earnestness as if she were in a hurry and trying to hide. Likely
they were friends or sisters, and what one did so did the
other. What a pity the girls were all going that way. No
sacred womanhood any more. He turned away and
paced the deck and tried to think of other things.

"Come, Lynnie," Dorothy was saying, "I was cross I

know. I was a fool. Forgive me. I didn't quite mean all that bunk I handed you. I just wanted to try you out I guess. Come on back and let's make up. You needn't dance, you needn't smoke, and you may preach at me if you like, but let's get out the trunk and try on the dresses. I'm bored stiff, and it isn't time to dress for dinner yet. Come on back."

Lynette went back and plunged into the beauties of Cousin Marta's wardrobe.

It was a gorgeous array as Dorothy had said. There were satins and silks of every hue in the rainbow, and cut in the most fantastic styles. There were sports clothes galore, with loud dashes of color in curious combination. There was a silver cloth as soft as a kitten's ear and a golden gauze that looked like spun sunshine. But there was nothing there save a smart little black dinner frock, and a white wool jersey that Lynette really fancied for herself, and in the end after she had admired to Dorothy's full satisfaction she folded them all carefully again and locked them away in the steamer trunk. Then she put on her own little blue crêpe frock that she had made herself and worn at home that last evening in the sunset, when Dana had walked away with another girl and left her life blank. The memory of it almost spoiled her evening, but she put it on bravely and went down to dinner.

"You're queer!" said Dorothy. "You might have had all those gorgeous things, and you don't want them. But you do look better in your own. You look sort of different—and more—well—like yourself. I guess there's something I don't understand. I wish I did. You're lovely anyway, and I'm glad you are you."

Lynette smiled wistfully and wound her arm about the slim waist of her cousin's attractive but brief little dance frock of rose color, and went into the dining-room. She wondered if perhaps life wasn't going to be even more complicated here than if she had stayed at home and worked out her problem with Dana and the little flapper girl.

Oh, how was she going to stand it alone? How know which way to turn in all the maze of paths?

"I will never leave thee nor forsake thee," rang a verse in her memory. She was not alone! It was all right. On water or on land! She would just trust!

XVIII

THE stranger was at a table not far from where the Reamers sat. He was so placed that he could watch Lynette's profile, but Dorothy was sitting so that she was straight across from him, and their lifted eyes frequently met.

"There's a perfectly stunning man over at the second table, Dad," said Dorothy. "He has blue plush eyes and a nice smile."

"Don't tell me he's smiled at you already, Kitten. I'll have to put him overboard if he has!" declared her father smiling at her indulgently.

"Oh, no, nothing like that yet," declared the wild child. "I only saw him smile at the man he is talking to at the table. But I'm dying to dance with him. I just know he dances like a breeze. You've got to chase him down and introduce him to me, Dad. I simply can't wait to meet him!"

"What if I don't like him, Dottie?"

"That's nothing in my young life!" chanted the spoiled infant. "You'll have to bring him or I'll get him myself you know."

"And what am I to do, Baby? Go trotting around the deck asking for a man with blue plush eyes and an enchanting smile? There might be more than one applicant for the position you know. Especially if I told him I had more than one beautiful daughter," and he cast a loving glance toward Lynette. "How do you know, now, but Lynette will cut you out, Dot? What will you do then? You've never had to compete with so beautiful a rival before."

"Oh, that's all right! Lynn doesn't dance. She's going to be stuffy just as Mamma said she would be. Oh, you needn't look that way, we've had it all out and shaken hands over it, haven't we, Lynn? We've agreed to be friends and each go our different ways, but it's going to be awfully dull not having Lynn to go to dances, and I've simply got to be amused or I'll be horrid. So it's up to you Dad! Go to it. You can get the names of the men at that table. You won't have any trouble. The others are only ordinary. One is old with white hair, and one is red and fat, and one needs a haircut. My man has blue plush eyes and faces this way, yes, the tall one, you can't mistake him."

"All right, Kitten, I'll do my best," said Uncle Reamer. "But what are we going to do to make Lynette have a good time? If she doesn't like the dancing we must get some nice young folks to walk the deck with her."

"Oh, Uncle Roth, I'd much rather walk with you!" protested Lynette in distress. "I don't really like to meet strangers, and I came on the trip to be with you. Don't you want to take a walk with me, you and Aunt Hilda?"

Aunt Hilda smiled comfortably.

"I think I'll just stay inside tonight dear. I really ought to keep Dorothy in sight, at least, you know. You and your uncle take your walk. I'm just too tired to move."

"Oh, stuffy again!" complained Dorothy. "You don't have to tag me around as if I were a Victorian maiden. That's old stuff, and I won't stand for it!"

"Well, I like to watch you dance, dear," said her mother gently. "I won't be in your way."

"It's rotten!" said Dorothy unfilially. "If I'm going to be continually shadowed on this trip I'll take the next boat back and do as I please!"

"There, there, Kitten!" pacified her father. "Just ease down on Mamma. She's tired you know, and she likes to think that you are her little girl yet."

"Well, I'm not!" pouted the rebel, "and I'll do something outrageous if you don't let up on this chaperoning business. Nobody else has to stand it and I won't!"

"Look here, young woman," said her father, a more determined yet still indulgent note in his voice, "if you keep on that strain I won't go hunt your plush man for you."

"Oh, yes, Dad, you're just kidding me along now. But I mean it. I'm grown up and it's time you knew it."

They hushed her up playfully, and turned the talk in another strain, but Lynette was left with the impression of unrest that brooded in the hearts of her aunt and uncle about their pretty wayward daughter. It perhaps was not going to be so pleasant in their company as she had anticipated. Was there always a trouble in every family, always a fly in every ointment?

She glanced at the two boys farther down the table, sturdy school boys, interested in their own affairs, discoursing about engines and propellers and powers and knots and various other matters of the sea. They had not yet reached the stage of rebellion where their sister had arrived, but they seemed as much aloof as if they belonged to strangers. They were a couple of wild young arabs who were engaged in getting as much out of their parents as they could comfortably extract. Of course they were nice and pleasant and funny about it, but they showed already that their interests were their own, and they felt no loyalty toward their family. Lynette wondered if here were a place where she might work? Could she win the boys and make them her companions? They seemed so much like Elim in some ways, and it would be less lonely if she had some one to depend upon. It was plain that Dorothy was a bird of passage and contact with her could only be established at intervals when she had nothing else to do. A great loneliness swept over her in the midst of the gay room full of people. She wished again that she had not come, and felt that she had been wrong to run away in a pet just because she was disappointed in Dana. There were other things in her home besides Dana, other interests in life even if Dana failed her altogether.

But there was little time for such thoughts.

People began to drift over to their table and stop to talk. New York friends of the family, and they all went on deck.

Uncle Roth went off in search of his man, but came back unsuccessful.

"His name is Alexander Douglas. That's all I could find out," he said sitting down between his wife and daughter, and giving them a smile that included Lynette and made her feel less homesick.

"I don't know whether he is Alexander the coopersmith or Alexander the Great, but anyhow he's Alexander Douglas, though nobody seemed to describe his eyes like that. But they said he was tall, very tall. He wasn't in the cabins and he wasn't playing cards, nor in the smoking room, and I walked the decks over pretty well and couldn't see anything-like him anywhere, so I guess you'll have to cut him out, Kitten."

"Cut him out, nothing!" pouted the child. "You keep your eyes open and bring him to me as soon as you find him. I'm just crazy about him. Is he married? Because I can't help it if he is. I'm simply dead in love with him!"

"Dorothy!" said Aunt Hilda in a shocked voice.

"Oh, Mamma, now don't be stuffy! That doesn't mean a thing in these days! Don't forget, Daddy, you've promised. Bye-bye Lynn! Too bad you won't come. I'd let you dance with him, just once, if you would. Oh, those dear plush eyes!"

Dorothy tripped away blowing a butterfly kiss as she poised in the doorway.

Lynette went to get a wrap and she and her uncle took a promenade around the decks, talking of many pleasant things. Of her college life, of home and mother, and what she intended to do next. She was shy about that, however. Her expectations had been so turned upside down in the last two days. She said not a word about Dana till her uncle asked:

"And what's become of that nice boy neighbor? Wasn't he studying to be a lawyer or something? Anything serious between you yet? I think your mother spoke of him once. His father used to be something."

Lynette summoned a laugh:

"You mean Dana Whipple I guess. We've always been good comrades," she said evasively. "Dana was studying for the ministry. He's through now, and I believe has a very good prospect for the future. He has a brilliant mind and seems to be in line for a city church. That will please his mother and grandmother who have great ambitions for him."

Uncle Rothwell eyed her keenly as they passed in the brighter light of the open doorway. Was there something hidden here? Some hurt? Was her voice just the least bit formal in talking so freely about this lifelong comrade? Uncle Rothwell was a keen man, and gifted with an insight into character.

"I was afraid he might get in the way of our plans," he said watching her. "Your Aunt Hilda seemed to think he would."

"Oh, no!" said Lynette trying to speak naturally but aware of the heightened color in her cheeks, thankful that color did not show by moonlight.

"Look!" she said eagerly, "the moon is coming up! Oh, isn't that the most wonderful sight!" And her eagerness turned her uncle's attention away from herself and Dana Whipple. Yet the brief passage had left its sting, and after they had walked a little longer her uncle left her at her own request to watch the moonlight on the water while he went back to see if her aunt would not like to come out and sit with her awhile in that sheltered end of the boat, which seemed to be deserted for the time being.

She stood still by the rail looking up into the face of the full moon, ignoring the chair her uncle had placed for her, lost in a profound wonder at the sight spread before her. The majesty of that brightness seemed to envelop and thrill her, and lift her out of the gloom of life. What did other things matter, when there was light like this in the world? She longed to drink it in and fill her soul with this illumination. She almost felt as if she had wings and could spread them and fly when she looked across the twinkling water and saw that radiance. It was as if the light were tangible, and if she were only near enough she could reach out and touch it.

So absorbed was she in her own thoughts that she did not see someone approaching nor realize that anyone was standing near her, until a voice, quite close at hand spoke:

"Clothed in light!" he said, and his voice was tinged with a strangely fascinating burr.

"What did you say?"

She spoke the words before she realized that this was a stranger who had spoken to her in the tone of a familiar friend. She felt like Alice in Wonderland.

The voice with the burr repeated the phrase:

"Clothed in light! I was thinking aloud. I was wondering if it will be anything like that!"

"Oh!" breathed Lynette with awe, turning her eyes from the tall stranger to look again at the glorious panoply spread upon the water.

"His raiment was white like the light," quoted the voice reverently.

"Oh, do you think it was like that?" breathed Lynette eagerly. She had no sense that she was conversing with a strange man to whom she had not been introduced. It was all most natural. Two mortals in the presence of God.

"It may be. Perhaps this is veiled somewhat for our weak vision that could not stand the full glory. But it seems as if He must be here. Listen! 'It is He that sitteth upon the circle of the earth. O Lord my God, Thou art very great; Thou art clothed with honor and majesty. Who coverest thyself with light as with a garment: who stretchest out the heavens like a curtain: Who layeth the beams of his chambers in the waters: Who maketh the clouds His chariot: Who walketh upon the wings of the wind.' It seems as though He must be here!"

"It does!" breathed Lynette filled with the wonder

of it, forgetting utterly that her companion was a stranger.

"The heavens declare the glory of God; and the firmament showeth His handiwork. Day unto day uttereth speech, and night unto night showeth knowledge. There is no speech nor language where their voice is not heard." The stranger's voice was low and clear, and the sacred words took on new meaning as he repeated them in this presence.

"Did you know," he went on with the voice of an old comrade, "that the story of the gospels is all written in the names of the stars, all about the serpent and the cross?"

"No," said Lynette, "how could it be?"

"Away back in the earliest ages of history the stars were named and arranged in certain figures, symbolic and significant. You remember they were to be for signs and for seasons. It's a strange thing, that all through the ages, though there has been many an attempt to change those signs and figures, they have been perpetuated in all the astronomic records of all the ages and nations since. And each one of those names and figures has a meaning which when translated gives a link in the story of salvation. Even the cross is there, the Southern Cross. Now if we start as the ancients did with the constellation called Virgo, which means Virgin and suggests the 'seed of the woman,' we circle the heavens and end with Leo. Do you remember how Jesus Christ is called in the Bible 'the Lion of the tribe of Judah?' Salvation is through Jesus Christ, born of a virgin, and coming again in the strength and kingly majesty of the lion to subdue all things unto Himself. Other signs of the Zodiac describe the Scorpion, forever striking to kill, and the Serpent, which also is typical of Satan, forever fleeing from the Lion. The rest go on in order until the whole story of the Cross is complete. Oh, it is a wonderful study! There is even a significance in the time at which certain stars have appeared and are due to appear again. All the history of the world is written there in bright language if man would only take the trouble to read it. How much do those in there know of it?" He moved his hand to indicate the lighted cabin with the moving forms, and the gay strains of music from the orchestra.

"I never heard of this before," said Lynette wonderingly. "I would like to know more about it. Is there a book that one could read? I mean just an ordinary person who is not a great scholar nor an astronomer?"

"Oh yes," said the man taking out a notebook and pencil, "I'll write it down for you. You can get it in London I'm sure."

He tore the leaf from his notebook and handed it to her, and then turned back to the sky:

"You see that bright star up there? No, over to your right more. Now that star is——"

And then they became aware of Mr. and Mrs. Reamer standing by their side, surveying the stranger coldly, questioningly, and Lynette came to herself and remembered the conventions with a gasp.

"Oh, Aunt Hilda," she said eagerly, and then stopped, not knowing quite how to proceed with her explanation.

"Who's your friend, Lynette?" asked her uncle. His voice was more cordial than her aunt's glance had seemed. "Won't you introduce us?"

The stranger turned and took the situation into his own hands:

"My name's Douglas, sirrr!" and there was a pleasant burr on his speech, "and we just got to talking about the stars." Lynette noticed that he said "aboot" and liked it. Grandmother Rutherford came of Scotch people.

Uncle Reamer perceived that he had found his man and that he was also a man of parts, and waived the conventions:

"My name's Reamer!" he said. "Rothwell Reamer. Wall Street. This is Mrs. Reamer, and this is my niece Miss Brooke. We oughtn't to stand on ceremony I suppose, all on a boat together. And I've got three more children, a girl dancing in there, and two boys, kids, racketing round somewhere. Shan't we sit down? There seem to be plenty of chairs."

"Oh, certainly," said the stranger courteously presenting a chair to Mrs. Reamer before her husband could make a move. But after all the chairs were brought Douglas began just where he had left off by pointing to the star about which he and Lynette had been talking when they were interrupted.

"You see that bright star up there? No, that blue one to the right——" And then they were off.

They sat there for an hour and a half, fascinated, while Douglas unfolded to them the wonders of the heavens, and even Aunt Hilda drew her wraps about her and stayed to the end. Uncle Reamer forgot entirely that he had promised to bring this tall stranger to dance with his daughter, and Aunt Hilda forgot that she was a chaperone. It had been like the unfolding of a romance, and held them all to the last word.

Then suddenly the speaker stopped, looked at his wrist watch:

"But I am keeping you all a long time listening to my hobby. I must bid you good-night now. It's been very pleasant to meet you," and was gone!

"He was really very interesting," said Aunt Hilda, drawing her wraps about her and preparing to go back to the dancing, as easily adjusting herself to the thought of it as if she had not just been fairly hearing the heavens declare the glory of God.

"It was all just an interesting evening's entertainment to her," thought Lynette, as she slipped away, pleading weariness. "But oh, I wish that Dana could have heard it! I must tell him!"

And then she remembered that for the present she could tell him nothing. And perhaps—well perhaps Dana would have sneered at some of the wonderful facts that man had told and called them fanciful. She could almost hear him doing it, with that new tone of superiority he had adopted, and somehow he paled before the great words to which she had been listening to-night. Oh, Dana, Dana! Must he fail of the highest and the best because he thought he knew it all? Wasn't there some way to make him see? If only he could have heard! But, would he have sneered?

A long time afterward, when Dorothy had crept into

her berth below, tiptoeing about because she thought her cousin was asleep, Lynette realized that for the space of the whole evening she had not but once thought of Dana and her troubles. The spell of the voyage was upon her. Perhaps she was going to be able to endure the long months of separation without such constant agony as it had looked at first. And then she opened her eyes and caught a last glimpse out the little round port hole of the moonlit sea, and was thrilled again at the wonder of God.

They talked it all over the next morning at breakfast, Dorothy eating grapefruit joyously and telling what a glorious time she had had last night.

"Yes, but do you know how your cousin cut you out? teased her father. "Here I had hunted the ship over to find your latest craze for you, and then I left Lynnie by herself just a minute to get your mother to see the moonlight on the water, and didn't I come back and find that sly miss had picked him up and had him on a line as nice as you please!"

"Daddy! Quit your kidding and explain yourself. Did you really find the man with the blue plush eyes?"

"No, I didn't find him, Dottie, your cousin did. I don't know where she picked him up. Ask her. But she had him all right. He was teaching her astronomy!"

"Oh brother!" said Dorothy frowning prettily. "Is he that kind! Isn't that horrid? There are enough stuffy people now. Well, but Daddy, if you found him why didn't you bring him to dance. You promised you would."

"Well, Kitten, I really forgot. It's the truth. He was so interesting I just forgot to speak. I kept thinking there would be a pause and after a while I'd get him. And then suddenly he stopped and bolted off somewhere, and I couldn't find him again."

"Well, I think you're mean you didn't come and find me then if you couldn't bring him to me. I could have listened a little while and then I'd have carried him off to dance. I never have any trouble with 'em!" And she tossed her pretty head and took another spoonful of grapefruit.

"I'll bet you don't, Baby. You fetch them every time. But there are several days remaining, and meantime we've paved the way. Try your hand at him yourself. I'll introduce you on the first opportunity, but don't forget your cousin had first inning."

They all laughed about him, and presently he entered the dining-room, and bowed pleasantly to them across the tables, but he did not come over and speak to them, and he left before they were through, for Dorothy purposely had lingered with her food hoping he would come.

Dorothy was playing cards all the morning with some young folks in the cabin, and Alec Douglas did not appear within her vision. Only once was he seen to come out of his mysterious retirement, and that to bring a book to Lynette who was sitting on deck beside her aunt reading.

It was a book he had told her about last night, and he lingered a moment to tell her more about its author, then vanished again as mysteriously as he had come. Lynette put down her magazine and began to read the book he had brought. It was about the pyramids, and held her from the first word. It appeared that the great pyramid had something to do with the Bible. That the gospel was written upon its walls in strange ways and devices. Why had she never heard of these things before? Did Dana know them? Who was this wonderful scholar who knew all these things and talked of them as freely as if they were wild flowers or beetles?

But Lynette was not allowed to read long. Aunt Hilda wanted to talk:

"He really is awfully good looking, isn't he? Scotch, your uncle thinks. I wonder who he is. I told your uncle to go look him up and see if he isn't something unusual. He has a manner like a nobleman. Those people of royalty do have such lovely manners. I suppose it comes of being at court so often. They really grow into fine manners. Manners are so important in life, don't you think, dear? You have lovely ones yourself Lynette. Your mother is a lady! And so is your grandmother. After all there's nothing like heredity and breeding! I do wish Dorothy would take on a little polish. I'm hoping she'll get over some of her hoydenish ways when she really settles down, but she is so mortifying sometimes. Why, the other day a friend of mine came to call who writes the most lovely essays on Happiness, and Concentration and things like that—I haven't seen her for twenty years, not since we were girls together in School—and Dorothy came in to be introduced and what did she do but stand back and bow and say in the most impertinent tone:

" 'Mrs. Dabney, I've heard a lot about you for years of course. You've written a lot of things haven't you? Of course I don't care for them myself, they're too stuffy for me, but Mamma just adores them!' My dear, I was mortified to death! And Lynnie dear, has she told you she smokes? It really keeps me awake nights, the things that child does. Of course I know everybody is doing it, but it's so against all the traditions of our family, and it doesn't seem respectable. Why, your uncle would kill me almost for not stopping it, if he ever found it out."

"I should think you would tell him, Aunt Hilda," said Lynette coolly. "He has a great deal of influence over her. Perhaps he could do something."

"Oh, my dear, I wouldn't dare!" said the poor woman, putting her handkerchief to her eyes. "You don't know your uncle. He can be almost severe with Dorothy sometimes, and Dorothy is so sensitive. Poor child, I do hope she won't have to bear the consequences of her own wilfulness."

There was a whole morning of that for Lynette, and the book with her finger in the page, had to be laid down at last, while Aunt Hilda poured out her troubles and laid them in order before her niece.

When she went down to lunch she felt as if another heavy burden had been laid upon her shoulders. She glanced over to the second table on the left, but Alec Douglas was not there. She wondered what he was doing with his time. Aunt Hilda voiced the curiosity of the family by saying:

"I believe that man is employed on board somehow, a clerical position or something. Rothwell, you better find out just what he is. I can't have the girl's going around with everybody, and it's very funny the way he appears at odd times and then disappears. He must be earning his way across! Dorothy, don't you go to dancing with him till we find out just who he is! Great mistakes are sometimes made by things like that!"

"He might be ill you know," suggested Dorothy.

"Hilda, we've not made any mistakes about that young man," put in the head of the house. "He's all right! I can tell that from his looks. And he's not employed on board in any capacity, I'm sure of that! Neither is he ill. He isn't a weakling. He's got bigger fish to fry than trotting around dancing with girls. You mark my words!"

XIX

Sunday morning after breakfast Lynette took refuge in her stateroom and sat down by the little round window to read her Bible. She felt reasonably sure of being alone for Dorothy was up on deck taking a constitutional, and Aunt Hilda was nursing a sick headache.

The sea had been smooth and the weather perfect. Scarely anybody on board had been seasick. It seemed an ideal day for Sunday, at least down here alone with her Bible and the sea breeze blowing her hair from her forehead gently. Somehow she was more reconciled to what she was doing this morning. She did not feel so keenly the wrench of parting, nor dread so much the prospect of a long time away, perhaps without any definite word from Dana. A kind of peace was in her soul after the anxiety of the past few days. Perhaps it was because of the great thoughts which she had been reading in the book the stranger loaned her. She was reading it avidly, and was growing more and more interested in that "miracle in stone," the pyramid, and filled with the wonder of the God who had planned the universe, and seemed to have written His plans in the secret places of this phenomenal building.

Suddenly Dorothy burst into the room in great excitment:

"Lynette! Who, *who* do you think is going to conduct religious service this morning? Guess! You never can in all the world."

Lynette smiled.

"How could I, Dorrie? I know hardly a soul on board. There might be the greatest preacher in the world on board and I not know him. Who is it? Some great bishop?"

"I don't know how great he is, nor what name they call him, but I know I'm simply crazy about him. Lynn, it's Plush Eyes, my beautiful Plush Eyes! Isn't that wonderful? My! I shall die of excitement. Which dress would you wear, my red sport frock or the black satin? I want to look my very sweetest."

"Oh, not your sports dress on Sunday, Dorrie!" protested Lynette smiling. "Wear the black. It's less conspicuous."

"But I want to be conspicuous! I want him to see me from the minute he steps into the room. I've set my heart on captivating him and I'm taking no chances. Don't you simply adore his eyes, Lynnie? They go straight to my heart. Oh, I've always been sure I'd meet a man like that some day, and now he's here!"

"But Dorothy! You oughtn't to talk like that even in fun! Suppose he should hear of it? Suppose he should be married?"

"Then I'll have him get a divorce!" said Dorothy tragically. "I shall give him up to nobody! Hurry, Lynnie, and get ready. I want to get a front seat. I wonder where my prayer book is. I'm sure Mamma stuck it in. She always does, and now the first time I've ever wanted it it's just my luck not to find it."

"Oh, Dorothy!" sighed her cousin. "I *wish* you wouldn't talk so crazily. It doesn't sound like you. You *try* to make yourself seem horrid, and you aren't really!"

"But that's the thing to do, darling! Everybody's doing it. Come, aren't you going to doll up any? Of course I know you don't need to powder your nose because you have such a perfectly stunning complexion, but don't you want to borrow one of my vanity cases just to have something to do between the hymns?"

"Dorothy!"

"Well, what's the harm? I always do at the symphony concerts. I think it's such a graceful little act; just get out your mirror and dab away at your face to see that it is all neat and nice. It shows you are well groomed and never let down on your job. I think it's attractive myself!"

"I don't think men like it, dear," said Lynette going slowly toward the door. "Come on, I think I hear the bell striking."

"Don't you really?" Dorothy paused as if she were actually considering the question. "Don't you think Plush Eyes would enjoy seeing me powder my nose? Well, then I'll leave my vanity case behind!"

And reluctantly she flung it on the bed and followed Lynette out into the corridor.

Lynette wondered. Who could tell how much earnestness hid beneath the frivolous pose of this sweet young butterfly of the world?

The room was filling up rapidly. Word had gone about that the great Alexander Douglas, the noted London preacher, who was making such a stir in religious circles with his original message was going to preach. Someone had requested that he be asked. The story was that he was traveling quietly, almost incognito, trying to finish a book, and that he had hesitated long before he consented to speak this morning. But the plea had been so urgent that he had finally yielded.

This was being whispered from one to another all about them, and Dorothy grew more and more excited over the idea.

"Well, they can't say I didn't pick a real one," she giggled to Lynette.

But Lynette was busy watching the still figure up behind the desk, as he sat quietly, his head resting on his lifted hand, his eyes closed, as if the moment were a hallowed one, as if the duty he was about to perform was one of deep responsibility. Was this her friend of the moonlight and the stars? She had scarely seen him since then, except the minute or two when he brought her the book.

So he was a great man, a noted preacher! She might have recognized the scholar in those wonderful words that fell from his lips as he taught her about the stars!

And then her heart sprang back to home, and Dana. Perhaps if he was very great Dana would count his word of some weight. Perhaps even Dana would think him great enough to listen to! Oh, if Dana could be here this morning!

Well, but he hadn't preached yet. He might not be so good a preacher as he was a teacher.

Yet when she remembered the reverent voice, the almost hallowed look on his face as he repeated those Bible verses, she knew that he would have a wonderful message. She felt that he was praying now, praying for the words, to speak. The message, then, would be from God. Would all those frivolous, card playing, cigarette smoking, wine drinking people who were crowding the seats and chattering about his greatness be open-hearted enough to take the message? Would they receive it gladly? Would Dorothy? Dear, sweet, naughty Dorothy!

She found herself praying now, for Dana, for Dorothy, for the dear home folks, and for the preacher that he might have a message for her tired perplexed soul.

And then the service opened.

It seemed that even the music was frought with deeper meaning than is usual on shipboard. People were very still during the prayer and more than respectful in the responses. And now the preacher rose to speak, and Dorothy murmured:

"Oh, you darling Plush Eyes!" close to Lynette's ear. How Lynette wished she wouldn't!

Then the reverent voice with the soft burr on the edge of the words began solemnly, and thrilled her anew as it had thrilled her when he stood beside her in the moonlight and said that wonderful sentence "Clothed in Light!" and gave her a vision of glory such as she had never had before.

"Except a corn of wheat fall into the ground and die it abideth by itself alone: but if it die it bringeth forth much fruit."

"Oh, what a horrid text!" whispered Dorothy. "If he's going to talk about dying I'm going out. It always makes me furious to hear about dying!"

The opening sentences of the sermon were lost in trying to get Dorothy to keep still, and when Lynette came in on it again he was saying:

"The greatest truth about Christ is that 'He was dead but *is alive again.*'[1]

"That life through death has controlled the world ever since and has made the world realize that, in spite of most determined efforts to destroy it, here is something which is indestructible. Great world systems, cults, and even empires have exhausted all their resources to blot out the Name and the continued vitality of Christ. But it is they which have perished. He still lives on victoriously."

Dorothy was watching the great preacher eagerly, studying the flash of those eyes that she admired, watching the well chiseled lips as they brought out the clearly enunciated sentences, admiring the sweep of arm, the fine broad shoulders, amused at the Scotch accent. The words he spoke meant little or nothing to her. But Lynette was drinking it all in.

"We never receive the *real* life of Christ until we too have been to the Cross," was the next astonishing statement. Lynette sat up straighter and listened with all her might. Was that a message for her soul?

"The real divine life—the life of Jesus Christ—" went on the steady quiet voice that yet penetrated to every corner of the room, and rang distinct above the beat of waves, and throbbing of the ship, and compelled the breathless attention of even those who were not near to listen. "This life is only known by what it does in men and women, in making them live on a plane which infinitely transcends the human level. 'I have been crucified with Christ, and yet I live, and yet no longer I but Christ liveth in me.' And again, 'For if we have become united with Him in the likeness of His death, we shall be also in the likeness of His resurrection!'

[1] Acknowledgment is made to Rev. T. Austin Sparks, D. D., the noted preacher of London, England, for permission to use the above extracts from his famous sermon on "The Threefold Law of the Cross."

And again: 'Like as Christ was raised from the dead, so also we.'"

"That doesn't mean a thing!" whispered Dorothy. "I like him best when he just smiles."

But the steady voice was going on, and Dorothy was compelled like all the rest to listen.

"If we are going to manifest that life of Christ, and if that vital indestructible something is going to bear its powerful testimony in the world, if that divine life—that very life of God himself—indestructible, victorious, is going to bear its mightly witness and make itself felt in the world in the members of His Body, the Church invisible, it is only through their oneness with Him in death and resurrection. Until we know this oneness our Christian life will count for little. We must take our place in one initial, all-inclusive reckoning with Him in death to the old self, and the old world with all its ambitions, desires, programs, ideas, and standards, and then allow that death to be wrought out in us daily in order that the resurrection life may be increasingly manifest in us. The life of God cannot come into the old creation, it is the *new creation life.*"

"He is looking straight over here," whispered Dorothy. "Do you think he recognizes who we are? He must have seen us together at the table."

"Hush, Dorothy, please!" pleaded Lynette, but she had lost the connection again. Oh, if she could but have come alone to hear this wonderful message. She had never heard anything like it before.

When she was able to give attention he was talking about how this law of life through death affects every relationship in life. How in learning new spiritual truths, even the great oft-heard doctrine of Christ's victory on the cross over sin, we have to get to the point where we give up utterly, in despair of ourselves, before the Holy Spirit can really teach and make a part of us the truth which before we had learned only with our minds. For then, in that hour of death, when we find ourselves at the end of our own power and we throw up our hands and say "Lord I can do nothing," then we find that truth which we thought was learned long ago, is the only thing which can grip us and bring us out into victory.

He spoke of service, how it, too, comes under this law of life through death. How we must die even to our service for Christ sometimes before it can be effectually used by Him. How there comes a time in our service when from sheer force of circumstances, adversity, and fruitlessness we feel that we are at an end. That is our testing time. When that time comes no self life is left, but only Himself in us, free now to work. Then is the time when we discover just how much of our work was a matter of popularity. Whether we were out to make a name for ourselves; whether it mattered to us when people said nice things about our work, or when they said mean things and criticized.

"From all this self life we have to be emancipated before God can use us," went on the preacher earnestly. "We have to get to the place where it does not matter in the least what people say or do, so long as God is satisfied and we are in the way of His will. This is the way of peace and the way of victory. But we have to go down to the realm of death, the 'I' has to be slain. It is just in the measure in which the 'I' has been crucified that Christ in the power of His resurrection can be revealed."

Dorothy was yawning prettily now, and one arm was slung across the back of Lynette's chair. Softly her hand stole up and captured a loose lock of Lynette's hair that hung in a little curl, escaped from the pins, and turning its ends in her fingers, began using it like a tiny paint brush, tickling Lynette's ear, her nose, her cheek, even her eyes were playfully attacked. It was most annoying and she did so want to hear this. It was something that Dana ought to know. Sometime she would have to tell him. She was convinced of that. And she must gather every word and remember it. Afterward she would write it out to fix it in her mind. Dared she write it to Dana now? Oh, if Dana were only here now listening, beside her! Her heart went up in a hungry cry: "Lord, save Dana from himself!"

"Please don't!" she whispered to Dorothy. "I want

to hear the sermon!" and at last Dorothy let her alone and turned her attention to another part of the room.

The preacher was talking now about the liberty that is ours through surrender.

"When the Cross has done its work," he said, "there is liberation from all human limitations, and Christ breaks forth from the grave in a way that gives Him mastery of the whole situation. Those who have been identified with Him in His death are raised by Him to a life on a super-natural level, and through them He achieves such things as were before utterly impossible."

"At this point Dorothy whispered again:

"I'm going out, Lynn. I'm dying for a smoke! I can't stand it another minute! Let me get by you!" and Dorothy arose in her slim black satin, with a smile, and made her pretty way out of the audience, causing not a little stir, and breaking through that silence that had come with the climax of the preacher's words.

When Lynette recovered from her vexation at Dorothy's thoughtlessness and got back to the sermon once more the preacher had reached his last point: Enlargement through Loss. He referred to the fifty-third chapter of Isaiah. "Here," he said earnestly, "we see the redeeming servant of God going into desolation. The whole picture is one of desolation. He is alone, despised, rejected,—terrible aloneness—His cross has cost Him everything. His own brethren do not believe in Him, His nearest disciples do not understand Him, and yet, how did that wonderful chapter close? 'He shall see of the travail of His soul and shall be *satisfied.*' From that point of the Cross and its promise of 'seed' we move on to the ultimate vindication: 'Behold a Lamb as it had been slain, in the midst of the Throne' and around Him 'great multitudes which no man could number out of every nation, and tribes and peoples and tongues.' There is the gain! The countless multitude, the result of His travail."

There was a breathless moment when the audience seemed to see the multitude around the great white throne, and to suddenly realize that the words they had often heard read from the Bible meant something tangible. It was almost as if an audible expression of this thought went through the room.

Lynette's heart almost stood still. Was this God's message especially for her? It was in some ways just what her mother had said, and yet—it went further. It was one thing to have something wrenched from you and to bow to God's will; it was a step farther to hand that precious thing over and let Him do His will. Was she ready to do that with Dana? Just give him up to the Lord? Maybe he would find the way to God and know all this deeper message some day, but was she willing that, in order to work this for him, and perhaps for herself too, she should hand over the thing she prized most in life?

The preacher's voice broke in upon her agonized thoughts, quiet, searching, as if he bore the message from the Understanding God and had a right to search their hearts.

"Very often it does seem as if God requires a lot of us: that this Cross makes tremendous inroads, tremendous demands, and sometimes forces the demand to the point of pain when we have to hand over to Him something very dear. We seem all the time to be giving, giving. It seems that the law of sacrifice is tremendously at work. But this is the road and the law by which, and by which alone, the infinite and transcendent gain can come.

"Are you prepared to let go in order to obtain? Let go the temporal for the eternal, the transient for the abiding, the earthly for the heavenly, the present glamour for the ultimate glory? This is the way to possess all things. Christ now has received of His Father's hands, eternal fulness, and by our union with Him through the Cross even these lives may become transcendently rich and unspeakably full. Some of us have proved that the things that we were most loth to let go—but which at length we gladly yielded up—have come back to us with a greater fulness or have been the way of enrichment transcending anything we knew before. The compensation is over-whelming as at the cross we lay our treasure in the dust. 'the gold of Ophir for the stones of the brook,' that the Almighty should be our treasure.

"Let us pray." The prayer that followed seemed to bring them before the very throne, and lay bare their lives to the eyes of God, and many eyes were bright with tears as the little congregation rose for the closing hymn. For the service was not following the regular order of the ship. The London preacher was bending it to suit his will, and more than one heart was deeply touched, as in silence they went out to the deck, and strove to assume an ordinary manner, glad that the sun was shining and the salt air tasting natural again, and they were back to the things that did not condemn. For there in that room where all was usually gaiety, and where there would soon move a free and easy group of worldly people intent on pleasure pure and simple, they had been made to think of eternal things, and it almost seemed as if God had come and stood just behind their chairs, waiting, waiting for something. What was it? Surrender. That was what the preacher said. Oh, not surrender! Not now, anyway! By and by perhaps when life was gone and hope was low—but now—Oh, No! On with the dance!

They spoke in lower tones at first as if they were not quite sure the Presence was gone out and past them into the infinite again. But then they grew more cheerful, and laughter began to creep refreshingly in, and women adjusted their beads, smoothed their Paris frocks, and life went on again in happy waves.

The preacher walked silently away, his head down, as if in prayer. Few ventured to speak to him till he came out into the sunshine of the deck on his way to quietness. Then one young matron bolder than the rest advanced.

"Oh, Mr. Douglas, I think your sermon was perfectly lovely! What a privilege this has been!" And then the mob let loose and lionized him.

Lynette could see he did not like it. He only smiled a sad wistful smile at them; as if to say: "Is that all that I have accomplished by my message?" and slipped away.

In the dining-room they hummed about his brilliancy, his talents, his eloquence, his gifts, but not a word did Lynette hear about his Lord nor the way of the Cross. Did nobody get it at all, or was the message meant just for her?

The preacher did not come to the table. Perhaps he did not want to hear their chatter. It seemed a desecration to Lynette to whom the message had meant so much.

Dorothy came late and had a queer look about her eyes as if she had been crying. Afterward she told her cousin:

"He made me weep. Wasn't that the limit? I had to get out or I'd have bawled right then and there like a baby. It stirred me all up inside and I felt horrid, and I just had to have a smoke or I'd have passed out. But isn't he precious? Darling old Plush Eyes!"

Had scatter-brained Dorothy really been touched by the sermon, or was this only a pose too? Lynette could not tell.

That night she stood alone for a few moments on deck looking out into the darkness. The moon was gone behind a cloud, and the sea looked very wide and black. She was thinking that it was perhaps like the place she was about to enter in her life, wide and black and alone, no stars even, save in memory, to guide the way. Then all at once he was beside her again.

"You helped me a great deal this morning," he said, just as if he had known her always.

Lynette looked up with surprise.

"Oh, but I was just wishing I might tell you how you have helped me," she said eagerly. "I needed it. I think God sent you just for me, to help me in the way I have to go."

"I somehow knew there was perplexity in your eyes," he said, "and perhaps pain. I thank God if you have found the way. I've been praying about you. Do you mind?"

"Oh, I am glad!" she said earnestly. "I have needed it so!"

And then, before he could answer, they were surrounded. The Reamers guided by the indefatigable Dorothy who had rounded them up even down to her two brothers, surrounded them.

"Oh, Mr. Douglas," gushed Dorothy, "your sermon was perfectly dear! I've been just crazy to hear you ever since I knew about you. Won't you take me for a little walk, just so I can say I walked with you, the great Mr. Douglas? I'd be so flattered. I want to tell the girls at home about it."

Dorothy lifted her vivid little impudent face wreathed in smiles, eyes full of pleading, and Alec Douglas laughed.

"With pleasure," he said, and turning to Lynette, "will you go with us?"

Together the three walked down the deck and around, Dorothy doing the talking, the preacher saying now and then, "Yes, quite so, quite so!" and "Fancy! I hadn't heard of it!" But when they came back to the door of the main cabin Douglas left them with goodnight, and just a lingering pressure of Lynette's hand as he took it before he left. She knew that he meant that he would remember her before the throne, and their eyes met with understanding, and then he was gone.

The next morning the boat docked at Liverpool and they saw no more of Alec Douglas. He had hurried away at once to meet an appointment.

XX

DANA had no intention of deliberately filling in the time of Lynette's absence with Jessie Belle. In fact it was several days before he would admit to himself that Lynette had really gone without further word to him. He had convinced himself so thoroughly that she was merely hanging around in New York, waiting for him to come down or write or telegraph, or do something, that he would not believe it was true. Of course he did not know the time when her relatives were sailing, and his pride was so great that he would not go to Mrs. Brooke and ask. So he blundered on, holding his head high, and trying to pretend to his family that he knew all about it.

And it was perfectly astonishing how many questions that family could find to ask him, right in public as it were. Even Grandma wanted to know if Lynette was going to Wales. She would have liked to ask her to call upon some old friends of her girlhood who had gone back there after several years in this country.

Dana grew to be quite an accomplished liar, although for the sake of his profession he generally managed to make his answers letter true if not spirit perfect. Dana had great respect for his office.

Amelia began to show interest in foreign tours; she also, plied Dana with questions.

And Aunt Justine was simply unbearable!

She kept asking if he had heard from Lynette yet. Every morning she asked that, until Dana told her lofti-

ly one morning when he got her alone, that it was none
of her business whether he had heard yet or not, and he
was tired of having to answer her.

And then came that unpleasant morning when that
cheap little flaring post card arrived while Dana was
out with Jessie Belle, and everybody in the house saw
it, not only saw it but read it and meditated upon it,
and seemed to roll it as a sweet morsel under their
tongues.

It bore a picture of Westminster Abbey and underneath was written:

"Have just been doing Westminster Abbey. It im-
presses me as having a lot of poise. I'm glad I came.
Lynette."

They passed it around and read it, one by one, Amelia anxiously, over and over, wondering what it could
possibly mean. Justine scornfully, knowing she would
likely never find out. Grandma with a chuckle, guessing
what might be behind the words, and keen to read between the lines. She admired Lynette more than any
girl she knew. She often said that she was more than
smart, she was good.

It was there when they got back, Jessie Belle with a
triumphant air. She had made Dana kiss her again. She
felt she had gained several points in the game. Dana
was half shame-faced, half vexed.

And there lay the post card, out before them all, and
it was obvious that they had read it.

"I wish that I could have my mail put away in my
room when I am absent!" he remarked severely, addressing his mother, but looking straight at Justine,
who usually got to the front door first when the postman was coming. He reached for the card, but Jessie
Belle snatched it from him:

"Let me see? What is it? Oh, just an old church. I
don't see what anybody wants of that!"

But Jessie Belle had read the words, and Jessie Belle
was nobody's dummy. She dropped her eyelashes and
smiled a queer little knowing smile. Grandma, eyeing
her furtively when nobody else was noticing, spoke out
quite clearly:

"What's the matter with you, Jezebel? What have you got up your sleeve? You look like the cat when she's just finished a bird!"

"Oh, Grandma!" giggled Jessie Belle immediately, dimpling and going into spasms of laughter. "How quaint you are! What will you say next?"

"I'll see when the time comes," answered the old lady sharply, and cackled to herself as she buttered a piece of bread.

Dana betook himself and his post card up to his room after dinner and did not come down again that night. Jessie Belle was bored to death but continued to show that triumphant little dimple at intervals during the evening. Grandma watched her furtively and grimly. She did not laugh the whole evening.

Dana had other mail beside the post card. One was a letter from a church in New York asking him to supply their pulpit the next Sabbath. Dana wrote an immediate acceptance and packed his bag that night. He was determined to get away from the house, from Aunt Justine's prying eyes—and from Jessie Belle.

Yes he had come to know that he ought to get away from Jessie Belle.

Of course his mother had spoken to him several times about taking her out so much and what the neighbors would say; and indeed he would have been more careful if she hadn't nagged him so much that he felt he had to assert his own will and show her that he knew what he ought to do and what he ought not to do better than she, a woman, could ever know. He was a man.

And then there was that annoying Bible verse that Grandma had presumed to pin to his sweater. Utterly inappropriate it was of course, but annoying all the same. Grandma needn't think that just because the money was all in her trust for him, or practically so, that she owned him body and soul. He wasn't a little child any more for her to cackle at and boss. He was a man! A full fledged minister! And it was high time that she understood. He would just go away a while and let them all understand that he was his own boss.

So he packed his bag and announced to his family in the morning that he was leaving. He had to go down and look over a church. He rather gave them to understand that the letter he had received was equivalent to a call, but that he wasn't at all sure it was worth considering till he went down to look the ground over.

Grandma eyed him keenly. She didn't hand over a roll of bills as she usually did when Dana was going anywhere, but she didn't lift a finger to stop him from going. So Dana went, but he came home Monday morning a trifle crest-fallen. The church had proved to be a little Mission Chapel in a new development of small houses among plain people and they had asked him to officiate at five services and had only paid him ten dollars! He was disgusted. Also, having no money, or very little, it did not seem wise to remain longer in New York.

He rather hoped on the way home that he might find Jessie Belle gone away. She had stated a number of times that he was the only thing that kept her from fleeing this barren waste of desert, back to real life again; and the moral, well-trained part of him hoped she had gone.

Nevertheless, as he neared home he found himself looking eagerly toward the house to see if Jessie Belle were on the porch or at the window, and he was glad when he saw her blue dress, and she came running down the walk to meet him.

Justine was glad to see him returning. That was most apparent. She had been getting uneasy. She was almost afraid he might run over to Europe for the week-end. And Ella Smith was relieved. She had been afraid that Jessie Belle would run away.

Grandma was distinctly *not* glad to see her grandson return. She felt he was safer in New York, and her acrid remarks told him plainly why.

As for Amelia, she frankly told Dana that he ought to have stayed and looked up some other church while he was there. That it was high time he was settled if he expected to get to work in the fall, and he ought to have something definite to tell people. It didn't look well to see him hanging around home and going out with a girl like that every day.

But Dana loftily told her that the church at which he was to preach in August was the church of his choice, and that it was as good as his now. He had practically been called, and everything would be settled in good time when the people got home from their vacations. Then he put on his knickers and sweater and told Jessie Belle to come along for a ride, and out he went into temptation again, although this time he knew he was going there. He was insane enough to think that the fact that he knew it would protect him.

That was the beginning of a very trying summer for all the Whipples. Dana had taken the bit in his teeth and did just as he pleased, and only Justine beamed. Amelia was raw with anguish. She went about the kitchen like a cyclone and came downstairs every morning with red eyes, and quivering flabby lips. They were not becoming to her large tired face. The neighbors were beginning to ask her, *who* was Jessie Belle, and *where* did Lynette come in? Was she satisfied?

"Well," said Grandma sagely one morning when they were alone, and without the usual cackle, "now that mortification has set in I suppose you'll try to do something about it, Amelia, but it's too late. You'll find it is too late. I suppose you'll blame it all on me, but I didn't bring your child up, and I didn't know a Jezebel was coming either, when I let Justine ask her. I'd have sent her away soon after she got here, only I thought Dana was safer with her here under our eyes. She's a little snake, and she'd have managed to have him come and find her, where nobody was around to bother them. But it seems Dana had to be tried out somehow or he wouldn't be fit to stand in his grandfather's pulpit. You brought him up, Amelia, and if you did it right he'll come through. I guess we can't do anything more. Dana's of age and he's got good sense if he's a mind to use it. It's up to him. But I'm sorry for you, I really am, even if you never would take my advice and make him mind."

"It was you brought her here!" broke forth Amelia

with a great sob. "A mother never would put temptation in her boy's way like that."

"Yes, I let her come, and I'm sorry for it, Amelia. I
don't mind saying that. I made a mistake. Still, if I
hadn't, the devil would have worked her in somehow.
The Bible says everybody's got to have his try out or
something like that."

"Yes, but it says 'Woe unto them by whom they
come!'" volleyed Amelia. "It wasn't up to you to plan
his testing."

"Well, I guess I'll get my share of the woe all right,"
said Grandma grimly. "The boy isn't exactly an alien to
me you know. He's my grandson, and I've been proud
of him."

"Been?" shrieked Amelia. "Oh, my soul!" and
breaking out in a great heart-rending sob, she fled up to
her room.

Neither was Ella Smith without her troubles.

She cried slow sad tears every night in bed, for an
hour or two after she had concluded her nightly plea to
her wayward daughter.

"Jessie—I mean Jessie Belle—you wasn't brought
up this way! You know your father would have told
you you were doing wrong. You are just leading that
young man on, and he doesn't mean a thing. He's engaged and he means to marry his other girl. He
wouldn't ever turn her down. His family think she's the
top notch. His mother spent all yesterday morning telling
me how wonderful she was, and what a high-up family
she belonged to, and how the families on both sides had
always been preachers' folks, traditions she called it,
whatever that is, and what a great help she was going to
be to Dana in his chosen profession. That's the way she
said it, 'chosen profession.' It sounded real solemn, and
kind of frightened me. I think she was kind of hinting
that the family wouldn't stand for Dana's making up to
you. And Grandma, she talks too. I shouldn't wonder if
she would send us off some day. She asked me when I
had to go back to New York. And Jessie Belle, I don't
know what we'll do. There won't be any more money

coming in from papa's lawyer till the last of October.
Jessie Belle, I wish you'd be more careful, and not go
off with that young man all the time and make his folks
mad at you so we can't stay here. Why'n't you get some
fancy work for yourself? Make some of that bead work
you're always admiring so much, or a sofa pillow to
give to Mrs. Whipple when we leave, or get some goods
and cut out a dress for yourself. I'll give you enough
money for the goods if you won't go over a dollar and a
half a yard. Justine will go with you to buy it. Or if you
don't want to do that, set around and read a little. My
soul! I don't see what you and Dana have to talk about
so much off alone together! It don't seem decent, it
really don't Jessie—I mean Belle!"

Said Jessie Belle:

"Oh, rats! Ella, shut up! I wantta go to sleep. I
wasn't asking your advice!"

Variations of this were played night after night no
matter what time Jessie Belle and Dana came in from a
picture show or a ride, and afterwards Ella Smith lay in
the bed beside her child and wept. Grandma felt sorry
for her too, in a way, though she was worse than Amelia she felt, in her lack of "git-up-and-git."

"Spoiled her child; that's what's the matter with all
of 'em," she told herself grimly. "I guess it's better to
have 'em dead!" and she sighed this time instead of
cackling. It had been long years since her son was laid
in the grave, but he had not been spoiled. Grandma
had never lacked "git-up-and-git."

Matters were drawing quickly to a crisis with Dana
and Jessie Belle as the summer began to wane.

The day before Dana went down to New York to
preach in that coveted pulpit, the last Saturday in August, Jessie Belle climbed into the car and settled back
in satisfaction, a gleam of triumph in her eyes. They
had spent the day in the woods and she felt mighty sure
of her ground.

"Well, Dana, I s'pose we better get married right
away, hadn't we?" she said nonchalantly.

Dana was silent a long time. She almost thought he

was not going to answer. His face had a haggard, hunted look, like one who had thrown away his birth-right
and had just found it out.

"I suppose we'll have to," he said miserably, with
white lips that struggled for their old dignity and found
it lacking. He had faced this thing for days and nights
and tried to fling it from him and now it had him by the
throat. Something inherent in his weak soul, or something about his conventional upbringing, would not let
him be a scoundrel and run away. He had made love to
Jessie Belle. He had been a fool! And now there was
just no way out of the consequences. He never meant
to be a fool. He had thought he was a perfectly cool,
calculating man, strong and self-controlled, and Jessie
Belle had shown him that he was not. Therefore he almost hated her. And yet so strong was her hold upon
him that he could not fling it off.

But now that she had brought the subject out in the
open and he had said the words that acknowledged her
right to do so, his soul reacted suddenly. Why, why did
he have to do this awful thing and spoil his whole life?
Yes, he saw in a flash that it would spoil his life. It
would affect his reputation too. How could he ever
take a girl like Jessie Belle into a congregation as the
minister's wife? Besides, he did not really want to marry Jessie Belle. He was getting deadly tired of her vapid
little chatter. It was only when she tempted him with
her white arms and her red lips that he crushed her
fiercely to him and was ready to sell his soul for the
privilege of holding her in his arms.

They were driving toward home now, and the way
reminded him suddenly of Lynette, and the things she
used to say about the flowers by the roadside. Such a
little thing as a clump of maidenhair ferns that he had
scarcely ever noticed before, conjured her vision among
the trees and wrung his heart with sudden recollection.

He stopped the car and turned in desperation to the
girl who sat beside him.

"Jessie Belle, I've been a fool!" he said almost humbly.

"You would," said Jessie Belle sweetly. "I saw that

from the beginning, Dana, but that doesn't make any difference. I don't mind."

"But listen, Jessie Belle. I can't marry you. Why, I'm practically engaged to Lynette Brooke. We've been as good as engaged for years. I can't go back on her! I really can't marry you, Jessie Belle. I shouldn't really have gone around with you. I didn't realize, I felt you were just a child—at first it never entered my head."

"I know," said Jessie Belle with a hard tone in her voice. "You were an awful fool, of course. But that's neither here nor there. You *did* go around with me, and you've gone too far, Dana Whipple. You're mine now, and I'm going to keep you. I don't care if you were engaged to a dozen other girls. That's nothing in my young life. I want you and that's that. You've gone too far to go back now and you know it. And what's more if you don't I'll take means to have you know it. If you don't turn right around now and take me off somewhere where we can get married before we go back to the house, why then I'm going to walk right in and tell Grandma and your mother and Ella and Justine exactly how you've acted from the start. I'll tell *everything*! And I'll go out to the neighbors. I'll go and tell Mrs. Brooke, and I'll write to your silly baby doll of a Lynette and tell her a few things she never heard before. And I'll write to your old New York church and tell them you aren't by any means the saint you set up to be. I'll spoil your wonderful career you're talking about all the time. I'll knock it all to smithereens. But you can't put anything over on me. I'm no infant! Now, will you turn around and go somewhere and get married?"

"Are you threatening to blackmail me?" Dana asked with some of his old time spirit, "because no man will stand for that!"

"Well, I'm not so sure you are a man!" snapped Jessie Belle. "We'll see! But it isn't blackmail, it's the truth, and you know it!"

Dana looked at her with miserable eyes and was speechless.

In the end she had her way.

They turned around. She would not risk passing the Brooke house till she had him hard and fast. She knew the very sight of it would make him falter again.

Silently, with set white lips and eyes that were hard and haunted, he drove the car at high speed, out across the county line, and on, across the state line, to a place where marriages were made easy and no questions asked, and Jessie Belle was well content to cease her chatter and let him drive. For once she knew 'twas best to keep her mouth shut.

They drove back a little before midnight, having eaten a wedding supper at a miserable little road house by the way. At least the bride ate heartily. The bridegroom gulped a cup of coffee and sat with shut lips watching her. It seemed to him incredible that he had come to this. He could not believe the thing was done and he was married to Jessie Belle! How had he ever allowed himself to get into such a plight? He saw his reputation ruined, his high hopes tottering. He saw the vision of Lynette as she stood on the porch that last night in the sunset. The last time he had seen her. Perhaps the last time he would ever see her in this life. His Lynette! Gone forever from him. And by his own act!

He was so miserable that he would have liked to put his head down on the cheap wooden table before him and cry like a little boy. And somehow the hardest thing about it all was that he despised himself. *Himself!* Had he himself done a thing like this? No! Surely it was not his fault. It was Lynette's fault for crossing his will and refusing to stick by him. For running off to Europe because she was peeved. It was Jessie Belle's fault for tempting him! "The woman Thou gavest me!" The old, old story of the Garden of Eden and the shut gate with the flaming swords. He was seeing himself shut off from the Eden that had been his. And yet there was no sorrow in his heart for what he had done, only for the things he had lost!

One proviso he had made, and Jessie Belle had acceded easily enough, because it suited her plans and besides she did not have to keep her promise if she did not wish to do so. Dana wanted the marriage kept secret! For the present anyway. She was not to tell a soul until he gave her permission. Well, it would serve as a good hold over him when she wanted anything. She would threaten to tell.

Dana was not sure what gain was to come from keeping his marriage secret. In the end it would have to come out perhaps, but he could not go home and face his grandmother, his grandmother who held the money in trust for him, just how powerfully he had never known, and have her know what he had done.

They drove home silently. Jessie Belle was sleepy, and yawned a good deal. It had been a strenuous occasion, this getting married, but it was done and she had the marriage certificate. Dana had wanted to keep it but she had insisted and it had been handed to her. She hugged it to her now, with a gleam of triumph in her eyes. What would that smug religious Lynette say when she found she was cut out? And she, Jessie Belle, meant to take pains that news of it traveled across the water soon, in one way or another.

They stole into the sleeping house and to their rooms, Dana creeping up the back stairs like a scoundrel, his shoes in his hand, Jessie Belle gaily, humming a light little tune, and flashing on the light regardless of her mother waking and weeping and waiting for her.

She shut the door and locked it and then turned to her mother her head up, her eyes shining.

"Well, you can say what you please now, Ella, I'm married, and on my own!" she anounced triumphantly.

"Jessie! Whatever can you mean?"

"I mean what I say. Dana and I were married tonight. Oh, it's all right. I got a certificate good and fast. He can't get away!"

"Oh, Jessie! My *bbba*-by!" sobbed the mother, burying her face in the pillow lest she should be heard.

"Oh, shut up!" cried the girl impatiently. "Whats the sense of bellowing like that? Didn't you expect I'd ever get married? I should think you'd be pleased that I got a good looking rich fella like Dana. There ain't so many of them."

"But Jessie! He don't belong to you. He was engaged! It wasn't honorable!" protested her mother sitting up in bed and getting tragic.

"Honor nothing!" said Jessie Belle impudently. "Shut up, woncha? Dana don't wantta tell them yet. If you boo-hoo like that the whole thing'll be dished and we'll haveta get out in the morning. But if you shut up and do as I say we can perfectly well get away with it and stay here all fall till your money comes. Dana's gotta get a job. I'm not goin' to stand for that religious stuff. You see me running a missionary society, doncha? Not on yer life. I've been thinking of the movies. Dana could act, and he's a looker, all right. I think we could both get in together. Great stuff, wouldn't it! Five thousand a week apiece and things like that. You could keep house for us, and have it soft, Ella. Didn't I tellya I'd get Dana, all right? Now, mop up and get to sleep. I'm just about ready to pass out! And in the morning keep yer mouth shut! Remember! No matter what happens, you don't know a darned thing. See?"

"Oh, Jessie," sobbed the distracted mother, "I feel just like a th-th-th-ief!"

"Oh, heck!" said Jessie Belle bouncing into bed. "If you don't cut that I'll throw some water on ya!"

And Ella Smith "cut it." But it was hours before she fell into a troubled sleep. She kept saying over and over to herself, "Oh, what would her father say? What would he say? He was always so honorable! What would he say?"

The next morning at breakfast Grandma Whipple watched the two come in with their guilty faces, Jessie Belle's face wreathed in smiles, Dana's in gloom.

She waited until the blessing was asked and the food was served and then she opened up, piercing Dana with her keen little eyes:

"Well, Ahab, what time did you get back last night?"

Dana dropped his knife and looked at his grandmother fury and guilt in his face. He studied her face for an instant, the color utterly leaving his own, and then he arose, white and angry, and stalked out of the room. He was not seen any more that day. But Jessie

Belle hung around and laughed and sang and played with the cat, and Grandma watched her incessantly, but she did not chuckle once all day, and Amelia thought she caught her wiping her eyes once.

It was the next day that the lawyer came for one of his occasional business sessions with Grandma Whipple and the door of the parlor was closed for two hours.

XXI

Dana went down to New York before lunch. He did not come back to the dining-room, and he did not speak to anybody but his mother before he left. Notwithstanding the low state of his exchequer, he refrained from going into the room where his grandmother habitually sat, and he even evaded Jessie Belle.

He had packed his bag and gone down the back stairs, climbed the back fence and walked to the station across lots. He avoided speaking to any of his fellow townsmen on the way. He held up his head and walked haughtily, as if he were the same proud Dana Whipple of the old days, but his heart was heavy as lead.

In his bag were his most brilliant sermons, filled with fine quotations, sparkling with his best seminary eloquence, not devoid of originality. He had not conned his great grandfather's sermons in vain. They had become a part of his fibre as it were, that is the rugged phrases, and the keen way of putting things had become his. That they lacked the deep spirituality that characterized the grandfather's mighty messages, and that they dwelt more on the note of uplift and peace and church union than upon doctrinal truths was a small matter in his eyes, in fact he felt that in this very point they excelled his grandfather's, they were all the more up-to-date; and his friends and professors in the Seminary were inclined to agree with him.

So Dana was not worrying about the morrow. He was reasonably sure he could get up in the pulpit and

go through the services without anyone suspecting that
he was in despair. He would be like a tall oak, neatly
sawed off at the ground, and standing yet upon its
stump. A breath perhaps might cause him to topple. As
long as he was in the pulpit he would be all right. Nobody would know that his life had been cut off down to
the roots, and all the sources of his happiness drained.
But if he had to talk with people, if he had to go down
among the congregation and answer questions, and
smile and do the conventional thing would he be able
to carry it through? He felt physically ill as he dropped
into his chair in the parlor car, and pulling his shade
down, and placing his hat over his eyes so that no
neighbor who chanced to be traveling that way also
would dare approach him, he felt that he would be glad
if the train would have a smash-up on the way down
and he would be killed.

Then he recalled that even so his stainless name
would not be kept untarnished, for Jessie Belle had that
marriage license, and she would extract through it the
last penny from Grandma, and then flaunt her position
before the world. Oh, he had been a fool, a fool, a
fool! Nevertheless so he did not search out the sin that
Self had brought into his heart. He began to tell himself
that it was all Lynette's fault for going off and leaving
him. "The woman Thou gavest me."

The elder who was to entertain Dana lived in a comfortable home on Park Avenue, and after dinner when
they were sitting about the gas logs which the coolness
of the late August evening permitted, the elder began to
warm up and tell Dana eagerly how interested the
whole congregation were in him, and how the session
was a unit in feeling that he would be the coming man.

Dana, his heart warmed by the genial atmosphere,
and his body comforted by the exceedingly good dinner
he had just finished, rested his comely head back
against the crimson cushion of the luxurious chair in
which he was sitting and began to look more like himself. He even expanded genially to the open flattery to
which he had been accustomed. It soothed his angry,
frightened, disgusted heart and made him feel as if even

yet there might be some way out, and life still be worth living. His face lost some of its becoming pallor, and his lips got back their habitual hue, and he warmed to the situation mightily. After all, this was New York. Grandma Whipple's ideas were quite different from those of the modern world. If he could only keep Jessie Belle in the background long enough, he could put this thing across, and once done, New York forgave almost anything. Also churches were not what they used to be. Christian people were no longer narrow nor hidebound.

"You may be interested to know what turned the tide in your favor at the last," went on George Avery Billingsgate genially. "It was the fact that you are reported to be engaged to the daughter of an old friend and former pastor of our senior elder, Mr. Tabor Vanderholt. Mr. Vanderholt was at first much in favor of calling an older and married man to our church. He felt that it had always occupied a prominent place among churches, that it had always taken a prominent part in our denominational government, been a leader in great and good movements, and that we needed a man of experience. A settled man who had chosen a wise wife, and lived with her long enough to have become one with her, and to work in perfect unison with her in our various organizations. But when it was mentioned that you were about to be married to Miss Lynette Brooke, I think that is the name, is it not, Lynette? it struck me at the time as being most unique and charming, and so clung to my memory—when as I say she was mentioned, Mr. Vanderholt gave immediate attention and asked if by any chance she was the daughter of Reverend Harrison Brooke, who had been his pastor for ten years before he came to New York. Of course then we looked up the data, and Vanderholt came over to our side immediately, which turned the vote in your favor. It is an interesting little item in the history of this affair that I thought you might like to tell Miss Brooke. I understand she is a very charming young woman, quite unusual in a way, and very beautiful——"

He looked straight at Dana's blanched face and waited for corroboration. Dana summoned his stiff lips and parched throat to reply, but no sound came from them. He merely bowed his head gravely. He had tried to summon a smile, but no smile had come. He felt that the man had stabbed him with a fine thin blade that had gone clear through to the chair, and when he pulled it out again his life blood would gush upon the floor and that would be the end of him. He wished that he might quietly pass away before this happened.

"And that she is remarkably fitted to be the wife of a city pastor." The elder went on smiling. "In fact we found no word of any thing but praise for her, in all our investigations. I was much amazed that she has even studied Greek and Hebrew to better prepare her for Bible study and teaching."

"Greek and Hebrew?" came to the startled lips of Dana before he could order his thoughts aright.

"Yes, remarkable! remarkable! And to take such high rank, and with such unmistakable scholars of authority as she has studied! I happen to have a brother out there in the college where she was graduated, and he keeps me informed about things. Of course when I found where she was I had no trouble in getting all the information I needed. And to think that she is as beautiful and winning in her personality as she is brilliant. It seems to me that you are a remarkably blest young man."

Dana never knew how he got through the remainder of that awful evening, nor what he said in answer to all the questions that were asked him, and the flattery that was dealt out to him. He only knew that he was the most miserable man on earth, when at last he was released on the plea of a desire to go over his sermon once more, and ascended the stairs to the guestroom, with the reflected halo of Lynette resting upon his troubled brow. Oh, what a fool he had been! What a fool! What a fool! What a fool! It rang over and over in his brain as he got out his most cherished sermon and assayed to go over it. He gave it up at last, snapped out his light and went to bed, but he did not go to sleep. Instead he went over the whole miserable business again from start to finish, his cheeks burning hot in the dark-

ness over his own part in his downfall. How he hated
Jessie Belle. How he loathed himself! Yet not for his
sin. Not even yet for his sin, only for its consequences.
It really had been all Lynette's fault. And now perhaps
she would never know in full all that she had missed,
and all that he had missed through her. He cursed her
and he loved her and he longed for her that he might
tell her in scathing terms just what she had done.

And now what was he to do?

They had asked him how soon he was to be married
and he had told them, "Not at present," and had spoken of Lynette's being abroad with her aunt. The elder
had raised his brows and suggested, oh, most delicately,
that perhaps it would be well to recall her and hasten
up the marriage in time for the installation and reception. It was always well for a man and his wife to begin
a thing like that together. It gave them a great advantage. He had even intimated that there was a house that
would be most convenient, and if Dana would care to
look it over Monday they could arrange that it would
be held until Miss Brooke could come on and look it
over. It really was an exceptional chance, and there
might not be another so good.

Dana was a most miserable man. And when he
thought of Jessie Belle he almost lost his mental balance. To think of Jessie Belle, his wife, occupying a position like that in a church like that! What a fool, what
a fool, what a fool he had been! The refrain began
again, and Dana lay and watched the dawn creep into
his room, a dawn without a ray of hope.

Somehow he got through the next day.

The attentive audience as usual perhaps went to his
head and lifted him above his circumstances for the
time being. He was all preacher now, and Jessie Belle
was not there. He had this one day at least in which to
shine, helped on by the soft light of radiance from Lynette Brooke's lovely life. He would preach as he never
preached before. He would show these people what he
could do. Himself should have its day, even if it were
but a day long. Himself should have the glory that he
had worked for so long and hard.

And preach he did! It almost seemed as if he were inspired, though not with the Spirit from above perhaps. The words came without hesitation, his perfect enunciation, his richly modulated tones, his becoming pallor, his handsome head and graceful gestures, all came in for pleasant comment by the eager audience. Here was a coming man, a great pulpit orator, who would make for their church a name and a fame in the annals of church history, as great as any that preceded him. They were unanimous in their delight over him. They had secured a prize. All about over the church could be heard the sibilant words, "So handsome!" "Such wonderful eyes!" "Such a clear penetrating voice," "Aren't his lips charming? I love to watch them move, they seem to make his words become living things," and one woman even said, "He looks like a young god!" He overheard the woman, and then he seemed to hear Lynette's voice, "Beautiful as the morning!" as she stood in the sunshine before the round hill, and looked at blue ruin raising its stately candles above the daisied cover of the hill. He almost groaned aloud at the memory. But he put it quickly aside. He must not let these people see he was distraught. He must get through this day somehow, receive his meed of praise this once, before all tottered and fell in ruin. Blue Ruin! He said that over, startled at himself, and wondered if he was going mad. And yet, Jessie Belle was like Blue Ruin who had stolen into his life and brough death. God! He must pull himself out of this somehow and get through the rest of the day!

He did.

He was surrounded by admiring women, and men who counted their wealth by millions. He was invited to dinner, and begged to stay over and take a trip with one of the members up to his summer home on the coast of Maine. If life had been going well with him he would have thought the millennium had reached him, for that was about his idea of the millennium.

But he declined them all, and said he must get away. His only desire was to get off by himself and think— think his way out of this horrible situation. It never occurred to him to pray. He would not have felt intimate enough with God to tell Him about it if it had. He would not have cared to speak of it before God. He would not have felt that his excuses would have had the sympathy from Him they merited.

Into the sharpness of the hour, as the tide of interest among the people became more and more apparent, there had crept one wild thought, like a ray of hope. He did not stop to think whether it came from above or beneath. It was that he must get rid of Jessie Belle!

Oh, he would do her no harm of course. But he would find a way to shake her off and hush her up. Nobody yet knew that they were married, and it was unthinkable that he should have all this phenomenal career stopped by one little silly schoolgirl! There were ways, perfectly respectable ways. Why not buy her off! Send her away! If Lynette ever came to guess anything about it—well, Lynette would forgive! He was not afraid but Lynette would forgive! And he would go and beg her humbly to forgive. Of course he had been wrong about some things. He knew that all the time. But she would understand. And then of course, he had not understood what an unusual college that was, quite exclusive, and really scholarly, unique in fact. He would humble himself and tell her that. He would bring her back with him. He would tell her the church wanted her, and all about the reception, and the beautiful house. They would be married! But! Jessie Belle! He couldn't marry Lynette, he was married to Jessie Belle! He must get rid of Jessie Belle! There would be some way. Just a few words and a little foolishness could never be so binding as to spoil his life forever. It couldn't! Of course it wouldn't be hard to get rid of Jessie Belle. She wouldn't mind. He would promise her plenty of money. His salary would be all he needed. He would always make a good salary, and Grandma would come across if she knew that Jessie Belle had got in the way. There would be a way! There must be a way. And Jessie Belle wouldn't care! She was just a kid. She would rather have the money!

Sometimes he realized what wild foolishness he was

thinking, and then it seemed that he would sink. He must bolster up his soul till he got somehow through this awful day and had a chance to think. And so he bolstered himself with saying that there would be a way. He almost convinced himself sometimes that he had not done any harm.

Back in the home he had left, Jessie Belle lay around and amused herself as best she could. She went and bought a fashion magazine and began to plan a trousseau. She manicured her nails, and shampooed her hair and spent a long time on her makeup, and sallied forth to take a walk, declining curtly Justine's offer to go with her. She hoped to meet that ugly little beast of a Brooke boy, and begin his subjugation, for she had decided long ago that that was the next step in her program. But Elim was safe away in the woods with Spud and Snipe and she came back disconsolate.

She settled down on the front porch in a steamer chair and lighted a cigarette. It was the first time she had dared. She had stolen off to the back of the garage for her smokes heretofore. If Dana had smoked it would have been different, but somehow she knew Dana had a tradition against it, and it wouldn't be wise to let him know. Now she was safe, what did it matter? Grandma was taking her nap, and couldn't get out to the porch anyway, at least she never did. Amelia had no sort of power, and she wasn't afraid of Amelia in any case. As for Justine she would be only too glad to keep a secret if she gave her one of her smiles. It wouldn't be hard to even induce Justine to smoke if she set about it. Maybe she would sometime just to horrify Amelia. It would probably make Grandma chuckle. Of course Ella would howl, but Ella didn't count.

So Jessie Belle sat on the old respectable, orthodox front porch of the Whipple house and smoked a cigarette. The neighbors came by, several of them, and saw her, for Mrs. Pettingill had a little tea that afternoon for a cousin from up the state who was visiting, and all the guests came home about five o'clock and saw Jessie Belle sitting on the old respectable orthodox front porch of the Whipple house smoking a cigarette! Jessie

Belle with her extremely short skirt and her long fine
legs in their nude, silk stockings kicking around carelessly, while the neighbors went by! Each group as
they came down the hill and passed almost stopped in
horror. For everybody knew that Dana Whipple had
been taking this girl out every day, morning, noon, and
night, and everybody also knew that Dana had gone
down to preach in New York in one of the oldest, most
respectable, most orthodox churches in the whole denomination.

Now Grandma Whipple was not asleep. She had not
been able to sleep at her usual nap time for three or
four days. Her mind was deeply troubled. In all the
years she had been conducting the Whipple homestead
she had never once had to acknowledge even to herself
that she had made a serious mistake in her administra-
tion. Until now, in this matter of having invited this
huzzy from New York to live under the same roof with
her cherished grandson, Dana, scion of the old Whipple
name and heritage. She was afraid it was even so bad
that she was going to try to do something about it. That
was equivalent to saying that she had been wrong.

She lay there grimly and thought about the different
things she might do. Of course she might tell Justine to
take her friends off to the seashore and she would foot
the bills. That would be an evasive way of getting
around it, but then they might return sometime.

She might pretend to get sick, and have the doctor
order quiet and everybody out of the house. But that
would be expensive, and she doubted if she could keep
it up long enough. She hated to stay in bed. She meant
to die in her chair at least if not on her feet.

Neither could she consider going away herself and
closing the house. That wasn't being done. Everybody
would think she had taken leave of her senses. Besides,
none of these means would bring about the desired effect of getting rid of Jessie Belle finally and forever. If
she was sent off in any such way Dana would merely
'trail after her. It had got as bad as that, she was afraid.

As she lay there mulling it over in her mind, a
strange new odor stole subtly into her open window. It

was sort of sweetish and pungent. But there was something about it that aroused her antagonism, she didn't know just why. It wasn't some of that heathen incense that Justine had brought in the other night to keep the mosquitoes away, was it? If Justine had dared have that around in a Christian household again, after what she said to her!

The old lady rose to a sitting posture and sniffed. She turned and put her stockinged feet to the floor. She sat and sniffed again. It wasn't Amelia baking cinnamon cookies, and burning them was it? Amelia wasn't herself these days. Poor soul! She was probably badly worried. No, it wasn't cookies, it was a new smell, more pungent, more like——

She hadn't walked without her crutches for two years, nor without her strong flat-soled shoes, but she managed to get over to the window and peek out the curtain. Her room was in an ell off the main part of the house, and she could just see the porch. From her window, she had a full view of Jessie Belle lounging, legs and all, smoking her cigarette and exhaling the smoke through her impudent powdered nostrils, her wide pink nostrils that somehow reminded Grandma of a little young pig.

Madame Whipple gave a snort of fury. She caught her breath and stood looking with steadily increasing wrath. On the street three women were passing, pausing an instant for the full view of the Whipple porch.

"Now, what do you think of that! My soul! Do you suppose Mrs. Whipple knows that? And to think of Dana!"

Grandma Whipple hadn't walked alone for months, but she managed to get herself to the chair where Amelia had stood her crutch, and she managed to open her door and steal down the hall, crutch in hand but not touching the floor for fear of making a sound. Feeling along the wall, she came to the door and got herself out on the porch as silently in her poor old lame stockinged feet as if she had been a butterfly.

Jessie Belle was mooning over a fashion paper, half asleep, and didn't see her till she stood over, her hand clutching the back of the chair, her crutch raised threateningly:

"Jezebel!" she announced in her deep old voice that had no cackle in it now. "Get out of that chair, and throw away that dirty cigarette! Don't you dare do that in my house again, or out you go!"

Jessie Bell rose lithely out of the chair and got beyond the reach of the crutch, then she laughed lightly:

"Oh, Grandma, you're so—"

But Grandma interrupted roughly:

"No, Jezebel, I'm not quaint any more! I mean this. Out you go, and if you don't throw that dirty thing away this minute you can go right upstairs and pack your bags and tell that pussy foot of a mother of yours that she can take the next train. I've stood all I'm going to stand. This has always been a respectable house."

But Jessie Belle stood her ground, her insolent chin lifted deridingly, one hand on her hip, her body slanted in defiance and coolly brought that cigarette up to her lips, and blew a long whiff of smoke out from her nostrils straight into the face of the irate old lady.

The next instant Grandma's crutch came crashing down on Jessie Belle's lifted wrist, and the cigarette flew to the ground where it smoldered in the grass, while Jessie Belle doubled up with a howl of pain.

Grandma Whipple stood her ground, a grand old nemesis, administering justice in spite of startled neighbors passing by in what seemed to Jessie Belle like throngs.

Grandma waited until the women had passed by, withered by her eagle glance which said as plain as words could speak:

"This is my business, not yours. Pass on."

Then, she turned again to the furious girl who was still holding her smarting wrist and struggling to keep the angry tears from her eyes. Not for anything would Jessie Belle cry now.

The lifted crutch went up again:

"Go, Jezebel!" commanded the old war horse.

Jessie Belle threw back her head, stuck out her chin

and tossed her lock of sleek black hair till impudence could rise no higher:

"You can't send me away, unless you send Dana," she taunted, her eyes bright with defiance. "Dana and I were married last night!"

The old lady halted not for amazement. Her brain was quicker than the lightning's flash. She came one step nearer in her wrath, and stood, untottering, straight as in her younger days, and strong. She lifted her crutch a third time now, and brough it down on Jessie Belle's shoulders, a strong quick blow that smarted on her tender flesh and bit deep, and made Jessie Belle run screaming into the house to her mother in a fright. Then the old lady turned and walked into the house again, holding her crutch but not leaning on it, upheld by the very strength of her fury.

Amelia had come from the kitchen, her hands and arms all floury from mixing biscuits, her eyes wide with wonder. Justine had come from a nap, her hair in crimpers, her face all cold cream, her old kimono clutched about her shoulders. She screamed in affright as she saw Jessie Belle rush in, holding the bruised shoulder, and still crying aloud with the pain.

"What is it, Jessie Belle, dearie?" she cried frantically. "Did something sting you? Did a bee sting my darling child?"

Ella came trembling from the guestroom where she had been mending her old foulard, and thrashing over her poor old problems feebly. But she did not cry out nor pity Jessie Belle. She knew she deserved whatever she had got.

It had come, then, the awful thing which she had been dreading. Jessie Belle had come to open war somehow, and they would have to go. She never doubted this, as she put her frightened face over the stair railing and looked down on her smitten offspring.

Jessie Belle had sunk down on the lower step of the stair and was making the most of the dramatic situation that her pain would let her make.

"Oh, oh! she tried to kill me!" she sobbed. "She's crazy! I believe Grandma's crazy!" and she sobbed on.

But Grandma had command of the situation.

"Shut up! Jezebel!" she commanded, waving her crutch with a menacing movement. Then she turned to her daughter-in-law as the only sensible one of the crowd.

"Amelia, this huzzy was smoking a cigarette on the front porch, in full view of all Mrs. Pettingill's company coming down the hill, with her long legs spread out for everybody to see. I came out and told her to throw away the dirty thing and go in the house and she defied me. She told me that she and your son were married last night, and that I couldn't send her away unless I sent him away too. Well, I'm sending her away! You can do as you like, but *she* can't stay in this house another hour. I hit her, yes, I hit her twice, and I'll do it again if she defies me. Ella Smith!"

She lifted her sharp gaze now to the balcony above and fixed the little trembling woman with her gaze:

"Ella Smith, I'm mighty sorry for you but you take your little devil of a brat out of my house right away. I won't have her here another hour. I'll give you money to pay your way, and enough to keep you at a boarding house somewhere a while, but I won't have you here any longer. Get out before the sun sets or I'll have you put out! Dana can go after you if he chooses. He always was a fool! But I'm done!"

"Oh, Grandma!" gasped Justine bursting into sobs. "Why, Grandma I never saw you like this before. Amelia, hadn't we better send for the doctor?"

"Shut up, Justine, you're another fool! I'm mistress of my own house, and I don't want the doctor. If you say another word or try to take this girl's part you'll go too, and when you go you stay, do you hear that?"

XXII

ELLA SMITH and her daughter left town on the seven nineteen. The sun was just dipping behind the farthest hill as their train moved out of the station and glided away into the evening.

Jessie Belle was a trifle cowed and tearful. She was still outraged at her beating, and still vengeful and determined to win out in the end. But the idea of going to a summer resort up in Canada pleased her immensely. Her mother had a sister up there working in a hotel office, and armed with plenty of money Ella Smith felt she could hold up her head with the best for a while. Grandma had agreed that Canada was far enough away, and they had wasted little time in packing. Justine had been whining and tearful, frightened lest this cataclysm might affect her also. She dared not speak to Jessie Bell lest the irate tyrant might see and carry out her threat.

Jessie Belle, uncomforted, angry, black and blue, and furious at Dana for forsaking her, sat down and wrote with her left hand a letter that she knew would make her newly wedded husband wince. She reminded him that he had told her the names of his New York friends, and she had not forgotten what church he was preaching in. He needn't think he could get away with anything for she was on the job. Then she walked boldly into Dana's room and laid the letter on his bureau.

The old Whipple house was very quiet all that long Sabbath day. The guestroom door was closed, Justine

Whipple's door was closed. Amelia's mouth was closed and set in a thin hard line of suffering. Grandma refused to come to the table, and sat part of the time with her old white head bowed on her folded hands on the little stand beside her chair, and part of the time with her head leaning back in the chair, her eyes closed, her hands folded idly in her lap, looking like death. She was walking through her valley of humiliation at last and she found it very bitter indeed.

Justine came downstairs about the middle of the afternoon. She had her head bound up with a bandage smelling of camphor, and her eyes were red with crying. She cast frightened glances at the old lady while she made herself a cup of tea, and when she had drunk it, and eaten a very thin slice of bread and butter she came meekly over and stood by the old lady's chair.

"I suppose you think that I am to blame," she began with her placating whine, but Grandma sat up and eyed her gravely, her old face haggard with trouble.

"Well, you are, Justine! You know it, and I know it, and it isn't worth while trying to prove that you aren't, for it can't be done. We've got this to bear, and it isn't going to make it any easier to have to prop you up by lies and try to make out you hadn't any hand in it. You know perfectly well you went about getting that girl here in an underhanded way, making us think she was a child. And now this is the result. It's done, and it can't be undone, and we don't want to hear you whine about it."

"Well, but Grandma, deah! Why do you feel so bad? Jessie Belle will make Dana a charming little wife! And Lynette nevah did——"

"Justine! That'll be about all from you! Go upstairs, and when I want your opinion on Dana's marriage I'll ask it. You can stay here because you haven't any other home to go to, but you can't bring anybody else here ever again, and you must keep your mouth shut. Go!"

Justine went.

Amelia brought a tempting tray and set it before her mother-in-law and seemed almost tender in the way she arranged the cushion under her feet. It was as if the common blow had brought a sympathy between them that had never been there before. Their idol was fallen. They must grieve together.

The Sabbath night settled down upon them waking in their beds, as it it had been a house of death.

Dana walked in on them late Monday afternoon and looked about for Jessie Belle, nervous, afraid to meet her, yet anxious to take her off somewhere and get it over. He felt almost confident now that he would be able to buy off Jessie Belle.

As he had walked in at the gate, Justine, just coming out the door to mail a letter scuttled back upstairs to her room a frightened look in her eyes. This was what they all had been dreading all day. What would Dana say? How would Grandma treat him? She hid upstairs in the dark hall, and tried to listen over the banisters.

Dana came into the hall, put down his bags, threw his hat on the hall table and flung into the dinning-room.

"Where's Mother?" he asked. "I want some lunch. I'm hungry as a bear."

Then he looked around for Jessie Belle.

Nobody answered him. There was a strange silence pervading the place. His mother appeared in the door-way, but did not speak. It was as if she were looking at a ghost. There was a reproachful look in her eyes, a sad strange look that he had never seen ther before.

"I want some coffee," he said crossly. "I've got a terrible headache. Make it good and strong. I want some bread and buter and cold meat. Is there any custard? I hope it's cold. I'm burning up! My soul but it was hot on the train. Full of foreigners too. There wasn't a place to sit down except by some ill-smelling brute. The parlor car was all taken."

He flung himself in a chair and dropped his head on his hand. Still his mother did not speak, and when he looked up irritated at the silence he saw that his grandmother was sitting with her head dropped upon her folded arms on the table.

"Heavens!" he exclaimed starting to his feet. "What a house this is! Still as a tomb! Where is Jessie Belle? Tell her I want her."

Then Grandmother Whipple straightened up and looked him in the eye with her old dominant glance.

"Jessie Belle is gone!" she said. "Jessie Belle will never come back to this house again!"

"Gone!" echoed Dana, bewildered, "Gone!" with a sudden relief growing visibly in his face. "Why did she go?"

The Grandmother faced him, still holding him with her eyes, but his mother spoke up, her voice strangely low and gentle, yet firmer, more demanding than he had ever heard it before.

"Dana, is it true that you have disgraced us all? Have you really married Jessie Smith, or was she lying to us?"

"Hell!" said Dana. "Did she say that?" He flew back and forth across the room and around like a caged thing suddenly gone mad.

"Sit down!" said Grandma, "and don't swear in my house again! You've disgraced your profession, and you've disgraced your grandfather's name, and you've disgraced your own reputation, but you shan't swear in my house. Now, if you've anything to say for yourself, say it, and then pick up your bags and go to your wife! Unless she isn't your wife, in which case you can prove it."

"But Grandmother!" began Dana flinging himself back in the chair, his elbow on the table, his head on his hand.

"Don't Grandmother me! Tell your story! I'm tired of blather and bluff. Let's get down to brass tacks. Did you marry that huzzy or not?"

"Oh, yes, I did," he groaned, "but—it wasn't really my fault. She——"

"Yes, Adam, I know, there hasn't been one of you sinned since the Garden of Eden but you found some woman to blame it on. I don't doubt she's to blame, but so are you and you might as well own it. I'm not interested in knowing what particular brand of devil Jessie

Belle is. I saw enough of her while she was here to make me sick of living. And I'm not saying I wasn't to blame to some extent myself for letting her come. But Dana, you're a fool! You knew what you were and you had a girl that was worth more in her little finger than five million Jessie Belles put together. And then you fell for that thing! Bah! You! The head of your class! The orator your professors decided you were. The future minister in a big city church. *You* picked out that little feather brain! You set her in the place that had belonged to another girl for years. You let that little flibberty jib fool you and bully you into marrying her? And now, Dana Whipple what are you going to do?"

"I have a plan, Grandmother," said Dana almost meekly. "If you'll just listen till I finish, I think, I know —I'm sure you'll approve."

"I'll listen," said the old woman grimly.

"I know that I've been wrong——" he began.

"You have."

"I know I was a fool," almost humbly.

"You are! There's no question about that."

Dana stirred uncomfortably, and then tried it again.

"But people have made such mistakes before."

"They have. There are a great many fools in the world, but we didn't think we had one like that in the family."

There was another long pause.

"Well, I've been thinking it over," Dana tried again, "and I can see only one way out. I didn't really mean to marry Jessie Belle. She got me in a tight corner, and I was so upset that I couldn't see what was the thing to do."

"Don't try to make excuses for yourself. That's our business hereafter. We'll have to be excusing you to ourselves the rest of time I imagine. Go on with your plan. Perhaps you've got a streak of honor left somewhere."

Dana got up stung to the quick.

"Grandma, I can't tell you when you meet me like that! I really can't!" he said with a trifle of his old haughtiness.

"Beggars shouldn't be choosers," quoted Grandma. "It was you that asked for the privilege of speaking."

Dana slumped into his chair and groaned, and his mother turned her face away to hide the contortion of sudden tears.

"You see it's this way, Grandmother," he straightened up at last, "Jessie Belle isn't the right girl, of course I know that. But she got me in a weak place. My eyes are open now, and I've got to do something about it. It's made a great difference for me to go down to New York and preach, Grandmother!" Dana's voice grew soft with feeling as if he had just met with some great spiritual awakening. "I wish I could make you understand how wonderful those people were to me, and how I preached yesterday. It was almost as if I was inspired, really, Grandmother! The house was crowded and it was perfectly still. They listened as if I was a great preacher, a really great one you know. And now, they are all ready to call me. They are only waiting for one member of the session to return from a trip abroad before they take the actual action."

He paused to get the effect of his words, but the two women were utterly silent. They regarded him with almost alien glances. It would seem that his work brought only deeper pain to them.

"Well, of course the effect of all this was to bring me entirely to my senses, and of course I have been suffering agonies ever since. I've been trying to think it out, and plan what to do. You see it is the more complicated because they have heard I was engaged to Lynette Brooke, and they have heard a lot about her. So it's absolutely imperative that I settle up with Jessie Belle immediately, and I've been thinking it over and I'm positive that I won't have any trouble—" he was hurrying to his climax now, afraid that they might interrupt him. But the room was still as death.

"I'm quite sure I won't have any trouble if I just had a little money," he went on. "I could make Jessie Belle understand that it was all a very unwise thing, and she wouldn't be any happier than I, and as no one knows

anything about it—I am sure it can all be hushed up—
of course I'd have to tell Lynette."

"Dana Whipple!" The old lady in her horror and
wrath had arisen to her feet and was standing straight
and threatening. "Do I hear your words right, or have
my ears deceived me? Is it possible that you not only
have disgraced your profession and the name you bear,
but you are planning to add cowardice and lying to
your sins?"

"But Grandmother, a marriage like that—nobody
really knows, and if Jessie Belle gets her freedom and
plenty of money she won't tell. I'll make her promise
to go away off somewhere. And if I get this church I
can live on the salary and you won't have to give me
anything else. Just give it to Jessie Belle. I'll never forget it, Grandmother, if you help me out of this terrible
mess. And really I've had my lesson. I'll never disgrace
you any more."

"Dana Whipple, have you forgotten *God?*" his
grandmother cried. "Get out of my presence! Get out
of my house! Your mother can do as she pleases. I'm
done with *you* from now on! The only thing left for
you to do is to go and live with your wife! You've
made your bed, now lie on it!"

The old lady dropped into her chair, and shriveled
back against the cushions a faded, frail, broken, old
woman, her white hair straggling down her furrowed
forehead, and over her wrinkled cheek.

Amelia answered in a lifeless voice: "That's your
duty now, Dana, since you've married her."

Dana looked at her for an instant as if he could not
believe his senses, and then dropping his head upon his
breast he staggered from the room. Dana the beautiful!
Dana the beloved!

In the small hours of the morning he went away
from the house that had sheltered him since he was
born, stumbling out into the darkness just before the
dawn. He had hastily packed some things, and his
mother had got money for him, and he was going away
to find Jessie Belle. He was doing the honorable thing

because they would not let him do anything else, but his heart was hot with rebellion and his punishment seemed greater than he could bear.

The winter settled down upon the House of Whipple in silence and desolation. Their glory had departed with Dana. There seemed nothing further in life to look forward to. Even Dana's letters ceased, after a few outraged protests. Then there was silence for a time, but later there came letters in a new vein.

He told them he had come to Canada as he promised, and he had taken a little house and was living with Jessie Belle. He was trying to make it a go. He did not know just what he was going to do. He had been preaching in a little chapel to some common people, "just for practice" and also he thought it would sound well to the New York people but he was not going to give up his ambitions. Jessie—he called her Jessie now, and tried to speak of her in his letters as if she had attained some new dignity by marrying him—Jessie had promised to take a course of study in a school up there, English and a few branches in which she stood sadly in need. She was also going on with her voice training. He thought it might be an asset in New York. He had not given up New York. He was trying to gloss his wife over with a veneer, and cover up the traces of what his family considered his disgrace. He gave suggestions also in his letter of things they might say to the neighbors. There was no need for anyone at home to know the true situation. He hinted that there might come a day when he would return with his young and beautiful wife and people would be glad to meet her, and would forget all the gossip there had been when he went away.

But the Whipples were not helping nor hindering gossip. They were keeping close at home. Justine seldom stirred beyond the door save after dark. Amelia went her daily route to market with closed lips and reticent air that few dared to approach. The old lady was failing visibly. People asked after her with lowered breath.

And in the Mite Society the woman talked of Dana

in whispers when the minister's wife was on the other side of the room.

"They do say," and "Well, I saw it myself!" and "How can his grandmother bear it?" And at last it reached farther up the hill and came to Mary Brooke's ears.

Elim had heard the study before, and believed all and more than he heard. Had he not seen enough with his own eyes? But Elim kept his mouth sealed. Let them find it out all in good time. Lynnie was across the water, and his mother's heart would only be distressed.

But Mary Brooke when she heard the whisper that Dana was married to the summer visitor at his Grandmother's house, went to the window and looked off across the meadows to where the blue ruin was long ago covered with deep white snow, and said, "Poor, poor Dana!" and then after a little, "But thank the Lord if that is so!"

Nevertheless she did not write the rumor to Lynette. She waited from week to week to see if her girl would mention her old comrade, or give some evidence that he had written. Surely he must have written once, at least. It was not like Dana to let things drop that way! Strange that Dana had not come near either to ask questions about Lynette, to get her address, or protest at her running away, or something. Yet was it strange? For Dana must have been very angry at Elim. And Dana must have changed as Lynnie had feared, or he never would have let things go on this way without some sort of explanation. Nevertheless, she was content to let the Lord take care of the matter, and glad too that her girl was safe on the other side of the world. Only, if Dana was married, how was Lynnie going to take it when she got back? Was she going to blame herself forever, perhaps even blame her mother for letting her go away in the midst of a foolish little misunderstanding which might have easily been put right?

It was all too deep for Mary Brooke, and so she took it to the Lord and left it there, and asked again for guidance. And by and by she did feel moved to write to Lynette and tell her all about the gossip and prepare her for whatever might be the truth when she came home, but that letter never reached her until long after she was back, for just at that time the Reamers had changed some of their plans, and their mail followed them from place to place, a good deal of it missing them entirely till they got home, so that Lynette while she was away, was not in touch with anything about her former lover, and had no news of him, save Elim's first outburst.

To that letter Lynette had written a beautiful reply. Elim read it over many times and rubbed his eyes with the back of his hand when at last he folded it away in his pocket.

Elim, dear brother (she wrote):

"I'm glad you wrote me that letter about Dana. Of course it was hard for me to read, hard to think you felt that way about him, hard to think he had done anything to lower himself in your estimation. But I felt the love in your letter that wanted to protect me from something you thought was a danger, and I appreciate it more than I can possibly tell you. I trust you, too, don't think that I don't. Of course there are such things as misunderstandings and mistakes in this world, and you know that my heart would hope there was some such explanation for what you saw or thought you saw, as you intimate in your letter. I know that you do not lightly speak real evil of anyone, even though you do not like them, and I know you would not have wanted to trouble me merely because you do not like Dana, so rest assured I shall feel that there is something that must be cleared up when I get back or Dana and I cannot be friends as we were before: Shall we just let the matter rest till I get home, dear? I've been learning to trust the Lord with my life, a lot more than I ever did before. I guess we can trust Him to this too. I'm glad I've got a wonderful brother anyway, and I hope I may be able to be just as good a sister to you as you are a brother to me."

Elim went out in the back yard and kicked the snow about and thought a lot about that letter. He could read between the lines that Lynn was feeling pretty bad. He wished he could do something about it. But he couldn't make Dana Whipple over, could he, not even if he were willing to, which he wasn't. Dana was a bad egg!

And up in a little Canadian lumber town, quite out of civilization as he considered it, Dana had chosen to hide himself and his humiliation, and was eating his heart out among the grandest scenery that ever a man could have for a background. The people to whom he almost contemptuously ministered on Sundays and Wednesday night prayer meeting were rough and crude in appearance but far his superiors in genuiness of character and strength of purpose, and might have taught him many a truth about the good old doctrines if he would have taken time to listen.

But Dana was only staying there to mark time. The New York elder was writing him again, saying the senior elder was on his way home, and soon they would be able to bring the matter of a call before the church, and he felt certain of the outcome if Mr. Whipple would only hold off from anything else for a little while. So Dana held off, for more reasons than one. He did not want the New York people to hear about his marriage until the matter of the call was a settled thing. And he did not want to bring Jessie Belle out into the open and introduce her as his wife until he had toned her down a bit and molded her into shape fit for a minister's wife. He had determined to show his mother and his grandmother that he had not done such a dreadful thing after all. That Jessis Belle had good stuff in her, and he could bring it out. If he was not fully convinced of this in his own heart, he yet so desired to convince others, that he felt he could do it in time.

But Jessie Belle, or Jessie as he now insisted on calling her to her utter disgust, did not take kindly to his teaching. She preferred to go her own willful brazen way. "Oh, rats!" she would answer to his lofty appeals. "What do I care for all that culture stuff? It don't get you anywhere. Oh a church mebbe, but I don't want a church and I don't want a preacher for a husband either. Religion is so long faced and gloomy. I want to have a good time. You know you don't believe all that bologny you hand 'em out every Sunday, Dana, and I'm not going any more to hear you either. What's more, I'm done with prancing around calling those old galloots. Old women that never saw a fashion magazine in the whole of their days, and think you're terrible if you wear your skirts short. It's none of their business how I wear my skirts, or how I talk and if I want to smoke I'll do it. I can't be tied up to your Grandmother's funny old ideas. You take that and swallow it. I didn't get married to hang around and study the catechism and I won't teach your dirty little kids in Sunday School nor try to act grown up and long faced either. If you cared anything about me at all you'd go out to Hollywood with me as I want you to. We'd both fit in there and have a wonderful time. I don't see what your grandfather has got to do with it. You know you don't believe a word you say on Sunday, and that's a fact."

Jessie Belle was not happy in the little backwoods town. She yearned for New York. She continually nagged Dana for new clothes, and to take her to the nearest town to the movies. She pleaded with him to take her to the dances, and when he refused on the ground that it was not the thing for a minister to do, that it would be as much as his position in the church was worth, especially at the present critical time, she stamped her foot and said she hated the old church and she hated him, and she wished she'd never seen him or his fussy old grandmother, and declared she would write to the New York church and spoil his prospects for him yet if he did not give her more money and show her a good time.

Dana was almost distracted.

This woman he had married was all and more than his mother and grandmother had warned him she would be. He could not mold her, he could not coax her, he could not do anything with her but endure her. For her physical attractions which had been all that had drawn him to her in the first place, had lost their charm for him. She was a lazy, selfish, spoiled woman who no longer cared to interest him, and who expected him to wait upon her. As Dana had always been lazy and spoiled himself things did not work out very well, and sometimes Ella Smith would come down from the hotel where she had got a position looking after linen, and creep in and set their house to rights. It was a sad state of things, and Dana grew more and more morbid. Only the hope of the New York call held him from utter desolation.

And then one day another letter came from the New York elder, apologetic, but cool. He was sorry, more than words could tell, that he had held up the young man so long. He had not expected things to turn out this way of course or he would not have presumed to tell him to wait. The senior elder had come home with his mind full of a wonderful preacher he had met in London. He had been approached before the senior elder had known of their interest in Mr. Whipple, but nothing had as yet been decided. He was enclosing his personal check for a hundred dollars which he hoped Mr. Whipple would accept as a slight token of his own appreciation of his work and in view of the fact that he had been kept so long waiting for the decision.

Dana's moral stamina collapsed under this blow, and Jessie Belle walked off alone to go to a dance that he had expressly forbidden her to attend. Things were getting worse and worse for Dana Whipple, and the end was not in sight.

So the winter wore away, and spring was upon the hills again, the blue ruin and the devil's paint brush, and the stars and gold of the daisy-and-buttercup broidery, and Lynette was coming home!

Her mother stood at the window one morning and sang the words to her heart, "My Lynnie is coming home." The little grandmother, a breath frailer than last year said it with a smile. Elim shouted it to his dog and went to get the fishing tackle ready. "Say, Snipe, Lynn's coming home!"

XXIII

GRANDMOTHER WHIPPLE had been slowly dying all winter. She did not seem to háve the strength to last from day to day. Her hands grew so frail that she could no longer hold the crutch under her arm, and her feeble knees would bend and give way. Twice she fell upon the floor when she tried to get up by herself, and Amelia and Justine were frightened at her gray look when they went to pick her up. After that she never tried to rise by herself, although she insisted on being put in her chair every morning. She would lie frail and grim against the pillows all day, only her bright keen old eyes as sharp as ever, seeing what ought to be done and directing, driving her slaves from morning to night although there was no need now for such intensive housekeeping with only the three to stir things up, and no young folks coming and going.

Amelia wrote to Dana that she thought he ought to come home, that his grandmother could not last long now, and he ought to make his peace with her, but Dana was proud. He would not go home till he had something to show for all his boasting. Grandmother had ordered him out of the house, had said she was done with him; very well now, let her send for him if she wanted him back. He would not come back till he could come with his head up and proudly as he used to come.

But Grandmother did not speak of Dana, and Amelia was afraid to excite her by doing so herself. The days slipped by and the old lady grew weaker till it seemed that a breath might blow her away.

Then, one morning, there was crêpe on the door, and the undertaker's car in front of the house.

Mary Brooke stood at the window and looked out across the way. She saw what had happened in the night and wondered what she ought to do. Would they consider it an intrusion if she went over?

So the frail old tyrant was gone! Gone with her heart broken by the grandson on whom she had counted! The pride of the house of Whipple, the descendant of the noble minister of God, hiding in the wilderness of Canada!

Mary Brooke finally called up, but met with such a sharp negative when she asked if there was anything that she could do—it was Justine who answered the telephone, and who seemed to resent her intrusion—that she merely sent down some flowers and let it go at that. It did seem strange at such a time to let petty differences come between households that had almost been united by one of the strongest ties that earth can weave. But the circumstances were peculiar.

Lynette was coming home the next day, too. And it would be Lynnie's birthday again, in two days more.

Would Dana be at the funeral? Would the two come in contact again? And what had become of Jessie Belle?

These questions troubled Mary Brooke until she went and laid them on her Burden Bearer, and sat down to wait for her child to return.

It would be hard for Lynette to have to go to a funeral the first thing. Perhaps it would be over before she landed. Boats were often delayed. Well, her girl was coming home after the long winter, and she felt that whatever came was going to be all right. The Father had somehow worked it out for her child's good. Perhaps Lynette would not feel it was necessary to go. Why would it be? An old person with whom she had had little to do?

But Lynette when she came looked grave.

"Oh, I would like to go, Mother. She was always

good to me. She used to like to have me come over
with flowers, or read to her. She enjoyed a good joke
too, and she used to tell me that none of the family had
a sense of humor, and it was a great lack. She thought I
had, and we used to laugh together over little things.
Oh, I think I would like to go to the service, and sort of
say good-by. I thought of her after I went away. I had an
impulse to write and say good-by or something, but
things were so mixed up that I didn't see my way clear
to do it, for Dana or his mother might have misunderstood, but now I wish I had. I think maybe it hurt her a
little that I went away without a word. It would. I will
just run over and say good-by. I would like to see her
face once more. It was a strong face I thought, and kind
of hungry for love. Not sweet like my Grandmother,
harder, but wistful."

And so it came about that Dana saw Lynette for the
first time since that night in the sunset, standing beside
his grandmother's coffin looking down into the rugged
old face that death had softened and dignified; and
there were tears upon her lashes.

He was startled at her beauty. He somehow had not
remembered how rare and fine she was. Getting used to
Jessie had taken the edge off from his memories. He
studied her without seeming to do so. Yes, she had
changed. She had acquired a certain something which
he used to call poise. He could see it in the very way
she entered the room, the way she stood and touched
the flowers, the way she smiled when someone gave her
a chair. In the Paris frock she wore, the chic little hat.

And he had thrown that girl away! Oh God, what a
fool he had been!

Through all the service he was watching her from
behind his slim white hand. There was the same sweet
serious brow, the lovely thoughtful eyes, the same gold
glint of hair, and upward curl of lashes, the delicate
complexion, an apple blossom pink—or was it wild
rose, or something still more delicate? How had he
been forgetting her all these months? How could he
ever have been attracted by Jessie Belle's rough skin,
coarsened by powder and paint, startling in its dead

white and carmine, when he had been used to this delicate lovely flower of a girl? Oh, well, he had been crazy, that was all. He had been crazy! And now he was
sane again. A man ought not to have to suffer forever
for a thing he had done when he was crazy.

The funeral service was long and deeply affecting,
for old Madame Whipple was well known and honored,
and came of a family who had been active in the
church and community; and tyrant though she had
been, they loved her in a way, and respected the things
that she always stood for, even though they thought her
hard and queer.

So there was much palaver about her family and her
husband, and the long and useful life she had lived. But
Dana heard little of it because he was watching Lynette. He scarcely noticed that no one mentioned him,
save in the prayer when the officiating clergy man
prayed for the bereaved friends, and mentioned the
daughter-in-law and grandson by name. That was all.
No mention of the brilliant descendant who was to carry on and follow in the footsteps of his noted grandfather, no mention of his prospects and attainments.
Dana would have figured largely in such a service as
this a year ago, for the town had been proud of him,
and was looking to him in a way to make the town
more famous, put it upon the theological map as it
were. But now Dana was wiped out. His reputation was
in question, his future a blank. He sat in the shadow
with his mother and Justine, and watched the girl he
might have married. He was nothing more than a figure, one of the mourners. How strange that such a
thing could happen to *him* in such a short time! And
back up there in Canada was Jessie Belle, *his wife!*
And here was Lynette, his Lynette, who was his no
longer!

People spoke afterwards of how sad Dana looked.
"He must have loved his grandmother a lot," they
said to one another as they walked away from the
house in the late afternoon sunlight. "I suppose it was
hard on him to have his grandmother send him off."
For somehow they had surmised that Dana had been

sent away or he never would have gone. And they
looked at Lynette as she walked sweetly by her mother
up the hill ahead of them, and wondered. Had Lynette
done this, or had Dana, or who? And what had been
done anyway? The town was not even sure yet whether
the story of Dana's marriage was false or true.

But there was a thunder shock the next day when the
news went forth that old Madame Whipple had left the
bulk of her estate to Lynette Brooke!

Amelia had the house and a comfortable income,
enough to keep her quietly, but not enough to support
Dana. Justine was given a small competency, with the
proviso that she live elsewhere. The remainder was all
Lynette's.

To Dana there had been handed an eveloped con-
taining a one hundred dollar bill and a Bible verse written in Grandma Whipple's cramped old hand. When
Dana opened it he read:

"Seest thou a man wise in his own conceit? There is
more hope of a fool than of him."

Dana's fury was beyond all expression. He simply
froze.

He spent a thunderous half hour alone with the lawyer trying to find some way of breaking the will, prov-
ing that his grandmother was out of her mind, or that
there was another later will, or something of the sort;
but when he became convinced that he had no chance,
he seemed to congeal like cold metal. He did not talk
the matter over with his mother, he brushed Justine
aside contemptuously when she attempted a word of
sympathy that he had been cut off penniless, and he
did not go near Lynette. He packed his bag and took
the next train back to Canada. It was up to Lynette
now, and of course she would come across and hand
him back his own. He could not think of Lynette as
keeping the heritage which she had always known was
his. Lynette was honest even if she had been exceedingly narrow. Lynette would hand it back of course. It was
only one of Grandma Whipple's crude old jokes. They
would both understand that, and as such he could receive it back without feeling any qualms. But he would

receive it proudly, as if he had not expected it of course. He could not go and talk to Lynette about it, for there was Jessie Belle! He would have to tell her about Jessie Belle. It was an awkward situation take it any way you would. And Grandma had known it would be. That was why she had selected Lynette, of course, instead of his mother. Now if it had been left to Mother, why of course it would have been the same as his, a little awkward perhaps to arrange the transfer, but he could have told his mother what to do and she would have done it. No, his grandmother had meant to mortify him, or else she was trying to make him break with Jessie Belle and go back to Lynette. Could it be possible that Grandma had some such subtle suggestion back of her act? That she was trying to let him know that she would be willing for such a thing? The thought was interesting. He put it away for a time of need, and went on with his other line of reasoning. Yes, of course, Lynette would give back the property. But it was going to be most awkward. He almost hated his grandmother to have given him this last ugly thrust in her death. To think a woman about to do such a solemn thing as to die, should be willing to hurt her cherished grandson of whom she had seemed to be so proud. He wouldn't have believed it of his grandmother. And that ugly Bible verse, too. He could almost hear her voice cackling with the old-time mirth, see her twinkling little eyes watching his face as he read it. Grandma had to have her joke even in her death! The old tyrant! The old wicked tyrant!

He said it under his breath, and felt better. Back in Canada he would wait for Lynette to do her part. It would not be many days. Lynette always did her duty promptly.

But two long weeks went by, in the which he haunted the post office at all hours, and was so unbearably cross at home that Jessie Belle took herself away to the hotel to visit her mother. And still no word came from Lynette. He had not told Jessie Belle that the inheritance was not his after all, for she had been counting on it. Unknown to him she had spent a lot of money on clothes and even a few cheap jewels. She knew the bills would be coming in pretty soon, and she was just as glad to be away when they arrived. Dana was not pleasant to live with when he was in that mood. She would stay away until the bills were well out of the way and Dana had forgotten them. There was no need for him to be so close any more, now that he had plenty of money. She would let him understand that right away. She wasn't going to skimp any longer.

In due time the bills arrived, and in a towering rage Dana went in search of Jessie Belle. The altercation that ensued made plain to both of them how utterly of separate worlds they were.

Jessie Belle flung her small contempt at him for being close, and said she wouldn't stand for it now that he had plenty of money. Dana told her a good many kinds of things she was and was not, and when she only laughed, in cold hate he told her that the money had not been left to him. He did not tell her where it had been diverted. That would have been too deep a humiliation, but afterward Jessie Belle wrote to Justine and of course got the whole story.

Dana stood haughtily in his mother-in-law's tiny fourth-story back bedroom, and delivered his last thrust to the girl who had married him because he was rich.

"Oh hen!" said Jessie Belle with a sudden pause in her gay contempt. "What an old devil she was!"

Then after a moment's thought:

"Well, that settles it! You've gotta quit this religious stuff. It'll never pay! You and I gotta start for Hollywood this week and get a *real* job, or I'm done. You're losing all your good looks mooning around like this, and it's time I did something about it. You go back and sell the furniture. That'll pay our way out. The bills! Oh, heck! *Ferget* the bills."

Dana went out from that interview humiliated, furious, and convinced that he and Jessie Belle could never make it go. He was done with Jessie Belle!

He told himself that several times on the way back to his desolate house, where soiled dishes and Jessie Belle's possessions held high sway. He sat down amid the débris and groaned aloud. He was tired and sick, and he was hungry. He was actually *hungry*. The story of the prodigal son came vividly to him. Even husks might have tasted good. He realized with a wave of horror that he had come to a place like that. He, the great Dana Whipple, with all his pleasant prospects, and sturdy ancestors! He was down and out! He hadn't but a dollar and seventeen cents in his pocket and there were all those bills! It would be two months before his next quarter's meagre salary was due, and how was he to live? Put Jessie Belle out of the question. How was *he* to live? Through his fevered brain ran a phrase from the parable, "And when he had spent all!" And when he had spent all! He flung the change from his pocket out upon the table and said it aloud and laughed a hard dry cackle, startlingly reminding him of his Grandmother Whipple, and then he dropped his face upon his arms on the table among the fluttering bills, and groaned aloud. But he did not remember what the prodigal did in like situation. "I will arise and go to my Father." Repentance was one of the things that did not belong in his new creed. It was unnecessary, because he no longer considered the possibility of sin. It belonged in the portions of the Bible that had been cut out and relegated to the dead past.

The next morning brought a letter from his mother. It enclosed a check for five hundred dollars.

"Lynette has insisted on giving all the property to me," she wrote casually as if it were not the most momentous business in the world. As if his very life did not hang on the words. He breathed a sigh of deep relief as he saw the check, and read the opening sentence over again. But why to his mother? Why not to him? But still, perhaps that was Lynette's revenge. She knew, too, that he would get it all if it went to his mother of course, only there would be the nuisance of the transfer, and Mother perhaps arguing a little about what he ought to do with it now and then. Still, it was good that Lynette had acted at last. He had known she would of course. Why had she been so long? He went back to the letter for further information.

"She went right to the lawyer the minute she knew it and had the papers made out, never even waited to tell her folks at home, never said a word to me till it was all done and registered and everything, and the lawyer came to me and gave me the papers.

"I went right over there of course as soon as I knew and told her I wouldn't have it. I told her Grandma loved her, and so do I—and that I was sure from things she had said that she was terribly disappointed that something seemed to have come between her and you, Dana."

Dana winced and drew down his brows at that, but went on reading—"and I said I couldn't think of taking the money when Grandma wanted her to have it. But Lynette just put her foot down and said she wouldn't touch a cent of it, that it belonged in the family and must stay there. And she was so sweet and nice about it that she made me feel it was all right. So I've taken it. I think you ought to write her a letter and thank her. You didn't treat her right, Dana, you know.

"I'm sending you five hundred dollars, because I feel you should have something, just now when you are having a hard time. Of course I know Grandma put the money out of my hands because she felt you needed to go through some discipline. She used to talk to me about it. I never dreamed she was going to divert the property, but now I can see she was trying to make me understand. She said if you ever got prosperous and had a lot of money it would ruin you. She was afraid you would lose your soul. Then, too, she hated Jessie Belle and I know she didn't want her to get any of the money. And I wouldn't feel right about giving you much, on account of what Grandma said. It was hers and she had a right to leave it as she did. Of course I shall leave it to you when I die, but perhaps you'll be a stronger man by that time. And anyhow I think Grandma knew that Lynette would do the right thing. Now, Dana, do try to get along plainly, and simply, and get Jessie Belle to settle down. Things will come out better for you some day if you work hard in your present parish and try to do right. God takes care of His own children, and you were dedicated to God you know."

Dana cast his mother's letter aside with a contemptuous exclamation, the last few lines still unread, and snatching up the check went out to put it in the bank and pay some of those awful bills.

So his mother was going to try to cut him out of the money too! His own mother! Well, she couldn't get away with that. He would pay the bills, and sell the things, and pack up Jessie Belle's clothes and send them to her, and then he was going home to settle Mother. That was only a little reaction from her long years of servitude under a tyrant. But he would soon make her see that he must have his rights.

So Dana paid his bills, sold his furniture, packed his things, resigned his charge, sent Jessie Belle's trunk to her the last thing, and started home again. He thought he was the prodigal going home for the fatted calf, but he still had not the talismanic words upon his lips. He had no idea in his soul of saying: "I have sinned against heaven and am no more worthy to be called thy child!" He almost felt that he was conferring a favor upon the Almighty by thus coming back and being willing to straighten everything else out and begin over again. He even cherished hopes yet of that New York church, after they were done following around hearing dumb Englishmen and realized that Dana Whipple was the only brilliant pulpit star still available in the universe. Let Jessie Belle go to her Hollywood if she wanted to. Nobody outside the family knew that he was married, only those people up in Canada. The world was too big to keep track of one man's deeds, and anyhow New York wasn't narrow. He could pose as a young unmarried preacher without telling any lies whatever, and if Jessie Belle made any trouble later everybody would pity the sad handsome preacher whose wife had left him, who was so faithful to his work—so eloquent, and who had walked so circumspectly in their midst. Then, sometime, surely, something would happen, things would straighten out—God wouldn't let his

future be utterly ruined by one mistake—and he could
marry Lynette after all.

Of course Lynette would be only too glad to forgive
and receive him back!

So Dana went home almost at peace with himself
again, having reconstructed his whole life with five
hundred dollars and a little brilliant soul hedging.

XXIV

LYNETTE was telling all about her wonderful trip.

The first trying days filled with the funeral and that awful will and its adjusting were over, and everything settled. Now they could talk in peace. They all felt as if a terrible scourge had passed over them, and held them in its grip for a few days, with a kind of threatening blight. But now that it was gone, and they all were safe, and everything was moving right.

True, there was over their dear Lynette, a grave sweet maturity that almost troubled them. They could not help but feel that she still was suffering from Dana's attitude.

But she said nothing about it, never seemed to brood or be gloomy and they drew long breaths of relief when the matter of the property was all settled up and out of Lynette's way. Grandmother Rutherford said to her daughter in the privacy of her own room with locked doors that it wasn't at all delicate of Grandmother Whipple to have done such a thing and brought Lynnie into the public eye in that way. It wasn't delicate! That was as near as Grandmother Rutherford would come to criticizing her rugged old dead neighbor.

So they sat themselves down one happy morning to hear all about the trip.

Of course they had heard bits before, but now they were to hear the special things, and Lynette was going to begin at the beginning and make a regular serial story out of it for the benefit of the family. Elim had given

up a baseball game with Spud and the rest to stay home
and hear it. Elim was seated by the dining-room table
whittling away at the model of a ship he was making. It
was almost completed. He had been working at it all
winter for Lynette's birthday present, and there were
just a few little finishing touches to be put on it. It really was a masterpiece, a copy of some rare old picture
that had fallen into his hands. Lynette was delighted
with it.

Grandma was seated by the window mending a bit of
fine linen with infinitesimal stiches, her sweet old face
wearing a light of utter joy and satisfaction. Mary
Brooke was beating softly away at the whites of eggs
for the birthday cake, the yellow bowl in the lap of her
big blue linen kitchen apron, beating carefully so as not
to miss a word of the story. Lynette was mending a
dress she wanted to put on, the same little blue dress
she had worn last year. Her grandmother had asked for
it again because Lynette looked so pretty in it.

They had heard the preliminaries of the first day out,
and Lynette had come to the stranger who stood beside
her in the starlight and told her such wonderful things
of the heavens.

"Gee!" said Elim pausing in his work of adjusting a
cord on a mast, and looked up. "I never heard of that
before. The names of the stars, and they are all in the
order of the things that happened? You say you
brought home that book? Gee, I'd like to read that!"

Lynette went on to tell how the stranger had
preached on shipboard, giving bits of the wonderful
sermon, and telling what people had said to him afterwards, imitating their voices in her own inimitable way,
telling how Dorothy had been crazy over him and
called him "Plush Eyes," but how his name was really
Alec Douglas.

"Why, yes, I've heard of him," said Mary Brooke.
"There's often a quotation from one of his sermons in
the religious papers. You remember, Mother, I read it
to you last Sunday. Why, Lynnie, he's over in this
country now, isn't he? I think that was the name. They
said he was to preach in one of the New York churches

soon, the whole month of June, or July, I forgot which. Let me see, which church was it?"

She named a church and Lynette looked up startled. Wasn't that the church that Dana had been so sure he could have for the taking?

"Yes, he's over here," she answered. "He came back on the same ship with us again. Wasn't that strange? And we saw him quite a little, his steamer chair wasn't far away from ours. He is a wonderful man. It was a privilege to talk with him. I shall never forget the things he said."

Mary Brooke gave her child a keen furtive glance and went on beating her frosting.

"You know I heard him preach again, in London. Yes, Dorothy and I happened to see in the paper that he was going to preach. We hadn't known just which his church was before that, and anyway we had just arrived there. So we went to church. It was the first time that I had ever been able to get Dorothy to go to church willingly. She hated it. So we went. And mother, it was even greater than the sermon on shipboard. He told such wonderful things about our privilege of victory through Christ. It was all a kind of continuation of the other sermon we had heard, all based on the condition of having died with Christ, that we might also live with Him. The text was: 'That I may know Him, and the power of His resurrection, and the fellowship of His sufferings, being made conformable unto His death, if by any means I might attain unto the resurrection of the dead.'

"It was a new thought to me that we might be having fellowship with Christ through suffering."

Mary Brooke looked up with a light in her eyes and nodded understandingly.

A look of quiet peace settled over Grandma Rutherford's sweet lips and gentle brow. Lynnie was safe. Lynnie had passed through the fire, and understood the way of peace!

Then suddenly Elim shoved back his chair harshly, and jumped up, his face expressing utter disgust:

"Good Night! There comes that dirty sucker!" he

said in a low ugly tone. "Lynnie, don't you ferget what
I told you. Say, you don't needta see him, do ya? Gee,
I'd go out an wallop him fer a cent! I'll go to the door!
Want me to, Lynnie?"

Lynette had dropped her sewing and looked out of
the window. There was Dana coming up the walk, with
almost his old gay swing. There was nothing dejected
about Dana.

Mary Brooke set the yellow bowl down on the table,
and stood looking at Dana, her eyes wide, a piteous
yearning expression on her face. And just when they
were all so happy, too! Why couldn't Dana stay where
he belonged? It surely wasn't here.

Grandmother looked out of the window, and paused
in her fine linen stitches, looked, and then remembered.
No, Lynnie would be kept. They needn't worry. Lynnie
had found higher ground than even Dana could pre-
sume to reach.

It was Lynette herself who arose to the occasion:
"Thank you, Elim, but I'll have to see him myself."

There was that about her tone that gave the excited
boy confidence in her.

"Well," he hesitated, "if you think you gotta, but—
Lynnie, I'll be right here at the back door. You just
whistle if you need me!"

Lynette gave him a quick smile of gratitude and reassurance and passed out of the room, slipping quickly
up the stairs. It was Mary Brooke who opened the door
for Dana, and ushered him formally into the parlor, a
thing that he couldn't remember ever to have happened
to him before in that house. He had always entered
freely wherever the family were sitting, even if it was
the kitchen.

She left him there and went to call her daughter.
There was a grave dignity about her that put a silence
to the gay greeting Dana had summoned to his lips. But
Dana was quick to adjust himself to the circumstances.
He entered with a grace of dignity all his own, as one
who has passed honorably through heavy chastening.
Dana had a way of placing his own blame on other
shoulders, just by his graceful manner.

Lynette entered presently, with a grave constraint upon her, and shook hands with Dana as if he had been a playmate of childhood very, very long ago.

"Lynette, I've come back!" he announced with his disarming manner. He grasped her hand and held it in a warm clasp.

Lynette disengaged her hand gently and stepped back a trifle, her chin slightly lifted, her eyes upon him, questioningly.

"Yes?" she said gently, "I know it's been very hard for you. You were very fond of your grandmother." There was genuine sympathy in her voice.

He waved his hand impatiently.

"Of course," he said almost brusquely. "But that's not the point. Lynn, I've come *back!*"

Lynette stepped back to a chair and motioned him to another.

"Sit down, Dana," she said gravely. "Just what do you mean? Come back to stay? Do you mean——? You've not given up your church have you? Your mother said you were preaching somewhere up in Canada."

"Oh, I'm not talking of such things. Don't you understand, Lynn, I've come back to *you.* I've come to throw myself on your mercy!"

"Dana!" she exclaimed in a troubled voice. "How? What do you mean?"

She thought he must be somehow thinking of the money, yet she could not see the connection.

"I mean," said Dana desperately, "that you are mine. Why, you've always been mine! I love you and I can't do without you. I thought when I came home that I was going to be able to wait until things got straightened out to tell you this, but now that I see you, looking so beautiful and so like yourself, only sweeter, much sweeter, I can't wait. I've had your image in my heart ever since I saw you at the funeral sitting beside my grandmother, looking like an angel. Lynn, you're *wonderful!*"

Lynette was very still, and white. She sat looking at

him in amazement. For a moment she could not summon words to her lips.

"But Dana," she said, wondering why his declaration of love had not given her the joy it would have done months ago. "No, sit still, please. There are some things that must be explained, and—there are——"

"Yes, I know Lynn. I'm coming to it all. I know you were sore about my forgetting your birthday, but I was so annoyed at being deviled over at the house about those people coming that I forgot everything. And then, that girl—Lynn, she was the limit! She made a perfect fool out of me. Of course I shouldn't have let her, but I was so upset about your going off that way without a word, just that nasty little crack about poise. You didn't seem to know that all I said was meant for your good."

Lynette felt a cold clutch settling about her throat and tightening so that it was hard to speak, but she wanted to control herself. Somehow she was seeing Dana in a light she had never seen him before, and he seemed weak—weak and childish.

"Do you mean, Dana, that you—made love to that girl that you brought over here that evening?"

Dana looked down at his shoes uncomfortably. "Yes —it amounts to that!" he answered still looking down. "But," he added eagerly, "I think I can get out of it. I'm sure I can, without any trouble. I think she is sick of it, too."

The cold clutch went on down and gripped Lynette's heart. What was this she was hearing?

"Do you mean that you are in some way bound to her?" she asked in a steady little voice that sounded very far away from herself. She began to wonder if she was hearing aright. Was Dana really saying all this, or was she dreaming?

There was a long silence. Somehow Lynette did not seem able to break it. She continued looking at Dana, the broad shoulders, the sleek well-set head. The same Dana her heart had cherished, the lover she had brooded over and prayed for all these months. Dana, saying things like that! It seemed in the nature of a confession, and yet he did not seem particularly sorry, only annoyed that he had been led into a breach of etiquette as it were. She saw everything with startling clearness now as she sat and waited for him to speak. Why had she never felt that way about him before? Was she still bitter at him?

At last he spoke, looking up with a kind of charming defiance.

"Yes, I married her!" he said, almost a smile upon his lips. "Of course I shouldn't have, but she made such a devilish fuss, and I didn't see any way out then. It really seemed as if I had to."

"You married her!" said Lynette, looking at him steadily, and rising to her feet, a new strength suddenly coming to her. "Is that what you are asking me to forgive you for?"

Her tones were hard, keen, like a knife going through him. He had not known that she could be so cold.

"Why, yes, Lynn. I shouldn't have done it I know, it was all a great mistake. She is not the kind of girl I could ever love. I have never loved anybody but you. Listen, Lynn, now don't get up in the air and go out of the room before I finish. You don't understand. You always did go off half cocked. Sit down now, and let me explain."

"There can be no explanation, Dana. You have no right to talk to me of love. You are a married man. It is too late to tell me that you love me. You belong to someone else."

"But that's just it, Lynn, I never did belong to her in the sense of loving her. She cast a glamour over me for a while, and when she got me right where she wanted me she threatened to tell everybody how intimate we had been, she threatened to—well, she would have played havoc with my prospects in New York. She had wormed out of me where I was going to preach, and she threatened to send them word of all sorts of impossible things about me. It was really blackmail of the worst kind. She demanded that I marry her at once. And—well—I was desperate, and I thought I had to. It was terrible to me to think of my family, and my professors and everybody hearing all those terrible lies about me."

"Dana, if they were lies they would not have mattered. The truth would have come out in the end!"

She looked straight through him as if she was reading the truth from his heart, and the slow color stole into his lean cheeks, and showed up the dark circles under his eyes. Dana had been suffering. That was plainly to be seen.

"Well," he hedged uneasily, "I was crazed. I couldn't use my usual judgment, and I married her!"

He flung the statement at her with his old defiance, and she did not answer, only looked at him steadily, sadly, as if she had suddenly grown years wiser than himself.

"But I do not understand," she said at last. "What is it that you a married man are asking of me? If it is forgiveness for having been disloyal to the love you say you had for me, you have it, my full free forgiveness."

Dana rose and stood beside her eagerly.

"It is more than forgiveness, Lynn, it is your love back again that I want. Your love and your trust. I cannot live without you. I have found that out during these terrible months!"

He tried to take her hands, but she withdrew them.

"No, Dana, don't touch me! You do not know what you are saying. It is too late to talk of love. You have no right to do that now. You belong to someone else. It is an insult to me and to your wife to speak of love to me now."

"You do not understand, Lynn! I am not insulting you, I am offering my purest love. I tell you I never wanted to marry Jessie Belle. I shall have no trouble with her. She is tired of me, and restless to get out to Hollywood and get into the movies. I could work it so she would have a good salary and be perfectly happy, and in time she would marry someone else. Thank God we live in a day when it is not a disgrace to get a divorce. Of course my grandmother was old fashioned, but people nowadays don't think a thing of it. Why the

New York church have heard about you, Lynn, and that was one of the reasons why they wanted me, some-one who knew your father years ago heard that we were engaged, and that was how I came to get the chance to preach there. It is hanging fire, now, because some old fusty from London has to be heard first be-fore they can give me the actual call, but if they knew we were to be married in a year's time, say, that would turn the trick all right. And I could begin life in earn-est. If you say the word I'll make all arrangements with Jessie and start proceedings for a divorce at once. Mother will finance it, I'm positive, and Jessie will be overjoyed to go to Hollywood at once. It can be done quietly you know. Scarcely anybody knows we were ever married. I took care of that."

"Stop! Dana!"

The words came out at last from lips that seemed stiff with agony.

Lynette was standing straight and slim and white by the door, her hands clasped, her fingers gripping till the knuckles showed white. Her face was so pale and her eyes so bright that she seemed like a beautiful spirit, an avenging angel.

"Dana, there can be no talk of divorce and marriage between you and me, ever," she said in a clear intense voice. "It is a sin! You and I are children of God. We do not belong to the world. It is a sin!"

Dana swung around angrily and paced the room back and forth.

"There you go," he broke forth, "condemning me wholesale when you don't know a thing about it. You don't know the circumstances. You just swing a whole-sale verdict, it is sin! What is sin, anyway? That's a bo-gey of the past. We don't push people back into hell nowadays and condemn them to worse than death the rest of their days because they have transgressed some mid-victorian view of hidebound laws. There certainly is more sin in living with someone you don't love than in breaking a ridiculous law that was made in the dark ages! I have no patience with these people who insist on living in the past. If the Bible were written today

you would find it to be a very different book. We are
not so gullible as they were in the days of the patri-
archs."

"Dana! God is the same, yesterday, today and forever! There couldn't be any change in the Bible because
He said that one jot or one tittle, just the little things
like the crossing of a *t* or the dotting of an *i*, should
never be changed until all was fulfilled."

"Oh, fulfilled! fulfilled!" he raved. "Don't go to
talking about prophecy to me. Don't be a fool. I have
no patience with the people who try to drag the Old
Testament into the New, and try to drag out separate
statements and apply them miscellaneously to their
lives regardless of circumstances. You have more sense
than that, Lynn, and when we get this thing straightened out and I can have time to sit down and teach
you, you will understand how narrow and confining all
those little musty ideas are you have imbibed. The Bible is a wonderful piece of literature of course, we must
not discount that, but there are many parts that are not
to be taken as anything but fanciful imaginings."

"Dana, please stop! I cannot listen to you. You are
beside yourself!"

"No, I'm not beside myself. I've had a good many
months to think all this over and get calm, haven't I?
And I say that if Jesus were here on earth today He
would probably talk quite differently about divorce
and a great many other things. We are not under law
any more. He came to put away law and give us love
for one another. He wouldn't want you and me to walk
apart all our lives when we love one another."

Lynette broke in with cool quiet tones that commanded his attention.

"Dana, you know perfectly well that what Jesus
Christ said about divorce is true. He said that even the
thought in the heart was impure when one belonged to
another. And look at the way he spoke to the woman at
the well. He said, 'He whom thou now hast is not thy
husband.' You remember how she felt. His look must
have gone through her heart with condemnation, when

she went into the village and said: 'Come see the Man that told me all that ever I did!' Dana, you could never be happy doing a thing like that. You don't realize what you are saying now, you are all wrought up. But you would be feeling the eyes of God upon you continually! The eyes that see all that ever we do!"

Dana's lip curled and he whirled on his heel again with his old impatient motion.

"There you go again," he said angrily. "That story's all wrong too. He never meant that. For how could He possibly know all that ever she did? He had no possible means of knowing all that ever she did. Oh, of course He might have heard some gossip about her as He came through the village, but that was all. He was just talking on general principles! That is the danger of people who are not students trying to interpret the scriptures. They are always trying to drag in the supernatural where it doesn't belong. It is a species of sentimentality! Now I can explain——"

But Lynette was interrupting him again:

"Dana, you must stop this. I cannot listen to another word of blasphemy about my Lord. If Jesus Christ did not know the thoughts and acts of the human heart He would not be the Son of God, the Saviour of the world. He is my Saviour, the Son of the living God, and I cannot let you insult Him in my presence. Once for all, I do not believe in divorce and remarriage because it is *wrong*! Not because your grandmother or mine or the town might or might not approve! Not because any New York church might wink at it. But because it is against God's law.

"But Dana, if you were free as air, and if you had never seen any other girl or showed anyone any attentions, I could never marry you. Can two walk together except they be agreed? We haven't any common ground to stand on. You have questioned my Bible which has come to be to me the guide to Heaven, the light of my daily path, and you have discounted my Lord, and we could never agree. You are not the same one whom I used to love!"

"There you go quoting the Bible again," snapped out Dana furiously. "You never loved me or you would not talk this way."

"Perhaps not," said Lynette sadly. "At least we have no common ground to stand on now. My Bible and my Lord are the greatest things in life to me now."

"And you would rather see me go to ruin than throw aside some of your narrow minded prejudices!"

"It is not necessary for you to go to ruin, Dana. The Saviour is always ready to help you if you will go to Him. But you have made it impossible for me to do anything for you except to pray. I will do that, gladly. You may have to go down into the valley of death, but if you will do that He will show you the power of His Resurrection, and put you on a new plane of life with Him!"

"Don't preach!" said Dana sharply, looking with eyes of anguish at the earnest face of the girl he had lost. "Oh, Lynn! I am so miserable without you! Won't you put all your hardness away and let us find a way out, somehow?"

He came suddenly closer and put out his arms. He would have taken her in them if she had not with a swift movement flung open the door into the hall.

"I am sorry, Dana," she said in a voice that a strong mother might have used, "but this is the only way out!" Then lifting her voice a trifle she called, "Elim! Did you call me?"

Dana lifted his haggard face to see Elim standing young and tall and forbidding just outside the door.

"Did you want me, Lynn?" he asked, but he did not take his challenging eyes from Dana's face.

"Yes," said Lynette, "I want you to show Dana the lovely ship you have made me for my birthday."

But Dana was gone, out the front door, down the walk, out of the gate, his shoulders sagging, his hat pulled over his eyes, his whole graceful body expressing utter failure, dejection, fury with his lot.

He almost collided with a stranger who was walking down the street, looking intently at the house, and did not see him till just as they faced one another.

Dana, his eyes full of anger, at this interruption, faced the man with the attitude of one who demanded an explanation for such interference, and for one long instant they looked into one another's eyes, the dark angry eyes, and the deep blue ones. The stranger was tall also, with finely chiseled features, and a look of knowing mien. He gave that long keen glance, and lifting his hat courteously passed on, looking once more intently toward the house, but he did not go in.

Dana, hardly knowing what he was doing, walked on and on up the road where he and Lynette had gone a year ago, not even aware that it was the anniversary, knowing only that he had fought his battle and lost, and that now he must walk, walk, walk, out of the world somewhere and never come back. He was not ready to face the cross. He was angry that there was a cross. His eyes were holden that he could not see.

He came at last to the little sanctuary on the mountain, sacred to the memory of Lynette and the years of their friendship, but desecrated by the memory of Jessie Belle.

It had been natural for his feet to walk that way without direction, it was as natural now for them to falter as the memories suddenly rose to torment him and accuse him, and he stumbled in and sank down groaning aloud.

Off in the distance the blue ruin blossomed lushly, and made soft incense rise against the rocky mountainside. Dana presently stood up and looked across unseeingly and moaned to himself in bitter agony, "Ruin! Ruin! Ruin! My life is gone to Ruin!"

"And now," thought he, when the darkness came down about him, and hunger was driving him home, "now there is nothing left but Hollywood, unless I can manage to make that New York church, and pull myself up. Pull *Myself* up alone!"

That was how he thought to do it, *himself alone!*

XXV

MRS. BROOKE had hastened lunch, and set the table with care, her heart praying while she did it. Grandma sat perfectly quiet taking her little linen stitches and praying too. Elim took his ship model from the table and put it away elaborately, hovering not far from the parlor door, keeping busy and keeping within call, Elim was not praying. He was doing the things a boy does in his heart when he is too shy to pray and is very, very mad.

Mrs. Brooke had felt that she must be prepared for whatever came. If this was a reconciliation, or even a beginning of that most delicate situation she must ask Dana to stay to lunch. So she made delicate little popovers, the kind Dana used to like, and got out the last glass of raspberry jam. If Lynette willed to take Dana back again into her life she would make the way as smooth as might be. No word or act or look of her mother's should reproach the boy whose face told that he had walked a rough dark way since last he was there. Still she prayed, and suddenly the rumors that had been afloat about him, the memory of the painted girl who had gone about with him, began to come to mind, and she shrank inexpressibly from the moment when that parlor door would open and the two would come forth, together or apart, to face the future.

She had a few terror-stricken moments when she blamed herself that she had not sifted down those rumors and found out just how much truth there was to

274

them. She had a wild idea that perhaps she ought to rush forth into the village and gather them up and trace them down to their source, now before that parlor door opened and it might be forever too late. And then she remembered and went on praying. It was too late now to do anything else.

Then at last the door was swung open and there came that clear call. It was not the voice of surrender, nor was it the voice of one whose cup of joy had been suddenly filled. It was a clear self-controlled voice of one who knew no weak illusions, and who was strong to order her life as God would have her do. Just that voice made Mary Brooke murmur softly as she passed her mother's chair:

"Thank God!" and Grandma Rutherford looked up and smiled.

"You didn't need to worry, Mary. Lynnie belongs to the Lord. He won't let her make a mistake."

Then Dana walked out and down the walk and disappeared out of their sight.

They ate that beautiful lunch together in a kind of holy union with one another. It was as if some great danger had paused at their door, and then gone drifting on. They spoke to one another with pleasant voices as people do who have escaped and come out into a surprising relief. They did not talk about the caller. They did not ask Lynette any questions. They just enjoyed the moment together, and noted awesomely that Lynette, though very quiet, did not look unhappy. It seemed more as if she too had dropped a burden that had long been upon her shoulders.

It was just as the close of the meal that she told them. In a quiet little voice as if she hardly had got used yet to the fact, but as if it would solve all their problems.

"Mother, Dana has married that girl that was here last summer! He came to tell me!"

Mary Brooke looked startled but she answered quietly enough:

"I wondered, Lynnie, there were rumors going around you know. Poor Dana! She didn't look the right sort. I'm afraid he had made a sorry mess of his life!"

"Yes," said Lynette looking up with a sad little smile, "he needs our prayers. The worst of it is, Mother, he doesn't seem to have any faith in God or the Bible to help him out!"

"Poor Dana!" said Mary Brooke, with a song of rejoicing in her heart that it was not "poor Lynnie" also, for Lynette was not like a girl who had received a sudden death blow. She was calm and sweet and almost placid as she looked up at them.

"Poor Dana!"

"The sucker!" said Elim frowning. "The dirty Sucker! He never did have any!"

But before they could reprove him there came a quick ring at the door.

"Good-night!" said Elim furiously. "Can't we have any peace? On Lynnie's birthday, I ask you, can't we have any peace? Has that poor fish come back? Here, Lynn, let me handle him!"

But Lynette arose from the table a stern look upon her face and went out into the hall shutting the door behind her.

"Aw Gee!" said Elim sinking back into his chair. "Aw Gee! Isn't that the limit? Now I suppose he'll stay all the afternoon and Lynn'll come back looking like two ghosts."

"Don't worry, Elim! I think it will be all right!" said his mother, though a trifle anxious. "Lynnie will know what to do."

"Everything will be all right," said Grandma placidly. "You see! Lynnie belongs to the Lord. She is shut into the hollow of His hand. Nothing can touch her to harm her any more!"

Elim blinked doubtfully.

They listened while the door was opened, heard a voice, a strange voice, heard Lynette's greeting, eager, wondering, joyous. They looked at one another in wonder. What could it mean? Who could it be?

They had gone into the parlor again, whoever it was. It did not sound like Dana's voice. And Lynette never would have greeted him in that tone, now, knowing all she knew. Who was it?

But in the parlor the two who sat and looked into each other's eyes and said the pleasant greetings that people who have not seen each other for some days usually say, were utterly oblivious of anything but their two selves.

"I hope you will forgive me. I had to come," said the tall stranger with the deep blue eyes. "I had to know what kind of a man it was that made the hurt look in your eyes. I've been hanging around for two days to see if I could place him. I think I saw him coming out the gate about an hour ago"—he called it "aboot"—"Am I mistaken?"

"Oh!" said Lynette, her eyes quite bright, the color rushing in waves to her cheeks, "How could you know?" Her voice was wondering, but not offended.

"I knew because I love you," answered the voice with the burr on the curl of the words. "If he had been all right, if he had been the kind of a man who could have taken the pain out of your eyes I should have gone on my way without calling, and left you to your joy. But when I saw him I felt somehow that I must come. Am I intruding?"

"No," said Lynette. "Oh no!" and her eyes told him more than her lips.

"Then will you come over here on this couch and sit beside me, and may I tell you how I have loved you since ever I saw you come on board the boat? Or am I too precipitate?"

She came, and he told her, in words that transcended all she had ever dreamed that such a tale should be. How tame and flat seemed all else in her life that had preceded this hour!

Two hours later Lynette came suddenly to herself. She had heard the clink of silver and glass, and realized that they still lived in a world where people ate, and that the family were awaiting her return disconsolately.

"Oh, but I must tell Mother and Elim and Grandmother!" she cried starting away from the arms that were about her.

"Why, yes," said the tall stranger. "Quite so! We should have thought of that before! How selfish we have been! And fancy having all those dear people! I have only an old aunt in Scotland, you know. Some day I must take you over to see her, my darling!"

She led him into the dining-room without waiting to announce him, a Lynette whose face was aflame with a holy joy, and who had no idea that she was flustering them all, from the quiet grandmother who had sat putting in her linen stitches all the afternoon, till she had darned up a whole inch beyond the hole, and was almost run out of thread, to Elim frowning in the kitchen doorway, restless as an eel yet afraid to leave lest he should somehow be needed, and her mother in the kitchen doorway, her hands all floury and her hair awry.

"Mother!" she cried, with a lilt in her voice, the old lilt that had not been there for a year. "Have you got a birthday party ready? Because we have the guest. This is Alec Douglas, Mother. I told you about him, you know."

Mary Brooke wiping her hands on her apron and going forward to welcome the guest heard her son murmuring behind her, "Aw Gee! Another sucker! Good-night! I'm going to beat it!" But Elim came obediently forward when his sister called, and looked into the eyes, and deep blue eyes of the stranger, and was won.

"He's a real man at last!" he said with a sigh of relief to his mother later in the kitchen while he was helping to dish up the dinner. "Gee, I'm glad we've got her fixed right at last."

For Alec Douglas had not waited for formalities. He went to the heart of his business at once.

"I won't deceive you, Mrs. Brooke," he said with an extra twirl of the burr on Brooke. "I've come because I've fallen in love with your daughter and want her to marry me. I know it's a great thing I'm asking of you, to share such a daughter as Lynette with me, and you don't know me yet. But I'll not take her away from you

if you will all deign to come and live with me. And I'll
try to be a good son to you, and worthy of your trust."

Then he turned to the sweet old grandmother:

"It will be a great thing to me to have a real grandmother again," he said. "My own has been gone to her
lang hame more than twenty years, and I've always
longed for her. I'd be pleased if you would take her
place."

Elim stood on the outer edge of things, uncomfortable and forlorn while these preliminaries were going on.
But at last the future brother-in-law whirled upon him
and gave him a real clap on the shoulder that almost
made him wince with the power of it:

"And you, lad, why we're going to have rare times!
To think I've got a brother at last! I've always yearned
for one. I'd only a baby sister and she went home too.
There's only a little stone with 'Janet' written across it.
But lad, I'll take you over to Scotland and show you
the castle, where the Douglases used to live, and we'll
climb the crags, and go fishing in the burn, and we'll
have a great time, shearing the sheep, and if you care
for golf we'll have some of the real thing. How about it
lad? Are we brothers?"

Elim gripped the great hand that held his, grinned
from ear to ear, and said:

"Sure! Go to it! I'm with ya. That's regular dope!"

They had their party at last. They sat down to the
bountiful table which Alec Douglas had helped to set,
entering into the heart of the family with great delight
to their exquisite joy. He cut the bread and he turned
the ice cream, spelling Elim who was sent down to the
spring house for water cress. He helped Grandmother
to her chair, and then asked the most wonderful blessing, till it seemed the Lord was right in the room,
pleased at their happiness, ready to bless them.

It developed that Alec Douglas had come over at the
request of a New York church who had called him
unanimously without hearing him or seeing him, on the
recommendation of their senior elder who had met him
in London. He was seeking the Lord's leading concern-

ing the acceptance of the call. It was all a question of where he was wanted most in the vineyard. And then he began to tell them of the two years he had spent in Africa as a missionary among the heathen, of his experiences with lions and leopards, and the natives who had never heard of Christ before. Elim found himself listening absorbedly to the greatest sermon he had ever heard, and saying to himself:

"Gee, he's a regular guy. I'd like to be a Christian if I could be like that! It hasn't hurt him not one little bit! There isn't a yella hair on him."

They sat long at the table talking, eager not to lose a word, and then Alec Douglas insisted upon helping them to clear off the table and wash the dishes, and while they went about their merry work and Lynette's laugh rang out happily, a silent figure came down the mountain in the darkness and passed that way. He looked hungrily at the lights of the house where he had once been the most welcome visitor, heard the merriment, caught the glimpse of the figures moving about, and drew his fine brows down in bitterness.

"And she can laugh!" he said in his self-righteous wrath. "She has ruined my life, and she can laugh! Ruin! Ruin! Ruin! And it was all her fault!"

Novels of Enduring Romance and Inspiration by

GRACE
LIVINGSTON
HILL

BRING ROMANCE INTO YOUR LIFE

With these bestsellers from your favorite Bantam authors.

Barbara Cartland

☐ 13942	LUCIFER AND THE ANGEL	$1.75
☐ 14084	OLA AND THE SEA WOLF	$1.75
☐ 14133	THE PRUDE AND THE PRODIGAL	$1.75
☐ 13579	FREE FROM FEAR	$1.75

Catherine Cookson

☐ 13279	THE DWELLING PLACE	$1.95
☐ 14187	THE GIRL	$2.25
☐ 13170	KATIE MULHOLLAND	$1.95

Georgette Heyer

☐ 13239	THE BLACK MOTH	$1.95
☐ 11249	PISTOLS FOR TWO	$1.95

Emilie Loring

☐ 12947	WHERE BEAUTY DWELLS	$1.75
☐ 12948	RAINBOW AT DUSK	$1.75
☐ 13668	WITH BANNERS	$1.75
☐ 13757	HILLTOPS CLEAR	$1.75

Eugenia Price

☐ 13682	BELOVED INVADER	$2.25
☐ 14195	LIGHTHOUSE	$2.50
☐ 14406	NEW MOON RISING	$2.50